A Viking Slave's Saga

(Jan Fridegård's Trilogy of Novels About the Viking Age)

Land of Wooden Gods
People of the Dawn
and
Sacrificial Smoke

Winner of the 1987 Translation Prize
of the American-Scandinavian Foundation

ARIZONA CENTER FOR
MEDIEVAL AND RENAISSANCE STUDIES
OCCASIONAL PUBLICATIONS

VOLUME 4

A VIKING SLAVE'S SAGA

(Jan Fridegård's Trilogy of Novels About the Viking Age)

LAND OF WOODEN GODS
PEOPLE OF THE DAWN
AND
SACRIFICIAL SMOKE

Translated from the Swedish with an Afterword and Notes by
Robert E. Bjork

ACMRS
(Arizona Center for Medieval and Renaissance Studies)
Tempe, Arizona
2007

Library of Congress Cataloging-in-Publication Data

Fridegård, Jan, 1897-1968
  [Trilogin om trälen Holme. English]
  A viking slave's saga : a trilogy of novels about the viking age / by Jan
Fridegård ; translated from the Swedish with an afterword and notes by Robert
E. Bjork.
    p. cm.
  ISBN 978-0-86698-375-4 (alk. paper)
  1. Sweden--History--To 1397--Fiction. 2. Slaves--Sweden--Fiction. 3.
Vikings--Fiction. 4. Historical fiction. I. Bjork, Robert E., 1949- II. Title. III.
Series: Fridegård, Jan, 1897-1968. Trilogin om trälen Holme.

  PT9875.F788V55 2007
  839.73'72--dc22

                                                            2007030341

∞
This book is made to last.
It is set in Adobe Caslon,
smyth-sewn and printed on acid-free paper
to library specifications.
Printed in the United States of America

CONTENTS

Part I
Land of Wooden Gods
(*Trägudars land*, 1940)
1

Part II
People of the Dawn
(*Gryningsfolket*, 1944)
119

Part III
Sacrificial Smoke
(*Offerrök*, 1949)
241

Afterword
357

I am deeply grateful to Steven C. Spronz, Esq., without whose timely and generous help this translation would not have been published.

ROBERT E. BJORK

LAND OF WOODEN GODS

The settlement was well-hidden among the fir trees, and anyone travelling along the cove down below had to already know it was there to notice it. Yet from inside the biggest of the timbered halls you had a clear view across the lake through a couple of openings in the south wall. A huge refuse pile stood by one of the longer walls, visited by dogs, ants, and flies. At night, when everything was quiet in the timbered halls and the smoke had stopped rising through the holes in the roofs, a sniffing wolf, a cautious fox, or a white-faced badger could grub for a minute in the pile while keeping watchful eyes on the dwellings.

About fifty yards from the main structure were two smaller dwellings, along with a stable and a pigsty. Their timber rested directly on the ground while the high hall stood on a stone foundation. In several places in the forest and on a slope by the lake, the earth was tilled in little patches where slender barley stalks, mixed with the tall, glistening grass, swayed in the light breezes moving among the blades. A number of footpaths began at the settlement and vanished in different directions through the trees. The most well-trodden path led to the lake.

Toward evening, the settlement's inhabitants came home from all directions. Indolent warriors with dangling swords, bows, or spears. Male and female thralls who, with cunning or uneasy glances at the high hall, went toward the two smaller dwellings, crawled in through a yard-high door, and disappeared. In one of the thralls' dwellings a baby started screaming, soon getting an even louder response from the main building.

Several thralls handed things in at the door of the main building. A string of fish, a hare, or a rough clump of bog ore. From a place a little distance into the forest the sound of hammer blows resounded all day long, and when they stopped, you could hear murmuring voices. They came from some thralls working at a smithy consisting of a metal wedge lodged between two protruding pieces of rock. They were forging tools and weapons.

In one of the smaller dwellings where the female thralls lived lay a figure who hadn't worked for a few days. She had fixed a bed for herself below her bench so she could rest better, and an older friend helped her when she gave birth. Someone would sneak in to her occasionally with some flowers or a handful of blueberries. Next to the straw bed was a bowl of roast fish. There was constant twilight in the dwelling, but just after noon, when the sun had started to sink, two shafts of light came in through the openings on the south side and shot to the opposite wall. The beams climbed toward the ceiling and disappeared in about an hour.

The smell of summer and pine needles penetrated the female thralls' dwelling. The mother cried all evening, rocking the baby in her arms. When her friends came home, they kept an uneasy look-out on the high hall so they could give word when the time had come.

After the chieftain and the warriors had eaten their fill, they leaned back in their seats, grumbled amongst themselves, and sucked the beer from their beards. After a while, the chieftain motioned to a female thrall attending table, and she walked to the thralls' dwelling with the message. The mother rose to her knees and, with the baby clasped to her breast, cried still louder.

The door to the high hall stood open to the summer night. Six or seven warriors sat on each side of the long table, and behind them their black and gold shields hung in rows with the bows above them on wooden pegs. The hall was cordoned off behind the chieftain; he lived there with his family. The shrine of the gods, with its mute wooden figures, stood at the far end.

The warriors slept on their benches in the high hall. A few male thralls—who were overseers or very skillful workers—had permission to stay inside the door during meals or when the warriors were talking or wrestling at night.

As the mother came crawling out of the little dwelling with her baby clutched to her chest, the warriors and thralls leaned forward so they could see her through the door. She stopped twice on the path between the buildings. With tear-filled eyes she thought about running and looked toward the forest, but the stare of the wolf pack inside the hall froze her and pulled her on. If she ran they would spring to their feet and seize her before she could find a place to hide. A dog got up from the grass by the path, yawned, and followed sniffing after her for a few steps.

She climbed over the two logs that formed the doorstep, tried to wipe the tears away on her right shoulder, and walked forward to the chieftain. The light of the fire and the departing day blended together, enlarging the figures around her. She laid the baby down at the chieftain's feet and tried to read his expression through the darkness. All the warriors sat turned toward him now, motionless. You could have mistaken them for wooden statues if one or another didn't twitch his beard either in excitement or sympathy.

The baby had a piece of cloth wrapped around its stomach but otherwise was naked. It screwed up its face to start screaming but caught sight of the fire and blinked in surprise. It had black hair, and two of the warriors looked meaningfully first at each other, then at the mother's blond mane.

The chieftain sat silent and motionless, leaning his head in his hand and looking down at the child. His short, thick legs were criss-crossed with leather thongs, and his sword-hilt was more beautiful than the other warriors'. His hairline began right above his eyebrows; his forehead was just a pair of red creases. His nose was thick, his beard brown. Like the other warriors' beards, his was darker around his mouth from food scraps and dirt. The mother stood before him, wringing her hands, not taking her eyes off his ugly face.

The thralls by the door, tired after the day's work, showed little interest in what was happening farther up in the hall. All but one. He crouched as if ready to spring, his head thrust forward and his eyes burning like explosive, menacing coals. He had broader cheek-bones than the others, and two black, evenly-clipped locks of hair fell down over them. Once the chieftain's eye wandered down among the thralls, and when he saw the dark warning in the thrall's face, his beard moved to reveal a contemptuous grin. A young woman looked out from the interior of the hall, troubled by the silence.

"Stor and Tan," the chieftain called.

Two of the thralls down near the door got up and came forward. The chieftain pointed to the baby with his foot and said, "Put the troll-child in the woods."

Tan bent down quickly, grabbed the baby, and walked toward the door, followed by Stor. The mother ran after them crying loudly, but the warriors got up and stood like a wall between her and the thralls who walked off with the child. It struggled and screamed when they got outside the door as the chill night closed on its delicate limbs.

The woman inside the hall shuddered and went back to her own child, who lay on the bed. When Stor and Tan were gone, the black-haired thrall turned and looked at the chieftain, who smiled for the second time at his threat. The baby might have been allowed to live if he hadn't encountered such defiance in his thralls, he thought, yawning hugely.

As soon as Tan and Stor disappeared, two warriors started wrestling in the open area between the fireplace and the long table. The other warriors gathered in a ring around them, and the thralls tried to see between their legs. The childless mother went out, holding one arm in front of her face.

The warriors crashed to the floor, and no one saw the dark-haired thrall slip out. Only after a while, when the battle was decided, did the chieftain notice he was gone.

"Where's Holme?" he asked, but no one knew. "Has he gone after Stor and Tan?" But the warriors answered that just a moment ago he'd been sitting in his place and wouldn't be able to find Stor and Tan after such a long time.

The chieftain went in to his wife, the warriors started yawning, a couple of female thralls arranged the benches for the night and then went to their dwelling. Two of the younger warriors talked quietly a while and then made off for the female thralls' dwelling. They stopped outside and softly called the names of a couple of the younger women. But no one came out that night; only the mother's sobs answered them from inside. From their dwelling, the male thralls were pleased to see the disappointed warriors returning to their beds.

Stor and Tan took long strides away from the settlement, Tan muttering peevishly about the baby's crying. When it wouldn't settle down, he held it to his chest with an embarrassed look at Stor and pulled part of his shirt up over it. The child quieted down and closed its eyes when it felt the warmth from the thrall's body, and Stor nodded approvingly.

Both men kept a silent look-out for a good place to abandon the child. They dreaded the moment when they would have to put it on the ground and walk away. They had carried a good many babies out but had always tried to find a place without ants. But what could they do about the sniffing muzzles and gleaming eyes that would soon approach stealthily through the trees? Or maybe the sun would find the child untouched when it came up and then keep it alive until the next night.

They laid the baby in the green moss on the south side of a large rock, still warm from the sun, and then hurried away. A song-thrush was singing very close by, and you could faintly hear dogs barking in a distant settlement.

The mother heard their footsteps and wailed louder. When they came in, they went to bed immediately, ignoring their companions' questions. They hadn't seen Holme and didn't care where he had gone.

Holme had run barefooted straight into the woods. He didn't know which way Stor and Tan had gone; they had different places where they left the babies and never used the same place twice. At first he ran haphazardly but soon felt resistance in his body and changed direction. That felt better, and he flew forward through the woods, silent as an owl.

He was standing behind a tree when Stor and Tan came walking home again. You could barely see the path they were following. Holme's teeth flashed, and he moved on in the direction from which they had come.

He saw visions that urged him forward. He imagined a wolf prowling around the baby, sniffing it, sinking its teeth into it, and carrying it off to a safer place to eat. He clenched his fists, longing to have the wolf's throat in them. Suddenly he slowed down and shifted direction slightly to the left.

In a small clearing in the forest he stopped again and listened. It was much brighter there; some light fell over the glade, although neither sun nor moon was out. Holme listened and retreated behind a tree trunk. He could hear snorting and twigs breaking on the other side of the glade.

A long, gray snout protruded from the brush, snorting and sniffing as the whole animal ventured out into the opening. Behind him came the other animals like a row of waddling, swaying blocks of stone. The wild boars followed closely in each other's tracks.

When the big lead boar was in the middle of the glade, it veered off for some reason directly to the left. The others followed, and soon the column of boars formed a right angle. All of them walked carefully out to where their leader had veered. A few half-grown animals trotted along at the rear. The bushes soon stopped moving as the last gray rump disappeared and the snorting died away. Holme gestured threateningly at the boars and rushed on like a shadow over the glade.

A nearly full-grown boar didn't find its way back to its herd until the next day. Where the herd had gone on in disarray in the forest, it had stumbled onto something strange. Soft and whimpering and smelling edible, it rolled away from his snout. The boar turned his head sideways, trying to tear the object with his left tusk. It slipped away again, waving its tiny paws. The boar lifted his head halfway, blinking and listening for the herd before continuing to investigate.

He had one of the tiny legs in his jaws when something came rushing up with a furious roar. The boar let go his hold and bolted away in a terrified wobbling gallop, making a hoarse, guttural noise with every bound.

Holme chased the boar a short distance but soon turned back panting and crouched down by the child. He turned it clumsily in his hands to see if it was hurt. Blood ran from one leg, and it screamed constantly. The severe creases in the father's face softened a little when he found that nothing serious had happened to the baby.

As Tan had done earlier, he held the child to his chest and folded part of his clothing over it. It whimpered for a while but eventually fell asleep from the warmth of its father's body and the swaying motion when he walked.

An hour's hasty walk brought him to a clearing, the middle of which was marshy and cold. He hopped on the tufts of grass, which rocked and sunk under his weight. A white night mist hung brooding over the area. On the other side, the ground rose more steeply, and several giant pines that had climbed down the slope marked the beginning of the forest. The earth was tepid under them, and their trunks shone a warm red against the west where the sky still glowed.

Holme walked up the rise, turned around, and looked back at the marshy ground and the forest beyond it. He was far away from the settlement now. The rage had left his face, and those black eyes, which few had ever looked into, bore a grave, searching expression. He loosened his grip around the child and looked anxiously at it. As if sensing the father's gaze, it revealed its toothless gums and let out a closed-eyed howl.

Holme continued over the gravel ridge and soon came into a soft, dark, spruce forest. Huge blocks of granite overgrown with foot-deep moss lay there like gigantic sleeping animals. A large bird off among the trees took flight with a rumbling of wings.

He walked straight to where some jagged boulders formed a cairn that reached halfway to the tops of the trees. Apprehension filled his eyes and he mumbled an invocation or a promise of sacrifice. Even the song-thrushes had stopped their singing. It was the darkest moment in the summer night, and the silence made his hair stand on end.

He soon found the cave opening. The stone and the dry spruce branches lay as he had left them. The moss inside felt soft and dry as he crawled over it, supporting himself on one hand and both knees. With his other hand he pressed the child against him and groped about for the best place to lay it. The cave was cool and smelled of earth and roots. He thought for a moment before he laid the child down, then took off his garment and wound it several times around the baby. He positioned the child as well as he could in the darkness and could feel that the little body was burning up. As he fumbled about to find if the baby had an air hole, he got one finger between the tiny, hard gums, which immediately closed on it and started sucking.

The soft cries were scarcely audible under the huge mound of stones. The father stood naked outside and rolled the stone back in front of the cave. He gathered smaller stones around it and finally put the spruce branches back in place. He listened again and walked a few steps in the direction he had come.

Then fear rushed in on him from all sides, fear for his child. It was safe from wolves, wild boars, and great horned owls, but he couldn't shut out the savage weasel, the cold snake, and the evil spirits. He returned to the entrance, examined it again, and shook a shivering fist out in the air at every terrible, dangerous creature wanting to eat the child. Then he ran through the forest moss, shot over the pine ridge, and flew from tuft to tuft through the white night mist in the hollow. The sedge slashed sharp and cold around his naked legs.

All the while he could feel the baby's gums close greedily around his finger, and he could visualize the mother's round, full breasts. He would unite them again, and he ran faster and faster back the way he had come.

"**W**as that Ausi who went out?" a drowsy woman thrall asked a friend next to her.

"Yes, she probably can't sleep. Probably has some pain too from her milk."

The thralls fell asleep again, but Ausi stood outside, wildly hoping to see Holme. Maybe he would come and tell her he'd found the baby. She had been watched herself until Stor and Tan had come back and night fell.

But out there, all was still. As she walked down the path toward the forest, there was a rustling in the refuse pile; a shadow glided out and moved off along the ground. Ausi could hear men snoring in the thralls' dwelling. Maybe Holme was inside sleeping, she thought bitterly. She had heard her friends say he was gone, but never before had a father gone out looking for his baby in the woods. Neither warrior nor thrall.

The forest was looming and black. Somewhere deep inside it her baby was lying on the bare ground, or maybe a wild animal had just discovered the little one and was closing its jaws around it. The thought doubled her over, forcing out a moan. As she walked up the path, the dogs growled in the warriors' hall, but a voice impatiently shut them up.

Where the woods grew more dense, she stopped and listened. A rivulet rippled softly down the slope, but there was something else too. From the woods a panting noise was approaching; then something passed by her and stopped a little ways below. She whimpered in fear before a naked body without head, hands or feet. The ghost leaned against a tree, breathed heavily and looked down over the settlement; soon she could distinguish its head and black shock of hair.

Holme's sun-tanned face, hands and feet blended into the darkness while the rest of his body glowed a soft white.

Her movement made him spin around, crouching in defense. She sensed more than saw his face relax when he recognized her, and in the midst of everything else she thought how strange he was, unlike any other man in the settlement. He was naked and he had probably been in a fight.

To Holme just then, the woman meant only food for the child lying under the stones. He took her arm and pulled her along with him as he uttered a few words to make her understand. But she already knew and ran beside the man she had hated and feared, happiness spreading through her whole being.

She felt the hot blood trickling down her legs from the fierce pace and as if in a dream saw the cool marsh where broad-winged birds flew toward them with anxious cries. She felt the warm gravel of the ridge under her feet and then the cool moss of the spruce forest again. While Holme rolled the stones away, she sat down trying to hide the blood that ran like black stripes down her legs. His white body ducked into a hole; she heard the baby squeal when it was touched, and then she had it in her arms.

The milk ran like a white thread down one breast while the baby nursed from the other. Holme stood leaning against a block of stone, looking on. He turned himself half-way away from the woman because he was naked. The threatening creases were gone from his face, and he looked calm and almost friendly in the first light of dawn. His garment lay beside the woman, and with one hand she ripped up some moss, wiped the baby's yellow excrement off the garment and handed it to its owner with an uncertain smile. She discovered with terror the blood on the child's leg, but the father said nothing about snatching it from the wild boar's jaws.

He had to go to the settlement again and knew it would be more dangerous now at dawn. But his ax and spear were still in the thralls' dwelling, his fishing tackle hanging next to them. The baby, full now, lay contentedly snorting at its mother's breast, but soon she would have to eat too. He couldn't afford to be without his weapons and tools, not even one day.

Gently but firmly, he pushed mother and child into the cave, told her to stay there, and carefully covered up the entrance before he set off. Ausi readily obeyed, thankful the baby was alive. From inside the cave, she heard his running feet withdrawing. She wouldn't have thought he could run that way; he always moved so slowly in the settlement, probably to annoy the chieftain.

The moss inside the cave was soft; smiling faintly, Ausi stretched herself out on it, as the child breathed lightly against her neck. A little way from her face there was a tiny opening between the jagged rocks, and gray light fell on a little patch of gravel and on a few pale blades of grass. After all the anguish, she felt endlessly calm and happy in the cavern, and she smiled again faintly in the darkness as she thought how long, long ago, people had actually lived in such places. She'd heard many stories about it.

Birds began chirping timidly outside. A pointed, black snout sniffed at the small opening; then its owner ran quickly off across the moss. The block's contours slowly became visible in the cave, and Ausi could see that it reached inside a ways but that the rock ceiling got lower and lower.

As she fell asleep, she wondered where Holme had gone and how soon he'd be back. She hoped he wouldn't go back to the settlement, where he could be killed. But he knew what was best; she didn't have to worry.

A slight murmuring whispered in the tree tops, and the uppermost layers of branches swayed. Then all grew quiet as the sun rose over the heathen land.

A couple of dogs got up out of the grass, yawned and wagged their tails as Holme approached the settlement. He petted them and listened before he went into the thralls' dwelling. A couple of his friends drowsily stared up but didn't see anything unusual in Holme's being awake and so closed their eyes again.

He took his ax, his spear, his fishing tackle, and a few little things that belonged to him and went out again. As he walked outside toward the main building, he thought about the warriors and their bows. It would be good to have one. He also thought about the bread chest standing just inside the door. He walked past a couple more dogs on the way down. They lay with their heads on their paws, looking up at him with brown, affectionate eyes while their tails swished in the grass.

The heavy door was not barred, and he carefully looked in. It was dark inside except under the hole in the roof,[1] where the dawn light fell through, spreading out on the floor below. He could see the fireplace's sooty oval opening and the warriors sleeping on the benches by the wall.

Silently he sneaked forward to the bread chest and opened it. It was filled with large, round disks of bread, and he threaded several of them onto his spear. Then he stood stock still, his arms outstretched. A warrior had lifted his head and looked down toward the door.

Holme stood there a moment, expecting the warrior to raise the alarm. But the head sank down again and nothing happened. The warrior had probably been half asleep, not quite comprehending what he had seen.

The bows hung like an ordered row of half moons, and Holme carefully lifted the closest one from its wooden peg. Everything was quiet as he went out again, closing the door behind him.

He stopped at the smithy. He couldn't be seen from there, so the danger was not very great. On one side of the forge lay large, rust-red clumps of ore and on

---

[1] Viking dwellings usually had a fire pit in the center of the floor with a smoke vent cut in the ceiling directly above it. On Viking architecture, see James Graham-Campbell and Dafydd Kidd, *The Vikings* (London: British Museum Publications, 1980), pp. 75–86.

the other side a row of ax-head material. He took some iron arrowheads, a knife, a sledgehammer, and a pair of tongs with him. For a moment he looked at an almost finished sword but shook his head and left it there. Swords were not for thralls; they got along best with axes and spears.[2]

Before walking farther into the woods, he looked out over the cove. A sea bird was swimming beyond the belt of reeds, followed by a column of chicks, chirping eagerly. The surface of the water straight across and below the forest was calm and black. You could see the white ring in the water whenever a fish would jump, though it was very far away. The settlement was still quiet when he disappeared into the forest with his bread and iron.

The mist in the hollow was dissipating. You could hear various birds cry in an area overgrown with reeds and alder wood.

Holme laid everything down outside the cave, listened at the small opening, and sat down after he recognized Ausi's deep breathing, broken up by the child's quick panting. A boulder lay beside him with blueberry sprigs shooting up from a crack like bristles on a wild boar's back. He picked a handful of blueberries and ate them.

It gradually grew more and more light, until suddenly a tree trunk here and there shone a glaring yellow on its east side. In the distance among the trunks a glade lay in the clear sunlight. The air was cold and calm; the rocks had a translucent gray border around them, and their edges dissolved in light.

As he waited, Holme surveyed his treasures, one by one, with pleasure. Then he hid them in the rocks, all but the ax. Fatigue crept over him, and he leaned back against the boulder. A little gray bird circled closer and closer, cocked its head, and peered at him. Finally it dared land and peck up the crumbs left from the bread.

One by one, the warriors awoke and walked out into the yard. Some went off to a pole nailed between two trees where they undid their clothes, squatted on the pole, and let their eyes wander across the glittering cove down below.

The thralls were already at work. Two of them let the pigs out of their pen and then followed the grubbing, grunting herd all day in the forest pasture. One swineherd carried a wooden container of meat and bread; a huge bronze horn hung over the other's shoulder. They always had it along, even though wolves seldom attacked during the summer. They appeared sometimes, fat and lazy, but drew away again with grinning jaws and wily eyes.

---

[2] Ebbe Schön, *Jan Fridegård och forntiden. En studie i diktverk och kallor* (Uppsala, Sweden: Almqvist & Wiksell, 1973), p. 143, points out that Fridegård probably got the notion that different classes used different weapons during the Viking period from a museum catalog published by the University of Oslo in 1932: *Universitets oldsaksamling. Tører utgitt ved samlingens bestyrer.*

A few other thralls went off to the slope where they'd been breaking a new patch of land for some time. They had a small, long-haired horse and an iron-tipped wooden ard.[3] A couple had wooden spades with foot blocks and iron edges. Sweat ran down their grim faces as they labored in silence. Below them they could see the warriors moving leisurely about the settlement or lying in the shade. Two were already reclining, one on either side of the game board,[4] contemplating it, their beards motionless.

Holme's two helpers sat by the smithy, looking indecisively down at the settlement. Their master was gone and they weren't used to doing anything on their own. They hoped to see him coming out of the woods before the chieftain woke up and came to the smithy.

The women thralls made their way to their own tasks. Two went into the high hall to straighten up after the night. Two others fetched grain from earthenware jars and carried it to the mill stone. They spread the grain in the worn groove, crushing it into flour with a rock pestle. They swept the flour together with a bird's wing. You could hear a rhythmic sliding noise, and a little cloud of dust rose up into the sunlit air around the women at their milling.

While the women thralls worked, they talked softly about the two who had disappeared. Mothers had gone into the woods before, looking for their babies for days on end, but they had always come back and started working again. Their tears had dried sooner or later. But a father had never gone to any trouble before, as Holme had. Even so, they'd probably both be back soon, take their punishment, and everything would be back to normal.

The chieftain's wife hadn't slept well that night. She didn't think much about the baby abandoned in the woods, but she couldn't forget the look in the black-haired thrall's eyes, which augured revenge and misfortune. She feared no one else, but that silent thrall could do anything with his hands, coming as he probably did from across the sea where people had magic powers. She knew well enough that even the warriors took care not to mistreat him. As far as she knew, none of them had touched Ausi, but two of the other women had told her that they had seen Holme subdue her after a long fight. They laughed and said that in the end, she had thrown her arms around his neck to choke him.

From an angle inside the hall, the chieftain's wife saw the hole in the roof like a blue, bottomless well, and she knew that the sun had come up. She heard the pigs grunting, the birds singing, and a horse whinnying in the distance. The

---

[3] An 'ard' is a simple pointed plow that cuts a groove in the soil but does not turn a furrow in it.

[4] We have evidence that the Vikings played board games, although we do not always know exactly what the games were. One game, called *hnefatafl*, is a kind of chess tha has only one king (the *hnefi*) defended by one group of game pieces (*töflur*) from another group. The game is mentioned in varous places in Old Norse literature, such as *Hervararsaga*, stanza 56.

bearded chieftain lay by her side, and a smell of smoke and filth rose up from him. A ladybug entangled in his beard struggled for freedom.

A couple of warriors were snoring in unison out in the hall. Then the first fell silent, and shortly after, the second; a mosquitoe's shrill whine pierced the air. Blades of grass, small pieces of charcoal, and dry spruce twigs lay on the hard-packed dirt floor under her feet. A distant seagull's cry came down through the roof vent.

Her baby woke up and she pulled it to her breast, which was soon sucked dry. The child had light hair and large hands, and it kneaded its mother's breast while it nursed. She thought again about Ausi's baby and wished that the chieftain would allow some thrall children to live from now on. Otherwise, their own child would be without thralls when it grew up.

When the chieftain awoke and emerged from the hall, he didn't think about what had happened the night before. He walked past the flies swarming over the sun-baked mud of the pigsty, then beyond the slope toward the lake where he kneeled down and washed and snorted in the clear water between the rocks. Without drying his face, he took out a bone comb and started grooming his hair and beard. Now and then he bent forward to look at himself in the water and seemed pleased with his fat, coarse face and the wild forest of beard engulfing it.

When he returned to the settlement, he walked around to the different work areas. He didn't speak to the women thralls but gave stern orders to the men digging on the slope. They either gave no response or looked up malevolently beneath shaggy eyebrows. It was already blazing hot, and the little horse's matted coat glistened with sweat. After the chieftain had walked on, the thralls straightened up and silently watched the short, coarse figure. They were all tall and knew the chieftain didn't like anyone taller than he was.

As he approached the smithy, the two helpers started fiddling with tools so as not to look idle. One examined some long-nosed tongs and the other hammered a bent spearhead. They shook their heads when the chieftain asked about Holme. When he realized that the smith had run away, his furrowed brow turned redder than before, but he turned back to the settlement instead of saying anything to the thralls.

Very shortly, half the warriors armed themselves and went down to the shore. They hid behind the clump of trees where the memorial stones[5] stood, concealed by leaves at this time of year. When the leaves dropped in the fall, the stones became visible all the way up to the settlement, only to be hidden again

---

[5] The memorial stones (*bautasten*) mentioned here do not have carvings or inscriptions on them. Those with carvings are called 'picture stones' (*bildsten*), and those with runic inscriptions or runic inscriptions and pictures are called 'rune stones' (*runsten*).

with the coming of spring. The stones, standing on green mounds, had been raised above the chieftain's father and grandfather.

The warriors were set to attack the settlement. They took cover behind the trees as they advanced up the slope. When they were still at a distance, the clear, sharp twang of a bowstring rang out, and an arrow sped like a white streak through the trees toward the attackers. It hit the ground short of reaching them, and the chieftain snarled angrily at the warrior who had shot prematurely.

From the clearing, the thralls snorted at such needless fighting. For them there was only the ax. That was good enough for both working and fighting.

The warriors had removed the iron tips from the arrows and had slackened their bowstrings. When the arrows started flashing back and forth between the two bands, they didn't come at deadly speed.

They shot at each other for a while, taking most of the arrows on their shields. One of the defenders suddenly leaped into the air to accomplish this, even though the arrow flew high over his head; you could hear the thralls mumble approvingly. The warriors fought silently; only the song of the bowstrings, counterpointed occasionally by clanging blows from the smithy, broke the silence.

At a shout from the chieftain, the warriors threw down their shields and bows, grabbed their swords, and charged each other. They hacked and parried a while, the broad iron blades flashing in the sun. The chieftain shouted again, the battle stopped, and all the warriors walked toward the settlement together.[6]

I n a small cooking hut, two of the older women thralls were preparing the meal. They built a fire in the central fireplace and slid the meat onto the spit. When it was done, they carried it into the main building where the clay floor had been swept and cleaned. Two of the south window-holes were open, and sunlight streamed in over the rough table and benches. The dogs sniffed greedily in the doorway, but the women screamed menacingly at them to stay out.

The smell of the cooking meat drifted over the settlement, and those who noticed it turned toward the buildings. The thralls glared down bitterly; they knew that the worst meat was being cooked for them, even though they had been working since early that morning. An old woman was cooking it and when she was through, she fetched the driest slack-baked bread from the chieftain's wife.

After the old woman set the pot of meat on the table and put the bread beside it, she went out and called shrilly for the thralls. At the same time, she got a jar of water from the well.

The thralls ate in the half-dark inside. They clutched the meat and bread, panting like dogs. Occasionally one would pick up his ax and crush a bone with

---

[6] According to Schön, *Fridegård och forntiden*, p. 144, Fridegård's description of Viking battle strategy was probably gleaned from the 1932 Norwegian museum catalog mentioned in note 2, p. 11.

a resounding hack, then suck out the marrow. After the meal, the earthenware jar was handed around the table.

Work would not begin again until the worst heat had passed. The settlement rested silently on the scorched slope; no one could be seen for the next few hours. The dogs lay panting in the shade or gnawed on bones thrown out to them. Down below lay the cove, and a budding field of flax, like a piece broken loose from it, was turning blue a short way up shore. A gull silently circled the settlement once before returning to the lake. Only the countless flies were constantly busy on the refuse pile and on the blazing hot timber wall above it.

When Holme woke up and took the stone away from the cave entrance, Ausi came creeping out, smiling. As Holme had done, she held the baby to her chest with one hand and steadied herself with the other. Both squinted into the strong sunlight pouring down over the hillside.

Holme held his ax so she would catch a glimpse of it, the corners of his mouth rising slightly with pride as she gasped in surprise. He showed her the other weapon, the work tools, and the bread lying there in a brown, delicious pile.

Ausi smiled again in happiness for the baby and the bread. A long time after waking, she had lain wondering what would happen to them. Hearing Holme's deep breathing outside, she had known that he hadn't left them, but how long would that last? One day he might be gone; he might get killed or just simply go his own way once he got tired of them. With his strong, skillful hands, he would be welcome wherever he wanted to settle down.

Holme turned back the garment to look at the baby. Scarcely a trace of the boar's bite was left. His dark eyes smiled at the child's thighs, no thicker than his wrist. Ausi, who stood looking at them, realized that her eyes had never met his even though she had been closer to him than anyone else had. When he looked up, all you got was a feeling of piercing blackness. She saw those eyes clearing now, moving over the baby's body, anxiously searching, and she was glad.

Holding the child so the sun would shine on it, she walked out onto the hillside. Below her the spruce thickets grew dense and mingled with the alder shrubs; there must be water there. Her feet sank into cool moss, and soon she came to a place where two glittering water veins met and gurgled gently out of a little hill coated with yellow-white lime. She washed away the yellow excrement from the baby's body as it whimpered and struggled because of the cold water.

When the baby was clean, she peeked through the bushes toward the cave. Holme was nowhere to be seen; he must have crawled inside. With the child under one arm, she quickly loosened the brooches on her clothes, scooped up water with her free hand, and washed her body, which still bore traces of the night's strenuous flight from the settlement.

Afterward, in the shadow of the boulder, they ate their bread while the baby slept. They didn't say much; Holme was thinking about meat for the next meal, meat or fish. Ausi began thinking about how close the settlement was, and she looked around nervously. A roaming warrior could happen by; the swine-herds might bring the pigs this way. They wouldn't hesitate to talk for some little reward or other.

She wondered if Holme intended for them to stay here. He was in the greatest danger. They'd take her back, but they would surely kill him. And the baby would be handed over to Stor and Tan for the second time.

When Holme went out hunting, he took the stolen bow, his spear, and his knife with him. The sun hovered above the treetops and was already shining intensely on the east side of the cairn. From a nearby tree, a bird warbled endlessly, and the anxious, indistinct sounds of the lapwings rose from the hollow. On a mossy shelf made from two boulders, Ausi sat watching him walk farther and farther away until the tall, smooth-trunked pine trees on the gravel ridge blocked him from view. She saw with alarm that he was walking toward the settlement.

When Holme was about halfway there, he stopped and listened. He was more cautious now, looking carefully ahead. The marshy area extended for miles and created little lakes here and there, partly overgrown with vegetation. By the shore of one of these, the settlement's herd of pigs walked grunting and grubbing. A few of them lay like gray blocks of stone in the cool mire.

Holme saw their herders a little farther away on a flat piece of rock. One was looking out over the marsh, but the other lay on his back with a huge water-lily leaf over his face to protect him from the sun. Beside the thralls, the bronze horn glistened brightly in the sunshine.

Holme thought for a moment about walking up to his companions and asking them about news from the settlement. Maybe they could give him one of the smaller pigs, too. One of them, Otrygg, probably would be on his side, but Krok would blab to the chieftain and the warriors. They would know he had stayed in the area and would search the whole district. Better to wait and not show himself; maybe the swineherds would fall asleep around midday.

He found a thicket where he could hide and look out over the little lake and herd of pigs on the shore. A school of small fish snapped at the air, making the water look like it was being pelted by a fine rain. Wild ducks and coots were quacking, and farther away a large brown bird hung flapping above the reeds. Two huge pigs started fighting, dancing, and squealing in the gurgling muck, ready to tear each other's belly open. The thrall who was sitting up bellowed at them, looking around for something to throw.

The sun rose higher, and more pigs made for the mud. The thrall turned his head constantly in different directions, and Holme got more and more impatient in his hiding place.

Close to noon he caught sight of a swaying bush a long way from the herd. He kept his eye on it and finally saw the back of a medium-sized pig grubbing in the thicket.

Watching the swineherds, Holme crept the long way round toward the bush. He stopped nearby, expecting the pig to go even farther away from the others. But instead, it became uneasy, lifted its head, and listened. Holme had to act quickly.

He put the bow down, grabbed his spear, and crept a little to one side, putting the thickest bushes between him and the pig. When he was only a few feet away, he rushed forward, bursting through the thicket. The pig, its snout under a root it was trying to tear off, let out a terrified guttural sound and threw itself to one side but fell down, rolling over again on its back. In the same instant, Holme's spear went through its throat into the ground. The pig was nailed fast and, as Holme had expected, it had not had time for a single squeal.

Holme bore down on the spear, keeping clear of the pig's frantically pumping hind legs. Frothing, bright red blood gushed into the hole the pig's legs had just dug. Holme could hear two other pigs from the herd squealing as they fought.

Gradually the animal's writhing abated; Holme pulled out his spear and wiped it off in the moss. Then he walked until he could see the swineherds. Both were sitting on the rock now with the rucksack between them. Maybe they would nap after their meal. Most of the herd was in the marsh below the rock and would probably stay there until the worst heat had subsided.

Holme walked back to his motionless prey, its bushy-white eyes shut tight in death. Big flies were already buzzing around the thicket. He had thought about covering the animal with juniper twigs and coming back for it at nightfall, but he changed his mind, deciding to take at least part of it with him. Ausi just couldn't wait until night for food.

He took his knife and cut around one of the shoulders to the bone. Then he stood on the other foreleg and yanked violently. The shoulder cracked and broke; he cut the sinews and pulled free a large, meaty chunk. It was easy to carry with the leg as a handle.

He covered the rest of the pig with fragrant twigs and then sneaked back. Both swineherds lay on their backs now. The pigs were rolling around indolently and playfully scuffling. Holme smiled maliciously at the thought of having deprived the chieftain of a pig. His black hair was heavy with sweat. Soon he was out of sight.

Toward evening when the thralls came home with the pigs, the chieftain stood as usual by the opening where the animals crawled into the pen, one by one. He held a long wooden staff, with a notch on it for each animal. He moved his finger notch by notch as the pigs crawled in, but one notch was left after all the pigs were inside.

He bellowed and yelled at the swineherds, who, tired and angry, had to trudge all the way back to the water-lily lake. They couldn't imagine that anything had happened to the lost pig except getting stuck in the mud. They didn't bother listening for it. They knew the pigs never squealed in the forest; they raised a terrible squealing and grunting only when the settlement was within sight and earshot.

Krok and Otrygg searched in vain for a long time and finally agreed that the animal must have gone out too far and drowned. The chieftain would stalk away from them, red in the face, but he wouldn't scold or beat them when it was clear that the pig was lost. They had known him for a long time, and he never made a fuss over something obviously hopeless.

All day Ausi wondered anxiously what the night would bring. Would Holme be with her in the cave? What would he do? How much did he understand, and could she talk to him?

He had gone to get the rest of the pig he had killed. They had cooked the meat on a flat rock he had built a fire under, but it didn't taste good without salt, and where could they get salt? The chieftain was very careful with his supply, which he got once a year in exchange for grain and iron from foreign traders. The meat wouldn't keep too long in the heat.

They had to think about moving on, too. The cave could be discovered any moment; every day the warriors wandered far from the settlement with their bows and spears. They might catch sight of the smoke and get curious. They knew where all the columns of smoke in the area should be, and if a new one appeared, everyone took notice and didn't give up until they knew where it came from.

They couldn't live in a cave indefinitely anyway. People had done that a long time ago, when they didn't know any better. Humans might even have lived in this very cave. Holme could build a house, of course, but they would have to go far away to be safe, deep in the countryside where farmsteads lay few and far between. And they'd have to do that before winter fell.

When Holme came back, he walked down to the spring with the pig's carcass and was gone for a long time. Toward evening, they ate a little meat and bread. The whole time Ausi thought about the moment they'd crawl into the cave for the night. She glanced at Holme from the side, but he never once turned his face toward her. What was he thinking about; how much did he understand?

Then he got up and started breaking twigs and carrying them into the cave. He wove a tight layer over the whole floor. Then he tore up big armfuls of the soft grass, warmed by the sun on the gravel ridge, and laid it on top of the twigs. She should have put the baby down and helped, but he might think that meant he could sleep with her and the baby in the cave. It was best to leave him alone to do what he wanted.

But she never knew whether Holme was planning to sleep with them or not. He was right behind her when she was ready to bend down and crawl in. Ausi turned around anxiously, put her hand on his arm, and wouldn't let go until their eyes met. She was startled by the bitter passion in them but she didn't turn away.

He knew immediately what she was thinking; she could see that and felt with relief she'd be safe. Now he could come in.

But he guided her gently in, showed her the best place to lie down, and then closed up the cave. She saw he had widened the opening between the stones to let more air and light in. The grass was soft and smelled sweet. She stretched herself out, smiling with satisfaction.

Holme could have slept in the cave, too, she thought before falling asleep, now that he knew she had to be left alone. But maybe he'd come in later. He probably still had things to do. She heard him now and then; he dislodged a stone and once he snorted like a dog. Then it got completely quiet, and you could hear the song-thrush even in the cave. But she sensed that Holme was very close by.

He sat on the rock with the blueberries on it, watching darkness approach through the trees. The sun shone now only in the tops of the tallest pine trees on the ridge. He heard weak, indistinct sounds, sometimes a distant call, sometimes a rustle or a thud nearby. He knew they came from forest creatures even though he couldn't see them. Maybe he could take them a token sacrifice, put a bit of meat and bread on a stone.

He could hear dogs barking in the distance; they stopped, then started again, and might easily be in the settlement. Barking carried a long way at night. He remembered they had to run out and pelt the dogs with rocks to keep them quiet when they started barking in the middle of the night for no good reason. But the older women thralls always shook their heads, mumbling about misfortune whenever the dogs started howling.

Now that things were quiet, he began thinking over all that had happened. He wondered what had come over him to run after a baby put out in the woods to die. Normally, no one ever did that, even if he knew he was the father. But Holme had had to do what he had done; his chest had ached strangely at the sight of the poor whimpering child at the chieftain's feet, receiving its scornful sentence. If he had been close enough with his ax or knife to the chieftain, there would have been trouble. But maybe they'd meet again.

A powerful snorting from the ridge caused him to crouch down and look up over the rock. After a while he could see something moving softly, something he had thought was a boulder. For a moment he saw the bear clearly silhouetted against the night sky; moving off, it hurried toward the woods on the other side of the hollow. Holme sat down calmly again. He had met the bear more than once before, and they seemed to tacitly agree to stay out of each other's way. But once he had seen an enraged bear—a spear and several arrows protruding from its body—almost demolish an entire farmstead.

When he felt his eyes growing heavy with sleep, he put the leftover grass down in front of the stone door as a bed. He kept hold of his ax. He heard the baby cry once, but the crying soon stopped, followed by a sucking noise. When it was as dark as it would get, he sensed something scurrying up to him. A small animal skittered across the rocks, its claws like rasps. But he felt cold when he got up, and so he sank back down among the rocks again.

The chieftain's child sat playing with some pine cones its mother had gathered. It reached out for more, and the mother picked them, murmuring and smiling. The warriors were busy with the boats by the shore; the thralls worked breaking the new field. It was cloudy, but warm and still, like just before a rain.

There was a thud next to the child, and a stone bounced in the grass. The child turned its head, looking at the stone with interest. The mother, sitting crouched down under a fir tree a little way away, didn't notice anything. She didn't see the second stone come whizzing either, hitting the child in the back just below the neck. She heard a noise and saw her baby lying still in the grass, its face ashen.

She snatched up the child and ran screaming toward the hall. The women thralls, terrified and curious, rushed forward; the men thralls straightened up and looked down the slope. They exchanged a few disdainful words, wondering what had gotten into the women this time.

From behind a boulder, a dark face looked out under a black shock of hair; then its owner slipped slowly from tree trunk to tree trunk until he was deep in the woods. There he picked up speed and was soon far away.

Holme, often drawn toward the settlement, had come upon a few things one night that could be of use to them in the cave. A bundle of cloth, a block of salt, a cauldron with iron feet for the fire, a pair of scissors, and a few tools from the smithy. He wanted to see what people were doing during the day now since he was close by anyway. When he saw the chieftain's son in the grass, his hatred for the squat, scornful man welled up until he could hardly breathe. He would pay him back for a night not too long ago. The ground was full of good stones.

After running a while, he slowed to a walk. At first he was elated at hitting the chieftain's child but he soon began to feel uneasy. He knew that neither the chieftain himself nor any warrior would ever stoop to throwing a stone at or harming a child in any way. On the other hand, they weren't above dumping them in the woods to be eaten alive by mosquitoes and ants or torn apart by wolves and foxes. He stopped while he thought about that. Maybe there was a difference somewhere, but he couldn't sort it out. He shook his head and walked on.

Holme knew what was happening in the settlement at that moment. A woman thrall would run down to the shore, screaming for the chieftain. He would come up the hillside, not running—that was beneath his dignity—but his short legs would move faster of their own accord. Once he had come up and gotten straight what had happened, it wouldn't be a good idea to be around. Holme smiled, thinking how everyone fled whenever the chieftain's face turned white instead of red, as it did for minor annoyances. Only one man stayed, the gigantic Stenulf. His job was to knock the weapons from the chieftain's hands, throw him to the ground, and hold him there until his face turned red again.

Then he got up and was calm once more. From the smithy, Holme had seen it happen many times. The chieftain would go inside without saying a word, and the warriors and thralls would emerge again from their scattered hiding places.[7]

When Holme got back, Ausi was sitting outside the cave. A soft, warm rain had begun to fall, and she soon crawled into the cave where the baby was sleeping. When Holme didn't come in after her, she stuck her hand out hesitantly and tugged on his clothes, pointing to the place beside her. He came in but sat with his back to her, looking out through the opening.

"Did you go back there today?" asked Ausi, who missed talking with her friends.

"Yes."

"What did you see?"

Gradually she pried out of him what had happened at the settlement. She felt intense, malicious glee thinking about the chieftain's child, but uneasiness about the vengeance he would exact. He'd know what had happened. Then he would take all the warriors with him and scour the whole district. They'd better be on their way as soon as possible—as soon as the rain stopped. The cave was fine, true, but they'd have to live in a house anyway like other people.

The rain increased, creating a gray stream outside the opening. Sometimes a breeze laden with a heavy smell of flowers and berries wafted into the cave. Through the hole between the boulders, big drops glided rapidly across the stone ledge and fell one by one on the gravel below.

It didn't stop raining all evening, and they stayed inside the cave. Ausi woke up once and through the hole saw a yellowish-blue sky; she knew the weather had cleared and night had fallen. Holme lay by the opening, sleeping noiselessly.

She loosened the brooches at her shoulders and waist before she fell asleep again. A cool gust or two passed through the opening over Holme's body. If only she had something to cover him with, she thought. But he probably wasn't cold—he was like iron and stone.

Everyone except the thralls clearing the new field gathered around the chieftain after his fit of rage had passed. He fingered the blue welt on his child's neck, shaking his head silently at the mother's talk about trolls and other spirits. He looked around and found both stones.

"It was a thrall," he said to the warriors standing around him, and they nodded silently. The chieftain looked toward the forest, estimating the distance from

---

[7] The chieftain's wild frenzies indicate that Fridegård probably means him to be a kind of berserk, perhaps even a caricature of a berserk, a warrior who derived his power in battle from Odin and was therefore invulnerable and not subject to the laws of society. For a discussion of berserks, see H. R. Ellis Davidson, *Gods and Myths of Northern Europe* (Harmondsworth: Penguin Books, 1964), pp. 66–69.

the large rocks lying among the trees farthest away. He knew now there would be no peace in the settlement as long as Holme was alive and free.

The child soon got a little color back in its face and started whimpering. An old woman thrall put an herb poultice on the wound, and after screaming loudly for a long time the child finally fell asleep. Within a few days, he had almost recovered, but the stone left a bump, and he couldn't turn his head. To look to one side, he had to turn his whole body.

After what had happened to the child, the chieftain set out guards at night. Holme, coming out to the edge of the woods to find a couple of traps, saw a tall figure outlined against the night sky north of the settlement. During the days, the warriors—two, three, or alone—roamed about in ever-widening circles from the settlement. Two of the dogs came up to Holme in the woods, licked his hands and wanted to follow him. He drove them away with the shaft of his spear, but they stopped a little ways off, looking longingly after him. One day they might lead the warriors to the cave, he thought.

It was probably best to move on. Other places, where he wasn't known, would be glad to have a smith like him. He had thought about just staying on his own, of course, but winter was coming, and living with a woman and a child in the cave wouldn't do.

Still there was no hurry. The nights were short and light yet, and a long string of warm days lay ahead. Then, too, Ausi needed to be a little stronger before they started a long journey. He had seen her wash off blood at the spring while she looked around apprehensively. They had to make clothes for the baby, too; it couldn't always be at its mother's breast. They had cloth, thread, and needles.

Ausi brightened when he told her some of his plans. She thought back on life at the settlement with greater and greater aversion now that she was away from it—away from the warriors who were too proud to look at the women thralls during the day but who came panting with lust at night, pressing them to the ground under heavy bodies; away from the thralls carrying repressed rage and treachery inside them; away from the quiet but dangerous chieftain; away from the gossip, the bickering, and the almost daily fighting among the women thralls. She was away from all that now.

The pork they had in the well-spring stayed good only a couple of days even though Holme kneaded it with the block of salt. It was tiresome, too, to have the same food day in and day out. The bread they had left was dry and mouldy. There was plenty of fish in the small lakes, and Holme started putting his fishing gear in order. A hazel bush was growing by the spring, and he cut himself a slender pole to tie the fishing line to. When he was ready, he told Ausi to take the baby and come with him, and she complied, happy and surprised. He was probably afraid that someone from the settlement might come to the cave while he was gone. But the danger was certainly just as great of someone running into them in the woods or spotting them by the lake. He had his weapons along, but what good would they do against two or more warriors?

On the way, she worried the baby would start crying, but Holme didn't think the sound would carry far because of the brush. Besides, the baby didn't cry often; it ate and slept, and for a while, it would squint into the light while it held on to one of its mother's fingers. Its leg had almost healed. Holme had looked at it a couple times with the hint of a smile on his bitter face.

When they reached the shore, Ausi sat down against a sun-warmed pine tree. Digging in the sand pile under the dead reeds that had washed up on land, Holme soon found a worm for his hook. Rushes and water lily leaves covered almost all the water's surface, and he carefully lowered the hook between them.

He caught a fish almost immediately, and it flopped down in front of Ausi after a glittering flight through the air. It had yellow scales and red fins. Holme, descending on it like a hawk, held it up in front of Ausi's nose while she laughed in delight. Holme flashed a smile too before starting to search among the reeds for another worm.

Farther out, a duck paddled out of the tall reeds, followed by a column of ducklings, but it turned around when it saw people. A pair of grebes fished a long way out, diving and shaking their heads when they surfaced. Dragonflies sailed back and forth over the reeds with a soft rustle of wings, past two others that were mating. Low yellow flowers grew in the short grass where Ausi was sitting, and a couple of bees, completely golden with pollen, wallowed in them. A brown bird with broad wings flew silently overhead, peering down on the humans.

The fish kept biting, and Holme soon had a glimmering pile of them in the shadow of a tree root. He threw the smallest ones back, and they lay still a moment, belly up, before coming to life and vanishing. The hook caught on a lily leaf now and then and didn't come loose until the long, cylindrical stalk broke from its root to be yanked up with it.

Farther to the left, a little sandy point of land jutted out, where the water was green and warm. The tiny, crystal clear waves had cut ripples in the sand. Ausi walked there to wash the baby before they returned to the cave. The sand oozed between her toes, and the water formed cool rings around her legs as she waded out. Mussels had plowed small, serpentine trails everywhere.

She put the baby in the warmest part of the water, and its large head on its little neck hung heavily against her wrist while she washed it. The black hair on the front of its head rose and fell with the pulse.

Meanwhile, Holme strung a thin twig through the gills of the fish to make them easier to carry. By then it was afternoon; the shadows from the pine trees on the slope moved closer, and the water by the shore darkened. He untied the fishing line and hid the pole for another time. He took the hook and line with him.

When they reached the rise, they could see the woods on the other side of the lake. There was a glade in one spot, a square part of it shining a yellowish green, probably a field of grain. Gradually, they also made out a small gray building near the field. The hole in the roof was just a black dot. Two people at most could live there, maybe a couple of fugitives like themselves. Ausi felt a longing for house, home and safety again, and even Holme walked pensively the rest of the way back.

After Ausi had settled the baby down on the fragrant grass bed, she walked to the spring to clean the fish. Holme, as usual, busied himself with his tools and weapons. As she walked past him, she noticed his quick, bronze hands and the lock of black hair falling over his cheek. For the first time, she was proud he was hers. Little by little, her fear had disappeared, and she thought that it was his silence that had seemed dangerous to her before she had gotten to know him better. His foreign origin had probably affected her too.

In a cleft outside the cave, Holme had built a fireplace out of round stones from the ridge. After the fish were cleaned and washed, Ausi rubbed a fine dust off the salt block to cover them, and then she kneaded the salt in with her hands. She gathered dry grass to make a fire. Holme, looking in her direction now and then, took the tinderbox from his clothes and handed it to her.

Ausi had to strike several times before a tiny spark took hold in the grass and stayed alive. It would flicker and then catch on, helped by a soft breeze moving through the stones. The grass soon burned, and she stuck in a few dry white sticks before she put the frying pan on. When the pan got warm, she put in some of the pig's reddish-white lard, which had kept longer than the meat. Soon the fish were sizzling among the stones.

The smoke rose like a pillar, and she looked up at it with concern. If anyone stood on a rise and saw it, he would know that it didn't come from any settlement. It could lead the chieftain and the warriors there.

Ausi looked at Holme and saw her thought reflected in his face. He broke off a large spruce branch and came over to her. He fanned the smoke with the branch, forcing it to spread out along the ground. When it finally did rise, it couldn't be seen for long.

Once the fish were fried, Ausi put them on a rock next to her, then freshened the stale bread over the fire. Standing with tools in hand and working his jaws, Holme sniffed the air, but he didn't come until she called him.

Ausi heard Holme, busy just outside the cave, take a sharp, deep breath. She looked out, feeling terror paralyze her.

A warrior was standing a few steps from the cave—the gigantic Stenulf. He looked in surprise at the cave, the man in front of it, and the woman peering out. Then it all became clear to him and he nodded. Without taking his eyes off the warrior, Holme bent down and grabbed his ax.

Stenulf had his sword but not his bow or spear. He furrowed his brow at the motionless thrall and ordered him to follow along to the settlement. Ausi trembled, afraid he might obey but also afraid it might come to a fight. No warrior could defeat Stenulf. What could a thrall do?

The warrior didn't come any closer, and the thrall didn't move. The baby started making a fuss in the cave, and again Stenulf's face took on a startled expression. He must have come upon the cave by accident and hadn't been out searching.

Again Stenulf ordered Holme to put down the ax and come along. His beard twitched in irritation, and he looked menacingly at his opponent. Ausi sensed that he'd prefer to be on his way but didn't think he could.

Even in the midst of the danger, she remembered that Stenulf had been the first one to pin her to the ground. She had managed to escape the warriors' and thralls' rough hands for a long time, but Stenulf's grip had rendered her powerless. She hadn't been able to do anything to defend herself. She thought he was going to do it again once, but it turned out to be Holme instead. Though she feared and hated Holme, she had been glad it was him instead of Stenulf.

When the warrior saw Holme wasn't going to obey, he hesitated. He didn't want to draw his sword on a thrall, but taking him bare-handed could be dangerous. Neither he nor any other warrior had ever given Holme a beating; he had gone wherever he wanted to, a silent warning emanating from him. In the smithy once, Stenulf had looked appreciatively at his shoulders and arms as the sledgehammer danced, thinking they could handle anything.

A few steps behind Stenulf there was a big piece of wood that Holme had found and hauled back to make something of. Stenulf went for it, but at the same time Holme charged him with the ax, enraged by the contempt the warrior had displayed by not drawing his sword on a thrall. Stenulf parried the blow with the wood, but it was knocked flying out of his hand. He dodged quickly to one side so he could draw his sword before the next blow. Despite his size, he moved unbelievably smoothly. Now the thrall, armed with an ax, stood before the strongest warrior in the land, his broad sword drawn.

Ausi could see by Stenulf's face that he took his adversary seriously now. He stood with his knees bent slightly and kicked away a stone with one foot. Holme stood motionless again, waiting.

They stayed that way a while, but the warrior soon lost patience. He came at the thrall, who retreated, ducking the long sword as he tried to hack his opponent. Ausi expected at any moment to see Holme fall before the sword. She and the baby would be dragged back to the settlement, and the baby would be handed over to Stor and Tan for the second time.

Ausi crept out and grabbed the spear leaning against the cave entrance. Holme had been moving in a half-circle, and Stenulf, following him, had his back to her. She took the spear in both hands, rushed forward, and thrust it into Stenulf from behind.

A severe jolt almost knocked her off her feet, and the spear shattered in two. Stenulf had swung violently behind his back with his sword, catching the spear in the middle. As he did so, he lost balance, reeled and was unable to fully parry Holme's blow. The ax grazed his neck.

Inexplicably, the fight stopped. Stenulf sheathed his sword and with a look of arrogance at the thralls, walked up the ridge toward the settlement. Blood pulsed from his neck, and he hadn't gone far before it was flowing down one leg onto the ground. The spear had pierced the back of his clothes, but no blood showed. Holme and Ausi watched him until he reached the crest of the ridge, sank down the other side, and disappeared.

If he had condescended to turn around and look at his adversaries, his eyes, dulled by loss of blood, would have seen the man and the woman approach each other hesitantly, then rush together in an intense embrace. They reeled toward the cave, the woman crawling in first, her supple arms gripping eagerly after the man behind her. The baby cried for a long time before the mother drowsily clasped it to her chest, wet with milk squeezed from her breasts.

For a while they talked about the fact that they couldn't stay in the cave much longer. Not because Holme thought Stenulf would reveal how he'd gotten hurt; he'd let them think what they wanted at the settlement. They'd surely think he'd fought some warrior from another settlement. But their hiding place could be discovered again any moment; soon Holme wouldn't dare leave mother and child alone while he was out getting food.

Holme didn't feel proud of the fight that had just taken place outside the cave. He knew well enough why Stenulf had walked away—because Ausi had jabbed him in the back. He knew it was beneath him to fight women and thralls. Holme thought he and the ax would have pulled through even without Ausi's help. He had kept clear of the long sword, waiting his chance to hurl the ax at his opponent's head and lunge for the spear at the same time. Then, if the ax hadn't hit home, the fight would have gone on.

Holme crawled out and looked at the traces of the battle. He had to make a spear shaft before they started their journey. He remembered with reluctant admiration Stenulf's swing behind his back. If Ausi had been standing just a little closer, she'd be dead.

He picked up the pieces of the shaft and put them with the others. Then he followed the trail of blood up toward the ridge. Ausi stuck her head out, watching him anxiously. Stenulf might not be too far away.

On the crest of the ridge loose boulders lay exposed, and Stenulf's blood painted a ragged ribbon across them. The sunny hollow lay far below with its tufts of sedge and cries of birds. On the slope was a gigantic boulder, split in two. One part remained in place, but the other had slid down a few meters, plowing a deep furrow. In its shadow Holme saw something that made him stop, clutching his ax. There sat Stenulf, his head resting on his updrawn knees. He didn't move. His sword jutted out diagonally from his belt and seemed to prop him up.

Holme stood looking at him for a long time before moving closer. Stenulf had ripped a thick swath off his clothes and wrapped it around his neck. Seeing that, Holme knew his enemy was badly hurt, perhaps even dead. He moved closer, but Stenulf didn't move and didn't look up. His face was ashen above his beard and his eyes were shut. His whole left side was crimson with congealed blood. Holme went back to the ridge to find a place to bury him.

After Holme left, Ausi heard a bumblebee humming drowsily outside the cave. Now and then she caught a glimpse of it in the opening; there was moss underneath, and it probably had a hive there. Ausi had gone out after such hives many times and robbed them of their clear honey while the bumblebees buzzed around her hands or whined shrilly when they got stuck in the moss.

Why hadn't Holme returned yet? He'd been away a good while. She got up to look for him and smiled at the tenderness in her shoulders where his powerful hands had recently clutched them.

The sun was setting, and the moss on the west side of the large rocks shone even brighter. The bumblebee still buzzed close to the opening. A little farther up she found some large, dark red, wild strawberries in a crevice, and she picked them for Holme.

She heard clattering and saw Holme standing waist deep in the ground. He had dug a large, rectangular pit. On one side lay a pile of stones and on the other, yellow gravel and pebbles he had scooped up with his hands.

In answer to her surprised question, he pointed silently down the slope. The sun had moved a long way since Stenulf had sat down in the boulder's shadow, and it shone on his bowed head now. His round cap had two straps criss-crossed over the crown. It took a moment for Ausi to realize he was dead, and then she thought there had been another fight. Neither had thought the neck wound could be fatal as they'd watched the massive warrior walk with dignified strides up the ridge.

It was, in any case, a great relief that he couldn't go back to the settlement anymore and give them away. They could stay there calmly now, at least over night. Ausi gave Holme a couple words of praise before turning back to the baby, but he didn't answer or look up. The pile of stones grew, almost hiding him. The pit caved in constantly, making it needlessly large and irregular.

Stenulf was a heavy load to drag over the gravel and stones. His cap fell off, and Holme retrieved it, breathing heavily from his exertion. Then he got down into the grave and let Stenulf slide over one edge while he kept clear of most of the blood. He arranged the warrior's body on the stones, undid the sword, and bent it double in toward his knees. He didn't know why he did that, but it was supposed to be that way. He vaguely recalled that the sword had to die too if it was going to be of any use to its owner on his journey.[8]

---

[8] Schön, *Fridegård och forntiden*, p. 116, refers to the 1932 Norwegian museum catalog as the possible source for the notion of bending a dead man's sword before burying it with him. The catalog reports that bent swords have been found in Viking graves.

If they'd intended to stay in the cave, it wouldn't have been good having Stenulf so near. He hadn't been burned—no one knew what he might do. Only the burned could move; the unburned stayed where they lay. But how could Holme burn him alone? You needed a huge funeral pyre. The pyre would billow thick smoke for half a day, and many people would come to see what was going on. But this was unjust; Stenulf should have been burned and laid in a great burial mound.[9]

Holme shoved the finer gravel in first, but it didn't cover Stenulf; it ran down both sides and he was still visible. So he put a layer of round stones on top of him, but it wouldn't do to lay them on his face. Holme got out of the grave and walked down to the cairn by the cave. He had seen a convex piece of stone there that had broken loose from the side of a boulder and slid down into the moss. He would cover Stenulf's face with that.

After the second layer of round stones, only a few whiskers poked up between a couple of them. The third layer hid the tips of the toes, and then Stenulf could be seen no more.

Holme piled stones a couple of feet above the ground. Then he got a larger and heavier piece of rock from the cairn and put that on top. When he was through, he overturned the stones that Stenulf's blood had dripped on so the red trail was less noticeable.

In the distance the sun was low, shining like clear fire among the trees. The gravel was warm under his feet, but the moss he stepped into was cool as water. Everything had gone well; he had overcome a powerful enemy, but he wasn't happy. He had no desire to crawl into the cave to the woman, even though he had just been thinking happily and with renewed yearning about doing just that.

Instead, he sat on a rock, letting his thoughts about leaving take more definite shape. In one way or another, people would soon know they were living in the cave; it could be surrounded at any moment. It would have been nice to stay where they were; finding a place among strangers would be hard. He'd get by, of course, but the woods and freedom would have been the best.

The chieftain wouldn't take Stenulf's departure so hard. He himself would be the strongest man in the settlement now.

Holme looked timorously at the mound where the warrior was pressed beneath many layers of rock. None of this was easy to understand. Just a little while ago, he had been standing there, wrinkling his forehead, huge and dangerous; now he was resting quietly under the rocks and would never rise again. Over there lay the pieces of the spear shaft he'd broken off.

---

[9] Although some scholars argue that the dead were frequently buried intact, others argue that in the area in which Holme lives, cremation was the rule. See Schön, *Fridegård och forntiden*, p. 115.

"Holme," Ausi called softly, but he didn't respond and she couldn't see him from the cave.

He had started thinking about what he should have done. He should have left Stenulf's body alone and sent a message to the settlement so they could burn him and put him in a proper burial mound. He and Ausi would surely have had time to escape. But he couldn't do it over again now; Stenulf would have to lie there unburned even though it wasn't right.

Holme's chest felt heavy from all the things he didn't understand. He looked at the trees, at the rocks, at his broad, coarse feet and shook his head. So much had happened the past few days, though he hadn't wanted any of it. He had been forced to do what he did.

In a little glade where the sun flooded in before setting, a meager swarm of big mosquitoes played. The mound was bathed in the yellow evening light, and the long shadow of a pine tree divided it in two.

Holme's hands trembled and ached from scraping against the gravel, and he walked down and washed them in the spring. Ausi waited in the cave with cold meat and leathery bread. Her eyes took on a strange new expression when she saw Holme coming, shaking the water off his hands. He had given her a great and strange happiness that afternoon, and already she was looking forward to more. Then they would move on to a safe place and everything would be better. She felt completely recovered from childbirth, and her body was as clean and firm as before. They could move on the next day.

Holme closed up the cave more carefully than usual before they went to bed. He didn't look toward the ridge the last time he was out, but still he knew that Stenulf's mound stood out against the night sky. He thought with relief about how strong Stenulf was; maybe he could travel on even without being burned. He could probably throw the stones off. He ought to have meat and bread with him too, but what they had was nearly gone.

During the darkest time of night, a lean wolf, the fur scraped off its flanks, happened by. It caught the scent of blood, pressed its snout down in the moss, and snorted protractedly. Then it followed the trail to the mound and circled it a couple times. It stopped and wedged its muzzle between a couple of the stones while the fluffy fur on its back rose. A weak scent of smoke and human being coming from Stenulf made the wolf run in fear and rage down the steep slope toward the hollow where the night mist hovered above the coarse, cool sedge.

The wolf stopped by the shore, sniffing the area. A dog barking in the distance caused it to turn around and listen. Finally, with its tail swaying for balance, it stepped gingerly out onto the tufts of grass and made for the trees on the other side.

When Holme emerged, the forest was light and cool, but the sun wasn't up yet. In the dark cave, he had just seen the baby, still asleep, holding its mother's nipple tight in its gums.

Holme carefully closed the cave and put the dry spruce branch in front of it. But the ground there was getting trampled down — a path to the spring, like a line drawn through the moss and grass, was already visible and was even more conspicuous in the morning when the grass rose in the dew. It was time for them to leave.

He took his bow and a couple of arrows he had attached nail-sharp points to the day before. Beyond the spring was a large, dried-out marsh area where dwarf pine trees grew on six-foot high tufts of grass. Big, heavy birds usually perched there with blinking, fearful eyes and would rumble and flutter into flight when you were almost on top of them. He could probably sight one while it was still perched.

Tall, glistening grass hedged the area, and the soft blades brushing against his hand were damp. Cow trails wound through the tufts, which the cows like to graze on. There were some fresh droppings, and a swarm of glittering flies was buzzing around them even though the morning was still chilly. Rotten tree trunks lay helter-skelter, twisted round with tendrils of grass. The area reeked of marsh tea and meadowsweet. Holme walked cautiously, glancing from side to side, but a couple of heavy birds saw him first and took flight. He surprised a brown bird of prey eating a duck. It flew off, its victim still blinking though its chest was torn apart and half-eaten. The sun came up, shining through the thin needles of the dwarf pines.

Two small animals suddenly popped up in front of him and scurried off in different directions. They were light-gray rabbits, about half-grown. One sat down again after a few bounds, rose on its haunches, and looked around. Holme carefully put his bow down and searched the ground. He soon found a stick, a fresh branch from a dwarf pine, the twigs standing out on it like pins. The rabbit remained still, not running until he was right on top of it.

The chase was on, winding through tufts and thickets. Holme was just a couple of steps behind the rabbit when the ground turned to marsh and his feet sank. The rabbit got ahead but stopped when it no longer sensed the pursuer. The chase began again where the ground was firmer, and after a great effort, Holme managed to get close enough to hit the rabbit with the stick. It tumbled a couple of times, and before it could get to its feet again, Holme had thrown himself over it.

He went back to the bow, carrying the rabbit by the hind legs. It jerked violently, and he hit it with a rock to finish it off. It would be just enough to eat before their journey. They had plenty of cold, fried fish as provisions for the trip, and they could always get something on the way.

Ausi was still asleep when he returned, and he flayed the rabbit by the spring. A crow sat silently in the top of a spruce tree, waiting for him to finish and leave so it could take the entrails. He rinsed the small, reddish-blue carcass in the cold water and cut it in the right-sized pieces before he pushed the stone away and woke up Ausi, who yawned happily at the new day.

When the meal was over, the fire out, and the skillet cooled, Holme tied his belt around all their goods to make them easier to carry, leaving only the ax free. Ausi, who was shivering a little in the morning air, walked over into the sun on the east side of the cairn while she waited. She had tied her hair in a simple knot so it wouldn't swing loose during the journey. The baby lay in her arms, still looking without expression up into her face.

They had thought about following the ridge into the back country but had no more than skittishly passed Stenulf's mound when Holme stopped. He had gotten an idea, which he briefly explained to Ausi. They would go the other way, follow the shore along the cove to the settlement's mooring. When night fell, they would steal the rowboat. That would be much better than trudging through the woods in the daylight.

Ausi understood but was anxious about what might happen at the mooring. The chieftain had probably posted a guard by the boats when he realized Holme was around. Still, it would be nice to sit in a boat, skimming along the shore at night and hiding during the day. Who knew what they might run into in the woods?

Holme had already turned back, and once again they passed Stenulf's mound. Ausi cast a longing glance down at the cave—things had been good for them there despite everything. But soon the days would grow shorter and the nights colder; they had to have a house to live in like other people. A long time ago, people had lived in caves, but not anymore.

Holme walked barefoot in front of her; he needed a pair of shoes. She had her summer shoes on, but she would probably never again have her winter shoes with the fur still there on the leather. She had left a few other things behind too: a necklace of wild boar teeth and a white armband she'd gotten as a little girl from a warrior. Her friends doubtless had those things now and were glad she was gone.

They passed the spot where the pigs usually were, but not this early in the morning. A large area on the other side was black and chewed up. The lake was completely hidden under the water lilies and leaves.

It was just a couple hours' walk to the lakeshore, so they took their time. A few young spruce trees growing in a circle formed a small room with a shining green grass floor, and they stayed there half the day. It was quiet and warm; they could hear only the chirping of some tiny gray birds engrossed in plucking caterpillars from the spruce tree trunks and the soft rustling song of the grasshoppers in the grass.

They each ate a couple of fish before moving on in the early afternoon. The closer they got to the shore, the larger the boulders on the ridge became, and the harder walking got. Once they saw a little hut on the slope. Tall grass grew all the way to the smoke vent on its sod roof—there probably hadn't been a fire there for a long time. Holme went closer and saw that a whole stone wall had collapsed. The hut was worse than the cave they had just left.

Soon they heard the wind whistling softly in the treetops and felt the coolness from the lake on their cheeks. The ridge sank in a huge, even slope to the shore, and rocks glistened in the clear water as far as they could see. Even from the crest of the ridge, they could see small fish. There wasn't a boat in sight in the cove. Beyond the point of land, the waves were rolling and breaking, even though there was little wind.

Holme, in a good mood the whole day, talked several times about the boat and how much better off they would be with it. And they could really provoke the chieftain at the same time. Ausi agreed with him about taking the boat; Holme had worked the most on it and so it should be theirs. Just so everything turned out all right! Holme was too impatient to sit with her; he paced back and forth on shore, yearning for nightfall.

The baby fell asleep again, and Holme finally came and sat next to her. They talked quietly about the future and which way they should go first. They'd better keep hidden during the day and travel cautiously at night.

After a while, Holme took out his whetstone and started sharpening his ax even though it couldn't get any sharper. Ausi lay down and napped beside the baby. The sun neared the tops of the trees, the wind picked up a little, and small waves began to lap against the stones on the shore.

As dusk fell earlier, the dogs barked more frequently and for less reason than during the lightest summer nights. Holme stopped far from the settlement so they wouldn't catch his scent or hear his steps.

He saw no guard and heard no sign of life. The flax was still on the root, but the barley was harvested and laid out to dry. He would have liked to go to the smithy but didn't dare. Although the settlement was far away, he sensed its distinct odor, inhaling it with a curious longing in his chest—the smell of soot, bread, and the garbage pile.

Holme walked down to the shore, emerging a short distance from the settlement. He noticed at once that the long ship was gone and felt great apprehension before he got close enough to catch sight of the little row-boat. He listened again before approaching it but couldn't hear a sound from land or lake. The warriors were probably either out on a long journey or waiting by the small islands to ambush some merchant ship.

He untied the boat, and it grated slightly on the stones as he pushed it out. No one yelled or threw a spear or shot an arrow at him. He rowed silently along the reeds, occasionally hearing a terrified quacking and splashing in them.

A cow suddenly bellowed among the alder bushes, and he stopped rowing in alarm. He heard a few snorts and the sound of twigs breaking. Ausi stood close to shore, trembling with anxiety and cold as he emerged from the reeds that thinned out and ended by the rocks. When he approached shore, she was glad to see a couple of old skin rugs lying in the prow. She had seen them before, and she knew that the warriors used them in bad weather when they were out fishing in the cove.

Through the darkness, she saw Holme's teeth gleaming triumphantly. He didn't say anything about the warriors being out in the long ship; he didn't want her looking around. He could both row and keep a look-out himself and she could rest.

He rowed silently. The darkness grew more and more dense, then lightened again over the lake and land. Ausi dozed in the stern with one of the skins over her, awakening only to see if her baby was all right. Sometimes the reeds opened up, and Holme could sense a farmstead by the faint smell of smoke, a horse neighing, or a boat lying on the shore. At dawn, it got cooler, and light mists floated across the water. The islets farthest out seemed like black streaks and dots against the sky, rising red from the lake.

For a while after the chieftain's child had been hit by the stone, the warriors roamed around, hunting the fugitives. They weren't very happy about it either, preferring to believe that Holme hadn't dared stay around after what he had done. Hitting the chieftain's child was probably just his parting gesture.

The thralls lived in suspense from morning to night. They looked toward the woods constantly, unable to rest until the last warrior had come back at night empty-handed. Then they were content; it was like a victory for them. They predicted misfortune for the warrior who ran into Holme alone, and his helpers at the smithy were sure that even two warriors couldn't bring him back against his will.

The women's suspense was even greater. They never tired of guessing what might be happening to Ausi. Unlike the men, most of the women would have been happy to see her brought back and punished. Their disappointment was clear every time the hunters came home without their quarry. The chieftain was silent, but his face was red and the furrows in his brow deep. Stor and Tan ran around officiously on the little patches of field, pushing their companions about when he approached. Everyone except Stenulf felt uneasy when he was around.

The boy had almost recovered, but he still had to turn his whole body to look to either side. The mother never let him out of her sight again, and she looked mistrustfully at the woods whenever she was outside with him. The chieftain had finally convinced her who had thrown the stone, and it wasn't a troll.

While the grain was drying, the settlement's inhabitants were busy harvesting leaves. It was over an hour's journey to a deciduous area where the surrounding farmsteads each had a designated place to harvest. People swarmed everywhere with knives, hacking and chopping. Small, shaggy horses hauled the fragrant harvest away on low wagons with oak trundles for wheels. Those without horse and wagon carried the harvest, bound with leather thongs in big bundles, on their backs. People were everywhere on the slopes and meadows where there was grass, cutting it off to dry—but without the harvest there wouldn't be enough winter fodder. As it was, the cows, sheep, and goats stayed outside as long as they could feed themselves. Their coats were thick from the cold, and they tore heather and moss up from the snow with hardened muzzles. During the long, cold nights they roamed the farmsteads crying out loudly, drops of ice hanging like glittering wreaths from their mouths. Only the hairless pigs had to be kept inside, and they would answer the snorts of their freezing companions from their sod-covered sty, a rectangular mound beneath the snow.

When Stenulf didn't come back, there was great wonder at the settlement. He couldn't have gone back to his old farmstead; it was many days' journey away and he was feuding with his father and brothers. And he couldn't have joined another chieftain, because his weapons and other belongings were still there. Something must have happened to him. No one imagined that a single man could have killed him. Who could defeat Stenulf?

The warriors started searching again as soon as they could. The hay and leaf harvest demanded every man's attention, and there wasn't much spare time. A warrior following the ridge happened upon Stenulf's mound. He noticed that it was fresh but didn't see the cave or the traces of blood. He didn't think either that there was anything especially peculiar about the thousands of flies buzzing around the mound or sitting motionlessly on the stones, almost seeming to think. The warrior shook his head, more bearded than wise, and walked on. He failed to notice the faint smell of corpse on the lee-side of the mound.

Stenulf's bench remained vacant with the black and yellow shield and his bow above it. A few warriors mumbled about black magic; some thought he'd run into a wounded bear. Only the chieftain suspected Holme. He knew that the dark, silent thrall was dangerous enough with an ax or a spear in his hand.

After most of the harvest had been brought in, the warriors stopped working, leaving the rest of the job to the thralls. There was still the flax to cut and lay out to rot; the clearing wasn't finished yet but the thrall foremen, Stor and Tan, could see to it that every thing was done. The warriors started making the long ship ready for a fishing voyage. The big fishbasket by the shore would soon be empty.

The ship had six pairs of oars but no dragon's head on the high prow. The sail was yellow and black. When the wind was up and the oars drawn in, the warriors sat with their shields over the side, alternating the black and yellow. It angered them that the ship wasn't larger and didn't have a dragon's head, but the chieftain often talked about calling in a shipbuilder to build a bigger ship. There was a clump of tall, young oak trees near the shore that he eyed frequently.

The second day out, they saw something approaching from the north: three dragon ships with furled red- and white-striped sails and rows of shields of the same color. The warriors rowed behind an islet, stepped ashore, and watched the foreign dragons approaching at a good clip. They passed very near, white foam rising before the gilded prows. The dragon heads—huge red mouths gaping amongst the gold—gazed relentlessly toward a distant adventure. Fourteen warriors sat on each side of the ships, their round helmet caps visible over their shields. One man sat in the stem of each ship and another in the stern by the rudder. They had soon passed, and the warriors saw the dragons' wakes, which were sucked hissing along after them.

Great dissatisfaction took hold of the men by the islet. They looked contemptuously at their own ship and almost threateningly at their chieftain. A furious longing to sail out, far out toward the west, gripped them at the sight of the departing dragons. They walked around the settlement summer and winter just like thralls, and it was never any different. It would be better to join a chieftain like the one who had just sailed by.

Even their chieftain looked disappointedly and enviously at the dragons, and he renewed his promise to build a ship. They would fell the oaks that year so the construction could start the following spring. But the warriors remained sullen and troubled during the whole fishing trip.

When they approached the mooring, Tan and Stor were standing at a distance, frightened, calling out that the little boat had been stolen. Who could contain the chieftain's rage now that Stenulf was gone? Something bad would surely happen. They called out in unison that Holme had probably stolen the boat, then moved up the slope out of danger.

The chieftain, angry already, turned white and hard in the face. He ground his teeth furiously, but the warriors stayed there in a grim group. They were angry, too, and felt no desire to get out of the chieftain's way. A spark of reason still flickered behind his wrinkled brow, but his rage had to have release. He slung his arms around a huge rock, carried it over, and threw it into the water with a violent splash. The color returned to his face, and he walked quietly up the hill. From the settlement, his wife, her child on her arm, looked apprehensively at him, and the thralls stood erect in the field. But the chieftain just calmly asked which night the boat had disappeared. When he found it had been two days before, he gave up all thought of pursuit. They would just have to make do for the rest of the summer with the big boat. When the boat building began, they could use the leftover timber to build a new boat for travelling among the islands.

Gradually the chieftain began to be glad that Holme had left with the boat. He knew that the dangerous thrall wasn't nearby and that he no longer had to fear for his wife and child when he was away. His biggest problem now was finding a smith as skillful as the one he had lost.

When the sun reached its peak on the second day, Holme and Ausi saw a vessel in the distance. It looked odd and could hardly move in the warm wind. Holme rowed the boat into the reeds and forced it close enough to shore so they could wade to land and escape if they had to.

They couldn't see anything through the tall reeds, so Holme waded to shore and watched the slowly approaching vessel. He sat on a bare hill, grunting an occasional word or two in answer to Ausi's anxious questions. Behind him rose a dense pine forest, carpeted with thick, green moss. Holme was soon convinced the vessel was a merchant ship and posed no threat. He was just about to wade back to the boat and move on when he caught sight of something else behind the wooded point to his right. A dragon ship appeared in the sparse reeds; the head seemed to rise above the reeds to gaze out. Behind it came a second, then a third. They had been hiding behind the point. The foreign vessel was almost even with them, and Holme could see men running frantically around on it.

Holme called softly to Ausi, and immediately she came wading ashore with updrawn skirt. The baby was asleep in the boat a few steps away. The dragons picked up speed, their heads gleaming brilliantly in the sunlight. Then they burst out of the reeds, and fourteen pairs of oars apiece propelled them toward the foreign ship. The men on it lined up by the rail, long swords glistening in their hands.

Two warriors on the closest dragon slammed their axes into the ship and held on. The two other dragons hauled to on the outside of the first, and the warriors on all three rushed on board the vessel. There was a short fight; a couple of the foreigners fell, and some were shoved overboard. Holme and Ausi could hear them splashing. The men sank immediately and did not rise again. The others soon capitulated and were disarmed.

Holme and Ausi could make out an unarmed figure clad in a long garment, holding up something shiny. The warriors encircled the figure as if they were listening to its words. It couldn't be a woman because he was as tall as the biggest warrior and had broad shoulders.

After a moment's deliberation, the warriors' chieftain motioned for the strange figure to get into the closest dragon ship. He obeyed after lifting his hands above the prisoners — his companions — he was leaving behind. The warriors rowed into a cove, disappearing behind a point of land. Holme and Ausi stayed hidden, watching those on the lake who were getting ready to take the foreign ship in tow. The disarmed men had to stay on board.

The third dragon returned without the foreigner, and when everything was ready, they rowed toward the north with their booty in tow. A belt of reeds gradually blocked the ships from view; only the dragons' gilded necks could be seen for a moment more over the brown spikes.

Once the dragons were gone, Holme pushed the boat out of the reeds with a pole, staying close to them as he rowed slowly. Behind the point of land was the cove where the warriors had lain in wait and where they had put the foreigner ashore. There was a narrow sandy shore, and the clear water looked black against the woods behind it. The thralls, peering cautiously ahead, could see the foreigner still there on shore. He was leaning forward on a stone, holding his face in his hands. Anybody could have sneaked up on him from the woods and killed him. You could tell that he came from far away, Holme thought, looking at him in wonder.

After a moment he took his hands from his face and rose to his full height. They could see his face from the boat now, a light, beautiful, and beardless face, unlike any they had seen before. Ausi whispered to Holme to row away; he was probably a sorcerer with the power to destroy them. He took out the shiny object, raised it toward the sky, and called out some strange words that made the thralls shiver.

Holme knew then why the warriors had put the foreigner ashore. He was a sorcerer whom they didn't dare kill or take with them. He was probably busy even now calling down a storm or some other evil on the departing warriors.

The foreigner put the shiny object away and started walking toward the woods without having seen either the boat or the two terrified faces staring out among the reeds. He walked calmly, not looking around even though he had no weapon. Holme surmised that he didn't need to fear arrow, spear, or ax. Soon the tall, gray figure vanished among the trees. Toward the north, they could still barely make out the dragons and the booty, just a row of dark specks.

Holme rowed to where the foreigners had fallen into the water, but there was no trace of them. A tinge of red in the water indicated they had been cut down by swords and tumbled overboard.

Toward evening of the second day, they ran into a mild current. Holme tasted the water, and found it less salty there.[10] Several times they had to get out of the way of ships coming up on them or bearing down. But the people on board paid no attention to the fugitives who were keeping as close to shore as possible.

The shores and islets had grown steeper and rockier; they no longer saw many farmsteads or animals. The thralls slept a couple of hours in the boat, then continued at first light. They saw several boats by the shore, but their occupants—except for one, who kept watch—were asleep under skin rugs on the beach.

The counter-current got stronger and stronger until they reached the spot where it came rushing down on both sides of an island. They rowed against the western current, but had to step ashore where it was strongest. Holme waded along, hauling the boat behind him. Fresh water was above the current, and a ways beyond the round islet was a long island where they saw people harvesting leaves on the slope by the lake. In front of them on both sides stood dark, towering fir forests.

The farmsteads were closer together here than they had been below the current. They saw grass-covered roofs and small white cows everywhere. Farther back, the land sank down again and there was plenty of deciduous forest. Holme and Ausi looked apprehensively at all the buildings and longed for their cave.

Toward afternoon, they saw a little, solitary hut in a sparse fir forest a short distance from shore. They decided to land and ask around. A dense belt of reeds by the beach provided good cover for the boat. It felt good to have solid ground underfoot again. Before them lay a meadow filled with tussocks. Farther away,

---

[10] Fridegård apparently intends for the settlement that Holme and Ausi are fleeing from to be in east Sweden, near the Baltic Sea. As they row west on Lake Mälar toward the Viking market town, they move into fresh water.

it rose in wave-like plateaus, densely covered with prickly green thickets and several varieties of small trees. No one was in sight, but numerous animal trails wound here and there, crisscrossing through the brush.

The sparse fir forest began behind the scrub brush. The little hut was made of mud and stone; from a distance, they saw a man sitting on a bench outside it. When he saw them coming, he got up and went into the hut, coming out again immediately and leaning the ax he had fetched beside him against the bench.

Ausi stopped short with the baby, and Holme went on alone. The man looked at him calmly, cordially answering his questions. The market-town[11] was a half-day's journey away, and they could get everything they needed there. He also thought that a skillful smith would be well-received wherever he wanted to settle down. If they wanted to stay with him for a night or more, there was nothing stopping them.

The man got up and opened the door. He left the ax behind by the bench; seeing that, Holme did the same. Ausi came closer and the stranger invited them into the dusky hut. There was a table, a few benches, and a round fireplace inside. The ceiling and walls were covered with narrow square timbers, but the mud stuck through a little everywhere and had plopped down here and there onto the floor, the table, or the benches. A tripod, a frying pan, and two cauldrons stood by the fire. White, crafted wood—a bucket, tankards, bowls, and spoons—glowed in a corner. Holme inspected them more closely and nodded approval at the craftsmanship. Their host took out bread, cold meat, and water.

They didn't talk about themselves, but Ausi thought the man had been a thrall just like them. After they had eaten, he said he usually rowed to the market-town to sell his wooden wares once he had enough of them. He said something about their probably meeting again if they, too, were planning on going there.

In the evening he took out a couple of skin rugs for his guests and let them have the best benches. He went outside to get the door, which had no hinges but did have a heavy iron ring and a wooden bar. It would be impossible to get in without tearing the hut down, and Holme wondered why the man had such a sturdy door.

The wind had started up, and a big spruce tree on the east side swayed back and forth above the hole in the roof, spreading light and shadow on the floor beneath. A whistling wind rose and fell. The hut's owner lay awake for a long time, burning with desire for the woman, but whenever he moved, he sensed the man's watchfulness permeating the room. He had also perceived that he would come out on the short end in a fight with the dark thrall. The woman and baby

---

[11] Fridegård never mentions the name of the market town, but it is unmistakably Birka, a major Viking trading center that was established around A.D. 800 and flourished for a bout two hundred years. Its ruins lie about twenty miles west of present-day Stockholm.

slept calmly as the sound of the wind descended through the opening in the ceiling.

After the stranger from the plundered ship had been put ashore by the Norsemen and had seen them disappear with his vessel and its survivors, he walked aimlessly into the woods. He had seen respect and a reluctant timidity in the pirates' eyes, and in that he saw God's hand. He didn't know they thought he was a sorcerer. They didn't dare rob him of his gold cross, which he had held out as a shield. Many of them wore metal objects around their own necks, shielding them from misfortunes of many kinds.[12] They considered him strange and wanted to be rid of him.

He no longer thought about his men who had been killed in the fight. He had seen much and knew that wherever his faith had gone forth, it had left bloody footprints behind.

When darkness fell, he still hadn't seen a person or a dwelling-place in the strange, heathen land. He ate a few berries, drank water from a brook, and lay down to sleep where the rising sun would shine on him. He didn't know what kind of dangerous animals lived in the northern land but was sure they wouldn't touch him. That the wild pirates hadn't killed him he took as a sign that he'd accomplish his mission.

He woke up once in the gray morning light and saw an animal, a dog, sniffing at him from a few feet away. When the animal met his eyes, it snarled, but slinked off, its hackles up. When it was a little ways away, it fell into a lopsided trot, one eye glancing nervously behind it. The stranger laughed, turned over shivering in the moss, and waited for the sun to come up. He saw the insects, which the evening before had sunned themselves on the west side of the rocks, come crawling over to the east side to wait for the sun, just as he did.

He suddenly thought he heard the weak clang of a bell and realized he had heard it a moment before in his sleep—a muffled, beautiful sound that came closer and then died away. Could it be a heavenly bell encouraging him, telling him he was on the right path and need only proceed? In this heathen land, deep in the wilderness, there couldn't be any real bells.

He heard it growing distant, going away, and he felt himself strengthened and full of power. And the small cows, one with a bronze bell around its neck, walked on to their farmstead for the morning milking.

The stranger ate red berries growing around the stones on the slope before going on. When the sun reached its peak, he was able to get some bread and fried fish from a couple of staring, terrified women by the shore, and was reminded

---

[12] Worshippers of Thor often wore amulets in the shape of Thor's hammer, Mjöllnir, which Thor used to protect himself and the other Norse gods. The amulet resembles a crucifix.

that his Lord had once blessed such food. He tried to talk with the women, but they gathered up their things and left. They were carrying plaited baskets full of some kind of root they had dug up with straight knives.

From a high hill, he could see the lake winding into the distance. Large and small ships went in both directions, some with gilded dragon heads like those that had captured his vessel. Finally, he recognized a broad, Frisian vessel approaching among the islets, and he smiled victoriously. He was on the right path and merely had to follow the shore.

Farther inland, the land sank and the forest became more and more mixed with deciduous trees. Passing the heathen farmsteads, he saw people busy with their patches of land or carrying home leaves in big bundles on their backs. Everywhere, dogs rushed out at him, barking, and the heathens kept a watchful eye.

The stranger saw many people gathered around a large, dirt-black mound in a clump of birch trees, and there was the smell of a fire. Before he could get any closer, they had all gone off toward a distant farmstead. The stranger saw a stone they had dragged up, probably to stand on the mound, and beside it lay a big, still-smouldering pyre. The heathens had dug the earth up around it for the mound, leaving a few of their spades behind. Beyond the new mound, you could see others the same size, green with grass and topped with stones.

Here, too, the dogs rushed at him, barking wildly. Some men came out and looked down toward the grove. The stranger kept going, but the dogs didn't quiet down until he was far into the woods.

When night fell, he was still wandering on, trying to keep the shore in sight. The land had become more desolate again, filled with wild thickets or dark, mossy forest. In the darkness, he walked past a little hut made of peat moss and stones. It smelled of smoke, but a stout wooden door sat in front of it. The wind had come up; the tops of the spruce trees swayed and whipped back and forth high in the sky above the low earthen hut. Between gusts of wind, he could hear the never-ending barking of dogs that they had been able to hear from the ship and that had followed him through the woods, near or far.

The day had dawned a little by the time he came down to the shore again. A low boulder went in step-like progressions down to the water, and he found a calm and protected place. Above him, the wind took hold of the branches and angrily shook them. Far away on the lake, he could hear shouting, but he decided to wait for daylight to try to see across. His journey's goal was on an island; maybe he'd be there soon. He who subdued the storm, the wild animals, and the heathens was with him guiding his steps—he couldn't get lost.

He fell asleep and heard the powerful wind even as he slept. But the storm subsided with the warmth of the sun, and it was almost calm when he woke up. He went down to the shore and looked around. To his left was a sandy point of land with footprints on it and signs that boats had been drawn up. He decided to wait there until some boat passed by or perhaps some person on land.

The lone man in the dirt hut followed his guests to the boat and showed them which way to row. It wasn't far; they could be there before evening. He went out in the water and helped Holme get the boat loose from the dense reeds. From the lake, they watched him walk into the grayish-green waves of brushwood and disappear.

Farther out, there were still white caps on the lake. A long vessel with many pairs of oars fought against the waves, winning slowly. Another ship, its sails furled before the wind, approached from a distance at sizzling speed.

Holme and Ausi kept off shore the whole morning. The man in the hut had told them about the town, and Ausi was curious to see it. Holme sat silent and would rather have rowed in the other direction where there were large, unpopulated areas. The many, strange-looking vessels made him uneasy.

In one place, where the reeds were shorter and sparser, a sandy point of land protruded below a boulder. Holme rowed toward the point so they could land and rest a while. There might be plenty of fish by the point, too.

Both Holme and Ausi had walked up on the shore before they caught sight of the stranger. He was sitting on a rock again, and they recognized him immediately. They didn't know that the distance he had walked wasn't half what they had rowed, and they stopped in astonishment. Holme clutched his ax, but the man stood up and walked toward them with a friendly smile. He carried no weapons and probably didn't need any. The object they had seen him raise in the air hung on his chest now.

Ausi retreated behind Holme, apprehensively hiding the baby from the stranger's eyes. She heard his voice but didn't understand a word. He pointed across the water in the direction the ships were going, then at himself and their boat. She hoped Holme wouldn't take him along, although it might be just as risky not to.

Holme soon decided he didn't need to fear the stranger. He had heard the warriors talking about merchants from distant lands who talked strangely; this man was probably one of them. The warriors who put him ashore had probably been afraid he was a sorcerer or posed some other threat. Or perhaps they knew him and didn't want to do him any harm.

Among the foreigner's words, Holme heard the name of the market-town, and he thought it probably wasn't too far away. He whispered to Ausi to sit in the bow with the baby and let the stranger have the stern. Then he could keep an eye on him while he rowed.

Behind the next point of land, the lake spread out almost endlessly in front of them. Two or three boats within sight went diagonally across to an island with a couple of larger islands beyond it. Holme rowed toward them, and the stranger nodded. He looked with kindness at the thralls, and Ausi thought that if they did him a service, maybe he could do something for them in return. He looked noble even though his clothes were simple. His hands were clean and white, and she could see a band of fine cloth around his neck under the grey cape.

The baby began to get restless, and she tried to turn so it could nurse without her having to remove it from inside her clothes. She finally managed after a lot of trouble and looked apprehensively at the stranger. He sat looking around. The soft smacking noises the baby made eating were obscured by the waves lapping against the boat. She met his clear gaze a couple of times but turned quickly away. His eyes radiated a cool friendliness she had never seen before. The warriors were sullenly proud and vain, but this was different. She felt inside somewhere that people like Holme and her should obey and serve a man like him. He was above everybody and probably wouldn't even fear Stenulf, if he were still alive.

At a distance they could see a number of vessels anchored off a point. Some distance up on the land, a gray stone tower jutted out of the leafy forest. The market-town came into view, but Holme and Ausi still didn't comprehend that what they saw on the shore around the tower were numerous buildings.

When the stranger saw the market-town, he said a few words and looked toward the sky. Holme rested suspiciously on his oars, glancing stealthily at his ax. He probably shouldn't trust the stranger more than he had to. Although fortune seemed to be with him — the wind kept dying down more and more until there were no whitecaps to be seen.

Holme looked at the town a long while, then set course to a peaceful and unpopulated looking place well to one side. The stranger nodded again, seeming to be of the same opinion.

They saw people moving in a constant stream between the buildings and the shore, many with large burdens. Some men on horseback came across the flatland from the west. Around the whole enclosure was a high palisade with intermittent towers, probably by the gates.

The shore wasn't really unpopulated anywhere, but they landed at the calmest spot — a few children playing, a couple of small patches of tilled soil, and beyond them, a small hut. A little fishing boat had been pulled up into the sand.

Once ashore, the stranger nodded a friendly farewell and walked directly to town. Ausi watched him with relief mingled with disappointment. He must be a powerful man and could have helped them somehow. She said so to Holme, but he grumbled indifferently as he dragged the boat far up on the beach.

Holme bundled up the skin rugs to take along. They would come in handy if they had to sleep outside a night or longer. He wasn't sure they would stay in town. He would rather have rowed on toward the great, dark-forested landscape on the horizon.

A broad, well-travelled road cut through two stands of scattered trees. They met many people on it, but no one paid any attention to them. Ausi was surprised to see a woman dressed in gold cloth with several women thralls trailing behind her. She must be some great and wealthy chieftain's wife or perhaps the queen herself. She looked at no one, sticking her nose in the air as she walked ahead, glittering. Holme looked furtively at the train but didn't respond to Ausi's admiring chatter and speculations.

Apprehensive about the reception they might get, Holme decided to leave Ausi and the baby some distance away while he walked in alone. If he was attacked, he could fight or run, but what could they do?

When they were near enough to see the people hurrying between the boats and the buildings, he told Ausi to stay where she was and wait for him. He left everything with her except the knife, which he kept concealed in his clothes.

Ausi sat on the skins, uneasily watching him go. He talked with a man who came out of a gate, and she expected to see them start fighting at any moment. The man was fully armed with sword and shield. He pointed toward the gate, and Holme went inside but came out again immediately and returned quickly in his bent-kneed walk.

He looked a little happier as he hurried up to her and told her that anybody was permitted to enter the gates. Many people inside were no better dressed than they were. The man Holme had talked to thought he could probably stay with one of the smiths who traded with the foreign merchants.

As Holme told Ausi all this, he was thinking he was good enough to be his own smith and barter his own work. But he didn't want to live inside the gates. The treetops were visible far beyond the town wall; maybe he could find some-place to live there.

When the stranger passed through the town gate, he took the road to the harbor. Many vessels were moored there, gangplanks out, and he boarded one of them. He found the merchant, and they talked for a long time about the situation in the heathen land. The merchant advised him against staying and offered to let him return with him.

Norsemen came and went on the vessel, and the merchant talked with them, sometimes in their tongue, sometimes in his. Many men in this land had trav-elled widely and could speak both eastern and western languages. The stranger with the gold cross watched them with great interest with detachment. The cool friendliness never left his face.

The conversation ended with his saying good-bye to the merchant and walk-ing back to town again. He looked at the heathens' wooden buildings—well-built, many of them with beautiful carvings around the doors. It struck him how quiet this town was compared with those farther south. Without a word, people met each other on the streets; without a word, they listened to the merchants' torrent of words when they offered their elegant goods for sale. A nobly dressed man quietly clipped off a piece of gold from a spiral rod in payment for some cloth of spun gold. Most of those he met looked sullen or morose, and he knew exactly why. They hadn't heard the good tidings.

The stranger had learned as much as he could about the people of the north-ern land before he had come. It was known the world over that they were fierce pirates. The only good thing about them was that they seldom tortured their victims; they killed them swiftly instead. It was said, too, that they did not like to fight anyone much weaker than themselves and that they treated their women well.

The stranger also knew that their gods greatly resembled the heathens themselves: strong, bearded warriors who got drunk on some brew and devoured masses of meat after their battles. And he knew that the Norsemen didn't boast about what they had already done as other people did but rather made promises about what they were going to do. They told about their life's adventures only when they sensed death approaching and then whether anyone was there to hear them or not. Naturally they thought that the battle god heard and drew them to him.

The stranger believed that his tidings would change the sullen faces to happy, gentle ones like his own and that the heathens were unhappy without those tidings. He had no idea that it was the darkness of the endless forests that hung over their faces and the eternal whistling of the wind that sang in their ears. He attributed his seeing so many reddish-blue cheeks to gluttony. He knew little about the winter's chalk-white iron ring around a settlement when the wind died away for a few days or about the wolf's howling outside that was answered by the dogs' anxious barking inside. Little too about the cattle bellowing loudly when they heard a snorting bear clawing at the walls of the livestock pen, trying to tear them down.

The Frisian merchant had advised him to find the king and talk with him before doing anything else. Everyone was kindly received by the heathens, and they didn't plunder within their own land. The merchant knew many others who had come with the tidings before, but they had all failed. And the merchant pointed toward a hunched-over carrier who had just walked ashore with a load on his back. He had come many years before on the same errand, but had been a chieftain's thrall for a long time. He never spoke, and his body had become bent. The merchant had offered him a return trip but he had refused.

As the stranger walked up the street, he decided to keep that thrall in mind. An extinguished candle could surely be lit again. He would probably be a good helper and would know everything about the heathen land.

When the stranger passed the gate through which he had come, he saw the family from the rowboat. The man looked defiant and the woman uneasy as they stood inside the gate. They were beautiful, distinctive human beings, each in his own way, and for the first time he saw that the woman carried a child. He nodded cordially to them, and the woman watched him until he was blocked from view by a building up near the fortress. She thought that the way he walked confirmed that he was an important man.

The guard outside the fortress stopped the stranger with his sword and asked who he was looking for. When he heard the foreign tongue, he called for someone standing farther back in the courtyard.

The stranger noticed that the fortress was a clumsy imitation of fortresses in his own country while the buildings in the town were of a kind he had never seen before. He noticed too that people who seemed well off bore weapons from the south and west while the others' probably came from the north. A woman walked across the courtyard, her shawl made of fabric with threads of gold that was such a good item for the Frisian merchants.

The warrior who responded to the guard's call was old and gray-bearded. He could speak the stranger's language, and as they walked into the fortress, he named several places he had visited in the southern lands. He also knew both what the stranger's cross meant and what his god was called.

They passed a long hall full of weapons and benches along the walls. Many men were inside either sitting or lying down. Several game boards lay on a long table. The side of the hall facing the lake contained a series of holes that could be shut up tight with heavy wooden hatches. The fire pit was almost as long as the hall itself, but since it was summer it was clean and filled with fresh spruce twigs.

There was yet another yard to pass through before they got to where the king lived, a smaller yard with green grass and a clear well encircled with round stones. The yard was shaded and cool from the walls on three sides. The fourth wall had a parapet over which you could see the harbor with its many jetties and vessels.

The king could be distinguished from his closest warriors only by the chair he was sitting on. His indifferent glance at the stranger seemed to come to life when their eyes met. There was no imploring or obsequious smile on the stranger's face; it showed the constant cool friendliness that had calmed Holme and Ausi and that had made the wolf in the forest retreat with a snarl. Besides that, he was a stately figure and his movements were deliberate.

The king's broad hand pointed to a chair beside him. The conversation among those close by stopped, and everyone looked at the stranger. The cross on his chest glimmered, and most of them recognized it. Many of them had crosses of silver or gold themselves, stolen or copied.

The king didn't understand the stranger's language well, so the gray-bearded warrior translated for them. To the stranger's request to be allowed to teach the northern people about his god, the king answered that anyone could say anything he wanted to. The king himself would like to hear a little about the god sometime. After a couple of questions about whether the stranger thought that additional merchant ships might make yearly visits there, the king ordered a room and a thrall for the stranger. He could eat in the fortress and take refuge there whether the king was present or not.

The old man followed the stranger out and showed him where he would stay. He said that many others had come on the same errand, but most of them had soon turned back. The stranger answered only with a smile, and the old man looked at him in surprise. He wasn't like his predecessors; he was more powerful than they even though he had come on foot and they in good vessels with expensive gifts for the king.

But when the stranger was alone with the bare gray walls, the table and the sleeping bench, the strength that had stood by him when he had faced the pirates, the wilds, and the deadly animals abandoned him. Doubts beset him, and he felt powerless before these strong men whose wooden faces were either silent or raging. He lay face down and felt as if his god were far from this land, with little interest in the people living here. He felt an almost irresistible urge to walk down to the Frisian vessel and sail home.

He lay there motionless for a long time, but then as the immense physical exhaustion abated somewhat, his faith began to sing again deep within him. He considered all that had happened to him during the journey, and once again he was aware of a great hand following and protecting him. Among the Master's disciples, there had been a strong man who was occasionally overpowered by cowardice. He must be very much like him.

Soon he could feel the Spirit's power filling his body with a joy that caused him to leap from the bench. He met a pair of sullen, watchful eyes in a bearded face near the door. The thrall had come in without his hearing him and stood waiting silently. The stranger was surprised again. In his homeland, a servant would have bowed submissively to get in his new lord's good graces from the beginning. This one looked as though he'd like nothing better than to strangle him and be on his way.

The thrall held a beautiful bronze dish full of water and a linen towel. He put them on the table, and when the stranger nodded, he went out. But he stayed nearby and no one tried to give him other work even though he spent almost all his time looking out over the endless mainland forests.

From a hole in the long wall, the stranger could see an almost boundless field of large and small green burial mounds among the deciduous trees and realized it was the town's graveyard. From the far end, smoke billowed above the green treetops. He knew that the heathens burned their dead and put their weapons and other possessions with them in the grave. He had come to save them from all such errors or forfeit his life in the attempt.

For a moment he thought about the thrall couple who had given him a ride in their boat. The woman had looked so timidly and wonderingly at him—surely she could be the first to reflect the light. Like his Master, he would go down among the workers and the overburdened—although it would be a great victory if the king could understand and accept the light and proclaim it to his people.

As soon as he attracted some followers, he would build a church. The king would probably give his permission, because even if he remained indifferent, he wasn't hostile. Only after he had a church and a congregation could he start thinking about seeing his homeland again.

Once he had washed himself, a nagging loneliness drove him out again to the harbor to look for the Frisian thrall, but he wasn't there anymore. The ship had been unloaded, so he had probably gone on to another looking for work as a carrier. There was another harbor on the other side of the point, but it contained no foreign vessels, only the heathen land's high-prowed ships, the same kinds of bright-colored animal heads on many of them as the pirates had had on theirs.

The stranger walked along the shore until he came to the opposite palisade and followed it upwards. The buildings were smaller and shabbier there, made of wood and branches and mud. Many children, close to naked, were playing there. They had small bows and were practicing sharpshooting at a piece of bark on the palisade. Soot and ashes from hundreds of fireplaces was everywhere. [13] The smell of burned bread hung over the entire area.

Farther away, the ground rose to a big hill, soft and open in the sun, and the stranger took a deep breath. The church would stand there—the poor would see it as soon as they came out of their huts. They could come there with their troubles and fatigue once their work was done for the day.

The stranger stood in the sunshine on the hill for a long time, imagining the church rising before him. Many curious eyes below in the town watched him standing there, tall and motionless, the cross glistening on his chest.

In their confusion, Holme and Ausi had walked straight through town and were soon standing at the opposite gate. Through it they could see an area growing more and more dense with mixed forest and a few small buildings here and there. The sight drew them on; being on the outside again made them feel they had escaped some great danger.

To the left, they saw the vast graveyard with its billowing smoke. To the right lay the lake, dotted with fishing boats. A path led toward the huts at the edge of the forest and they followed it. Cows were either grazing or lying down everywhere. A few horses stood in a clump of trees, their long tails switching.

Many of the small huts seemed to have fallen into disrepair and were uninhabited. An old thrall tending the cows was glad for a chance to talk to someone and told them that anyone who wanted could take over the huts. If the owner came back, you just had to move to another. Several had been empty all summer and winter; their owners had gone east or west and never returned.

Holme brightened as he listened to the old man. He felt better there with the woods at their backs. He'd be able to see an enemy approaching from town and take shelter in the woods if he was outnumbered. Ausi was happy too. The town had frightened her, but she was still curious and wanted to know more about it. If they stayed here, they could walk in as often as they liked. Maybe she would see the strange foreigner again and could learn more about him as well. The thought of him made her strangely uneasy. She wanted to be near and serve him so that his clear, gentle gaze might fall on her again, as it had done a few times during the boat trip.

---

[13] An area of about thirty acres at the center of the Birka ruins has been dubbed 'The Black Earth,' since ashes and other organic materials from human habitation have greatly darkened the soil there. See James Graham-Campbell, *The Viking World* (New Haven and New York: Ticknor & Fields, 1980), pp. 96–97.

A hut just beyond the first few trees was in pretty good shape. The mud had fallen off, exposing the timber in a few places, and most of the birch-bark had come off the roof, but the wood was solid and strong. The door seemed to have had an iron lock once but was only propped shut now. Inside, long benches on two walls met in an angle, where there was a table with a top made of split logs.

The thralls looked around the hut with satisfaction. The fire pit had fallen apart, but an iron cauldron remained with its black, splayed legs still intact. The smoke hole was eaten away, crumbling around the edges; some grass and a couple of frail yellow flowers leaned over the edge, looking down into the dark room.

Ausi fixed a bed in the corner for the baby and then helped Holme, who had already started clearing out the room. He cleaned the ashes out and put the stones for the fire pit back in place. A leaky chest with a broken lock and bound with iron bands stood in another corner. Ausi was glad to have it and asked Holme to repair the lock as soon as he could.

The air in the hut was raw and chilly, so Holme brought in an armful of sticks and twigs. There was still some dry grass inside, and soon a fire was crackling and casting its flickering light on the walls. The baby woke up, and her dark eyes glistened in the reflected firelight. For the first time, Ausi seemed to see a smile in the ugly little face, and she told Holme about it delightedly.

Dozens of moths and other flying insects woke from their slumber in the chinks in the walls and began to flutter about the fire in a wild dance. In a couple of places by the wall some little mounds of dirt had been scratched up by forest mice.

Holme and Ausi smiled at each other across the fire. They had never dared hope that things would go so well for them. Holme hung his bow on a peg above the door, thinking how nice it was to have such a fine weapon. It was probably part of the reason for the journey's success. It had certainly helped them be mistaken for freemen—a thrall would seldom carry such a bow.

In several places on the outskirts of town Holme had heard hammer blows that sang in his ears. They came from smoke-billowing smithies, and in one of them he had heard the bellows whistling and squeaking. He longed intensely for the smell of coal and iron, for the heat of the hammers and for the tongs, from the longest kind for taking iron out of the fire, to the smallest for making seams and nails. After he had put his hut in order and fixed a lock for the door, he would go to the smithies and ask around. If only they were in the woods. But no doubt, the iron had all came by ship; there was no ore on the island and no bogs—nothing there for a miner to do.

That evening he rowed the boat closer to his new home. The lake was almost calm, and beyond the expansive, glistening water rose the mainland forests, black and jagged against the sky. He heard a yell from town now and then, a banging door, and dogs barking everywhere. A herd of cows came out of the woods near the hut and ambled toward town, their heads bobbing. Holme rested on the oars, not knowing what he wanted. The woods tugged powerfully and incessantly at him, but like Ausi he wanted to get to know the town a little better—to stay a little while, especially since they had a good place to live. Maybe the smiths here knew more than he did and had better tools. He wanted to find that out most of all.

Small boats littered the sandy shore, and he put his among them. A number of them weren't locked; there probably wasn't anybody around who had to steal a boat.

He saw the town wall with its look-out towers in the distance and wondered what enemy they were afraid of. Who could come across the water with enough warriors to defeat the town's defenders? They wouldn't even be able to land; he had seen dense pilings outside the harbors, and only someone who knew about them could navigate a merchant ship to the unloading docks. Of course, he didn't know how far the island extended on the other side. Maybe danger was luring there.

The fire was still burning in the hut and the air was warm and dry. The moths had stopped swarming and were crawling on the floor, dazed. Ausi had moved the two benches together and had put the skin rugs on top so all three of them could sleep there. After a quiet conversation filled with laughter, they both took off their clothes after so many days of cave life and flight. A little embarrassed, they sat next to each other, letting the warmth of the fire and the coolness of the night dance around them. The baby slept under the skin, her head a little black speck over the edge.

They talked of the distant settlement—of their friends, the grain, and the flax. Ausi wished that the envious women thralls could see her living in a hut she could call her own.

In the silence, both longed for their work and companions—for the smell of the fire, for the pigs, the outlying buildings, the woods behind and the cove below the settlement. The new place, with its mass of buildings and throngs of people, intimidated them.

Before Holme lay down, he propped the heavy table against the door. Ausi lay white and soft on the bench, chewing on a strand of hair and following him with her eyes.

When the first snow-squall came rolling across the cove, the whole settlement was ready. The barn had been stuffed with hay and leaves, wood had been stacked in huge piles, the roof and walls had been examined and repaired. The pigs, still outside during the days, ran, long-bristled and squealing, toward their pen for shelter. The swineherds let them in with a laugh, and they got to stay inside all the time once the snow began falling; during the winter, the thralls fetched them one by one, although they put up a fight, their protracted screams echoing across the cove and ending in a death-rattle. A few drops of blood would be left, enticing the dogs to lick the snow and magpies to flutter around the area until the next snowfall turned it white and clean. When spring arrived, only the boar and mating sows would remain.

The cows came home from the woods and stood around mooing for a couple of hours, but when no one paid any attention, they lumbered off again to the trees. At dark, they tried again and were allowed to go into their stable overnight once a little snow had fallen. In the last gray daylight falling through the light holes, the women thralls squeezed the milk from the cold, limp udders.

Both thrall dwellings were empty and dark during the winter. The chieftain thought it unnecessary to heat them, so the thralls were permitted to stay by the door in the high hall. The long fire extended almost that far and kept them warm. The area was divided by a couple of skin rugs hung over a beam, and the women slept on one, the men on the other side of the partition.

The first few nights, a thrall would sometimes try crawling under the skins or a warrior from outside the hall would try sneaking in to the women. But the older thrall women raised a fuss each time, whether to the joy or disappointment of their beseiged younger companions. The thrall or warrior vanished quickly before anyone could see who he was. In a couple of instances of a long-standing relationship between thralls, the old ones remained quiet or enabled them to meet undisturbed in an outlying building or in the woods.

In the autumn, all kinds of work was done to prepare for winter. The hides were cured, thongs scoured, awls and needles sharpened with small slate whet-stones. The loom would bang all day; when one woman stepped away from it, another stepped in. Holme had made one weaver's reed out of iron; the chieftain's wife had bartered in town for another made of whale bone.

The women spun flax and wool thread by the fire. They kept an iron or bone spindle-whorl on a rod spinning constantly with one hand, and worked the thread with the other. Each one owned her own spindle-whorl and often had it buried with her.

The chieftain's child crawled around by the fire or pulled himself up, grop-ing along the benches for support. He still had to turn his whole body in the direction he wanted to look. The stone had left a hard lump, but on the chief-tain's orders, the old woman had stopped her poultice treatment.

One of the younger thralls began to show signs of pregnancy. The chieftain's wife noticed and talked several times with her husband about letting the baby live. Their own child would need someone to wait on him and be his playmate when he got bigger. Finally the chieftain growled his consent. From that moment, his wife saw to it that the pregnant woman got the lightest work possible, and occasionally she would point out the good fortune awaiting the child.

After the snow cloud had passed, a thin layer of snow glittering in the dusk covered the hard, frozen ground. The chieftain and a couple of warriors stood outside in the enclosure, wondering how the winter would turn out. They hoped it would be mild and brief. A long, long time ago, the summers had been longer and warmer.

The sound of thralls and squealing pigs came from the pigsty. It had been divided in two, and the thralls had to keep the animals in the two sections separated. Sometimes a skinny, gray pig, kicked and sent flying, stood still a moment grinning into the cold wind, then returned to the fray. Outside the sty stood big piles of acorns and roots for the pigs' winter fodder.

The warriors urinated on the ground, making the earth peek through again in black, steaming patches. Going into the hall, they laughed at the thralls' battle with the pigs. The long fire burned, and gray smoke hung under the ceiling's sooty beams. Close to the fire, the shoemaker sat with his work. He wandered from farmstead to farmstead, staying as long as he was needed. Neither warrior nor thrall, he was still widely known and sought after. He brought all the news from town, the farmsteads, and foreign lands.

The skins for winter shoes had the fur left on them for warmth. Around the shoemaker were piles of old shoes needing repair before he started making new ones. A couple of warriors already sat beside him, listening to his talk. After the evening meal, he would be the center of attention.

This time he brought news that another man from the south had come and had the king's permission to stay in town and teach the people to believe his new god. But he'd probably be driven away by the people pretty quickly or maybe even slaughtered in the nine-day sacrifice — hung up in one of the sacred trees or perhaps drowned in the sacrificial well. It had happened before. As they were all aware, the king had no power to save anyone the people had sentenced.

Stenulf hadn't been seen or heard of anywhere, and the shoemaker was very surprised about his disappearance. He had probably displayed arrogance to one of the gods, and they had killed him in the forest. One of the warriors said that Stenulf had never carried any protection against evil spirits or trolls; maybe he'd had a run-in with them.

The shoemaker hadn't seen Holme or Ausi either. But he had come by land and they had undoubtedly taken the coast route since they had the boat. Sooner or later, though, he'd surely run into them. Probably nothing much had happened to them — they'd just been allowed to stay at another farmstead.

In a partitioned storeroom lay a great many forged iron rods. Those that weren't used at home at the settlement were taken to town on the winter trip. So too with grain and meat if it looked like there'd be a surplus. Sometimes a bundle of cloth, some hides, and various wooden utensils would also be brought along for bartering.

After the midwinter sacrifice, when the sun was strong enough to make the snow on the roof soggy and heavy but not to touch the ice, everything would be loaded on sleds for the journey to market. The chieftain, his wife, and most of the warriors would go and stay for a few days. The best harnesses hung ready, bronze fittings and chains holding the hames together.

Up until then, there had been no roads leading to the settlement, only a sled path from the lake. Winter fishing was the warriors' only outdoor pastime. Among the barren trees in the grove, you could see the memorial stones with caps of snow on their gray tops. Great swarms of various kinds of birds flew from the forest, looking for spilled grain between the outlying buildings or scouring the garbage pile.

A few snowflakes fell intact through the smoke vent in the roof, creating tiny wet specks on the clay floor. The chieftain's stiff-necked child watched them with interest, poking them. Whenever anyone came in the door, the smoke by the vent went wild from the draft. Large and small iron containers stood by the fire, and a wooden tub with iron bands around it filled with clear spring water stood in a corner.

When everything was quiet, you could hear the murmuring waves from the cove through the smoke vent. Toward morning, the blanket of smoke under the ceiling disappeared, and it got colder inside. The snowflakes settled on the floor, glistening a moment before melting.

Outside, snow and darkness, wolves, bears, and wild boars would hold sway for a long time to come.

Ausi hadn't seen the stranger again the whole autumn, but Holme told her he was still in town. He had come to the smithy once to talk to the smiths. They couldn't understand everything he said, but the master smith, who was from the stranger's homeland, interpreted most of it for them.

Holme had heard too that the king had taken up the stranger's cause and was protecting him. Some of the people from town followed him almost everywhere. At his place in the evening, he would talk with anyone willing to listen. A few had even let him pour water on them so they might become like him.

Ausi thought a great deal about that when she was alone all day. How could they become like him? She had heard a lot about the old gods and had seen much sacrifice to them, but they didn't care about women and thralls.[14] From what Holme said, the stranger had more women than men among his followers. That was remarkable and encouraging. If only she knew more about it.

She walked to town a few times while it was still summer, but carrying the child with her was cumbersome and difficult. She also noticed that Holme didn't like her going even though he didn't say anything. Since autumn had come, cold wind blew almost constantly from the lake, and neither of them had enough clothes. Holme got cold too walking back and forth to town, but he said nothing. Soon he would have worked enough for winter outfits for all three of them.

Shortly after they arrived, Ausi saw the three dragon ships with red and white sails steering in toward town. They didn't have the stranger's ship with them. She noticed they stayed for a few days, but she had no way of knowing

---

[14] Schön, *Fridegård och forntiden*, p. 104, observes that Fridegård could not have found any historical support for his notion of the Nordic religion's being undemocratic. Thor, for example, was considered the people's god. See the afterword to the present volume.

that the stranger had also recognized them and, with the king's help, had gotten back a few small items. The ship belonged to one of the men who had fallen, and nothing more was said about it.

The days seemed long at the edge of the forest, and the fire had to burn all day. Holme told of dreadful, evil rumors from town—the sun wasn't coming back; everything would freeze into oblivion. Someone kept daily watch from the tower; people often stood on the rocks and hills watching for the sun. Every day, the air was thick with sacrificial smoke. Many people thought the stranger had angered the gods, and they demanded that he be sacrificed or at least driven away. Then one day, the haze lifted and the sun burst out over dazzling fields of snow. A thousand-voiced shout of joy rose from the town and scared Ausi into locking the door.

From the doorway, she could see the narrow path Holme had forged. It led straight as an arrow to the town wall. If anyone approached on it, she would shut herself in and would not open up, no matter how hard they might beat on the door. Black cargo wagons moved slowly across the frozen lake's endless expanse.

Ausi knew that two such wagons would soon be coming from the settlement; they usually came a little while after the sun returned. Some days she would gladly have gone back to the settlement if only she could have kept her baby and Holme with her. She longed to be there now when the ground was bare under the pine trees on the slope and the snow slid down off the roof, causing the dogs to dash up barking.

But the next instant she would think all was well. If they went back, they'd never get away again. She'd never learn more about the town or the stranger and his teaching. If only she dared go where he talked to people who wanted to listen. They congregated in the evenings after the work was done for the day.

Should she suggest to Holme that they both go? The baby could sleep by herself for a while. No, Holme would never agree. Maybe she could go alone once the evenings got a little lighter. Maybe the stranger would recognize her and talk with her in front of the others. The thought made her cheeks burn with pride.

When Holme came home, he said he had seen their old chieftain and a couple of his warriors. They had come into the smithy to sell some iron, rods that Holme had once forged himself. They hadn't recognized him; they hadn't looked at the smiths and Holme's back was to them. They had had to go on someplace else since the smithy already had enough iron, but the master smith had examined it anyway and had said it was fine, pure iron.

Holme said no more to Ausi, but the settlement stayed in his mind all night. He almost missed it; he had been master there and had had two assistants. No one ordered him around. When work was over, he had always enjoyed gathering with the others to hear about the day. Occasionally someone would show where the chieftain had hit or kicked him, but never Holme.

But when summer came, he would move on with Ausi and the baby. There must be some farmstead in the mainland woods that needed a smith. A man could roam widely there without hearing waves lapping and without always running into the shore wherever he turned. The forest was dark and the moss deep. Here you never heard a wolf howl, or a fox bark, or wild boars squealing in rage as they fought.

His friends in the smithy urged him daily to move inside the town walls. Didn't he know that only outcasts lived where he did? You had to be an outlaw or crazy. And if the town were attacked from land some night, he would be the first killed and his woman taken away into thralldom or something even worse.

Holme already knew that. But he was more comfortable outside town. Besides, why should anything happen just now? A big assault on the town was only possible during the summer when the lake was open. He didn't care about his neighbors; they didn't bother him and he seldom saw them. Only narrow paths in the snow and the smoke from the roofs indicated that anyone lived in the little huts.

Work was fine, but he always looked forward to the day when he'd be on his own. He was just one of five here, but he wanted to be first or on his own. There was nothing for him to learn in the big smithy; he had done everything before. They made weapons, plows, knives, pots, and frying pans, and he had made all those things at the settlement. He could test out new ideas back there, but here someone else determined every blow of the sledgehammer.

The days in the cave had been the best of his life. He would never forget his happiness when Ausi had taken hold of him and drawn him to her in the cave. But he had gone into the woods so she wouldn't see that; she shouldn't know. He had never dared believe that she, the most beautiful woman at the settlement, with her cool disposition, would be his the way she was in the cave and had been ever since.

He didn't want her walking around town alone. Some powerful man, perhaps the king himself, might see her and force her along with him. When summer came, they would leave, and in a good forested area somewhere, he'd build a better house than this one. He'd see to it that he had various kinds of tools with him, and they would own some cows or at least some goats so Ausi would have something to do.

Ausi felt a strong urge to turn back about half-way to town; she was so unused to going alone. Holme had finally given in to her, though hoping she would hear the stranger once and have enough.

It was half light; the snow had melted slightly in the midday thaw, forming a crust on the surface. The lake was still covered with blue-gray slush, but showed an open, clear black rim near shore where a couple of birds were swimming. A distant flock flew off with a whistling of wings.

Holme had sullenly given her directions. Past the fortress, up the slope, a nice big building with a cross on the door, like the one the stranger wore on his chest only made of wood. Besides, she couldn't get lost; the stranger had someone standing outside, luring in any passersby. Sometimes he was successful, but once in a while he found himself lying flat on his back. Served him right; he had to learn to leave people in peace.

Heart pounding, she walked through the gate without looking at the little guard room. She heard the guard jump up from his bench and knew he was watching her, but he didn't call. She wished she were a little better dressed, but it would soon be dark.

Many men on their way home met her, but they didn't even notice her. She felt a little safer passing the fortress she knew was full of warriors. She thought about the people from the settlement, but they had gone home a long time ago. Holme had kept an eye on both their sleds, and finally one day he saw them disappear on the distant ice.

At a distance she saw the building and hesitated again. Two women came up behind her, and she let them pass. They walked purposely straight toward the building, and she followed. A man opened the door and gestured them in.

Some benches lined the wall and others ran straight across the floor. A good many people sat there, and she saw a couple of well-dressed warriors in the first row. One of them had a gray beard and friendly eyes.

The stranger alone sat at a table. His head was bowed, and something rested in front of him. Ausi shivered and her heart pounded. This was both upsetting and delightful. A strange candle stood beside the stranger's head, a kind she had never seen before. It burned noiselessly as though out of great respect for him. How could a flame be so quiet and still?

A few more people came in, and then she heard the man close the door. He walked forward, stood behind the stranger, and waited. The stranger kept sitting there, and not a sound could be heard in the hall.

After a while, the stranger rose and slowly looked out over the congregation with a clear gaze familiar to Ausi from the boat journey. In a soft voice, he spoke and she listened without understanding the words. Her head swam, and she wanted to crawl on the floor to his feet. By the time she had calmed down, he was speaking short sentences, and the man beside him translated them after him. It took a moment before she knew what it all meant, but eventually she was able to follow along and understand almost everything.

It was as Holme had said; the stranger's words were even for women and thralls — in fact, for them most of all. Ausi anxiously looked at both the warriors, but they sat quietly, calmly. They didn't knit their brows and stomp arrogantly off even when the stranger clearly said that the first would be last. This was all very odd. The chieftain and the warriors at the settlement surely would have torn the whole building down if they had been insulted in that way.

She saw the faces of the women and thralls light up with joy when the stranger said that the new god demanded nothing; no animals had to be slaughtered for him, no silver or gold buried in the ground. The warrior wounded in battle or the thrall woman sick in the forest — both could crawl forward to the Powerful One, be comforted and healed.

When the stranger had finished speaking, a man rose from the bench by the wall and said in a harsh voice that he didn't believe the stranger's words anymore. Nothing had improved for him even though he had done everything he was supposed to. He had always had bad luck and still did. He was leaving and would not return. He might just as well stick with the old gods or have none at all.

The stranger didn't look at the man who spoke and didn't seem to hear him. He picked up the candle and walked among his listeners, saying a few friendly words here and there. All eyes followed him, sparkling with reflected light.

When both were standing in front of Ausi, the stranger looked at her in surprise. She was looking down, and her long eyelashes cast shadows on her cheeks. Her chest heaved under the bronze brooches. The stranger searched his memory and soon placed her. He was glad and took it as a favorable sign that she had come there of her own accord. Her black-haired husband wasn't along, but maybe he would come eventually.

The stranger spoke a few friendly words with his hand on Ausi's head, but she got up and walked toward the door when she realized she would burst into tears at any moment. She couldn't get the door open, but the interpreter was just behind her to help. Just as she went out he said something that she didn't understand. Probably something about coming back another time.

The town was deserted now, and she walked between the rows of silent buildings. She didn't meet anyone, but a fire burned in the guard room, shining on everyone who passed by. She hurried quickly through and heard the guard get up again and come out. His voice followed her, laughingly suggesting she come into the guard room with him. He had such a nice bench in there.

The spring night was silent outside town, and the air was mild. The footpath was a dark stripe in front of her. Melted snow trickled across the path in one spot, and when she walked under a big spruce tree, a couple of heavy drops fell on her. She felt the moisture seep through her shoes and spread out under her feet. But she'd be getting new shoes and clothes soon.

It wasn't so dark she didn't see the numerous footprints that had appeared since she left. Several times, Holme had walked out about half-way and back. He had been anxious about her and that made her happy. Holme, the baby, and the hut—they all seemed more pleasant and dear after she had been away for a while.

Ausi had wondered if Holme would be gruff and angry, but he was himself. He listened to her story without scorn but also without great interest. He had warm food in the cauldron for her—a meaty bone with broth and cooked roots.

She held the baby to her breast with her left hand and ate with her right. She talked, and Holme finally showed some interest when she said that the new god didn't want anything for what he did. That was why he was so good for thralls and other poor people.

"And you shouldn't burn your dead anymore. Someday the new god will come back and wake them, and then you have to be unburned so you can arise. Anyone can understand that . . ."

"Is that what he said?" Holme asked, getting up suddenly from the bench. "Don't you think he's lying?"

"No, I don't."

Holme lay down again pensively. If that were true, then the strange god could awaken Stenulf. Holme had often thought of him uneasily. He would tell the stranger approximately where he was so he wouldn't be forgotten.

Then the nice, white god could see a real warrior. Holme imagined his huge shoulders shooting up out of the mound, hurling the stones down the hillside. It was good he had his sword with him. The strange god would be glad to count Stenulf among his warriors.

As he thought these things, he watched Ausi. She was like a completely different woman. Her cheeks were red and her eyes glowed. He felt uneasy again when he saw how beautiful she was in the firelight. He must take care that no powerful chieftain caught sight of her. If only the summer would come soon; then the woods would hide her.

Naturally, she could attend the stranger's meetings again sometime since she seemed so pleased with them. There didn't seem to be any harm in that. She said herself that only a couple of warriors were there, otherwise mostly men and women thralls.

He was glad to know about the unburned being called to life again by the new god. He wouldn't forget to show where Stenulf was.

Ausi was wide awake and excited by her experiences. She told the whole story again, except for the stranger's putting his hand on her head. She had a feeling that might make Holme suspicious. He wouldn't understand how the stranger had touched her. It was like a father's hand she had felt on her hair, yet different. He was so young and tall.

She moved restlessly on the bed, unable to decide what she wanted. Holme lay quietly, perhaps sleeping. Her body was tense and warm; she wouldn't be able to sleep for a long time. If only Holme would take her; tonight she needed the limpness and heaviness that followed. She had been wanting that ever since coming home and the thought lingered, burning.

She raised up on her elbow and looked carefully over his ear and the black lock of hair. His eyes were open, and he looked up with surprise and joy. Their eyes met, lingering and enticing, and then lost focus. Holme had longed for the moment when she would come to him again of her own free will.

The dying fire caught an unburned twig and flared. It crackled, lighting up the room a while longer. By the time it went out again, Ausi was asleep in Holme's rugged arms.

From the door of the hut, Ausi could see the lake grow darker and darker in the sunshine, and one day a warm and strong wind started blowing. The ice rumbled and sang; it shot up on the land in big floes that glistened in the sun as far as she could see. The snow was gone except in the woods, where isolated drifts grew dark with pine needles and yellow birch leaves.

The evenings were light now when Holme came home, and he often looked off toward the mainland forest that rose up dark against the spring sky. Restless and uneasy, he busied himself with his tools and kept acquiring new ones. Once the ice was gone, he worked several nights putting the boat in repair. A couple of friends from the smithy helped him lower it into the lake.

Ausi followed all this anxiously, knowing perfectly well what it meant. But she didn't want to go back to the woods; too much was holding her where she was. She had been to the stranger's house several times and understood more and more of what he said. She had gotten to know a couple of the women, and she longed to see them again and hear their voices. It had been so long since she had been able to talk with other women.

Memories from the settlement and the cave came to her less frequently now. She had so much to be happy for; here no warriors tried to rape her, no dangerous animals lurked in the forest, and then there was the stranger. A pack of wolves approached over the ice one cold winter day; she saw them when they were only small black dots in the distance. But they stopped, sniffed toward the town, and then ran diagonally past the island toward the other shore.

It would be good if she could get Holme to go see the stranger with her. But he wouldn't listen. All he cared about was that Stenulf wouldn't be forgotten if the unburned were truly to rise again some day. He had asked her to describe to the stranger as well as she could how to get to the mound.

But she'd eventually get up the courage to discuss her problems with the stranger. He'd probably know what to do. She didn't consider for a moment staying behind if Holme left, but her heart sank whenever she thought about the forest that would hide her for all time.

She saw the group as it passed through the town gate, and she began getting the baby ready. They were walking along the shore, and if she took the road through the woods, she would catch up with them. She could recognize the stranger and the old warrior bringing up the rear. Some women were walking in front.

Her new clothes were light-gray linen, and Holme had come home with two large bronze brooches for them. She carried the baby in a woolen sack, and as she walked, the baby laughed and reached for her nose and chin. For a moment she thought of the chieftain's child and the stone Holme had thrown at it. She still thought it had served them right—why had they put her and Holme's baby in the woods? Besides they could have more children if that one died.

Her new clothes and the times she had been to the stranger's assemblies had made her less timid. She walked boldly up to the people on the shore, and everyone greeted her warmly. The women came over to admire her baby. A couple of them had children with them too.

The group continued along the shore a ways and beyond a point that blocked the town from view stopped near a little cove with a sandy bottom and calm, clear water. A couple of ducks flew away, arced in a half-circle and landed again nearby.

The stranger had already explained what his god demanded from his followers, and everyone thought it was simple. Somehow, of course, he had to be able to tell them from the others. With a few words, the stranger called for God's presence, and Ausi looked somewhat nervously toward the edge of the forest. She half expected to see a figure as tall as the spruce trees even though she'd heard often enough that you couldn't see the new god.

The stranger walked into the water without lifting his clothes. When the water was above his knees, he turned around with a smile and stretched out his hand toward the gentle, gray-bearded warrior. Ausi was glad she wasn't first.

The god didn't request much. The stranger bent the warrior toward the water, scooped up a handful and poured it on his head as he spoke a few words. Then the warrior splashed to shore, wringing drops of water from his beard. As the warrior walked to the grass between the beach and the forest and sat contentedly to watch, the stranger stretched out his hand to one of the women.

When it was Ausi's turn, she handed her baby to one of the other women and waded trembling out into the cold water. She saw the stranger's gentle smile; he reached out his hand and steadied her. Then she felt one arm supporting her as the other slowly pushed her head down. She heard the stranger's voice speak to God with warm intimacy.

Just as the stranger bent forward to dip his hand in the water, Ausi saw a sudden and wonderful sight. The cross he wore around his neck was reflected under her gaze, shining brilliantly on the smooth, black water. Then his hand moved it again, and she felt the cool water running over her hair.

Afterwards, everyone sat in the grass, and the stranger told them as he had many times before that they were all alike, with the same rights as the children of one father. Ausi felt proud to belong to the group and looked surreptitiously at the warriors, but they seemed calm and satisfied. The water that had run off their clothes and down into the sand soon dried, and Ausi felt a slight warmth permeate her wet shoes. A short distance back in the woods, some women stood looking in amazement at what had happened by the shore.

Ausi thought that leaving with Holme would be a little easier now. No matter what happened to her, the stranger's god would be watching and would come to her aid. He kept track of all those who had water poured on their heads, even if they were killed and buried. But she would still prefer to stay in town.

The stranger told them that they would build a house, a temple for the new god. It didn't need to be decorated with gold and silver as he had heard the temple of the old gods was. God Himself shone brighter than all the gold in the world, but He wanted a place where His followers could meet before Him, a place not to be used for anything else. The bare hill above the smithies would be a good place, and surely that was why God had let it remain untouched.

No one spoke, but most of them knew that a great deal of human blood had flowed on that hill. It was an ancient place of execution, so who would want to build anything there? But the new god could do so much; surely He would cleanse and sanctify the hill.

That evening, Ausi let Holme know how much she wanted to stay. With her arms around his neck, she said she didn't want to go to the forests just then. Maybe later. She really didn't know why but she didn't.

Holme answered laconically as usual, but she could tell by his face that he was puzzled and disappointed. He hadn't considered this for a moment. And he shouldn't have to; a woman ought to follow her husband, but just then it was very hard. She was in the middle of something important and had to finish it. She would gladly go later.

From that moment, she saw mistrust in Holme's eyes when she told him anything about the town or the congregation. He said nothing about the baptism; there was no harm in what happened under the open sky. And it was so little compared with what the old gods wanted. He had seen a nine-day sacrifice once.

When Ausi hadn't wanted to go to the woods, he had searched for a reason for the misfortune and concluded it had to be the stranger's fault. Under Holme's low, broad forehead, hatred for the stranger was born and began to grow. Everything was so well-planned—the tools prepared, the axes and the spear sharpened, nails of all sizes forged, and the boat ready by the shore. And then this.

Holme realized vaguely that he couldn't drag Ausi down to the boat by the hair. She wasn't like that. She had to come willingly; whatever you took violently from her or forced her into wasn't worth much. He would have to wait.

The stranger had done this evil deed to him, but the stranger was not invulnerable.

Once he had made the decision to leave, the town became dreary. He would sit for hours on a rock, looking east toward the rugged black mainland forest standing against the blue-green sky. He contemplated building a house and owning a smithy that people needing a master smith would seek out.

The baby crawled across the grass, grunted, and lifted herself up against his legs. He didn't pick her up, but supported her back with his hand. The chieftain's child stuck in his mind—was it still alive or had he delivered its death blow? He drove the thought away; it was always unpleasant. But the chieftain should have been on his guard.

The summer had just begun; he should settle down, not worry about a trip. Maybe Ausi would want to leave someday. She would probably tire of the new god eventually. He never bothered about such matters himself, but women were different. No god existed who cared about thralls. It was all the same anyway, but if this one could raise the dead, it would be good for Stenulf's sake.

The baby slid to the ground again and crawled away, turning her head right and left. She would soon be standing up and walking; it might be a good idea to wait until then to move anyway. She was getting hard to carry, and if she could trudge along a little on her own, it would be better for Ausi. All he could carry himself was tools and weapons, he'd acquired so many.

He hadn't told Ausi what had happened in the smithy when the stranger came to talk about his god—how Holme had winked at his friends and then raised a din with his sledgehammer on the anvil. His friends understood immediately, and four other hammers joined in. A scream wouldn't have sounded any louder than a rat squeak. They revelled in their nasty trick, the whites of their eyes and their teeth glowing in their blackened faces. The master smith hadn't tried to stop them but instead had stood there in amusement, waiting to see what would happen.

But the strange man didn't get angry, and he didn't try to out-shout the hammer blows. He had just smiled cordially like that time in the boat, then walked away. When they stopped hammering he was standing in the door saying in a gentle voice that no noise could drown out the quiet message he wished to give them. But he could keep his message.

He got a taste of how preaching to us is, Holme thought, brightening at the memory. Every time he thought how Ausi and he could be in a good place on the mainland then starting to build, he felt a passionate hatred for the stranger. If only he had thrown him in the lake instead of rowing him to the island. No one would ever have known.

The stranger had done him a lot of harm, and one day he would repay him. Holme could have dragged another woman from the settlement—any other—down to the boat by the hair, but not Ausi. That was unthinkable.

The fire was burning, the bellows clanging and hissing as the smiths laughed scornfully at the stranger walking out the door. He knew that one of the smiths was Ausi's husband; he recognized the broad cheekbones, the black shock of hair, and the hostile look. It would not be easy to bring a reflection of divine light to those eyes. Of course he was happy about the ones who already followed him, but there were so lamentably few. Heathens were swarming everywhere, unassailable in their strength. He was probably too weak to stand alone in this heathen land, endless and uncharted.

Part of the lumber had already been dragged up the hill. Perhaps things would move more quickly once they had a little church. He had asked one of the Frisian merchants to bring a bell back with him on his next trip. It would ring over the district, calling the heathens to the church on the hill. He must pray for a miracle for them, a great miracle. They would never pay attention to anything else.

The king, who had left town to visit one of his farmsteads, had been friendly and obliging, but he hadn't concealed why. He wanted more trading ties with the Christian lands, more ships loaded with goods. Even so, he did nothing to limit the pirates' ravaging. The Frisian merchants never knew whether they'd reach their destination with life and cargo intact. There were those who claimed the king himself had dragons out plundering.

The darkness the stranger had to conquer was boundless. The blackened, scornfully laughing smiths had made that clearer than ever for him. If only he could walk on board one of the merchant ships and return home. Someone stronger than he was needed here. Or, if that were impossible, he would stay and suffer a bitter but ennobling death by knife or fire.

Only two freemen had joined him; the rest were thralls. And the younger warrior was already wavering, probably tired of the thralls' company and his friends' scorn. The older one stood firm and had ordered the timber hauled up for the church. The hill was free and no one could stop them from building there. They would start as soon as possible and raise it with their own hands—himself, the old warrior, and the thralls. The women would help however they could.

During the summer, he had talked from the hill, with the people sitting in the grass. Many passersby stopped, and the hillside was often gray with people. They sat with motionless wooden faces, concealing whether or not they felt anything in their hearts. He was so tired of these hard, cold people who were never moved, who never cried or rejoiced. They were either infinitely calm or raging beyond measure. There was no singing or playing among the adults and scarcely any among the children. Their poems were long, strange descriptions of by-gone events and people who had died long ago.

Even the young girls wore dignified expressions, and the boys played with bows and arrows. More than once a blunt wooden arrow had hit him from some hiding place. No one except the warriors and the noblest women escaped the boys' annoying war games.

Some day he would go to the heathens' temple, a few days' journey away. It had been described to him as glistening with gold and silver and having gigantic statues of the three noblest gods who were worshipped with blood sacrifices; even human beings were slaughtered when the gods' wrath had to be appeased. The third was also worshipped wantonly, in both word and deed.[15] Perhaps there, in the very center of abomination, his Lord's intention for him would be manifest.

However, first the church must be erected so his little brood would have a refuge. A few rows of benches and an altar with the gold cross on it would do. The gray-haired warrior could be in charge if he himself ever had to be away.

---

[15] The stranger refers to the pagan temple at Uppsala, which Adam of Bremen, the great German medieval historian described ca. 1070 as being completely adorned with gold and surrounded by a gold chain over the gables. He said that statues of three gods stood inside the temple: Thor, Odin (Wodan), and Freyr (Fricco). Thor, god of the skies and thunder, was the most powerful of the three for the Swedes and was flanked by Odin, god of battle, and Freyr, god of fertility. See E. O. G. Turville-Petre, *Myth and Religion of the North* (New York: Hold, Rinehart, & Winston, 1964), pp. 244–46.

And if he were gone forever, certainly someone stronger would come along one day. Perhaps by then nothing would be left except a legend about a man with a gold cross who had come there once and then was gone. A few had followed him but even they soon forgot everything he had taught them.

All day and all night, the stranger visualized the jeering smiths, and he agonized over his mission. With ravaged face, his cross clutched between white knuckles, he stood on the fortress's parapet the following day watching a Frisian ship putting out to sea and disappearing among the islands toward home.

On the first day of work, they levelled the area and stacked rows of logs chest high. It wouldn't be long before they had their own church. Ausi wasn't there; she didn't dare ask Holme, and the site of the church was too easily seen from the smithy.

He had grown more and more quiet and brusque as summer wore on. He no longer talked about moving, but he rowed out for long periods during the evenings, sometimes all the way to the mainland. Many times, he was gone all night while she lay awake, afraid that something had happened to him.

At midnight, three or four figures approached the newly begun church, which looked like a big box in the night. They whispered scornfully about the construction and laughed softly. Holme took the lead, prying loose the upper layer of logs and throwing them down the hill. His friends joined in and soon nothing was left but a jumble of logs at the foot of the incline. Then it was time for the cornerstones; blackened, powerful hands heaved them over and rolled them down the slope toward the logs. Holme wished he had his ax with him so he could chop the corner joints off the logs and render them useless for rebuilding.

The next morning on his way to the smithy, he saw the stranger standing on the hill in the sunshine. His god certainly wasn't worth much if he hadn't been able to stop them that night or even put the logs in place again. And to think that Ausi believed He was there, watching everything. He probably wouldn't even be able to wake up Stenulf when all was said and done.

The church builders were reluctant to begin again. They were convinced that evil spirits were responsible for destroying their work. The hill was no good; too much had happened on it; the earth had soaked up too much evil blood.

The stranger had noticed sooty handprints on the logs and stones, but he didn't say anything. Instead he started pushing a log back up the hill. The nearest person lent a hand, and soon everything was in motion again. But there was no speed or joy in the work; most of them were silently dissatisfied with the new god who was incapable of better protecting His interests. The building was for Him, after all.

Every now and then, the stranger saw sooty faces peering out of the smithy. He knew the same thing would happen again the next night if no one kept watch. The first night, he would stand guard himself. He might be able to change the vandals' minds. Or they might kill him. That seemed his secret desire. To die under the bottom layer of logs as the first martyr in the heathen land would be a blessed release. Especially since he didn't seem to be the one destined to spread the light there.

When night came, the gray-haired warrior offered to lend him his weapon if he really thought living beings had torn the building down. Iron was effective even against invisible powers. But the stranger refused; if the cross couldn't protect him, neither could a sword.

He sat on the logs as the sun went down, and darkness enveloped the town. Smoke from hundreds of ceilings grew thick, then thinned out again after the food had been cooked. A few women came out of their huts, dumped ashes or food scraps by the door, and then went back inside. The dogs pricked up their ears, snarled, and fought over the morsels. A ship left the harbor, its six pairs of oars rowing toward the mainland. When it passed through a ray of sunlight, the monster on its prow flashed bright red. The boats always sat high in the water as they left town, but they came in heavily laden with iron and grain.

This was a hard and strange land. It was beautiful and luminous, but that only made him heavy-hearted. It surely wasn't meant to be inhabited; that was why the people were so hard and contentious. The night was mild and warm, and he didn't need to be afraid of being killed, but even so, there was something ruthless hanging in the air. Maybe he had misunderstood God's voice; maybe He hadn't meant this land whose inhabitants listened only to the language of weapons. Not even the thralls would accept freedom; instead they clung sullenly to their servitude. For a thousand years, the people there had bought their gods' favor with sacrifices, and now no one believed they could get something for nothing.

The stranger needed help and support from his homeland. On the other hand, if he were the right one, his power should grow day by day.

In midwinter when the sun was gone, many had come to him in their anxiety. They wondered if his god could bring it out again. If so, then they would be willing to sacrifice cows or goats to him. Not even then did they believe that God in His goodness would give them the sun again. When it returned, they forgot everything.

He saw a small boat out on the lake, and he could guess who was in it. It disappeared in the dark water below the wooded point, but it wasn't long before three figures came up the street. They stopped near the new building and once again began to deride it. But they suddenly fell silent, staring at the tall, gray figure striding toward them along one of the long walls.

Two of the smiths retreated to the foot of the hill. The third stood his ground, and the stranger looked into piercing black eyes between two shocks of hair. He recognized Ausi's husband at once.

Holme heard the gentle voice but didn't understand the words. He was angry and confused; he would have preferred the stranger to attack him. He didn't want to back away as his friends had, but he didn't want to listen to that friendly voice.

The stranger put his hand on the heathen's shoulder and in the same instant felt a violent blow that knocked him to the ground. For a moment, he could neither move nor breathe, but he could see the three figures walking down the street. The friends boasted, a little ashamed, about Holme; they hadn't thought the creature coming out along the wall was a living being. Holme scarcely knew himself why his bewilderment had taken such violent form. He had just wanted to be rid of the stranger and his fist had shot out.

The pain from the blow gradually subsided and vanished. Somehow the stranger was glad this had happened; it seemed like the beginning of something. He had been permitted to suffer for his cause. The smell of fresh lumber reached him occasionally, and as he lay there he imagined the completed church. The bell, if he ever got one, would be suspended between two tall poles so it could be seen and so the ringing could be heard far away. The heathens on the mainland would hear it, and curiosity would drive them to the shore. Finally they would climb in their boats and venture across.

It was lovely to lie there, struck down for the sake of the Lord. For some reason, Ausi's husband hated him. God grant that he not take it out on her! It was odd that her husband didn't stop her from attending the meetings. But the women in this strange land often had considerable power over their husbands; eventually she might even win him over and bring him along. He would discuss that with her. She was the best of his women followers, noble and straightforward.

For a moment, his thoughts focused on her beautiful face and shapely body, but he drove them away at once and castigated himself. What a poor wretch he was, faced with this boundless task. So far, most of what he had sown had fallen on barren rocks.

He got up, his chest still tender from the blow. He could go to his quarters in peace now; the smiths wouldn't return tonight. The church would be finished while summer still flourished.

The thrall who was his servant had made himself scarce after the king had left. He would sullenly bring in a little water or arrange the bed but then would be gone until the next day. You couldn't talk with him; he would recoil, snarling like a dog. Obviously he knew nothing of friendliness and was more suspicious of it than of blows and kicks.

When the stranger returned, the thrall was standing by the parapet, looking across the nocturnal lake. The stranger thought he saw a touch of satisfaction in the thrall's eyes. But it couldn't have been that the thrall had missed him; it was more likely that the king had ordered him to guard the stranger's life as his own.

The bed was made and the bronze dish filled with water. He would stand guard again the next night if neither warrior offered to. The smiths wouldn't respect a thrall and the younger warrior had begun showing more and more indifference; he might soon leave the little congregation. The pain of losing one was greater than the joy of finding another.

Soon they would ask for some reward for following him, some proof and compensation. What would he say, what would he give them? They were deaf and blind to the core of his preaching, wanting only to see immediate, tangible results.

The baby was asleep, and Ausi sat down outside with the door open. The day was hot and still; no one was around. The cows sought the hills for a little coolness in the soft breeze.

She trimmed her toenails with Holme's smallest knife as she thought uneasily about him. He wasn't himself anymore; the friendly looks that had given her such joy had become more and more rare, and he never said a word. The expression that had frightened all the thralls at the settlement and made the warriors leave him alone had returned to his face. She'd probably have to go with him into the woods, but maybe it wouldn't be so far she couldn't come back to town occasionally.

Every day she expected the new god to intervene and help her. The stranger said she need only have patience. Either her wish would be fulfilled or something even better would happen. But such things were hard to believe all at once. She'd never heard of the old gods doing anything, even for the warriors, without gifts and sacrifices. And she was just a thrall.

On the side of town away from the lake, she saw a small band carrying a large object through the gate. It must be a corpse since they were heading for the burial mounds. Thick smoke would soon be billowing over the distant trees. She had witnessed it many times and had been tormented by the stench whenever she was downwind.

Almost simultaneously, a lone man walked out the gate on the west side, closest to her. She had been watching the funeral procession, and he had walked a long ways before she caught sight of him. She stared, the color rising in her face. It was the stranger, and he was coming in her direction.

She jumped up and ran into the hut. She left the knife lying in the grass, and a couple of tiny flies lit on the handle. Ausi swept the blades of grass and pieces of charcoal into the fire pit and straightened up a little. The iron cauldron on the chest was full of water; she quickly looked at her reflection on the dark, smooth surface, and fumbled to redo her hair. Then a shadow appeared on the floor, and the stranger was in the doorway.

Once he started talking, she managed to calm down and even look at him. In his gentle voice, he expressed sadness about Holme's antagonism and wondered if she couldn't do something about it. He surely wouldn't listen to anyone else.

When he had finished, there was total silence except for the flies merrily chasing each other in the spots of sunlight on the clay floor. The warmth and the fragrance of summer permeated the hut. The stranger looked quietly at the woman, having forgotten the rest of what he had to say. He beheld her beautiful face—the long eyelashes, the sky-blue eyes seeking and avoiding his, the chest rising and falling under the bronze brooches. As though in a dream, he stepped closer and put his hands on her shoulders. She stood motionless, looking down at the floor.

Her cloak, loosely hanging because of the heat, rustled to the floor behind her. The stranger's fingers trembled as they pulled down the skirt strap from her bare shoulder, causing the brooch to slide to the side and the breast to fall free. It bore a red mark from the brooch but was round and firm. The stranger, trembling from head to foot, took her breast in his hand like a fruit.

A tiny noise from the bench made Ausi turn her head. The baby had awakened and was looking at them with Holme's fathomless eyes. When Ausi felt the stranger's grip loosen, she walked over and turned the baby to the wall. She didn't mind being turned, and then all that was visible of her was the little neck and soft hair, damp with sweat, sticking out in every direction.

When Ausi turned back to the stranger, all she heard was a peculiar sobbing noise as he disappeared through the door. He didn't take the path toward town but toward the woods behind them instead. She walked slowly after him; as he moved out of sight among the tree trunks, she automatically pulled up the shoulder strap and put the brooch back in place.

Once back inside, she turned the baby again, who looked just as unconcerned as before. The stranger's behavior had surprised Ausi. At first she thought he must have seen Holme coming. Then it really would have been time to run. But there was no one in sight.

She recalled how his back looked as he hurried off—as if he expected to be struck from behind. She hadn't seen men flee very often, even from a much superior force, and he had fled from nothing. She was somehow disappointed but soon realized it was for the best.

Besides, there might be things she didn't understand. She knew he wasn't afraid of anyone. Maybe his god had summoned him from the forest even though she hadn't heard him, and then naturally he had to run. What did a thrall like herself know?

The day seemed so long and warm in the solitude; she would have liked it if he had stayed and talked a while. He could have sat there on the bench talking with her alone. They probably could have figured out what to do about Holme. Maybe he'd be satisfied and stay if the stranger's god would give him his own smithy.

She went out and looked toward the woods several times, but the stranger didn't return.

Fewer and fewer were helping to build the church, and they worked without any great enthusiasm. Three nights after the stranger had stood watch, everything was destroyed again. The logs lay at the bottom of the hill, and this time the vandals had chopped off the joint pins. If they used the shorter logs now, the building would be smaller.

This time all of them said they didn't want to work there anymore. It seemed clear that either those executed on the hill were at work or the gods had found out what was going on. Most of them thought the new god wasn't very strong if he couldn't protect his own property. If someone had treated the old gods' temple or other possessions that way, his days would have been numbered.

The stranger didn't try to reason with them anymore. He thought about how worthless he was; he couldn't be the one who would build the first church in the world's darkest heathen land. His vision was not clear enough; it had even been clouded by lust for a woman in his congregation. At the last moment, he had been saved by her baby. It hadn't occurred to him until his eyes met those of the child that the mother was a temptation put in his path.

Still, he didn't want to give up; maybe he'd see a sign that would tell him what to do. Maybe, despite his guilt, the highest honor of all was imminent, the Master's way—painful death at the heathens' hands. Everyone was talking already about the great festival of sacrifice coming in the spring, the older ones with expectation, the younger ones, who had never been there, with curiosity. They never tired of hearing about the festival, which would last for nine days.[16]

The stranger would attend the festival and stare their noblest gods right in their blood-stained faces. Perhaps he would learn the meaning of the call to the north that he had felt so distinctly. It didn't seem to him as if he could achieve his potential here on the island; the power drained from him in the face of the heathens' defiance and ill-will.

Maybe he would be the first Christian ever to witness the heathens' great, mysterious sacrificial festival, legendary in every land. After the next snow-melt, it would begin. Until then he would endure where he was.

He had seen a small sacrificial feast the past spring through an open door. It had taken place at a rich family's with its own shrine, and all the relatives had gathered there. They had sat eating around the fire that shone on a wooden image painted with blood, and most of them were drunk.[17] The stranger had stood watching the ritual for a long time, praying for strength to go in and strike down their idol. But time had passed, the men's beards grew tousled, and their eyes shone with a wild and repulsive gleam in the firelight. It would have meant

---

[16] Adam of Bremen describes this festival as occurring every nine years. See Turville-Petre, *Myth and Religion*, pp. 244–45.

[17] Turville-Petre explains drunkenness at these ceremonies: 'Alcoholic liquor is a drug; it raises man into a higher world, where he is inspired by loftier thoughts. Its emotional affects [*sic*] are like those of poetry, and that is why, in the myth of the origin of poetry, poetry is identified with the precious mead' (*Myth and Religion*, pp. 259–60). For the myth of the origin of peotry, see Kevin Crossley-Holland, *The Norse Myths* (New York: 1980), pp. 26–32.

his death to go in and desecrate what they held holy. His courage had faltered, and he had walked on merely to see the same sight and hear the same uproar repeated in almost every house with a shrine. That night he had felt more powerless than ever before.

After fleeing from Ausi that day he had sat at the forest's edge until evening, and he saw an old woman walk up to an aspen tree standing in the sun apart from the other trees. She was holding something that she buried in the ground by the foot of the tree. She had barely finished before a soft wind rose, and the leaves of the aspen began rustling back and forth. The woman looked up delightedly and went home, certain that her wish would be fulfilled, whatever it might have been. Then he noticed that the whole area around the tree had been dug up. A fox or a dog had clawed a hole, bringing up tiny white bones from a previous sacrifice.

If he had been the man he thought he was, he would have walked over and persuaded the old woman to forsake that tree for the tree of everlasting life. Instead, he had sat struggling with a passionate, sinful desire to return to the beautiful woman he had just escaped. He could still feel her breast in his hand, and he could still visualize every move she had made as she turned the baby so it couldn't witness what she thought was about to happen.

While the stranger sat in the forest all day, his flesh conquered him one more time. He walked back until he saw the little house, but smoke was coming from the vent, carrying the smell of cooking meat. The shadow of the spruce trees behind the hut fell on it, extending far out onto the plain. Ausi came outside to fetch a bucket of water from the well by the deserted hut next door. She didn't see him and seemed completely preoccupied with her domestic duties.

A moment later, a dark figure appeared on the path, and the stranger drew back into the woods, wondering if the woman would tell her husband what had happened. He didn't discount the possibility; there was something truthful and candid about her. Maybe she would no longer be part of his depleted flock now.

Someday a believer stronger than he would come and perhaps hear about the monk who had tried to clear the way for him. An irresolute monk who had come through the forest, robbed of his possessions but full of faith, whose light had flickered momentarily then died in the boundless darkness.

That autumn the stranger could already see intense expectation rising among the heathens, and it grew as the winter progressed. It gripped the remainder of his little flock, and soon nobody was attending the few meetings he still held. Some avoided him on the streets; others responded to his words with doubt and scorn.

The looms were pounding throughout the hall, and craftsmen of every kind had plenty to do. Calves and foals with unusual markings were carefully guarded. A great deal of strong beer was brewed and stored in wooden vats that gave it an odd flavor. The usual winter sacrifice was either played down or cancelled altogether in anticipation of the big festival.

This winter was milder than the previous one; the ground was bare just after midwinter, and the lake had never completely frozen over. Trade continued briskly as usual. Chieftains and their women required a great many things from the foreign merchant ships that year. Gold-laced cloth, necklaces and arm rings, ornamented swords and knives—all these coveted items carried back to their farmsteads to be saved for the festival. Like turtles, ships from the settlements came to town loaded down with grain and iron but rode high in the water on the way home.

The king visited the town once during the year. He saw to it that the stranger lacked nothing but remained cordially indifferent to his mission. The king did wonder, however, if he might not need some helpers. If so, they could bring various goods along on the ships then, too.

But the stranger didn't want to send a message to his homeland, and he didn't want to return there. He had no results to show except a handfull of thralls still hoping that the new god would give them something or at least help them avenge themselves on their enemies. The old warrior was still his friend but was spending more time with his friends in the fortress than he had before. Only a miracle could open the heathens' eyes now, and he wasn't one who could summon fire from heaven.

The stranger had been completely alone the last few days. His thrall had shown up once but finally had said sullenly that he had to leave for a while. There was water out in the courtyard, and a couple of old women would be home. He could get food from them.

But even as the first few wagons left town to board the ships, the stranger was walking down to the shore to find passage. He got it on a family boat in exchange for holding onto a goat during the trip. The goat bleated, staring with terror-stricken, yellow eyes at the waves. Its owners, a middle-aged couple with a nearly grown son who did the rowing, were in a festive mood already. They said the goat was food for the journey; they would live off it for many days. The wife opened a small chest and showed proudly how much bread they had to go with the goat meat.

The man, who clearly realized who was in the boat with them, talked amicably about the festival. He had been to two before, but this would be his son's first. He looked at the stranger's simple attire and said a man could easily go unarmed the whole time. No one would touch him. But on the way home, he should be careful; then he wasn't safe until the beer left people's bodies and they were themselves again.

When the stranger released his hold on the goat and stepped ashore, he looked back. In the distance lay the Sodom of the north, clouds closing in on it, followed by shadows. Numerous boats of various sizes were coming that way. Some people would doubtless travel by water as far as they could; others, those without boats, had to go by land. He was offered a day's ride in the boat, but he shook his head and walked into the forest. He wanted to be alone with his new hunger for pain and death. He walked northeast, and the oarsman called to him saying that if they met at their destination, he could have some of the goat meat.

The forest wasn't as endless and dreary as it had seemed from town. Cultivated glades and clearings were not far apart. The sun warmed the peaceful areas; a boggy patch of ground was completely covered with yellow flowers though the ditch was lined with dirty snow. He could hear horses neighing and cows mooing in the barns. Two panting dogs dashed by oblivious to him and copulated farther up on the path.

Beyond the forest, the path fed into a larger road, well-worn by both solid and cloven hooves. The droppings on it were still steaming, and off in the distance, he could see a group of travellers plodding along. Three or four cows, heads bobbing, followed them. This was the right road; the stranger could even hear mooing behind him where the road came out of the woods. The festival grounds wouldn't be hard to find.

Small clumps of mixed forest dotted the landscape, and there were farmsteads near most of them. At one secluded farmstead, people were preparing to leave, and a couple of cows were already quivering outside the stall. A boy in the group caught sight of the cowbell hanging on the wall, took it down, and started ringing it as he ran around the building. It was a bronze bell with a beautiful, delicate tone.

The stranger heard the distant clanging of bells, and his heart trembled. He stopped and listened. Now there was no sound, now it intensified, diminished, and was gone again. Tears welled up in his eyes—he thought he had heard the same bell two summers ago as he had walked through the forest. Back then, he was walking the road the Lord had designated; since then he had gone astray. He was walking the right path again now. He looked up to heaven, blind with tears and happiness. He hadn't been forgotten; the Lord's eye followed him—He had made an angel ring a bell to give him heart on his journey.

The stranger heard the bell again above and around him. After the boy had circled the building for the third time, the father had gruffly ordered him to put the bell back where it belonged. If the stranger had listened more carefully, he might have heard the man's voice, but his ears were full of the melodious ringing, and he wept, his arm before his face. The heathen land had regained life and meaning; the sun shone down gently, and heaven was bluer than ever before. God had broken His long silence. All was well.

His movements, which had been tired and labored, were rejuvenated, and he felt his old strength come back. The air was alive with singing birds, and the melting snow rippled joyously everywhere. He took out meat and bread and ate as he walked. Suddenly a woman dashed away from a level rock in a field he was approaching, so he walked up to it. There were small indentations in the rock where the woman had laid some fat, undoubtedly a sacrifice to the harvest god. A narrow, well-trodden path connected farmstead and altar.

The stranger walked on, gazing into the heathen land's future. The ringing from the first church's bell would wash away the people's veneration of wood and stone; they would turn their eyes upward, toward the heaven that was clearer here than anywhere else. He knew the day was coming. He was the first indication of it, just as a lone gray bird is a harbinger of spring. His failure seemed necessary now. The Lord Himself had failed while here on earth.

Toward midday, the entire landscape came to life. Wagons, horseback riders, and wayfarers appeared from everywhere, all drawn in the same direction as if by some great force. A couple of times the stranger was offered a ride, but he refused. He didn't want to miss a moment of the most significant walk of his life. A band of riders passed by and a young, arrogant warrior forced the stranger off the road with his little, shaggy horse. The older ones yelled roughly at the stranger, and the band trotted on, their sword hilts glistening in the sun. The leader wore a helmet like those from the stranger's homeland; it must have been bought or stolen there.

When night came, he wasn't concerned about taking shelter or finding someone with a fire. The air was humid, and drops of water were falling from the trees. A thick haze passed before the moon, but there was still some light in the forest, and he cast a faint shadow. A whitened baby skeleton lay near a rock in the woods, the skull no bigger than his fist. One arm lay a few steps away, its tiny fingers scarcely visible. The stranger stopped and asked his god to receive the tiny soul and to forgive those who had left the child to die.

He walked all night and saw many fires surrounded by dark figures. Toward morning he rested at an abandoned camp where the embers were still glowing. A meaty bone, crusts of bread, and other scraps of food littered the ground. A thick bed of spruce twigs by the fire indicated that the travellers had slept there.

When the sun rose and a breeze stirred the gray-white ashes, he got up and continued on his way. The thawing ground had acquired a thin crust of ice from a couple hours of morning frost, but water was gurgling constantly through gullies and crevices. Many of the flowers had closed up, looking like tiny yellow points topping reddish-brown stalks. But out where the forest's shadow couldn't reach them, they were already shining, opened up in the sun.

The day was as clear and warm as the one before, and the area he passed through didn't change much. He had to walk around a little lake, and he got a boat ride across a bigger one. The owner was alone and had laid his ax beside him before rowing out with the stranger. He didn't say anything and didn't respond to the stranger's friendly words. Occasionally he glanced anxiously at the cross, and when they reached the other side, he quickly hopped out of the boat. He waited a few steps away while the stranger stepped ashore, then watched until he disappeared among the trees.

Toward evening, the landscape began to open up. The forests turned to groves and islets, the roads improved, and in many places stone bridges spanned the rivers. The number of travellers behind him grew, and he left the road for the fields and meadows to be free of the shouts and taunts. The moon rose behind the spring haze as it had done the night before, and campfires glowed near and far. Various signs indicated that his goal wasn't far away.

The stranger consumed his last meat and bread in a crevice. He slept for a while but woke often from the cold. Distant shouts and laughter reached him now and then. He smiled as the cold penetrated his shivering body, but he had no fear of sickness or death. He felt he was being guided and cared for and that he need only walk on with a thankful heart.

The crest of the hill was even with the treetops, and when it grew light, he walked up to it. Before him lay an endless plain, punctuated by pools of clear water. A couple of wooded rises teemed with travellers and animals.

At sunrise, he was still standing on the hill. Far down on the distant horizon the burgeoning light reflected from something. He could guess what it was — the heathens' golden temple. He would be there by evening, and perhaps the festival of sacrifice would begin the next day.

Once he was below the hill he could no longer see the dazzling spot. He set out across the marshy meadows where quacking sea birds were swimming on the pools or flying between them. A reddish-brown animal stood stock still looking at him, then darted off as he drew near. He saw it melt into the landscape and vanish.

The stranger walked all morning in soaking wet shoes. When the sun reached its zenith, he sat down on the south side of a little rise and took them off to dry in the sun.

He still couldn't see the temple that had glistened on the horizon. The land had grown more forested again and was rising. He deduced that a larger plain lay farther ahead, and from there he would be able to see his journey's — and perhaps his life's — final destination.

The ringing of the heavenly bell had ended his vacillation for all time. Oh, that he hadn't understood the magnitude of his mission earlier! Alone in this remote land, he would suffer death for the heathens' salvation. The bells couldn't mean anything else.

A large group on foot passed at a little distance. There were men and women, but no animals. He thought he saw Ausi, and with terror he drove away the memory of how she looked. Some rough voices wafted to him now and then on the cool breeze that smelled of water, and he suspected the smiths were passing by with their families. A few days ago, they had sent off several boatloads of weapons and iron goods to the big festival marketplace. He had seen many craftsmen moving in the same direction, lugging their wares on their backs — huge living bundles of tankards or other wooden vessels lumbering along on two legs.

There was one last forest between him and the temple. He emerged from it in the afternoon when the sun was going down. From a ridge he saw an almost endless plain, and a river wound and glittered across it from the direction of the temple. As far as the eye could see, boats of various sizes were heading up the river.

He could survey the whole temple area, which was swarming with life. The temple was in the center, but the sun shone behind it now, making the facade lofty and dark. Nearby the ground seemed to mount up in three massive waves. The roar from the throngs of people and the animal noises reached him even across the great expanses.

His courage flagged again as he felt the threats of death accompanying the roar like cold rays. He looked into the endless blue for help, his eyes burning. This was his Gethsemane, and he trembled with a feeling of endless isolation. His country, where he could still live for many years, was far away. Why didn't he turn around and catch a ship home? He could do penance there for the rest of his life.

But this was his last battle. No bell or any other outward sign answered him, but when he walked down the hill, he harbored a strength that would not desert him again. His mission had been revealed to him in the clear light; that was his answer, and there was no turning back. He would strike a blow at the heathens' heart by means of their notorious temple, the pride of the north.

In the patch of meadow still before him, no one noticed him. Numerous roads and trails merged here; strange creatures came from the depths of the forest many days' journey away. Wild, bearded recluses—everyone except out-laws—were safe within the sacred area. Deadly enemies met and ground their teeth, but their swords hung at rest by their sides. He had heard it described that way; now he would see it with his own eyes.

He passed an area cluttered with wagons, animals, and people. Farther away were long rows of cases, tables, and chests. That must be the market square. Even at a distance, the temple still towered ominously above everything around it. The facade, with its vertical, rough-hewn logs, resembled a gigantic, golden pipe organ. Next to it was a grove of knotted trees with dense, sprawling branches. A few oddly dressed men moved among the trees and near the temple.

What had resembled three huge waves from a distance were right in front of him now—gigantic mounds of equal size, covered with grass and probably raised by the heathens ages ago. These mounds showed the signs of centuries of wear from feet pounding trails through their yellow grass.[18]

---

[18] Snorri Sturluson in chapter 29 of *Heimskringla* claims that these huge, seventy-yard-wide mounds were occupied by the 6th-century Swedish kings Aun, Egill, and Athils, but there is no conclusive evidence to support that claim. The mounds are tradi-tionally referred to as Odin's, Thor's, and Freyr's mounds.

The stranger walked around the temple, examining it carefully. Close behind it grew a clump of small fir trees; from there you could get right up to it unseen. A couple of low hills nearby were completely covered with people.

On the temple's other side, too, were line after line of wagons and animals. Cows mooed continuously, goats and sheep bleated, pigs fought and squealed in the pens. Countless dogs prowled everywhere. The people conversed in shouts in order to be heard above the noise. Beyond the wagons lay a big pond of melted snow, and flocks of ducks, wings rustling, flew back and forth without daring to light on the water.

More groups kept coming from all directions on horseback, in wagons, or on foot. But there were no children; the young people walking around, their eyes hungry with expectation, were full-grown. Only a handful of older women were there but plenty of older men.

He saw rows of huts nearby, but he avoided them and walked toward the wooded area to be alone for a while. The sun had just gone down in the distant forest; this might be the last time he would see it set.

The master smith had invited the others and their wives and grown children to go with him to the festival. Holme balked for a long time. He knew what went on there and was afraid something would happen to Ausi, but his friends' arguments finally won out, and he and Ausi agreed to go. She was happy for the change and immediately began putting clothes and other things in order. The master smith promised to take care of any tax money or sacrifices they might have to leave there. The small children could be left to be cared for by various women for the nine days.

The group went by land and sent their wares and most of their provisions by water. The smiths took beer along and were half-drunk night and day. Even before their arrival, one got punched in the face for trying to take Ausi into the woods with him from the campfire. Holme was never far away, and his friends had to intervene to save the lovesick smith from Holme's rage.

Ausi hadn't seen the stranger again, but Holme told her that no one went to his sermon hall anymore. For a couple of nights the stranger had stood alone staring at the door, but soon it was closed and forgotten. The pile of timber at the foot of the hill grew smaller and smaller as dark figures walked off at night with the logs and took them home for firewood.

In his terse way Holme tried to make Ausi see that there couldn't be anything to the new god. Why hadn't he protected his temple? It could have been finished a long time ago. Could she point to anyone he had helped? He didn't even help his own servant. Everyone had seen him walking around like an outlaw, averting his face even though he lived under the king's protection.

Ausi, who had trembled under the stranger's friendly gaze and hand, wanted to deny she had but she couldn't. How could Holme understand what she didn't understand herself? He was right, but things still weren't as he implied.

Ausi was the only one of the group who had seen the tall, gray figure walking across the fields and flooded meadows far away from the road. She recognized the walk and posture, which was unlike anyone else's. Once again she had felt a curious longing to follow and serve him, to be his thrall. For a long time, she could see him and the flocks of birds taking flight before him.

When he was gone, she looked with aversion at her companions and listened with disgust to their talk. There was something entirely different about the stranger, something purer and better. He should have taught her what it was so she could be like him. Perhaps they would meet there. She still belonged to him even though she hadn't been able to go to his house for a long time. But he had put his hand on her head and poured water on her. She still remembered the way his cross had reflected in the water.

Maybe the stranger's god would appear at the festival and reveal his power. The thought comforted her and she clung to it. She visualized a battle between a huge, fair-haired man and three blood-stained ones. Maybe that's what the stranger was waiting for. It was such a long time between the big festivals. Last time, she had been a little girl at the settlement, but she could still remember how peaceful it had been with only the old people and children at home.

Holme, of course, had been to the festival once, but he never said anything about it. The master smith said laughingly that Holme was sure to have problems because of Ausi. It was a wild time when the god of the harvest and fertility received his offerings. The most beautiful women were wise not to be around then, when the songs were sung and the beer steamed on the hot stones. They'd see for themselves now whether it would be like the last time.

Soon they could hear the thousand-voiced cry from the animals, and they reached the barrier of wagons shortly after the stranger.

From the hill among the clump of pine trees, the stranger could see the king arriving with his large retinue. No one slept that night, a night aflame and smoky from countless fires. Inside the temple enclosure, three large pyres burned, but from the clump of trees the stranger was unable to see what the heathens had there. He tried to reach the temple once but was pushed back by the throngs of people.

He heard strange and terrible sounds all night. A curious excitement had gripped the seething mass. Sometimes songs flew toward the night sky—a single roaring noise concluding with some shrill cries. The fires shone on innumerable faces around the temple enclosure.

He couldn't complete his mission that night; he couldn't get to the temple. But surely there'd be a more peaceful moment, perhaps toward morning.

Many dark figures walked past him but no one took any notice. At dawn the noise subsided, and the densest throng around the temple dispersed, though the area was never completely empty or quiet. People—mostly old people—were asleep on the carts and on the ground around the fires. In the market place, the merchants began taking out their wares. The stranger saw several who were doubtless his countrymen, probably Christian, but he had no desire to approach them to talk. Still, a thought quickly blossomed, spreading a light within him. Surely the merchants would carry home the story of all that happened here and would speak his name. God's plan for him had foreseen even that.

With this thought, the last trace of depression fell away. His life and struggle would not be drowned and lost in the eternal whistling of the heathen woods. He had been afraid of that, yet had bowed in submission. But now those who came later would hear about him, and it would be a little easier for them. His memory would live on in Christian lands, and maybe in his home district a church would be erected in his honor.

This was the angel in his Gethsemane. How could he have doubted? God's clear eye had seen the sorrow in his innermost soul, the sorrow that all was for nought, and He had sent witnesses to what was about to happen.

The stranger wandered around the marketplace a few times and heard his language spoken among the merchants. He managed to overcome the temptation to converse with them and tell them his name. It wasn't his place to intervene in the plan.

The sun rose and the temple gleamed red and yellow. From where he stood he could make out three gigantic figures in the darkness of the hall. In the grove, many temple attendants were busy tending the tree regarded as holy. Today the festival of sacrifice would begin; everything that had happened during the night was merely preparation.

The stranger was one of the thousands forming a wall around the temple enclosure as the sun reached its high point. Closest to the temple were rows of benches where the land's noblest men had taken their places.

Everything happening before him seemed unreal, like a dream — the huge temple with its three gigantic gods standing in front of him now, the quivering animals who were to be slaughtered and whose blood was caught in large round tubs, the strange songs and ceremonies. He watched the king step forward, dip a branch into the blood, and smear it on the images of the gods. The throng stood in silent expectation, but he sensed they were waiting for something else, a climax. Rumor of past festivals and the stifling feeling in his chest told him what was to come.

He didn't see the major offering appear, but it was suddenly standing there, a tall, young man, ashen-faced but calm. The people around the stranger began breathing heavily, restlessly shuffling their feet. An ornamented bronze container was brought out so that none of the noblest offering's blood would be lost.

As the knife was raised, the stranger dropped his head and stared at the trampled yellow grass under his feet. He couldn't watch what those around him strained not to miss. He whispered to his god, "You who watched over the thief, take this wretched heathen to you too." He didn't hear a scream, just a soft flowing sound mixed with the hiss of breathing around him.

Suddenly the silence was shattered as a shrill voice sang a few notes. A mass choir responded, and while the antiphon proceeded, he saw the king step up to the place of sacrifice with branch in hand.

The stranger pushed himself away through an impatiently grumbling and glowering crowd. He wanted to escape the atmosphere and the smell that made the heathens' nostrils flare and their eyes burn. Those gathered farthest away had dragged different things up to stand on so they could see, but the market square was empty. The sun shone on burnished weapons and whitewood household utensils. Water glistened on flooded patches of land in the distance.

In the afternoon the stranger approached the temple again and saw the heathens were preparing great masses of meat. Large pieces strung on iron spits were rotated over the fires by two men. Beer tankards formed long rows on the tables. Now that the crowd had thinned out, he could see many of the kingdom's noblest men in their glittering garments and weapons. Beautiful, smiling women, fair-haired and dark, with jewelry glistening in the sunlight, moved happily smiling among the men.

The morning's sacrifices were hanging in the sacred trees. One animal of each kind, from horses and cows to sheep and chickens. In a tall tree with strange foliage by the temple the man was hanging in a leather sling, and the soft breeze twisted him around so the stranger could see his young, white face, its eyes closed fast. The three blood-smeared gods looked rigidly out across the place of sacrifice. Two of them governed battles and victories, the third, harvest and fertility. The nine days' sacrifice would bring victories and good crops for nine years to come.

It was dark before the moon rose, and no one noticed the stranger sneaking behind the temple. The crowd, dull with fatigue, was eating, resting, and sleeping in expectation of the next event in the festivities.

Under his arm the stranger carried a bundle of dry grass and dry resinous sticks he had taken from a wagon. He crammed the bundle against the temple wall at a place where a stone prevented the end of a log from penetrating the earth. He struck a flint and soon a spark caught hold in the grass, blew up in a gust of wind, and caught fire. The oily sticks began burning fiercely, emitting black smoke, and the stranger fanned out his robe to hide and protect the fire.

A moment passed, then, pleased, he saw tongues of fire licking the logs. The reddish substance smeared on the walls seemed to burn easily. He heard voices close by, but no one yelled or grabbed him.

Then suddenly he heard a muffled cry followed by an uproar inside the temple. The temple attendants, seeing the smoke force its way in between the logs, had sounded the alarm. Soon they came rushing from both directions to find the source of the smoke.

The stranger defended his fire as long as he could. He saw the heathen faces drawing near him, puzzled or threatening. He pushed away those trying to cast themselves over the fire and for a while managed to fend them off. But then a loud, commanding voice was heard, and some warriors threw themselves on him; their iron grip on his arms convinced him that further resistance was futile.

To his sorrow, the heathens soon extinguished the fire. They came running with pots and wooden buckets and threw water up the wall. Soon only a singed spot was smoking. No one struck or insulted the stranger, and he suspected it was because the protected area shielded him. The warriors handed him over to some of the temple attendants and ordered them to watch him carefully all night.

He was thankful they didn't tie him up. He was made to sit on one of the front benches in the temple, surrounded by his mute guards. The moon rose, big and round behind a comb of forest far away on the plain.

The rumor of his deed spread, and group after group came by to look at him. Most of them pretended to be just passing by and looked at him without stopping. No one abused him. A dog came up, sniffed him, and stayed for a moment, its bushy back level with his knees. Suddenly it noticed something out in the murky moonlight on the plain and rushed off.

The temple stood before him, the facade's gigantic vertical logs giving it a massive stature. He hadn't succeeded in destroying it, but that was already troubling him less. He had given all to his Lord and thought that perhaps He had other plans for the temple. Maybe it would be destroyed when the heathens were converted.

Once during the night, his guards fetched bread and meat. They picked out the best for him, and he ate greedily while he marvelled at them. There was something magnanimous about them even though they were heathens. They didn't torture anyone for the pleasure of it, and they stood by their word. They would be a great people once the light had spread among them.

The sacrificial grove, hung with dark carcasses, stood in the dark haze of the moon. A few servants walked about protecting the carcasses from the dogs that were prowling and sniffing everywhere. The stranger had heard that the victims would hang there until only bones remained. Huge flocks of scavengers would descend on the grove all during the first summer, and their calls would be heard for miles.

The stranger sat listening to the different sounds of the night. Even now he could distinguish the dull roar of the crowd, and once the furious shrieks of cats fighting cut through it. That, in turn, was drowned out by dogs barking wildly, and a clamorous hunt started across the field toward the pine trees.

The moon rose quickly over the forest but inched slowly across the sky now, surrounded by a ring of haze. His guards exchanged words now and then about the festival or themselves, but never mentioned him or his fate. Through the darkness, they glanced furtively at the gold cross glistening in the moonlight, the cross that he held to his chest all night.

At dawn, the stranger saw the moon pale and seem to lift. Out on the bogs, gulls screeched shrilly at the rising sun, and the crows answered hoarsely from the pine trees. The heathens put new wood on the fires and cleaned up around the temple. People cold from the morning came from every direction to warm themselves after their few hours' sleep in the wagons or between skin rugs on the ground.

The king's first glance at the stranger was troubled and full of reproach but betrayed no recognition. He ordered him taken to the assembly place, then walked there himself, surrounded by his top men. The crowd rushed after him, streaming in from everywhere.

Some other prisoners were awaiting sentencing, but the stranger was brought up first. A ring of raised stones stood around him. Someone spoke his name and described his activities up to the previous night. The voice ended by censuring the king for permitting the stranger to work against the gods, provoke them, and thereby bring calamity on the land and people. Even as he spoke, he was interrupted by a roar of agreement.

The king made a speech to defend himself. He pointed out the important trade connections with the stranger's country and stressed how little harm a single man could do. The king didn't believe for a minute that the gods had noticed his presence, and besides, he himself had seen to it that the stranger's activities would come to nothing.

The prosecutor's next speech dealt with the stranger's attempt to burn the temple, their pride and joy, the dwelling-place of the gods, and so draw irremediable harm over the land. Many signs during the night indicated that the gods were incensed and that a prompt sacrifice was necessary to appease them. The human sacrifice of the day must be the stranger; they surely wouldn't accept anyone else.

The stranger heard the uproar around him, loud screams and thumping. He heard the king try to save him, suggesting instead that he be driven away as an outlaw, but that prompted an even greater uproar. The crowd was adamant, and the king had no power over it. In response to a general, threatening demand, he decreed that the stranger would be sacrificed to satisfy the gods he had angered. The guards bound his hands with a strap, and he was taken back to the temple.

While he awaited the king's return from the judgment place, the stranger watched the heathens putting everything in order for the day's sacrificial feast. Various kinds of knives were lined up on a table, and he realized that each sacrifice had a particular knife, according to size and appropriateness. The sun was already getting warm, and when it reached its peak, his last moment would be at hand. A heathen would be allowed to live, the one whose place he was taking as the day's sacrifice.

His eyes were drawn to the row of knives, but he focused them on the sky where a veil of clouds passed slowly toward the west. He longed for a new sign that everything was as it should be. He was already oblivious to everything around him, and he saw the three idols in the pillared hall as if in a dream vision.

A thought still tormented the stranger. Would he be forced to be the day's final offering, to live and witness the whole terrible slaughter as columns of animals were slowly drained of their blood? He prayed that they take the human being first that day.

The crowd was gathering, and the noblest ones were already beginning to take their places in the front rows. There was a light cool breeze, and the women had shawls with golden brooches over their shoulders. An occasional raw, musty odor floated on the wind from the sacrificial grove.

A great fatigue overwhelmed the stranger, and he longed for the moment. He understood that this was God's answer and drove away every thought about himself, his land, and his relatives. The past was the past; he was standing at the gate now, tired of wandering. Soon the gate would open.

After the king arrived, the temple attendants took the stranger to a spring and splashed water on him. He got to stay there while the animals were led to the slaughter. He didn't look in that direction often, but he could hear the horse resisting violently, almost breaking away from its tormentors.

For a terrible moment, he told himself there was nothing other than what he could see before his eyes, no God, no meaning, no life after the slaughter of his body. But the thought passed instantly when his destination was revealed to him. Who had guided him, who had saved him, who had sent the celestial bells when he teetered on the verge of doubt? He prayed that his faith would persist until the end.

When the moment came, the stranger was led out. Only one knife was left on the table, the most beautiful. The king stood there, splattered from head to toe with blood. Blood stained everyone nearby, and the gods had been smeared with it again and again. Never once turning to the stranger, the king held the branch in his hand.

The stranger watched the golden bucket brought closer but felt no terror. He prayed only for strength to endure patiently and to show himself worthy of his great predecessors. The surrounding crowd stood completely still. A white feather came floating on the wind, stuck in a pool of blood, and swayed slowly, trying to free itself. In the next moment, he felt himself seized and lifted by strong hands, carried a few wavering steps, and laid on a bench. He felt his upper body being exposed, and the sun shining directly in his eyes blinded him.

He focused all his force of will and all his strength around a single thought: the nails that were driven through the hands of his Lord, the spear in His side. He hardly felt the knife. The sun just faded away; soon he could look right into it, and he seemed to be moving toward it. It was transformed into the eye of God, and he felt secure because that eye forgot no one and would never be closed. It drew him on, and he was almost there when the motion changed into a gentle rocking darkness to which he gladly surrendered, a darkness filled with sunlight and hope.

The king tried to avoid dipping the branch in the golden bucket; he asked his top man to take his place, but the fierce grumbling from the crowd forced him to perform his ancient duty. The foreign merchants who had managed to force their way forward were astounded to see that the king was merely the people's obedient servant.

The large wooden statue stared lifelessly into space as the king smeared it with the stranger's blood. The multitude felt relieved; the god had to be pleased with the sacrifice. It would give them victory over their enemies, the grain would grow dense in the fields, and the animals would produce offspring in abundance.

The temple attendants brought forward the stranger's gold cross, which they had been able to tear from his hand only with great effort. The king took it and after consultation with his closest advisers, hung the cross on the chief god. The king and many of the warriors understood what it signified, but the masses thought it was a differently shaped hammer and murmured approval.

The Frisian merchants had already returned to the market-place, unaware that the day's human sacrifice was one of their countrymen.

The cross gleamed in the afternoon sun, but the stranger hung with closed eyes in the sacrificial grove's most sacred tree.

Even before nightfall, Ausi had tired of the festival. The first few hours were dreamlike; she had never known there were so many people. But they had pushed their way through the glistening armaments and gray hoods of thralls until she was fed up with everything. They could see nothing of what happened by the temple.

She wished Holme's iron hand would let go of hers a while. He had dragged her along all day in a firm, mistrustful grip, and his look was ominous. She hadn't seen what prompted him to do that—the lustful looks of the men they met, their deliberate pressing up against her in the crowd. Her thoughts were mostly on her baby, wondering if the woman they had left her with was feeding her properly. Sometimes she wondered if they would run into the stranger. But he was undoubtedly closer to the temple with the most distinguished people.

At night after the crowds had dispersed, they walked to the temple. The first day's sacrifices hung in the grove, but a guard kept them from going any closer. Ausi looked at the three gigantic gods and wondered how the stranger's god could stand up against them. But the stranger had said his god was the most powerful in the world.

If only she could see him there. He would probably be surprised to see her. If Holme would let go of her hand for a while, she would go look for him. But he held her so tightly that her arm went numb. She almost hated him for that. No one else had such a grip on his woman, and no one else glared around so fiercely.

At night they shared camp with the master smith and his friends. A few of them teased Holme about his bad humor, and one took out a couple of silver articles and offered them in exchange for Ausi for the night. Holme was furious and growled a warning what would happen to him after the festival.

All night, Ausi remained locked in his grip and every now and then he made sure that none of the others had come any closer. She lay thinking of how to escape, if only for a little while. She would try the next day. His dark glance and the fierceness of his hold made her weary of everything.

Ausi heard vague reports about what had happened the day before. About an attempt to burn down the temple, about someone's trial and death. She felt a nauseating fear that it was the stranger. So his god hadn't helped him and wouldn't help her either. The good that the stranger had talked about would never be; everything would remain the same.

Holme was pleased and grunted contemptuously about the stranger and his god. He hoped Ausi's restlessness would vanish with the stranger and that when they got home he wouldn't have to watch her standing in the doorway looking toward town several times a day anymore.

Holme had no respect for the three idols either. While an anxious Ausi gazed at them in wonder, he gave them no more than a cursory glance. He'd always been told that they didn't bother with thralls, and he returned the favor. Deep in his rebellious heart something told him the images were nothing to fear.

The second day passed; Ausi still was not able to find out which foreigner had been sacrificed. At camp that evening, the master smith said that if the festival turned out as it did nine years ago, then the third day would be a happier one—a day of offerings to the harvest god, who provided grain, babies, calves, foals, and eggs.

"A man can't be as careful and stingy on that day with his woman as you are now," he said to Holme, laughing. "Otherwise, he can stay away. That god likes everyone drunk and happy."

Ausi heard his comment without really understanding it completely, but she hoped something would happen. One of the smiths lay red with fever by the fire and couldn't get up; sometimes she wished it were Holme.

The third day passed much like the two before, but instead of thinning out at dusk, the crowd around the temple grew even more dense. Holme and Ausi came along in the wake of a large group of warriors who ruthlessly pushed their way ahead, followed by their women. When they could look around again, they were standing in front of the temple.

Ausi saw more meat than she had ever seen before. Huge slabs turned on spits over the fires or simmered in cauldrons. Beside them lay piles of meat, spitted and ready to roast. There were enormous vats of beer, and long rows of beer tankards were lined up on the tables.

The people standing closest were all nobly dressed, and she looked at them anxiously. But no one seemed to notice that Holme and she wore humbler clothes; everyone seemed excited about what was happening in the temple enclosure. The king's place was still empty, but there were good indications that he'd soon be coming.

The image of one god had been moved in front of the others. It glittered with gold, and around its neck hung a wreath of yellow and blue flowers from the muddy field at the sunny edge of the forest. This god was unlike the two gods of battle; his body was almost feminine and his mouth was turned up in a smile.

The mood was lighter and happier than it had been the past two days. An accidental push or shove didn't bring about angry looks and words. Here and there, you could hear laughing and joking, always about the same thing. The air became more and more charged, and the god's smile reflected itself a thousandfold on the faces before him. The sacrifical grove, its three-times-eight ornaments hanging motionless in death, stood out against the blue-green spring sky.[19]

Ausi saw a huge number of attendants arranging a half-circle around the temple for a gigantic meal. They brought tables and benches for hundreds from a storehouse between the building and the grove. They put large baskets of bread and clay plates for the meat on the tables. The beer tankards were lined up in rows, but golden drinking horns glistened at the king's place and a few others.

Ausi caught a glimpse of the king and queen through the people standing in front of her. He was a tall man, somewhat stooped, with a pair of good eyes peering out from under his golden helmet. The queen was very young and seemed delighted with her beautiful garment. A group of expensively dressed women and men crowded around them.

The crowd moved forward and Ausi wasn't able to see when the king signalled for the meal to begin. But when a couple hundred people sat down near the temple, she got a better view. The king and queen had higher seats than the rest and could be seen over the entire area. The god stood smiling in the glow of the fire at the front of the temple. The eating and drinking had already begun.

Those in the back row or standing weren't forgotten. Smoking cauldrons of meat were hauled around on poles, followed by bread and beer. Many got what they wanted for themselves at the front of the enclosure. The temple attendants joked, laughed, and passed out things from huge stock piles. A cheerful, friendly mood spread through the crowd. Friends and strangers talked, clapped

---

[19] Adam of Bremen reports being told that a total of seventy-two sacrifices are made during the nine-day sacrifice. See Turville-Petre, *Myth and Religion*, p. 244.

each other on the back, and drank to each other. They no longer paid attention to differences in clothes or station.

Holme and Ausi didn't sit down when they had the chance, so they had to stand in the first group of people behind the tables. New fires flared everywhere; anyone was welcome to sit by them. In front of the god's feet, beer was offered on hot stones, sometimes completely hiding him with steam. Smoke hung over the entire area, and the moonlight went unnoticed although it forged broad yellow paths through the distant melted snow.

Ausi was chewing on a fine big mutton bone with meat. Holme had fetched a beer tankard, and she took a couple swallows of beer, strong, bitter, and frothy. Soon she grew animated, laughing at everything she saw and heard. Even Holme bared his teeth in an occasional smile though his eyes never lost their vigilance.

As far as the eye could see, fires were shining on rows of laughing faces or dark backs. The thralls, driven by curiousity, dared wander far in among the chieftains' tables, but no one chased them away. Drunken and smiling, the temple attendants ceaselessly dragged out more food and drink, more wood for the fires. At the market-place, a few merchants were selling mead, and a great throng surrounded their table. The god stared out over his people, smiling.

Strangely dressed people began gathering within the temple. The people turned around in their seats so they could see inside. The murmuring quieted down, and you could hear the fires crackling. From the darkness beyond the fires came loud, drunken laughter.

The singers gathered around the god, and the crowd fell completely silent. A man's loud, clear voice began singing, and Ausi listened, half dazed. But what she heard couldn't be possible! What thralls talked of only when they didn't think there was a woman around he was singing about in front of everyone. You just didn't sing about such things! Everyone joined in; then the voice was alone again, still describing all that could happen between a man and a woman in private.[20]

Ausi's cheeks flushed, but she couldn't keep from listening, soaking up every word. She was aroused and transported. She heard heavy breathing around her, and when she turned, she met a forest of eyes glistening in the firelight.

The singer stopped, replaced by another who sang a different song but described the same things, even more blatantly. The song thanked the god for the pleasure and enjoyment he provided and carefully described how he should be honored. When certain words were repeated, everyone raised a tankard.

---

[20] Schön, *Fridegård och forntiden*, p. 109, points out that Fridegård found the detail about obscene songs being sung in honor of Freyr in Helge Ljungberg, *Den nordiska religionen och kristendomen. Studier over det nordiska religionsskiftet under vikingatiden* (Stockholm: Hugo Gebers förlag, 1938), pp. 261ff. Schön shows that Ljungberg's book was one of Fridegård's major sources for his knowledge of Nordic religion. See the afterword to the present volume.

Among the long rows of silhouettes, Ausi could see men and women edging closer together. Hands sneaked into secret places; legs sought each other under the benches at the song's arousing words and melody. A man on her left grabbed her hip without Holme's noticing it, and she stood absolutely still. It was a kind of revenge for the firm grip on her right. She looked furtively at the man, who was tall, but young and beardless.

The singing continued, but something else was in the air. The singing vanished into the temple, and the attendants put more wood on the fires so that the whole area was lighted up. Two people, a man and a woman, emerged from the temple. Both wore only a light skirt and were the stateliest figures Ausi had ever seen. She felt both men tighten their grips on her hand and hip. A murmur like the squall of a storm rose among the crowd and fell as fast as it had risen.

The man and woman performed a dance, revealing enough of what the skirts hid to drive the crowd wild. Ausi was burning with a flame that had to be quenched. She resented Holme's hold more and more and pressed harder against the unknown man's hand. People behind them forced them forward a couple of feet, but neither man let go of her.

The dance of tribute to the fertility god ended with the beautiful couple partially blocked from view behind his effigy. There they enacted, actually or symbolically, something that made the crowd boil and surge like a forest in storm. The crowd could catch only rapid glimpses of one or the other's movements and then finally the woman's head on one side, cast back, flower-adorned hair hanging down. The god's body concealed the rest, and he grinned as if in mute empathy with the spectators.

Ausi felt Holme's hand trying to drag her away, but she struggled defiantly. The other man was now holding onto her arm. Then, like a wedge, the crowd behind them came with brute force between her and Holme. She felt his fingers clutching at her fingertips, desperately trying to hold on. The next instant there was nothing but a flood of strangers where he had been a moment before.

Without a word, the man plowed through the crowd with her. She followed, drunk with the beer, the song, and the spectacle. Soon they were beyond the press of people, and she could see a dark clump of pine trees rising from a moonlit plain. The man pulled her into the blackness, swept her into the air, and dropped with her to the ground.

Hard roots and stones under her back joined with the couple in their tribute to the god. The lust, like rivers ready to burst their banks, had swelled for hours, and scarcely had they imagined the possibility of release before they threw themselves into each other's arms and were united. When their passion ebbed it was replenished once more as if from a hidden spring. Ausi heard voices and laughter nearby but neither could nor would move.

She was still in the ebbing throes of passion when the man disengaged. Surprised at her beauty in the moonlight, he stroked her clumsily on the cheek.

He was young and awkward and once his warrior body had spent itself, he left her without a word.

Ausi felt the cold rising through her clothes but was still too weak to get up. She didn't think about anything, but wished she could stay where she was and sleep. The dull roar of the festival seemed far away and unrelated to her. A few couples hurried by, breathing heavily.

She sensed someone next to her and sat up. A man with a long beard was kneeling beside her. Grinning, he put his hand on her breast to push her down again.

Disgust and rage gripped her, and she hit him hard enough to knock him off his feet. When he got up again, she was already running across the moonlit plain. Before she reached the temple area, she stopped and straightened her clothes. She had dark wet spots on the back of them, but she saw many other women who were wet and muddy too.

Ausi was constantly accosted by drunken men and had trouble getting free. She tore herself from the roaring crowd again and walked toward the smiths' camp. No one was there but the sick smith who, red with fever, had rolled himself closer to the waning fire. His teeth chattering, he said that Holme had been there twice and had gone off again.

Ausi put more wood on the fire and warmed some beer for the sick smith. Then she lay down between the skin rugs and smiled contentedly. There was a smell of fresh pine twigs; she saw the moon swaying in the smoke above the fire and heard the distant uproar and shouting before she fell asleep.

Holme didn't wake her when he came back the third time. He had charged through the crowd in every direction, enraged and worried. A woman seeing his dark, grim face reached for him even though someone else already had an arm around her. He saw couples hurrying off into the darkness and searched all the more frantically.

When he saw Ausi was asleep, he sat next to her, staring quizzically into her face. It was calm and innocent; nothing could have happened to her. She hadn't been separated from him for long; they'd probably just kept missing each other in the crowd.

The fourth day was like the first two. It was the supreme battle god's second day, and fresh blood flowed, new sacrifices were hung in the trees. The wind blew hard, and the bodies swung back and forth, the large ones ponderously and slowly, the small ones rapidly. The scavengers flew screeching into the storm or sat quietly in the pine trees. Ausi saw the stranger again that day, and she wept softly into her arms until nightfall. No god cared about women and thralls after all; the stranger had been wrong. Or perhaps he had fallen into disfavor with his god, and who could survive that?

On the other hand, this god might have been there and been powerless to help his servant against the three massive gods in the temple. They had to be powerful and dangerous; anyone could see that. Huge and motionless, they stood there glistening with gold and blood. One of them wore the stranger's gold cross around his neck as a token of victory. He held a big silver hammer in his hand, and someone next to her told her he was the mightiest of the gods.

The sixth day belonged to the fertility god once more, and the scenes of the third day were reenacted. Holme was already dragging Ausi away when the songs started. He didn't drink any beer that day and didn't let Ausi have any. They sat in camp, listening to the murmuring rise and fall. Anxiety and sorrow filled Ausi's heart, and she longed to mingle with the crowd and escape everything, to frolic and be seized by unfamiliar hands. What did it matter now that all she had hoped for and been happy about was gone forever?

The sick smith had died and was lying under a skin a short distance from the fire. The next day he would be burned in a place set apart for the ones who weren't taken home after they had died or had been killed during the nine-day sacrifice.

On the ninth day, the smiling god's last, Ausi had disappeared by noon, and Holme couldn't find her. Strangers fetched her mead and meat; she heard new songs and once again saw the beautiful couple, who were even bolder now than on the first day. With flushed cheeks she witnessed everything that happened behind the god and felt an intolerable burning inside as the steam, rising from the sacrificial beer, obscured them.

She drank more beer and sweet mead, was led away, and was soon oblivious to everything that was happening. She must either really have been inside the temple or, had she dreamed of a soft, red lair and half-naked people, men and women wantonly joined? Hadn't the handsome priest of fornication who had danced around the god come and lain with her even though many beautiful women were tugging at his clothes?

Someone helped her past the three gods in the dawn, and for a moment she caught the terrible smell on a wind from the sacrificial grove. Then she found herself wandering around the marketplace where the merchants were gathering their remaining goods together and getting ready to take them away. Ausi's head gradually cleared, and she saw people leaving in every direction. No one looked at her; the men were sullenly and crossly arranging things for the journey, the women, officiously. Everywhere people were collecting their things, and in one place two women were arguing over a bronze dish.

Suddenly she was gripped by a strong desire to be away from it all, home with her baby. Today they would begin the return trip; she must go to the camp. The ground was well-worn everywhere, and it looked like a tilled field in front of the temple. Meaty bones and scraps of bread lay trampled in the mud everywhere. The temple attendants silently carried the tables and benches away to the storehouse or scoured the inside of the temple before the feet of the indifferently staring gods.

She saw Holme through the thinning crowd. His face was drawn and tired; he had probably searched for her all night. He didn't ask her anything or get angry, just said they were ready to leave camp. He noticed a mark she had under one ear, a mark from two rows of strong teeth, but said nothing. He had feared he'd never see her again, that some chieftain had left with her, and deep in his sullen heart he was relieved.

On the way back, they heard a yell from a large group breaking camp, and suddenly found themselves standing before the chieftain and people from the old settlement. There was a momentary silence while everyone stared in disbelief; then the chieftain turned red in the face and harshly ordered them back to the settlement with them. They'd get what was coming to them there.

Holme was confused for a moment; then he whispered to Ausi to run to the smiths' camp. He'd follow soon. As she responded, she saw him pull out the knife he had under his clothes.

The chieftain hesitated before ordering Stor and Tan to take Ausi. With quick, frightened looks at Holme, they started running, but he rushed them with the knife, chasing them in a semicircle out toward the field.

People all around stopped what they were doing and watched the spectacle. Someone yelled that fighting was forbidden in the temple area. A band of riders on their way home galloped up.

Stor and Tan had stopped out in the field, and a little ways away stood Holme, knife in hand. He asked them scornfully why they didn't want to fight him. Was abandoning babies in the woods and catching women all they were good for? All the time, out of the corner of his eye, he was watching Ausi, who soon reached the smiths' camp.

The chieftain, seeing there might be trouble and unpleasantness, yelled irritably for the thralls to come back. The court had already sat, and he knew that he had no legal right to Holme. They had found him, a black-haired, angry boy, on an islet—a "holme"—and that had given him his name. But Ausi had been born at the settlement, so she definitely belonged to him. He was running short of thralls and would have been glad to have both of them home with him again. He had missed his skillful smith many a time.

The festival and the court were over, but maybe there was some other way to get the thralls back. You could never just talk with Holme; you had to do something else.

Stor and Tan returned like big, chastised dogs, and the warriors glared contemptuously at them. The chieftain ordered everyone to go on and break camp and forget Holme until later. Off in the distance a group of men came running from where Ausi had fled, doubtless to help Holme. A fight here would never do. Holme walked toward them, and they gathered in a menacing group a short distance away. The smiths held their long-handled axes close to their bodies so they wouldn't be noticed in the sacred area.

They stood there a moment, but the people from the settlement ignored them and kept working. Holme explained the situation in a few words to his friends, and they were all on his side. He was too good a man to be a thrall for the short-legged, broad-nosed pig of a chieftain they saw over there.

The smiths gradually retreated toward their camp, where the women were clustered in an anxious group watching them. The beer was gone, the food spoiled, and the older women knew that there was usually trouble on the way home. Many of the groups hauled a silent body with them under the skins for many days so he could lie in peace in the earth of his fathers.

Seeing his former thralls had provoked the chieftain, and he plotted how he could get them back to the settlement. He sent Stor and Tan to see which way they had gone. Maybe he would get his chance if they were travelling in the same general direction.

He didn't want to attack them openly. He had seen the big smiths with their axes; it would be hard to overpower them. But he could follow them for a while; maybe they would split up farther down the road, leaving the thralls alone. Smiths travelling by foot couldn't walk very far the first day.

Ausi watched the temple and the huge mounds recede into the distance and disappear on the horizon. They trudged sullenly and silently all day, enjoying nothing. Wagons and bands of riders splashing along the muddy road passed them continually.

Though she missed her baby, she recoiled at the thought of returning to town. Everything had seemed so bright and joyous while the stranger was there; now, since he had brought light and then disappeared, it was even darker than before. But he had said there is no death, so maybe he'd return. She'd have to be there in that case so he could find her.

Holme had said nothing about her running away and performing every imaginable act with other men. She shouldn't have done that, but it was his and the beer's fault. And the singing and dancing! She didn't want to think about it anymore, but no wonder things had gone as they did. She would never think about doing those things with other men at home.

If they would only set up camp early now so she could sleep. None of them had slept more than a couple of hours at dawn for several days. And she hadn't slept at all the last night. She must have taken a wrong turn since those were nobles she had ended up with in the temple. She remembered expensive clothes and gilded walls, soft beds. They might have thought she was some chieftain's daughter. A man had whispered the smiling god's name in her ear, saying she was his loyal servant. But she wasn't—she must have been mistaken for someone else.

The smiths and their women looked for their old campsite and stayed there again. The spruce twigs were dry and warm from the sun, and there was plenty of firewood. No one had to tend the fire; it could go out and they would be all right under the skin rugs the rest of the night.

Many people passed by, and some camped near them, but they didn't hear the laughing and yelling they had on the way there. After the smiths had eaten meat and old bread, they immediately lay down under the skins and slept heavily.

It wasn't completely dark yet when a noise awakened them. The softly burning fire shone on men standing around the camp. The smiths groped furiously for their axes, but they were gone.

The chieftain spoke calmly, saying he didn't want to harm them; he only wanted his due. They'd better give him Holme and Ausi. Then they could lie down peacefully again to sleep and they'd get their weapons back.

Ausi's first anguished thought flew to her baby. What would happen to her if neither parent returned? They might carry her into the woods again if there was no one to answer for her.

The chieftain and the master smith exchanged a few words, but it was already clear what would happen. At least twelve armed warriors were surrounding five unarmed smiths. Holme was holding his knife, but what good would that do against several swords? He was ordered to give it up.

"You can have it when you come back," the master smith said quietly to him, certain he wouldn't remain long in servitude. Everyone was watching him, the warriors vigilantly, Stor and Tan anxiously. Finally, he handed his knife to the master smith and gave himself up. The master smith asked the chieftain to treat him and his woman well but got no response.

The prisoners walked between Stor and Tan toward the large camp not far away. The chieftain's wife looked uneasily at Holme's dark face. In vain she had asked her husband not to bring the two thralls back. She also noticed with hatred that Ausi had grown even more beautiful since the last time she saw her. Surely the tranquility now characterizing the settlement would vanish once Holme and Ausi returned.

No one tied the prisoners, but two men at a time kept guard over them at night. Holme finally managed to ease Ausi's mind about the baby; she knew they'd take good care of her. The master smith was expecting them back soon, so he'd obviously protect the child.

Holme had already decided they'd go back to the settlement before trying to escape. He couldn't free himself and Ausi without weapons, but he'd soon have some once he got to his old smithy.

Stor and Tan looked extremely uncomfortable at the idea of having Holme back. He noticed that and smiled ominously at them. The chieftain and the warriors ignored the prisoners once they had them secured.

They broke camp early and travelled on miserable forest roads, where a few patches of snow still dotted the north sides of boulders. Toward evening of the second day, Holme began to recognize the area, and after a while, they could hear dogs barking from the settlement. The dogs had caught their distant scent and soon came bounding and barking merrily toward them in the forest. A couple of them recognized Holme and almost ate him up. He smiled contentedly and patted their heads.

The road passed the smithy, and he looked in with curiosity. Everything was in disarray, and he snorted scornfully at the work that was lying in view.

Before the chieftain left them and went into the hall, he made a little speech. He said they deserved to be severely punished, but everyone was tired, and he would let it go if they would work faithfully and behave. If they tried to escape again, nothing could save them.

Holme listened to the threats with only half an ear, but Ausi was alarmed and cried about her baby so far away. Holme was usually right, though, and he had told her several times during the trip that the baby would be taken care of until they could get back to town for her. She hoped the wait wouldn't be long.

Ausi got her old place back in the thralls' quarters. Her friends were endlessly curious about everything that had happened to her while she had been away. They told her that the oldest woman thrall had died and that her ashes lay under a barely visible mound above the fields. And the mighty Stenulf was no longer there; he had vanished just after they escaped.

The next day, both Holme and Ausi looked with malicious pleasure at the chieftain's child, who ran around with a rigid, forward-bent head. He was a big, spiteful child. His mother was always nearby, watching him with uneasy eyes. When he caught sight of Holme, he stared at his face a moment, then ran screaming for his mother.

The concern for his baby could not drive away Holme's satisfaction in being his own master again. His helpers busied themselves officiously around him, anxious to please. Plows and spades stood outside awaiting repair for spring; kettles with broken handles, bent swords, and blunted spearheads were strewn everywhere. Most of the ax material was still where he had seen it last.

The chieftain listened contentedly to the new ringing in the sledge-hammers' song. He had secretly posted guards during the night, but no one had tried to escape. He had used a couple of the least valuable thralls so the loss wouldn't be too great if Holme had killed them. But the night had passed, and they were still alive and trembling when day broke.

The long ship lay on shore, almost finished. It was more beautiful than the old one, and the dragon head was still bare wood. The chieftain and the warriors kept busy with it all day, and Holme had orders to produce some smith-work for it that his helpers couldn't do on their own.

Ausi wandered around, her heart heavy with longing for her baby, but at the same time she was a little proud of her clothes, which were much better than her companions'. She talked about the town, too, their hut, and the treasures she had there. If it hadn't been for her baby, she would have gladly stayed, at least for a little while. But as always, Holme would decide what was best for them. That night maybe she'd hear what he had figured out.

The new clearing was finished and had borne a year's worth of crops. The pigs were already out, skinny and dirty after the winter. They grubbed in the refuse heap and plowed long furrows in the ground with their snouts. There was still a layer of dry leaves and grass in the barn for the horses and cows.

The chieftain marked out a new patch of ground for the thralls to clear in their spare time. He was convinced that this year, the first after the abundant sacrifices, would be a rich one. That's how it had been the last time.

Ausi's first job was to help with the spring cleaning. The provisions shed and storerooms had to be swept and aired, the big hall and holy room scrubbed and decorated. The shrine had only one inhabitant, a war god, his crude wooden statue painted red and gold.

The second night, two warriors wandering the forest came home while there was still a little daylight. They headed toward the women thralls' building, wrangling over who'd get the one who had just come home. They talked about how much more appealing she was than other women in the settlement.

But a dark, motionless figure sat guard on a rock on the hillside. The warriors stopped outside the building when they caught sight of him, then hesitated, talking in low voices. They both knew who was sitting on the rock. They couldn't mistake the broad shoulders and head lowered like a wild animal ready to spring.

"Get out of here!" one of the warriors ordered in a harsh, muffled voice, but the figure neither answered nor moved.

The warriors thought a while longer. The silent figure outside made them lose their desire for the women. Besides, they might get a knife in the back when they turned to crawl in through the low door. It always annoyed them to have to bend over and crawl; it was demeaning and made them feel helpless.

They withdrew from the thralls' dwelling in a rage and walked toward the high hall for bed. They would rather have cut the thrall down with a sword, but the chieftain wanted him there, and besides, there was no telling how the fight might end. The thrall was strong and wild and couldn't be scared off; there would have to be a fight.

The next day, Holme and Ausi agreed she would call for him if any warrior tried to pay her an evening visit. They both knew that none of the thralls would dare even look at her. Holme also told her that he would soon have weapons and equipment ready so they could leave. He had paid attention to the road and was confident he could find his way back to where they'd been ambushed.

They stood in the dusk a while, holding hands, talking about the baby and their hut. Deep down, Ausi felt like crying at the thought of the stranger's not being around anymore, of not being anywhere.

A thrall from another farmstead came panting through the woods a little after sunrise. His message caused the chieftain to assemble his warriors with an angry roar. His wife stood mute and ashen-faced while the stiff-necked son bent back to see his father's face.

The thrall came from his father-in-law's farmstead, asking the chieftain for help. The farmstead was under attack from a hostile family, much greater in number than the defenders. No one had seen the thrall or known that he had run for help. He had taken off before sun-up.

In a short time, the warriors were ready. The chieftain gave brief orders about the work and animals to those staying at home. He ordered Stor and Tan to come along, thought a moment, then gestured toward Holme. "We'd better take you along," he said. He didn't worry about Ausi; he knew she'd do nothing without Holme.

Holme hesitated only an instant. He knew if he refused, he'd be cut down before the warriors left. The chieftain was always on the brink of rage.

The chieftain didn't say good-bye to his wife and child, but he cast a strange, almost sorrowful look at them before rushing down to the ships at the head of the warriors.

The farmstead was located on the other side of a large cove, and they would save a lot of time by sailing across instead of running around it as the thrall had. Those staying at the settlement saw them hop into the old ship, and soon seven pairs of oars were slicing through the water. Farther out the wind picked up, and the black and yellow sail filled.

After they had disappeared beyond the point, the chieftain's wife ordered a year-old male calf to be slaughtered. She went to the shrine and anxiously studied the battle god's forbidding face. The thralls came soon with the frothing blood, and she ordered the oldest one to make the offering. As a woman, she didn't dare provoke the god by smearing him with the branch. He would doubtless rather have a man do that, even if it was a thrall.

Ausi walked into the high hall to put it back in order after the hurried departure. The warriors had sorted through their weapons and thrown the ones they didn't want on the floor. She was sure Holme would return before the others so they could get away with no one there to prevent them. What could women and thralls do against Holme?

In the middle of the day, the chieftain's wife sent a couple of thralls up on the look-out hill. When they came down, they said smoke was rising from her father's farmstead. Ausi watched the edge of the forest almost constantly and put in order what she could, but no one came. Still she did not grow anxious. Holme always knew best.

The forest on the north side of the besieged farmstead was dense, and the warriors could have gained a great advantage if they had circled around and attacked from there. But their pride urged them over the glade by the most direct route. Holme felt contemptuous, realizing how many they could have killed with arrows or spears before anyone even knew they were there.

A joyous cry from the besieged women and children greeted the new arrivals. Their assailants quickly retreated toward a large feed shed to protect their backs. A warrior lay to one side by a rock, holding his side and looking at the newcomers. The spear that had wounded him lay beside him. Several arrows were stuck in the timber wall.

The chieftain ordered the thralls to stay back during the attack. Stor and Tan hurried straight into the woods, and Holme sat down on a rock at the forest's edge. The men at the shed were shooting arrows, all of which were either deflected by shields or missed their marks. The men from the farmstead rushed out to join their allies.

Several men on both sides got spear wounds but none so serious they couldn't continue the battle. The women urged the wounded man by the rock to try crawling to them, but he shook his head. Gradually, one by one, the enemy was forced into the shed they were trying to keep at their backs. A couple stationed themselves in the doorway to cut down anyone trying to break in.

The shed was set off from the other buildings, and the air was calm. The two chieftains conferred together and then gave one of their men an order. He sneaked behind the shed and struck his flint in the dry grass by the sun-warmed southern wall. He crammed it in under the logs and listened with glee as the leafy branches started crackling inside.

The men in the shed had no way of putting out the fire, which raged in the bed of dry branches left over from the year before. They knew they'd backed into a trap, but they hadn't imagined their enemy would burn his own building.

They left their shields behind as they rushed out. The warriors outside, not expecting them so quickly, stood with shields in hand. Confusion spread among them, and a couple of them fell before the blows of the onrushing men.

Holme saw a big, raging group of men, swords flashing. His chieftain charged like an angry wild boar, and more than one man gave way before him. One of the enemies, unable to hold his ground against him, dashed away, picked up a spear, and flung it at the chieftain even though they should have been using only swords then. It hit him, lodging under one arm. The chieftain reeled, and another man hacked him with a sword as he fell.

The spear came out when he got up again. His face was white above his beard, and with wild, unseeing eyes, he rushed straight into the battle. He swung his sword wildly, and both friend and foe had to duck. He fell again closer to the fire, crawled a short distance, then collapsed. Holme watched him tensely, thinking that it would be a simple matter for him and Ausi to leave now whenever they pleased.

The heat forced the warriors back, and Holme had to move to another rock. The battle became less fierce after the chieftain fell, and then suddenly the enemy chieftain called loudly for a truce. His warriors gathered around him while the defenders placed themselves between the enemy and the farmstead. Holme alone saw the fallen chieftain suddenly kick his short legs out and then lie still. He could barely see Stor and Tan in the woods.

After the feed in the shed had burned, the fire continued to lick the charred walls a while but then weakened and sank toward the ground. When the battle was over, the women and thralls from the farmstead came and threw water on the hissing timber. The burned feed lay inside the shed, a smoldering black mass.

The warrior by the rock had bled to death; the chieftain and three other fallen warriors had stopped moving too. Many others had bloody faces and arms. A young woman came from the hall and sat silently beside one of the dead.

The rock Holme was sitting on was cold, so he moved to some sun-warmed moss. He was almost indifferent about the outcome of the battle now that chieftain was gone. A woman ruled him and Ausi now, and that practically meant they could go wherever they wanted. Even the warriors might not stay at the settlement but instead find another chieftain or go home to their relatives' farmsteads.

He saw the two bands of warriors reach an agreement. The outsiders lifted their dead on their shoulders and walked down toward the lake while a dismal group of warriors surrounded the chieftain's body. He had buried his face in a layer of mouldering leaves on the ground. In the sunshine by one of the other fallen warriors, a woman sat as motionless as the warrior.

Stor and Tan approached from the woods. As they stood by the chieftain's body, they feigned dismay, but Holme knew they had trouble hiding their glee. They'd have even more power now that just a woman ruled over them.

The woman's father, the old chieftain of the farmstead, ordered the thralls back to work. But he asked the thrall who had independently run for help to step up and made him foreman over the others. The thrall received new clothes from the storehouse and walked out beaming to abuse his underlings.

The warriors carried their chieftain to the ship, then returned to the farmstead to eat and drink. Down by the door Holme could hear them talking about what would happen now. The old chieftain could take his daughter and her child home with him until the boy grew up and was able to take over the settlement. The thralls could stay and tend to everything the same as before. He'd send someone to keep an eye on them if none of the warriors stayed on as overseer.

But no one responded; the warriors had wanted adventure for many a summer and had no desire to tie themselves to a farmstead. They thought silently of the dragon ship that would soon be ready. No one had more right to it than they did. What would a woman do with a war-ship? The old boat would still be good enough for the fishing grounds.

There was no cry of rage or promise of revenge for the chieftain: his in-laws had nothing to say about him, good or bad; Holme, Stor, and Tan felt relieved and thought of the advantages his death would bring; the warriors seemed a little more enthusiastic, glad their lives were about to move into a new phase.

The chieftain's wife had been standing in the yard of the settlement almost all day. The thrall who periodically descended the hill had reported that the smoke had thinned out and disappeared just before noon. The work was almost done; earlier the crops had been sown, and the chieftain himself had participated. Arms swinging and a bushel basket hanging from his waist, the stocky figure had walked up and down the fields the last two days. On the hillside above the fields was a little stone altar where he offered sacrifices to the harvest god before and after the sowing.

A dog at the forest's edge suddenly started howling protractedly, and a shudder ran through the whole settlement. It must mean one of their warriors had fallen, one or many. From way below the hill, they could see the thrall shaking his head as the howling reached him. After a moment, he came running down and said he could see the ship in the distance. The wind had settled toward evening, so the sail wasn't up.

Ausi wasn't anxious about Holme despite the dog's howling. She knew he wouldn't be allowed to fight even if he wanted to. But when the ship approached, she was standing right beside the chieftain's wife like her equal. Both had a husband on the ship. Both shielded their eyes with their hands when the ship moved into the dazzling sunlight and out of sight for a while.

Ausi had been more independent since her return, and the chieftain's wife eyed her with distaste even in the midst of her apprehension. How dared she stand there in the courtyard waiting for the ship even if her thrall husband was on it?

As the ship approached, the thralls began moving again. No one knew what kind of mood the chieftain was in or whether he was watching them. A sow was farrowing in one part of the pigsty with a thrall watching over her. Whenever she tried to bite one of the squirming piglets, he kicked her in the snout. He announced the arrival of each new piglet with a loud yell toward the hall. A sow that already had a litter ambled on the hillside, surrounded by piglets. From a distance she looked like a big rock capping a mound of little ones.

The chieftain's wife did not see the familiar squat figure step up on the gangway first, as he usually did. She saw the men tending to some heavy objects in the ship, and Ausi noticed her lips turn white and rigid. She looked around for her little boy and picked him up though he kicked and flailed his arms.

Ausi had seen Holme's black head already, and then he hopped ashore, followed by Stor and Tan. The thralls waded in the water and steadied the gangway for the warriors to walk over with their heavy loads.

With eyes wide, the chieftain's wife again searched the group of men, but they were all too tall. He had to be among the inert forms they had lain on the ground as they looked apprehensively toward the settlement. They picked them up now and started up the path. She backed all the way to the wall to make way for them. Standing there with her little boy as they walked past with the dead, she listened to their heavy steps, but their eyes stared grimly ahead. Almost all of them had bloody faces and arms.

The little boy in her arms held still now, watching the warriors. Ausi walked toward Holme, who had anchored the ship and was coming across the field toward the thralls' dwelling. Stor and Tan positioned themselves silently near their mistress to await orders.

Now that no one was guarding Holme and Ausi, they were no longer so eager to leave. Holme wanted to see what would happen to the settlement. Ausi was curious about how the chieftain's wife would handle everything, the funeral feast and building of the burial mound. Both felt a profound sense of well-being in knowing the chieftain was gone forever. Standing at the edge of the forest where the blue flowers were fading and losing their petals, they agreed to wait until all this was over. Holme assured her again that they would get their baby back safe and sound.

After the warriors had carried in the dead, there was complete silence. You could distinctly hear the sea-birds screeching and the shouts from the pigsty whenever a new piglet arrived. The thrall watching over the sow hadn't realized anything was happening in the settlement. The other thralls stood, their eyes fixed on the chieftain's wife, waiting for something to happen.

The warriors saw the remains of the offering at the shrine and asked who had made it. They shook their heads at a thrall having wielded the bloody branch; now they knew why things had gone so badly. The battle god had been insulted. It would have been better if the chieftain had made time for the sacrifice before they went into battle.[21]

No one talked at all that night. The chieftain's wife took her place after leaving the child with a woman thrall. From the high hall, she heard the warriors clearing their throats and chewing their evening meal. She saw the god's image in the darkness of the shrine, and the smell of blood drifted out. The child and the old nurse lay in the bed she had shared with the chieftain.

A couple of moldering leaves had stuck in the chieftain's beard, and she plucked them out. His clothes were bloody and torn near his left shoulder. The warriors had put his sword with the ornate hilt on his chest. Through the window behind the god, she saw a couple of motionless treetops against the sky, which grew darker and darker.

Once she heard some mumbling outside; the pigsty door closed, and then all was quiet. A warrior snored heavily in the darkness. The chieftain gradually disappeared from view into the gloom and was gone an eternity. His sword hilt was the first thing to catch the rays of the rising sun.

---

[21] See p. 52, note 14.

The warriors started digging the grave the next morning. The chieftain would lie beside his father and grandfather in the grove of memorial stones. The thralls gathered a huge stack of dry wood together for the funeral pyre.

In the hall, the chieftain's wife prepared food for the dead man's journey. Some chickens were killed and cooked; a bronze pot was filled with soup.

The memorial stone was already in the grove, taken there by the chieftain himself. The spades struck rock scarcely an arm's length into the earth, and everyone said it was deep enough.

At midday, two dragon ships from the relatives' farmstead sailed up to the jetty carrying the chieftain's father-in-law, brothers-in-law, and other relatives with women and children. Some sacrificial animals were also brought ashore—two goats the old chieftain wanted to sacrifice for the dead man's success on his journey.

The funeral pyre was ready and the chieftain was carried down to it. He had on everyday clothes but no weapons. Only his knife remained in his belt, its bronze sheath shining. A flint and some other little things were left in his pockets. Behind the warriors carrying him, everyone walked single file, the noblest first and the thralls last. The wood in the pyre had been artfully stacked as in a charcoal mill, and there was a skin rug on top.

Before the father-in-law lit the funeral pyre, the chieftain's wife threw handfulls of blue and white flowers on the corpse as a gift to the gods. They rained down over the chieftain, setting like stars everywhere, in his hair and beard, on the skin rug and the wood.

Powder-white smoke from the dry leaves poured out of the pyre after the father-in-law lit it. It rose up and floated among the tops of the young aspens, which had begun sprouting tiny leaves and long, pendulous stems. The birds fell silent and flew off toward the forest.

The fire, crackling and popping, took hold in the wood, driving those standing closest to it away with its heat. It looked red and malicious in the sunshine. A gust of wind pushed it to one side, revealing for an instant the chieftain's ghastly head with the hair and beard burnt off.

The heat intensified, and the fire crept into the half-dry grass. Thralls stood ready to throw dirt on it with their spades. They called to each other under their breath and laughed when no one was looking. It was a good day for them—a real change and some light work.

The flames reached higher yet, and there was something festive in their roar. The warriors watched with approval, thinking it was a good sign for the chieftain. The child laughed at the fire consuming his father, but the mother stared into it with a rigid face.

Ausi and Holme dared stand next to each other and watch the funeral pyre. They felt relieved and happy; they could go wherever and whenever they wanted. And the man they hated above all others lay burning on the pyre in front of them, the one who had despised them and condemned their baby to death, who had brought them back into slavery. There he was now; he could never do anything to them again.

Ausi watched the smoke, wondering when the chieftain would continue his journey to the realm of the dead. Sometimes she imagined she saw his bearded face high up among the white-gray smoke billowing toward the blue sky.[22] The stranger had said that there was only one home after death, and that was with his god. The chieftain couldn't go there. It was difficult to understand it all, and now she had no one to ask.

An unexpected puff of wind drove the smoke among the onlookers, forcing them to one side. The smell was foul and was sometimes accompanied by a soft hissing sound. The child played by his grandfather's memorial stone, hiding behind it and peeking out. He turned his whole body in the direction he wanted to look.

Holme had long since tired of it all and wanted to be on his way— back to the smithy or the forest. But that would cause offense, and there was no need for any disturbance with everything turning out so well. He wanted to see what it would be like at the settlement now and who was going to stay on to run things. It might be someone from the other farmstead.

He had already made weapons and hidden them in a safe place. Ausi could get food for the journey, at least bread; there was enough meat to be had once they were under way. A few days' journey through the wilds would be enjoyable.

His thoughts returned to the chieftain on the pyre. That's how it should have been for Stenulf, too— Stenulf, who was a much bigger and better warrior than the chieftain. He had been lying under the mound on the ridge for three summers.

Maybe he was still there, unable to move on and without food for the journey. The stranger's god hadn't even helped his own follower; he couldn't raise up Stenulf either. Ausi believed the stranger would return, but she was a woman and believed all sorts of things.

The swineherd was busy at the sty, the only man not by the pyre. Some women, occasionally visible between the high wall and provisions shed, were preparing for the feast. The sacrificial goats gnawed on the tender grass, looked toward the lake, and bleated. After the pyre had burned and the mound had been raised, they'd be sacrificed to the gods.

---

[22] In chapter 9 of the Old Norse *Ynglinga Saga*, the first part of the *Heimskringla*, Snorri Sturluson explains the importance of smoke at a funeral pyre: 'It was people's belief that the higher the smoke rose into the sky, the more elevated in heaven would he be who was cremated' (Snorri Sturluson, *Heimskringla: History of the Kings of Norway*, trans. Lee M. Hollander [Austin: Univ. of Texas Press, 1964], p. 13). See also line 3155 of the Old English poem Beowulf, where the poet describes the hero's funeral pyre and burial: 'Heaven swallowed the smoke.'

The roasted birds and bronze pot were a little ways from the fire. Holme figured the food would only last a couple of days for someone who ate as much as the chieftain did. But he might be able to find something on the journey if he had to.

The pyre would soon burn out; the smoke no longer billowed as before, but was hot and blue. The child had fallen asleep by the memorial stone; the woman thrall sat next to him keeping watch. Everyone knew the grove was full of snakes; they lived in cairns during the winters and would come out and sun themselves as soon as the ground was bare and the previous year's leaves dry.

There were good-sized waves out on the cove, but the belt of reeds checked them so only tiny, glistening swells rolled in among the stones on shore. The warriors glanced frequently toward the new ship painted dark-red with gold trimming on the prow and stern. On the shore lay some leftover oak that the chieftain had intended for a fishing boat to replace the one Holme had stolen.

After the flames had died down, the black mass of ashes that had once been the chieftain was still hissing slowly. His father-in-law took a spade and pushed aside most of the cinders; some metal objects glistened in the ashes. The thralls were ordered to throw water on the smoldering ground so he could walk closer to the pyre.

When it had cooled off a little more, he took the ash urn, an ornamented clay pot, and began scooping the yellow-gray ashes, remains of the chieftain's flesh, into it. The fire hadn't touched the bones; they were still intact, smoking from the heat. He piled them beside him and continued scraping up the ashes. A clasp or some iron fittings sparkled now and then in the heap of ashes. The chieftain's wife, her face pale, looked on.

When he finished, the old chieftain washed the bones and laid them beside the urn. Finally he laid down the provisions for the journey. The people standing closest to him handed him rocks to stack around the burial objects to protect them. He covered the urn with a flat stone. Then he got up, and numerous spades starting throwing dirt back into the grave.[23]

When it was level with the ground, he said they would leave it that way until later. They'd finish after they had eaten, raise the memorial stone, and finally offer sacrifices to the battle god for the chieftain's good reception.

Most of them found it hard to hide their pleasure at the thought of leaving the hot burial grove, getting washed, and sitting down to eat. No one missed the chieftain except his wife; his death had created new vistas for the others and brought relief to their lives.

By the time night fell, three memorial stones stood an equal distance from each other in the grove. They were visible from the settlement now, but the

---

[23] Except for the wife's throwing flowers on the corpse, the details of the burial scene are based on archeological evidence. See Schön, *Fridegård och forntiden*, p. 116.

foliage would soon grow dense and hide them for some months. The new mound would be bare the first year; in the second summer, sparse blades of grass would creep over it, and after four years, it would be just like the other two. A thousand years later, one of the stones would fall down, but the other two would still be standing, and the mounds would remain unchanged. By then the shore would have receded a good distance from the grove.

The old chieftain decided how the settlement would be managed after he left and took his daughter with him. The thralls would take care of everything by themselves until he designated someone to come and take command.

He called the people together and determined which jobs and duties they had had up until then. Stor and Tan stood by watching smugly; they were sure they'd be named foremen since they were so conscientious. Holme stood farthest away, watching it all indifferently, but he noticed the old man's eye searching for him. The chieftain had seen many weapons and tools by Holme's hand and even carried a sword of Holme's making fastened to an expensive foreign hilt. He realized the thrall was stubborn and dangerous, but then he probably had to be because of the chieftain they had just burned. The escape and recapture had been related to him, and he realized no one could keep the smith and his woman there now against their will. The chieftain was old and wise, and in most matters, his vision was clear.

"You'll be in charge here," he said amicably to Holme. "You know how everything should be. I'll come back now and then and see how it's going."

Stor and Tan cleared their throats in surprise and disappointment, but the chieftain didn't pay any attention to them. Holme smiled self-confidently and straightened up when he was convinced the chieftain was serious. Yes, he could do that as well as anybody. The dead chieftain's wife started to object, but her father silenced her.

The warriors lost all interest in the settlement and absorbed themselves in the ship. In a few days it would be ready. No one denied their right to take the vessel they had built with their own hands. The old chieftain had asked if any of them wanted to stay on and take over the settlement and his daughter, but all remained silent. They had been waiting for too long for a chance to sail to distant lands.

After making his request, the chieftain boarded ship with his daughter, her child, and all his household servants. Ausi looked at Holme proudly and happily; they were like rulers now. She could repay her companions for all the harm they had done her.

That night, they sat alone in the large, empty hall, talking about retrieving their baby. Holme would return alone in a few days; he didn't think the thralls would dare do anything to her while he was away. He could be back in three days if he went by horse.

They considered sleeping on the chieftain's bed but went to the thralls' dwelling instead. There was no need to provoke the warriors, who would be leaving soon anyway. The women thralls had just come in and were setting the long table with the warriors' meal so it would be there when they returned from the lake.

In the thralls' dwelling, friends were talking, both men and women, in sullen, threatening tones about the new situation. They'd gladly work for the chieftain's wife or some new chieftain, but Holme and Ausi weren't as dependable as they were and shouldn't try lording it over them.

The battle god stood mute and forgotten in his shrine. The old chieftain had ordered a sacrifice out on the field, but he hadn't said anything about the god inside. A farmstead without warriors was in no need of his favor.

A warm wind was blowing across the hillsides the day the warriors sailed away. They hauled ample supplies down to the ship, whole chests of bread and meat. Holme had examined their weapons and given them new arrows.

The long glistening red grass surged around them as they walked down to the shore around midday. The freshly gilded dragon gaped toward the cove, its spiky red tail turned toward land.

The thralls stood in a group at the settlement, watching the warriors sail away. After they had passed the point, the sail fluttered out, filled, then stretched toward the open sea. The dragon picked up speed and ducked behind the point, its length glistening as the oars were pulled in. The next instant, it was gone.

The thralls sat down where they were, not knowing what to do. It felt strange, almost unsettling not to have to fear the chieftain's hard eyes. Holme was nowhere to be seen; naturally he was thinking about leaving and he wasn't their master anyway.

A rhythmic shuffling noise came from the provisions shed. Ausi and Holme were amusing themselves by grinding with the new hand-mill the chieftain had gotten while they were away. It consisted of two round, notched stones, and the upper one was pulled around with a heavy stake set in a hole. You could mill many times faster with it than by rolling a stone in a worn groove to crush the grain. The old millstone lay discarded on the hillside now, and when rain fell, sun-warmed water stayed in it for many days for the birds to bathe in and the dogs to lap noisily.

When Holme left the seed the chieftain had sown had already sprouted, lightly covering the gray field. Nettles and oily grass were growing high up the pigsty wall. He had told the other thralls what to do while he was away, and they had answered either with scornful grins or silence. But he knew the most important things would get done anyway. He had also told them that if anyone touched Ausi, he wouldn't live to see the sun set in the forest the day Holme returned.

He had fixed up some old riding gear and had made a new bridle to go with it. He wasn't accustomed to riding and so he walked long distances, leading the horse by the reins. He followed along the ridge by the cave and saw Stenulf's burial mound again. The top stone had fallen down, but he would put it up again on the way back. The footpath between the cave and the spring was no longer visible. He longed for the days he had lived with Ausi in the cave.

His ax hung by a loop on the saddle so he could grab the handle. People he ran into looked with surprise at the powerful, melancholy figure on the little shaggy horse. His broad cheek bones and black locks of hair made him look like a wooden god.

By the next morning, he could recognize where they had been ambushed by the warriors. There were still some dry twigs and soot left from the camp. The chieftain hadn't derived much joy from what he had done that day.

Riding became easier and easier, and night was still hours away when he passed through the last forest and came to the shore. There was the wide, blue lake, there the market-town with its swarms of ships, people, and animals.

Holme left his horse at a farmstead near the ferry. In the boat, he enjoyed the thought of how surpised the smiths would be when he came striding into the smithy. "I'm back for my knife," he'd quip to the master smith. Then they'd hear how well things were going for him and Ausi now.

On shore, he walked straight to where Ausi had left the child before they had gone to the festival. The hut was on the outskirts of town, and a middle-aged woman had been well-paid for caring for the child during those nine days.

In a garbage pile near the outskirts, a couple of dogs were scrounging for something to eat. Holme, looking indifferently at them, noticed something moving in the trash. He discerned a tiny black head and a pair of skinny arms and hands digging in the garbage and occasionally putting something in its mouth. With a roar, he rushed up the slope, and the dogs dashed away, snarling.

The child's hair was a single twisted knot of dirt, and she was holding a crust of bread in her hand when he picked her up. At first she just chewed listlessly, her dark eyes staring at him; then she began trembling and screaming with joy as she reached for her father's face. She had a little skirt on, but her arms and legs were bare, dirty, and scratched.

For the first time he could remember, Holme felt tears running down his cheeks. But his rage exploded at the same time, and, still weeping, he raced down the garbage heap toward the hut, the child under his left arm, his ax in his right hand. A couple of women who had seen it all ran after him at a distance to see what would happen.

The woman responsible for the child was standing in the doorway. She saw him coming, the child under his arm and the ax in his hand, and she ran screaming from the hut to seek protection. She ran toward the fortress, looking frantically around, screaming with fear. Holme pursued her silently and swiftly.

Terrified faces peered out from everywhere, and a warrior coming out of a side street stopped and watched them.

They were still a good distance from the fortress when Holme caught up with the woman, whose legs were almost paralyzed with fear. Without breaking stride, he hit the back of her neck with the flat of his ax. She tumbled on her face, and he kept running toward the lake.

The oarsman said nothing about Holme's haste or his strange cargo; instead he quickly began rowing. Soon several men and women appeared at the shore, screaming and pointing at the boat. Holme glared grimly at the oarsman, who pulled even harder. His passenger's face made it clear that his own life wouldn't be worth much if he tried turning around. He was an old man and no match for this black-haired man who looked as if he was made of granite.

Out in the middle of the cove, Holme realized he hadn't even had time to visit the smiths. Everything had happened faster than he would have wished. He couldn't turn back. He didn't regret teaching the woman a lesson, but it was good that she only got the flat of his ax. He could sense the blow hadn't been fatal, but she'd certainly have a headache. Maybe the smiths would hear about his visit and figure out what happened. They could have kept an eye on the child, though.

A long ship set out from the market-town, and the oarsman gestured at it as he tried to row faster. It had to be the town guard after them. The child clung to Holme, never taking her eyes off him.

Before he jumped ashore, Holme clipped off a piece of silver rod twice as long as the oarsman should have received. The other boat was still a good ways out but approaching rapidly. The horse with the riding gear still on was grazing outside the farmstead. The forest was just behind them so they could surely get away.

He looked around at the farmstead and could see he still had a little time. He ran into the house and asked for milk for the child; the woman brought a pitcher immediately. As the child drank greedily, the woman watched, feeling great pity for her.

The long ship touched bottom just as Holme disappeared into the woods, and the little horse scurried like a rat into the brush, its bridle dangling. Holme knew it would find its way better than he could. He had re-shod it, so it climbed the rocky slopes like a cat.

He heard the shouting as his pursuers reached the farmstead, but soon everything grew quiet in the sun-warmed forest. After he had passed through the trees and the plain beyond, he stopped at the edge of the next forest. The horse began grazing immediately, and Holme sat down with his child. He tried to put her in the grass beside him, but she resisted, refusing to leave his arms. He gave her some soft bread and meat, which she ate voraciously.

For a few hours that night, she slept lying on his clothes, he sitting half-naked beside her. When daylight broke, he rode on, the child sleeping against his chest. As the day grew hotter, she drank spring water from her father's large, dark hand and ate the last of his provisions.

Holme rode past Stenulf's mound in the middle of the night, his left arm numb from the child's weight. Even then, a night mist hovered over the marsh far below, and somewhere a bird called. On the other side of the ridge, he could hear squeals from the wild boars mating and fighting in the dark, ancient forest.

The settlement was quiet, but the horse under him whinnied wildly when it smelled home. The child woke up and clasped her father tighter. He got off and released the horse, which trotted off at once to find its companions in the pasture. Someone bolted toward him from the women thralls' quarters, snatched up the child in the darkness, and snatched her with tear-filled eyes.

Holme later tersely described the journey, and when he told Ausi about the woman he had hit with the ax, she reached out and caressed his cheek for the first time in a long while. The child was soon sleeping in her mother's arms, and they walked to the chieftain's quarters inside the big hall. It was empty and quiet inside; a couple of bows left behind by the warriors still hung on the wall. Ausi glanced furtively at the shrine where the figure of the god was standing in the darkness, silent and grim. What would he think of thralls occupying the chieftain's bed and so close to him?

The chieftain's wife had taken the best skins with her, but those she had left made a bed good enough for the thralls. Outside the skins, the clay floor was cold and hard. They talked softly until the gray light shone through the hole in the roof and the songthrush in the aspen grove sang its morning song. The sun was soon shining on the west edge of the light hole, and a bird's shadow occasionally flickered by. Around midday, when the door was open, swallows would fly rapidly in, making a pass through the swarm of mosquitoes under the ceiling, and disappearing through the hole. Sparrows fluttered in frequently, sitting on the wooden pegs in the wall, or hopping about on the clay floor.

Before anyone else awakened, Ausi was already up putting out a pot of water for the sun to warm. It wouldn't be easy to get the child clean. She thought with satisfaction about Holme's clubbing the woman with the ax. She must have just kicked the child out to fend for herself. What if Holme hadn't shown up?

When Ausi got up she felt dizzy and sick and realized she'd felt this way for some time now. She'd better ask for a potion from the old thrall woman who knew about medicinal herbs.

Three summers had passed now since the child was born and they had lived in the cave. Everything had gone well for them, and now they had their child back. There were a few pieces of cloth in a chest; she finally dared take one to make clothes for her child.

But when day came and she asked the old woman for some medicine, she got a scornful laugh in reply. The woman turned her back on her and said that the evil would probably pass toward autumn.

"Don't you understand?" she asked, turning around and pointing at the child Ausi was washing. A foreboding gloom descended on her, and she thought immediately about the festival of sacrifice. She had wondered many times what had gotten into her then and was ashamed that she hadn't behaved as she should. What would Holme say? He couldn't say anything until the child was born and he could take a look at it. But something inside told her it wasn't Holme's.

The black-haired youngster was soon clean, and she ran laughing in the sun, her hair still wet. When Stor and Tan walked by, Ausi couldn't resist asking them if they had noticed that the baby had made it home from the woods. Hadn't they done their duty three summers ago? The thralls didn't respond but looked with surprise at the child they had abandoned by a rock that summer night so long ago. Now it was running around here, perhaps destined for something special since it had been permitted to live.

Within a few days, the trees had come into leaf, hiding the three mounds—two green and one dirt gray—in the aspen grove. The thralls had only begun to fully realize that the feared and hated chieftain was gone, that they never agian would have to hide from his fits of rage. Holme wasn't as bad an overseer as they had feared; he stayed in the smithy most of the time and let them take care of the fields and meadows as they pleased. He fixed the warrior's discarded weapons and didn't say anything if one of his fellows went off to the woods with bow and arrow.

The old chieftain showed up now and then and was invariably satisfied with what had been accomplished. The grain looked splendid, and the store of weapons and tools in the smithy grew. He never mentioned anything about sending a new chieftain to the settlement.

Each time, he offered a sacrifice on the altar by the fields, but he entered the shrine only once. The battle god stood there; woodworms had eaten tiny round holes in his head, dropping wood particles onto his shoulders. The smell of blood had almost completely disappeared on the warm wind wafting in and out through the constantly open light openings.

The north wind played with the hair of the woman sitting on the rock as she contemplated her fallen chieftain and husband. It was a hard and bitter memory he had left behind, but he was still her husband. Her son played beside her, looking like a bull calf because of his stiff neck.

Soon the wind rustled the leaves in the aspen grove, making sun and shadow dance and twinkle on the three burial mounds, two green, one gray. Many hours later, the sun reached a flotilla of dragon ships. The settlement's warriors had recently joined it with their new ship and were happily following a powerful chieftain to distant lands for war. The chieftain's ship was the biggest they had ever seen; a full-grown man could sit in the dragon's red maw.

The rumor soon reached the warriors that this flotilla would join another even larger one farther away; they were astonished. Their big new ship was looking small and shabby, but they still felt fortunate to be part of the large fleet.

And so the summer, warm and calm, passed by in the settlement. Holme exercised his power only in the smithy and turned everything else over to Stor and Tan, who contentedly strolled through the meadows or fished in the cove. In the evenings they would stand and count the pigs and other small animals as they came in, just as the chieftain used to do. The responsibility did the thralls good, and the settlement was run as well as ever before.

When the grazing was good in the forest, the cows didn't come home for the milking, so the thrall women with their wooden pails had to search for them. They walked mostly through a large, dried-out bog where white and pink orchids rose candle-like from the grass as far as they could see. The sun was always low at milking time, so the bog soil was cold both morning and night. Dwarf pine trees grew on the grassy tufts, and brown birds of prey thrived there.

Sometimes the herd of cows came running toward the settlement at a wild, snorting gallop, and surrounded the outlying buildings with anxious bellowing. Stor and Tan would count them quickly and frequently would find an animal missing. Then they knew that a bear stood in the bog somewhere eating, peering around with small, fierce eyes. Once it followed the herd all the way to the settlement; heavy and ponderous, it lumbered into the courtyard but retreated soon from the blaring horns, the shrieks, and the spears that spit up dirt all around it.

Ausi had begun to show signs of pregnancy. Her walk got heavier and her hair lost its luster. Occasionally she met Holme's eye and saw a question there, but she said nothing. It was best to wait and see. She didn't dare hope that the child would be dark-complected and black-haired like Holme. The thought of that drunken, lascivious night among the pine trees when she had trembled between a large, hot body and the ground was too firmly embedded in her memory. The child was from that night. She sensed it; she knew it.

With the warriors gone, the thralls began living in couples. Two older women were left alone, but they had tired of men long ago. Several couples moved into the high hall and made themselves at home. Ausi watched disapprovingly, but Holme let them be. After all, they themselves were living in the chieftain's quarters. When the old chieftain came, he didn't care where the thralls were living. He saw that the fields were tended to and the animals cared for, and he was content. It seemed obvious to him that all this was a result of his sacrifices to the god of harvest, and he continued to bring offerings every time he came.

In a few years, his stiff-necked grandson could take over the settlement himself, with his mother's help. With that in mind, he encouraged the thralls to take good care of their children and to bear many. Quite a few of them were growing old and would no longer be alive when the new chieftain grew up and needed thralls for his settlement.

One day during the leaf harvest, Holme walked to the cave. A couple of years' worth of spruce needles had fallen on the rock by the door, indicating no one had been there. There was a hollow in the ground by the narrow opening; a badger had probably thought about settling in the cave. But the stony ground had been too hard to dig in, or perhaps it still held the scent of human beings and had scared him away.

The grass was still lying there, but the needles fell off the spruce branch when he touched it. He lay down for a while and thought. Deep inside he longed to live in the cave again, to stay in it forever. Of course, things were going well now — he was living like a chieftain. But sometimes he wanted to walk into the heart of the forest where there wasn't a single soul. There were men who lived in caves or small dens of earth and stone. Fugitives and outlaws with long hair and beards, resembling wolves in their animal skins. He had always felt drawn to them.

But Holme had come to replace the stone on Stenulf's mound. Stenulf had been a mighty warrior and should have had a chieftain's funeral. If the stranger's god had been good for anything, he would have called Stenulf up from the dead, but as it was, he couldn't even save his own priest. The stranger was hanging in the sacrificial grove; by now the flesh of both animals and humans had probably rotted off the bones.

Holme plucked away the small stones so he could anchor the top slab better. It wouldn't fall over for many lifetimes now. As far as he could see into the future, whoever walked by would see that Stenulf was lying there.

But after he fixed the mound, he still wanted to stay a while; it was so isolated and pleasant on the distant gravel ridge. Down in the hollow, a few of the tall, long-legged birds were walking, looking very much like sheep from a distance. Once when an old thrall had tried to catch one, they had attacked and almost killed him.

Plenty of good grass was growing between the cave and the ridge, and for a moment he thought about bringing the others from the settlement to retrieve it. But he changed his mind at once; someone might discover the cave. He wanted to be the only one who knew about it; he never knew when he might need it again. Ships might come sailing into the cove some day carrying warriors from across the lake. Then he'd only have to drop everything and flee as fast as possible, now that there was no defense. Such things had happened in other places.

He'd visit the cave again one day and hide a few essentials. An ax and a spear, a bar of gold. He had one such bar from the town but had no use for it right now. At the settlement, you had everything you needed without having to pay for it the way you did out in the world.

From the ridge, he could see far out over the forests, fading into blue in the distance. Smoke was rising here and there. The dark fir forest was broken by an intermittent patch of deciduous trees, especially where the land sank toward a river or lake.

He walked home across the hollow, keeping an eye on the large birds, which had flocked together watching him as he passed. It would be strange indeed if he couldn't break the necks of a few birds if they attacked him.

The smaller birds that fluttered around your head chirping during the spring now sat silently among the tufts, only reluctantly getting out of the way. Their nests were doubtless nearby. Maybe this was where the women usually came to gather eggs.

As everyone expected, it was a good year after the great sacrifice. Grain and grass grew thick and tall, the animals retained their beauty and had numerous offspring. Many women who hadn't had children by their husbands for many years felt the results of the tribute they had brought to the fertility god in the spring nights during the festival of sacrifice. At many farmsteads, a field was consecrated to him, and he got his allotted share of all that was born and grown.

The thralls finished their work in good time and had a few free days between harvesting the hay and the grain. Nothing had happened during the whole summer even though from the look-out hill they had seen several flotillas of dragon ships sailing south. The chieftains doubtless wanted to test their luck in battle, which ought to be good after the great sacrifice. A wanderer told them that a vast flotilla of dragons was on its way west to conquer lands and property. Warriors from all over the north had joined it.

All during the late summer, Holme worked on a little boat he was making from the leftover oak wood from the long ship. The old ship was too big to fish with, and besides, a little boat might come in handy. No one knew how long the halcyon days of peace would last.

Ausi's movements became heavier and heavier, and her features hardened. The anxiety gnawed constantly, but she hadn't responded to Holme's silent question. She realized more and more how closely the time coincided with those two insane nights. Around the midwinter sacrifice, the difficult hour would be at hand. She could see that Holme's figuring was the same.

If it only had come during the summer so she could go out into the forest when the moment approached. There she could examine the child alone, and if it looked like Holme, she could go home again with joy. If not, then at least she would be alone to decide what would be the best thing to do.

If only there were someone who could give her advice and help. The stranger was gone, but she couldn't have talked to him about this anyway. And his god probably wouldn't help her. But if the stranger had told the truth, then neither he nor his god could really die; they were there but couldn't be seen. Maybe she could go into the forest and tell them how difficult it was for her right now. Maybe they would hear and understand. The stranger had usually held his hands together and looked upwards when he talked with his god, and she could do the same.

He had said that since they had had water poured on their heads that day they belonged to his god. Then he ought to help her now, too. If she walked up on the look-out hill, then he would surely see her as long as he wasn't too far away.

Holme saw Ausi gathering pieces of cloth together, tying them up and wrapping them in an animal skin, then taking them outside to hide. She would step timidly to one side whenever they met and tried to hide her condition as much as possible.

A thin crust of snow covered the ground, but the lake was still open. The sheep and goats stayed out during the days, gnawing on the hard-frozen ground and bleating, their yellow eyes directed at the outlying buildings.

Toward evening, Holme saw Ausi standing in a corner, clutching the back of a bench and groaning. He decided to sleep in the hall with the others that night so she could be alone with the old thrall woman who knew a little about everything. He was glad the worst would soon be over. When the baby was gone and Ausi was healthy again, everything would get back to normal. Neither would talk about it, and no one else would ever know what had happened at the festival of sacrifice.

Actually, the fertility god should probably receive an offering so everything would go well. When the chieftain's wife was having her baby, the chieftain stayed by the altar in the field the whole day. But why should thralls make offerings? They usually bore their children just as well without sacrifices, and it would probably be no different this time.

Out in the high hall, the thralls had built a fire, and it flickered on the wall in the chieftain's quarters. Holme realized he hadn't seen Ausi for a long time. She wasn't usually still outside at this hour, and she hadn't wanted to be with the others for some time.

He went outside and looked into the thralls' dwelling, but it was quiet and deserted. They had all moved in for the winter. The hillside was white with downy snow, but the sky was dark with a heavy vault of clouds. Where could Ausi have gone?

Suddenly remembering the bundle she had hidden, he checked its hiding place. It was gone. He went in and asked around in the big hall, but no one had seen her.

"You've probably driven her out in the woods," said the old woman thrall scornfully. But what did she know? Stor and Tan laughed. All the men were fixing shoes or carving bowls and spoons. The women were busy with flax or wool. The meat was cooking and filling the entire hall with its fragrance, but Holme's anxiety drove him back out again.

If there had been a little more snow, he would have been able to see her footprints. She had to have gone to the woods, and he thought of the wolves and wild boars. He hurried along, his eyes glued to the ground in the fading light.

Where a trickle of water had run down the hillside from the stables, he caught sight of a track. The water hadn't frozen so hard that her foot couldn't break through it. At least he knew which way she had gone.

In the woods, he followed his instinct more than tracks. He found another sign by the shore of the marsh—a footprint again, filled with water and black against the snow. Farther out she had taken a wrong step, and both feet had gone through. She must be wet and cold.

Holme was soon across without sinking into the marsh once, whereas Ausi had slogged for long stretches through the mire. He paused on the hillside and listened. He heard a strange shriek, but it wasn't a wolf or a great horned owl. He had never heard it before. It stopped, and he hurried on. He thought about Stenulf and a shudder passed through him, but he had to pass by the mound.

Just below it, the howling started again. Fear ravaged him fiercely for a moment, but then he understood. Could a human being sound like that? He made no move forward but instead stood behind a boulder until the shrieking abated and stopped once again.

Holme wondered how she had managed to budge the stone from the cave opening. Once a long time ago she had tried but couldn't. It was a good thing there were still twigs and moss inside.

When there was a long silence, he sneaked up to peek through the opening. To his surprise, he saw a light inside. Ausi was just sitting up then, lighting a piece of wood with the one just burning out, and then wedging it in the air vent. It crackled, flickered, and shone on her as she lay back down again. Soon the screams started again, and he moved a short distance away so he wouldn't have to hear them so distinctly.

This time it was worse, and he paced around anxiously, wondering what he could do. For one fleeting moment, he thought it served her right; that's what she got for the festival of sacrifice.

When it grew quiet, Holme sneaked closer again and saw that Ausi was sitting up. He heard a strange sound and saw her take the stick from the wall and shine it on something in front of her. He sensed disappointment and despair in her swollen face as she put the stick back and began busying herself with the thing in her lap.

Holme waited a long time before he went in. She screamed when she saw his black-haired head in the opening, but when she realized it wasn't a wolf or a bear, she threw a skin rug over everything before her. Then, filled with agony, her eyes probed his face. He noticed with surprise that she had carried a pot of warm water with her through the woods.

"Give it to me," he said.

"You won't have to look at him; I can keep him out in the hut, you know . . ."

"Give it to me!"

Sobbing, she lifted the skin and brought out the baby, who was screaming through a contorted red face. Long fair hair clung to his head. Ausi wrapped all her pieces of cloth around him and wanted to wrap him in the skin, but Holme stopped her. No sense wasting a good skin out in the woods. It was better for the baby without it, too.

Ausi wouldn't hand him the baby but laid it beside her instead. It looked like a big bundle of cloth. Holme took it and crept backwards out through the opening. Ausi heard the faint cries die away, then stop.

Holme was glad all had gone well. It was unpleasant and almost beneath him to carry the child out, but who else would do it? No one else must know anything about this. He didn't care what the thralls thought. Ausi was herself again, and everything would soon be back to normal between them. Her beauty would return, and her hands, which had pushed him away for so long, would pull him to her once more.

He didn't have to walk far. Beyond the glade bright with snow, the forest was so dense that he couldn't see the trunks until he was on top of them. He left the baby beside a tree. When he reached the middle of the glade again, he listened, but all was quiet.

Ausi had stopped sobbing and asked him to wait outside until she said he could come in. He had to wait until she had the strength to walk; she didn't dare be alone. He responded gently to her and began pacing back and forth outside the cave. A couple of times, he heard her change the lighted stick. She must have brought a whole bundle of them with her. No wonder she had sunk in the marsh with so much to carry.

When he finally got to come in, she showed him where to sit. If he would wait while she rested a moment, they could go home. Neither mentioned the baby; Ausi thought about him with anguish but it was mingled with a strange hostility because of his fair hair. She had hoped to the last it would be Holme's baby even though she had a gut feeling it was not.

The night outside seemed endless; new stars came and went in front of the cave opening, and the silence was complete. The sticks were all gone, and they missed the light and mild warmth. It got gradually lighter, but it wasn't the sun coming. Far beyond the mound hung an oblong moon, which had risen after midnight and had slowly climbed above the black forest.

Holme would rather be home before anyone awakened, but he said nothing to Ausi. She sensed what he was thinking and suggested they leave. Her feet were getting stiff from the swamp water that had filled her shoes, and she needed to move. She too longed for home, fire, meat, and bread.

Holme's hard arms supported her the whole way, and this time the marsh held under her feet. A fox barked hoarsely, morosely. Toward the end of their journey, the forest started smelling of morning, but they would still probably make it home before anyone could see them and figure out what had happened.

Already Ausi thought less despairingly about the baby left in the woods. It had surely already died, without having suffered too much. She had accepted long ago that it wouldn't be allowed to live, so now she felt as though something important had finally been settled. She would never drink beer and watch the priests of fornication again. In fact, she'd gladly stay home next time there was a festival of sacrifice.

Everyone was asleep when they walked through the high hall. Holme built a fire at the far end of the fireplace where the ashes were still hot and some embers were glowing.

But deep in the woods a tiny blue face shone rigidly and questioningly back at the moon, which gradually sank among the dense branches of the spruce trees. The baby's new mother—cold—had not taken long to lull it to sleep.

The old thrall woman who knew about medicine lit into Holme the next day. How dared he put that baby out when the old chieftain had said the babies should live to be thralls for his grandson? She'd tell him about this the next time he came.

The old woman pursued him, scolding him, even though Ausi stuck her head out and defended him. She said it was hers and Holme's business what they did with their own child. Not until Holme bent down for a stone did the old woman turn and run into the hall, dogs leaping around her excitedly.

Holme took her threats calmly. All he had to do was tell the chieftain that the baby was from the festival of sacrifice, and he'd understand. Not many of the babies conceived by the temple that spring night escaped abandonment in the woods some midwinter night.

But the thralls didn't need to know how poorly Ausi had behaved after she had drunk beer and witnessed the priests of fornication.

The days had grown longer, and the blanket of snow dazzled the eyes. But the ice was still thick when the thralls saw a sled approaching from the north with three or four people on it. It turned toward the settlement, and the onlookers saw a little boy trying to take the reins from the driver. Beside him sat a woman with fair hair under her cap.

As they got closer, everyone recognized the woman and child. It was the chieftain's wife and son, but beside her sat a blond-bearded stranger. When he stepped out of the sled, the thralls could see he was as tall and thin as the dead chieftain had been short and stout. They all suspected he was the new lord.

The chieftain's wife had changed entirely. In a gruff voice, she told the thralls that the good days were over now. She was furious over their having moved into the high hall and having set up house inside. Everyone had to move either down by the door or into the thrall dwellings immediately.

She looked at Ausi and Holme strangely and talked softly with her new husband, who nodded meekly to everything she said and then approached Holme. In an indifferent voice, he ordered him and his woman to leave before the next day and never show themselves again. He had been defiant and had played the lord long enough. Besides, he had injured the child over there; he'd never be like other children.

Stor and Tan regained their authority as foremen and looked triumphantly at Holme and Ausi. But it was no broken-hearted Holme who walked to the smithy to gather up his belongings. He had anticipated a hasty end to his chieftainship and was just as glad for a change from the monotonous life at the settlement.

The chieftain's wife, who had expected resistance and defiance from Holme, forgot her old fear of him. This might be her chance to be revenged for the rock he had thrown from the forest. In the afternoon when the thralls were ready to depart with their burdens, she walked up to them, followed by her obliging husband stroking his blond beard. The little dark girl, now as clean and well-clothed as a chieftain's child, was standing between Holme and Ausi.

"She stays here," the woman ordered, pointing at the child. "My son will need thralls when he gets bigger."

Her husband nodded assent. Beside them, the group of thralls stood in tense and silent expectation. Stor and Tan were smiling maliciously at the front of the group.

Before Holme fully grasped her meaning, it became so quiet everyone could hear a dog crunching a bone on the refuse pile. Feeling the rage surging to his head, Holme scanned the crowd before him to see if anyone was on his side. Only Stor and Tan supported the chieftain's wife, and he wasn't afraid of them. His helpers let him know with a wink where they stood.

Holme told Ausi to go on with the child; he picked up his bundle in his left hand and his ax in his right. The chieftain's wife repeated her order, but her voice had lost its authority. Holme, glancing back over his shoulder, saw her stop her spider of a husband from coming after him with his sword. But Stor and Tan were ordered, as before, to take the child from them. They followed hesitantly on the forest path, and Holme laughed loudly and scornfully, his woman and child walking before him.

Ausi hadn't really felt afraid the whole time. She knew no one at the settlement would dare tangle with Holme. But they had a long and hard road ahead of them. They were warmly dressed and had plenty of food, but it was still winter. She had heard the wolves howling one night not too long ago. The protracted, desolate howling had forced its way in through the smoke vent, and she hadn't been able to fall asleep for a long time afterward.

They weren't at a loss about where to go this time. Holme would probably be welcome at the smithy, and the hut still suited them. Their only regret was leaving the boat Holme had built, but the ice hadn't broken up yet.

The first day's journey was the most difficult because there was no road to follow in the snow. Toward nightfall, they took turns carrying the child, who couldn't stay awake any longer. The weather was mild, and they could rest wherever they wanted, on a rock or a tree blown over by the wind. They had long since passed the cave; it was only a short day's walk away, and it no longer enticed them as it had before, with all that had happened at the time of the winter sacrifice.

It was late when they reached a farmstead and went into an outlying building. A few emaciated cows were standing around, and the moon was shining in through the ceiling hole. Holme found some dry grass for a bed and then went out with a wooden bucket to find water. Ausi had eaten snow the whole night. He soon found the well's black circle in the snow, and after a meal of meat, bread, and water, all three slept heavily until dawn. They didn't see anyone at the farmstead when they walked on.

Toward nightfall three days later, they were by the lake. A broad road, dark with horse droppings, led toward the town. There were deep tracks after the midday thaw, but the water had frozen crisp on the surface, and they saw only a few people on foot.

They headed off the road toward the forest where they had lived before. It was just as well not to pass through town. Holme thought now and then about what had happened when he had gotten their child back. He might have hit the woman a little too hard, but he didn't think she had died. He probably had nothing to fear after such a long time. At the worst, he might have to give her something in recompense.

Not until they were standing in front of the hut did they see the faint smoke rising through the hole in the roof and a narrow path leading up to the door. They hadn't once suspected that it might be occupied while they were away. Ausi looked with fatigue and despair at Holme. The surprise on his face changed to ferocity before her eyes. He was tired too and had looked forward to a fire, some food, and rest.

Holme put his burden down and picked up his ax. Then he walked up and knocked on the door. It was opened immediately and a middle-aged man appeared. He was holding an ax too.

The man stared with surprise at the man and woman looking at him with wild hatred in their eyes. He didn't know them and couldn't have done them any harm.

"Get out," Holme growled through clenched teeth.

The man answered that he had lived there the whole winter and had a right to stay. They could find another empty hut.

He didn't get to finish talking and didn't have time to raise his own ax more than halfway. There was no sound except the ax blow and the soft thud when the man hit the floor. Immediately Holme grabbed him and dragged him out into the woods.

Ausi went inside, grateful for the warmth. Their old skin rugs were still there, but there were some new things too. She laid the sleeping child on the bench, went out for some snow, and sprinkled it over the blood on the floor. The man had gathered up a big pile of firewood, so Holme wouldn't have to go out into the woods for several days.

They said nothing about the man when Holme returned, but lay down to sleep on the familiar benches. He was undoubtedly an outlaw no one would miss.

Spring found the king at one of his farmsteads, taking counsel with his top men. Trade with the Christian lands had fallen off and they were afraid it might stop altogether. There was much that they needed from other lands.

Several envoys had returned with the message that trade would increase if the northern people would receive those men wanting to spread the new teaching, if they would protect their lives, and let them build a church.

The king talked it over with his men, and they decided to meet the Christians' demands. The foreign priests would be allowed to come; they'd see to it they didn't do any great harm.

New envoys boarded ship, and the king carefully instructed them which goods were needed most and first. He gave them a special token so that everyone would recognize them as his envoys and would give them safe passage.[24]

That summer at the settlement, sparse blades of grass began to sprout on the chieftain's mound. His wife reigned while his bull-necked son ran loose, and his light-bearded successor walked around in an ineffectual daze. All he had to do was take care of the sacrifices. The high hall remained empty and cold unless relatives came to visit.

In the town's largest smithy, Holme had become the master smith. His predecessor had drowned on a fishing trip. Holme, Ausi, and the girl now lived inside the town walls.

The stranger's bones whitened along with the others. Many remembered him and his words, but only two with hunger and sorrow in their hearts. One was the old warrior; the other was Ausi. She was still waiting; he wasn't, he couldn't be, gone forever. Surely some day, he would either come himself or send a message.

Far to the south in the Christian land, new men were equipping vessels to sail to the Norsemen with the light.

---

[24] The Swedish King is Björn, the Christian king, Louis the Pious (788–840), son of Charlemagne and emperor of the Holy Roman Empire 814–40.

PEOPLE OF THE DAWN

A few years passed peacefully in the settlement after the chieftain died and Holme and his family had been driven away. The chieftain's wife ruled the aging thralls and her new, spindly-legged husband with a heavy hand. A little thrall girl also lived there, and the woman's stiff-necked son tormented or played with her at his whim.

The spring night formed a grayish-blue ring around the crescent of the moon as foreign ships were quietly rowed toward shore and tied up at the dock. A large group of men with foreign appearance stepped ashore, whispering among themselves as they moved up the slope. They spread silently out among the buildings, listening and signalling to each other. Their chieftain tested the solid door, shook his head, and waved for his warriors to gather round him again. After some more whispering, they spread out again around the building.

The thralls who woke up in their hut peered terror-stricken through window cracks, and soon they saw smoke creeping gently up the walls of the hall while dark figures lurked outside the door. After whispering together in perplexity, the thralls decided to run to save themselves.

The warriors heard something, then saw terrified faces in the doors of the thralls' hovel, lit up by the flames catching on the long sloping roof. They caught sight of some old thralls running toward the woods. A couple of invaders gave chase, but the chieftain called them back; they returned laughing quietly in their beards. The old thralls, their gray hair fluttering, disappeared among the trees.

Then there was a shout, and chaos broke loose inside the hall. The bolt was yanked clattering back, and some people dashed out, choking on smoke, not being on guard. The spindly-legged master was holding a sword and blinked in confusion before the grim enemy band. Blindly he rushed them with sword raised but was immediately hacked down. He kicked with his skinny legs, and one of the enemies walked up and delivered another sword blow. Then he lay still.

Only three women — two middle-aged and one old — were standing before the thieves now. A young boy and a little girl were behind them coughing and staring with wonder as the flames, reddish-yellow in the morning light, angrily licked the walls around them.

The alien chieftain pondered the group for a while, then ordered the younger women and the girl taken to the ships. The old woman wasn't worth anything, and the boy, with his stiff neck and fierce eyes, looked like he hadn't been born of normal parents. They could just as well let him go.

Two laughing men dragged the chieftain's wife down the slope; she struggled and kicked, trying to bite their hands. The thrall woman walked of her own free will and watched her daughter, who walked calmly in front of the group, holding the hand of a gray-bearded warrior.

Those thralls who had escaped to the woods saw the light from the fire grow brighter among the tree trunks and heard the chieftain's wife screaming in shrill despair for her son. The pigs squealed shrilly, too, as the men dragged them to the ships. The neglected old thrall woman soon joined her fellows in the woods and told them what had happened, but the boy was nowhere to be seen.

All the thralls, except Stor and Tan, left when they saw the fire leaping to the other buildings. Someday they might return to survey the damage. Right then, though, it was best to go to the nearest farmstead for protection and to give warning about the invaders. No doubt they would try to harry the whole district.

It was broad daylight when the thieves rowed away. Stor and Tan could hear the mother's voice receding as she screamed for her son, "Svein, Svein!"

The old thralls cautiously approached the burned area, inching their gray-bearded snouts out from behind the trees like trolls. Suddenly, they saw Svein coming from the other side. When he heard his mother's scream from the lake, he stopped and listened but didn't respond. He picked up a long stick and disinterestedly started scratching in the hot ashes, blue smoke still rising from them. The stick caught fire, and he slapped the ashes with it to put it out. He soon found a ring of iron with the stick and laid it in the grass to cool off while he squatted next to it, waiting. Then he rolled it down the slope.

Stor and Tan, mumbling to each other, decided not to approach the boy. He'd only mean trouble. Besides, who knew what might become of him, all alone out there in the woods? They were already talking about his being the settlement's only surviving owner. Once he was gone, they'd build a little hut for themselves. They could forge tools and weapons and cultivate sections of the fields. The cows were grazing in the forest, and a couple of pigs had escaped the thieves and were rooting on the slope. They'd come home in the evening.

They could still hear a distant scream from the lake. The boy ran and got the iron ring, rolled it down the slope again, then grabbed his stick and retrieved a short sword, burned blue, that lay smoldering before him. Stor and Tan waited to see what he'd do next.

The sun had risen and was shining on the gray ashes and hot blue smoke rising from the center of the fire. The boy looked up, twisted clumsily around, and gradually seemed to realize that he was homeless and alone. He threw down the stick and looked across the lake, but the ships had disappeared behind the peninsula, and his mother's scream was no longer audible.

Suddenly, the boy started howling like a dog as he ran toward the woods. A short distance up the path, he turned around, still howling, and took out the blue sword. He ran past Stor and Tan's hiding place, and they didn't give themselves away. They could hear his howl for a while before it died away among the trees, and then all was quiet. The only sound was the song of the birds in the trees around the burned settlement.

The thralls soon dared to walk around the area, which was still very hot. The pigsty with its sod roof wasn't damaged, and the pigs rooting in the burial grove would probably find their way home.

The spindly-legged master's body was half-burned, but it was still too hot upwind of him for them to approach. His sword, glistening in the sun which shone radiantly above the cove, poked out from under his body. For some reason, the thieves had left that behind.

The old thralls waited all afternoon. Then they salvaged many useful utensils and tools from the ashes—intact pots and pans, knives and hooks they could repair in the smithy. Toward evening, they fixed up the pigsty so they could sleep there temporarily. The three pigs approached distrustfully, grunting and blinking, before being shut in.

The cows came home at dusk. They stopped at the edge of the forest, mooing in bewilderment at the sight of the burned settlement. It took a long time for them to calm down and stand still so the thralls could milk them. All night, they bellowed and pawed at the ashes, but in the morning they stood peacefully chewing their cud on the sunny slope and gradually walked into the woods.

For the first time the thralls noticed that the boat was gone. The thieves had taken it. But Stor and Tan were old anyway and decided they could catch the fish they needed from shore.

They talked about the chieftain's wife for a while. They had served her and both her husbands for a long time, and now she herself was probably some chieftain's thrall far across the lake. It was all very strange, and they couldn't do anything about it. They were only a couple of old thralls and couldn't even offer a sacrifice to the wooden god for her deliverance.

They'd build the new hut among the trees so it couldn't be seen from the lake and entice passing ships to plunder it. They'd live on their own in their old age. If one of her brothers showed up, he couldn't very well object to their having stayed and done what they could for the settlement.

In the burial grove, three level mounds were silhouetted against the water. If the chieftain in the freshest grave were alive, the thieves would have had a different reception. Maybe he could hear his wife's screams as the foreigners dragged her past the mounds.

The thralls pulled a large wooden block, formless and charred, from the ashes, once they had cooled. They found it where the shrine had been, so it had to be the household god. It still had a roughly human shape. They carried it respectfully to a big rock to make it visible from the surrounding area. It might protect and help them, now that it had nothing else to do. People could see the black guardian from far out on the lake, and that might keep them from coming ashore.

They dug a grave on the slope for the spindly-legged chieftain whom they almost despised now because they had no need to fear him. They buried him unburned with his sword at his side. They had heard that a lot of people do that, and those who had visited distant lands always wanted to lie unburned, with their weapons whole and ready for use.[1]

The skinny-legged warrior didn't have any provisions for his journey either. Only a gray heap of gravel showed where he lay, but later the thralls rolled rocks on top of him—big rocks so he couldn't toss them off and come hunting them.

On the second day, they saw something moving at the edge of the forest, then dart anxiously away. They kept watch for hours, finally discovering a terrified old woman who in turn was watching them from behind logs and boulders. It was the oldest thrall woman, and they called for her to come out. After she ate some fish and milk, she told them she hadn't had the strength to follow the others and had been abandoned in the woods. A wolf had stalked her from a distance, and she wouldn't be alive now if he hadn't already eaten. Afraid of being driven off, she praised the old thralls for staying put.

They soon agreed she could be of some use. She could tend to the animals and milking while they were busy building. During the long evenings, it might be nice to have another person to reminisce with.

They dug a fire pit in the pigsty and huddled around it during the cold night. Behind the fence, the pigs grunted and peered out at the thralls who were talking about everything that came to mind—the chieftain and his burial mound, his captured wife, Holme and Ausi. The old thralls hoped their enemy was long dead. They still secretly feared seeing his rugged frame and black hair at the edge of the forest. There was no one left to protect them from him now.

But they'd build their little hut so it couldn't be seen from the lake or the road at the edge of the forest. Whoever came would see only ashes of the burned settlement, and perhaps the charred wooden god might scare them off. No one would suspect that anyone still lived here.

After Svein had run howling a while, he started coughing. When he stopped, he looked around. The forest was quiet; the path wound through the thickets, and he could hear the faint noise of a tiny gray bird climbing up the trunk of a pine tree. From old habit he picked up a pine cone and threw it at the bird, which flew off. Then he was completely alone.

He felt a vague anger at his mother, who wasn't there when he needed her. He still didn't realize she had been dragged away by force. His grandfather was

---

[1] Fridegård apparently was aware or became aware after the publication in 1940 of *Land of Wooden Gods*, that some debate existed over the question of Viking burial practices. Although some scholars argue that the dead frequently were interred whole, others argue that in the area described here, cremation was the rule. See Ebbe Schön, *Jan Fridegård och forntiden*, p. 115.

dead, but his uncles were still living at the other farmstead. He'd go there and complain. They had gone by water before, but if he stuck to the path by the shore he should get there.

Svein kept the burned sword in his hand, occasionally hacking the thickets with it. He had a smaller sword of his own, but that was in the hall. If he had grabbed it, maybe he could have hacked one of the invaders to death. But he had run after his mother, his throat and eyes full of smoke.

He thought suddenly of all the danger in the woods, and he ran as far as he could. The path was scarcely visible at several points, but a long, narrow, grass-lined pool of clear water showed where feet had been treading for many years.

Svein happened onto the cows in a glade. They seemed to offer companionship and relief, so he approached one of them. But she glared, snorted, and loped away when he tried to pet her. He had pulled their tails or hit them with a stick too many times for them to be friends with him.

He stayed with the cows for a while anyway, but they ignored him, and he vaguely sensed their animosity. They began grazing and moved into the forest on the other side of the glade. Svein continued dawdling toward his relatives' distant farmstead. Several times he heard the cry of seagulls far to the right of him, and at one place he found the skeleton of a big fish a little way off the path. The shore couldn't be far away.

Twice he had to run as fast as he could. The first time, a massive beast, with dangling snout and long legs, was standing to the left among the small pine trees, ogling him. Later, the path had been chopped up by huge, sharp hooves, and there was a lingering, pungent smell of wild boars. He thought he heard them snorting in the marsh below him and sped off again.

The sun was high overhead when he caught a glimpse of the cove, and an islet that seemed familiar. It was near the farmstead. Shortly thereafter, he smelled smoke far in the forest just as he had done when he left the house with smoke still faintly clinging to his clothes. He smelled it again where the forest began thinning out, but didn't give it another thought, just started running, eager to tell his uncles what had happened.

When he reached the edge of the forest, he thought in the first surprised moment that he had circled back home again. Huge piles of ashes rose before him, hot blue smoke drifting away from them. The heat waves shimmered against the woods on the other side. He stopped and soon grasped what had happened. He hunched over even more than usual and looked toward the lake, but the thieves had gone. The small boat was there, but the big one had vanished. Fresh green reeds sprouted among the yellow ones from last year. Beyond them, little black birds were swimming in fits and starts, and a couple of silent crows, turning their heads right and left, sat on the drying poles for the fishing nets.

Svein approached cautiously, then saw several men lying near the ashes. One was badly burned, and his swollen red skin shone through his rags. A round cap with golden wings on it lay at his feet, and Svein grabbed it; the metal band was carved full of signs and figures he couldn't understand.

A horse whinnied shrilly from the forest, and Svein dashed off and crouched behind a rock. From there he cautiously watched a horseman emerge from the forest, then freeze at the sight before him. He galloped forward, leaped off the horse, and approached one of the fallen men. The horse looked indifferently at the ashes, neighed, and ambled off to graze on the tender grass behind the back building.

Svein had feared a new enemy but, recognizing his uncle Geire, rushed happily out of his hiding place. The man spun around, drawing his short sword in defense.

Geire was silent while Svein talked and then shook his fist toward the lake. He examined the winged cap and determined that the thieves had come from the other side. He'd go after them someday, and when he was through, their farmsteads wouldn't look much different from the way his did now.

The thieves had taken their dead and wounded with them, except for the one who got burned; they couldn't get to him because of the fire. Their bodies had left pools of blood in several places, and Geire counted them with grim satisfaction. There were more pools than there were people from the farmstead. He dragged the dead men to one spot, having decided to get help to bury them later. After he had taken the boy to the closest unburned farmstead, he'd come back to guard the bodies from wild animals.

Once the warrior and boy had disappeared into the forest, the farmstead was quiet. The crows hopped closer, flapping their wings, watching the row of silent men. A wolf sat at the edge of the forest sniffing the air and grinning for hours, but didn't dare come closer. A narrow trail of blood led down to the lake, ending in a few drops on some of the round stones protruding from the sun-warmed water by the shore.

The dry white sand on the beach dazzled both men as they waded ashore.[2] No one was in sight, but a boat with high prows fore and aft tossed and rocked

---

[2] Fridegård does not name any of the historical characters in his trilogy, but these two monks are clearly St. Ansgar (801–65) and his companion, Witmar. The date is ca. A.D. 830, the year when Ansgar undertook the first recorded mission to Sweden, and the monks' ship has been captured by pirates off the southwest coast of Sweden, a considerable distance from Birka, the main Viking trading center of the period and the monks' unnamed destination. Fridegård's source for most details concerning events surrounding Ansgar's and his successors' activities is Bishop Rimbert's *Vita Anskarii* (see Schön, *Fridegård och forntiden*, p. 102, and the afterword to this book). Fridegård's account begins with chapter 10 of Rimbert's. For an English translation of Rimbert's work, see *Anskar: Apostle of the North*, 801–865, trans. Charles H. Robinson (London: The Society for the Propagation of the Gospel in Foreign Parts, 1921).

near a log landing a few stone throws away. A ridge along the shore rose before them, blocking the land beyond from view. Behind them, the water swelled, endless and dark blue.

The men fell to their knees and thanked their god for saving them from the swords of pirates and the watery depths. As they looked to the heavens, they failed to notice a wild-looking man watching them from behind a bush on the shore, distrustful and half-terrified by their strange words and postures. When the strangers got up and started exploring, the man was careful to keep the bush between himself and the men. After a while, he clambered up the ridge to take a better look, and when they turned around to look at the lake, there he was, an apparition that had sprung up from the ground they had just walked on. Supported by a heavy stick, he was silhouetted against the lake and the heavens, and the breeze caught his flowing beard. The strangers marveled and looked all around again but still found no sign of a settlement or people, other than the man and the boat.

Before them lay a rolling, limitless flatland, broken here and there by clumps of broad-leafed trees. It was still morning, and fine mists scurried across the land, pursued by the sun.

The men soon came to a road and followed it. They could see dwellings in several directions, and a village lay straight ahead of them. Huts with low, green, sloping roofs and smoke rising from holes in the sod. All around were small patches of arable land, but there was no one to be seen. The ground was trampled down near the buildings, and the smell of animals and sun-warmed mire greeted the men. They continued north, and surprised faces watched them through a half-open light opening. Two dogs, discovering them too late, gave chase, barking in disappointment.

The men had no idea how long their road was; no one knew how far north the heathen lands extended. The heathens had built a stone bridge across a marshy area and had stuffed peat down between the stones. Coarse wheel tracks had cut through the peat. A couple of long-legged birds, wading in a pool, leaped chattering into the air and flew rapidly away. Here and there a dog bark penetrated wood and field, or a cow could be heard mooing in the distance; otherwise they heard only the birds and the silence. Around midday, the mist lifted, drifting away in white clouds toward the blue sky.

The Christian strangers wondered how such fierce pirates could come from such a peaceful land. The ground beyond the village swelled into a rise, and the sun warmed the sand in the wheel tracks. Cows walking on a nearby road chewed indifferently and watched the two gray figures as they passed. An old man with a staff in his hand was standing on the far side of the cows by a gray willow tree, but the strangers didn't notice him.

Inside the dense leafy forest, the grass grew in patches, and the foliage shut out almost all the sunshine. Prematurely yellowed leaves fell quietly, sometimes nearby, sometimes at a distance, but they could be seen long afterwards, always in the peaceful light between the tree trunks. An animal with huge horns had been watching the men for a long time, but when they approached, it sped away as swift as the wind, its horns cast back. After a while, more light began to filter through the trees, and soon the plain again took command.

Around midday, the men got bread, meat, and water from a silent old woman, who lived alone in a sod hut. When she saw them coming, she put out the bowls, and they thought she probably gave food to anyone who came by, no questions asked.

The road north soon opened up more and became easier to follow; they encountered wagons and horsemen. The farmsteads were bigger, too, and not as far apart. The people they met looked at them with hard, blue eyes, but no one bothered them. At the farmsteads, the children stopped their playing, crowded together, and looked mutely at the strangers.

The two figures on the sunny flatland plodded on toward the north.

The dismal autumn rain poured down over town and lake. Beyond the lake and the rain, you could see the forest on the mainland, a dark, grayish-blue strip. No vessels had left the harbor, and all the sails had been taken in. Only the ferry man occasionally rowed someone to town or the mainland.

Holme walked down the empty street, muttering about the rain. A soaked dog tagged along with pleading eyes, careful to stay out of kicking range. A woman in a dirty skirt stepped out of her hut and hastily dumped a pot of hot ashes; they hissed gently as the rain drops fell on them.

A number of white winters and clear blue summers had passed in town since Holme had returned and become master smith in place of his old predecessor, who was sleeping in one of the burial mounds. He had built himself a new hut on the outskirts of town and had adorned its door hinges with many-headed dragons and snakes that people frequently stopped to admire.

He passed the hill where the peculiar stranger had once tried to build a temple for his god. The logs were long since gone, but some of the rocks still lay at the bottom of the hill, looking more and more like they had always been there. Holme shook his head when he thought about the stranger. He had been dead and forgotten for a long time, and his bones were probably lying with many others in the field of bones near the big temple. Only Ausi still talked about him; she believed he'd return or send someone in his place, but no one listened to her. She ought to know that death is a journey from which no one returns.

For the most part, these had been good years for the smiths and craftsmen but bad ones for anyone earning his living by tilling and sowing. The farmers had sacrificed half their livestock in vain for a better harvest, and, enraged at the gods, had armed themselves and sailed out on a raid. Holme had received orders for as many weapons as he could make.

For a moment, his thoughts wandered back into the darkness of the past. He thought of the old settlement and the slope by the lake where he had been a thrall, wondering what it might look like now. Wondering if the chieftain's wife was still there with her spindly-legged husband. Stor and Tan would be old, of course, if they were still alive, gray and hunched from their cowardice and the frequent bending of their backs.

Many times during the past few years, he had felt a great need to return. He would approach through the forest like he used to and survey the settlement unobserved. Neither he nor Ausi had forgotten their thralldom, even though their lives were good in every way now. Spring and autumn, winter and summer they talked about that former time, remembering the various chores at the settlement.

Before Holme entered his hut, he looked across the lake toward the mainland. Someday he'd move back; he had never felt at home in town. His black hair had started to show some gray, his daughter was half-grown, and he could afford to build a house anywhere he wanted. Wherever he went, he could have a smithy. Ausi talked now and then about how she wanted someday to have a plot of land and a few animals.

As Holme stood there gazing toward the mainland, the three-day rain stopped and a brassy yellow stripe of sky rose slowly from the earth in the west. The sun broke through a crack in the clouds for a moment, casting its brilliant evening light on soaking wet log walls and green sod roofs. The rain water ran a moment longer, trickling in rivulets along the rocky streets.[3]

After the sun had passed the narrow crack, he walked into the forest. Dusk fell. Holme listened to the sounds—the gentle rippling of water, the barking of dogs, the yells and noises from the harbor. On the distant mainland, someone lit a fire that sputtered reluctantly, then finally burned strong. Holme shook his head at the memories from that place and walked into his hut.

Two homeless people, Svein and his uncle Geire, came through the woods on the path connecting the two burned farmsteads. They had just passed Geire's and had seen the piles of ashes. A summer's wind and rain had compacted them, making assorted objects stick out—here a hinge, there the black legs of a tripod. The path to the lake was harder to see than before, and the log landing, whitened by sun and rain, had collapsed on one side.

Geire walked with a gloomy face, and Svein plodded along silently. The rain gradually stopped, and the evening sun shone between the tree trunks. For a moment, everything was lit up in the yellowish-green glow after the rain—stones,

---

[3] Stone paving would have been unusual during this period. Archeologists think that the streets of Birka were paved with wood. See Bertil Almgren, ed., *The Viking* (London: C. A. Watts, 1966), p. 39.

tall ferns, blades of grass, and the branches on the ground. In the open areas, sparse swarms of large autumn mosquitoes still danced in the last rays of sunlight.

Once the sun had gone down, the woods quickly grew dark, and a raw chill rose from the hollows. The bow hanging on Geire's back creaked with every step he took. Svein constantly looked to the sides, turning his whole upper body. Several times, he thought he saw trolls lurking in the darkness. He thrust his sword at them, and they came no closer. The winged cap, with the unfamiliar insignia, hung on a thong over his shoulder.

In the last of the dusk, they recognized the look-out hill and the slope running from it to the settlement. Cowpaths were visible here and there in the thickets, which Geire was surprised to see freshly trampled—the smell of cattle filled the air. They hadn't seen any animals at his farmstead; the raiders had undoubtedly stolen them.

"Were the cows here when it burned, Svein?"

"No, in the woods."

So they were still there. They caught a glimpse of them among the trees. But who had milked them and why were they still going home to the burned settlement? Maybe some outlaw had taken refuge there. There might be trolls, too, or some other forest creatures now that no humans were around to keep them at bay.

They walked around the piles of ashes but saw nothing unusual. The pigsty was still there in the darkness, but they didn't think of entering it. They made a bed of spruce twigs on the damp ground close to the cows. Geire took some meat and bread out of his birch-bark box. While they ate, it occurred to him that he could get a little milk for the wooden tankard they had with them. The cows belonged to him and the boy, but they couldn't take them along. Maybe they'd find a farmstead where they could sell or barter them for a couple of horses and better equipment. His sister and her skinny-legged husband had kept no horses the last few years.

One cow stood chewing indifferently and let him milk her. She showed signs of already having been milked that evening, and again he thought about trolls and highwaymen. Where were they now? Had they hidden, waiting for him and the boy to leave? He had better keep an eye open; an arrow or a spear might come flying silently through the darkness.

The ground was damp under the twigs, but they sat down anyway, their legs heavy after the day's journey. Svein lay down on his side and was soon asleep, but Geire didn't dare lie down. The outlaw might not have a bow or a spear, but he could sneak up on a sleeping man with an ax, a stick, or a rock. Geire kept diligent watch, and many strange noises came from the dark and silent night.

He would rather have moved on before nightfall, but Svein needed to sleep. The boy was a hindrance, but they were the only two family survivors; they had much to avenge. He was a peculiar boy, sulky and strong like his father, but with his mother's blonde hair and plain features. And his stiff neck, the legacy of the smith's stone, might not be as noticeable once he was grown and had long hair and a beard.

Svein's mother was probably a thrall now for some chieftain in the east. If Geire heard of someone going that way on a raid, he would join him. The gods would surely help him ferret out the invaders. He was a single man and had no desire to rebuild the farmstead. He would spend the rest of his life offering his arm and sword to some marauding chieftain.

Geire's thoughts were interrupted by something like a door thudding shut, followed by distinct grunting. You could hear such things in the night where people had once lived for a long time. Somebody probably hadn't been properly buried. In any case, he ought to move on with the boy; it was no good staying there. Just then, he thought he heard the ashes mumbling. His beard stood on end and chills ran up and down his spine. He reached out to wake the boy but hesitated. Svein was sleeping so soundly, his face white and fatigued in the soft glow of the moon.

A moment later, he saw something moving on the slope. The creature was all hunched over, its hair a radiant white under a kerchief. It was neither man nor woman and looked most like a gray rag floating fitfully along, stopping intermittently. Geire mumbled something and placed his sword between himself and the ghost, which glided toward the ashes and disappeared in front of them. A cow standing higher up the slope turned its head and gave out a prolonged moo, and the sound of splashing waves suddenly roared loudly across the slope as if the shore were getting nearer. Then everything fell quiet again.

Geire didn't dare wait for what might happen next. He shook Svein's arm, and the boy sat up peevishly. They didn't say a word; Geire got up and started walking with Svein following him as before. They didn't know that two relieved old thralls watched them from behind the pigsty. Against the hazy sky in the west, Stor and Tan saw the stately man and the stiff-necked boy silhouetted for a moment before they disappeared down the forest path.

A few mornings later, the thralls awoke to a noise and cows mooing. They peered cautiously out, suspecting wolves or bears, but instead saw strangers catching the cows. The ones they couldn't catch they drove into the forest. The thralls watched bitterly but didn't dare show themselves. They knew this was the result of Geire's visit. It wouldn't be easy to get by without cows once winter came.

A few days' journey to the south, two gray-clad men were wandering north. They had walked for several days after the pirates had put them ashore. Many times, death—in the form of outlaws and half-wild heathens—had peered at them from the forest. Perhaps their impoverished look saved them. Other times they had slept peacefully under the roofs and eaten the food of friendly heathens. They passed graveyards filled with numberless burial mounds and, a couple of times, containing tall gray stones bearing mysterious symbols. The land seemed endless, and the leafy woods had become an expansive dark pine forest. An icy wind blew from the clear blue horizon in front of them, and all day frost clung to the north side of the lingonberry tufts.

The men plodded on without rest, hoping to reach their destination before the heathen land's hard, white winter set in.

Ausi and the other women waiting in the harbor saw the milk boat approaching at a distance from the mainland. Every morning they carried their wooden tankards down to fill them with milk still warm from the udder. There weren't many cattle on the island, and they couldn't supply the whole town.

The autumn morning was cool and gray before the sun came up, and the icy water lapped the dock's wooden pilings. As the boat came closer Ausi could see its foaming wooden prow, the oarsman, and two identical figures. People came across with the milk boat every day, but something about these two made Ausi stare and gave her a strange feeling. Her heart began pounding when one said a few words as he handed the oarsman something. The foreign sound and gentleness of the voice called the sacrificial stranger back from the darkness of the years enveloping him. She could see him standing in the clear blue water again, smiling, offering her his hand that day of the summer baptism. She remembered his cross reflecting in the water below her bowed head. The two new strangers were walking across the gangway now, and she caught the first one's eye. He had the stranger's gaze—gentle, unfathomable.

The sun rose over the town's sod roofs glaring yellow-green in the first rays of light. As if in a vivid dream, Ausi saw a cross flash on the new stranger's chest as he stepped down from the gangway. It was the cross from the past. Without thinking, she started following him, until the oarsman's laughing voice caught up with her, asking if she planned on going home with an empty tankard. The sight of the wind rustling a clump of reeds brought her to her senses, and she turned around.

The oarsman knew that the men were Christians from a far away land. The king had sent for them, and they were men of high station, even though they had come by foot. The oarsman asked the women if they remembered the stranger who had tried to build a church on the hill. But Ausi didn't answer and didn't hear the oarsman's comment that you could live as a Christian only with the king's permission.

She was still watching the two figures walking west along the shore toward the fortress. Neither was the sacrificed priest, but he had to have sent them. He had said that he or someone else would come until all the people had cast off their wooden gods and turned to Christ, the One who could and would call the dead back from the grave.

Ausi was filled with anxiety and happiness all the way home. The hunger in her heart, which she remembered from when the stranger was there, had returned. She didn't know how she could stand waiting until she heard more about the strangers. Maybe they knew a little about her, that she had been baptized. The look one of them had given her was full of something like love, but was nothing like what the men in town expressed when they ogled her now and then. She knew perfectly well what they wanted.

Maybe the strangers could perceive that she had had the water poured on her head once—that she belonged to those who would not die and be gone forever.

The thought bloomed inside her like a radiant, beautiful meadow, but a black shadow soon fell in the midst of it: Holme. He loathed the Christians, and his look darkened whenever she talked of them. And Tora, their daughter, was just like her father. Holme never traded with Christian merchants and had once laughed derisively at Christ, saying he was a lesser man than the wooden gods—pale and feeble as a woman—whose followers refused to fight, had timid eyes, and cried easily. Holme knew many Christians in town even though they had no priest. He, on the other hand, had always managed without either the wooden gods or Christ.

As far as Ausi knew she was the only one left who had been baptized back then. The old warrior now slept in one of the green mounds outside town; the younger one had sailed off to a distant land and didn't return with the ship. She hadn't seen the women for a long time—they probably weren't in town any more. If the new strangers didn't look for her, she would go and tell them about her baptism. But Holme would be enraged again, and the peace of the last few years would be gone.

Ausi was afraid to go back to Holme and Tora with her heart full of such joy. Both had piercing, dark eyes, and it wasn't easy to hide anything from them. They had already opened the light openings, so it had to be fully lighted inside, and Holme would see from her face that something had happened. She didn't want to tell him about the strangers, not yet. He'd remember everything from the past, and that could jeopardize their lives. Back then, Holme had been a runaway thrall but still dangerous; what couldn't he do now that he was a respected man? Many would stand at his side against the Christian strangers. Christ was powerful, but who could stand up against Holme?

She saw the men once more before she reached her house. The two figures in the distance were walking slowly up the slope toward the fortress. The wind had turned cold, and snow was starting to fall from the blue sky. The mainland was scarcely visible through the veil of flakes. Snow usually didn't fall from a clear sky; this might be a sign from Christ that his men had reached their destination. Or it might even be a warning from the wooden gods. The men stood at the gate as if hesitating to go in, after all. But then maybe the guard had stopped them.

The snow fell harder, and soon she could see only those buildings closest to her. The soot piles, the garbage, and the roofs soon glittered white, and when she looked up, the blue sky had vanished in a gray-white chaos of flakes. She could tell Holme about the strange snowfall, and he wouldn't notice anything unusual in her face.

Holme was sitting on his bench deep in thought when she came in with the milk, and Tora was asleep, her black hair encircling her face. Finally Holme spoke a few words about his dream of the mainland, but Ausi felt resistant again. She didn't want to leave town now—not before she had received a message from the one coming to life again in her heart.

After breakfast, Holme walked to the smithy at the edge of town. He was often in a bad mood in the morning and didn't want to talk to anyone. The pigs were grubbing in the road, and one that didn't get out of the way got a kick that sent it flying.

His helpers, already waiting outside, started talking with their quiet master. A couple of them had been there in the old days when they tore down the stranger's new church; the others were thralls Holme had bought and set free. Holme, never forgetting his own days as a thrall, divided the smithy earnings equally among those who worked there, much to the surprise of anyone hearing about it, and much to Ausi's anger. He had thralls and craftsmen for friends, although merchants and chieftains both sought him out and would have liked to have him as their guest.

The smiths opened the windows, and a ray of light shot into the smithy, which smelled of soot and iron. Completed weapons were hanging on the walls; half-finished and newly-begun weapons lay in rows by the hearth. Anvils sat on the sooty, earthen floor, fastened to heavy oak stumps. Stone molds were strewn on a bench.

There were other smithies nearby; the clang of sledgehammers and the song of the smiths could be heard throughout town, if no other noises drowned them out. Other craftsmen had their huts and sheds close to the smithies. Some made combs, boxes, and other things out of horn or bone; others were silversmiths and potters. Craftsmen from everywhere flocked together, as windows and doors opened to the new day.

Many kinds of people visited the town to buy or barter for various goods. Farmers came from the mainland with grain and meat; beautifully and expensively dressed merchants came from the foreign ships with ornamented earthen ware more beautiful than that made in town, gold-laced ribbons and silk fabrics, glass bowls and pearls. Warriors came to Holme, wanting new edges on their swords, spears, or arrow tips, and farmers came, needing points for their plows or wanting other tools and fittings.

It was still morning when Holme and the smiths saw two figures standing in the door, an older warrior and a boy. The two blinked at the darkness for a moment before coming in, and the vague memory their presence awoke in Holme puzzled him. The boy had a short sword that had been in a fire, and the warrior asked if Holme could repair it. Or would it be better to buy the boy another sword?

His blue eyes opened wide, the boy watched the dark figure of the smith the whole time. He recognized Holme from his mother's description and his own nightmares. As long as he could remember, his mother had warned him that if he ventured into the forest alone, a dark man would come and hurt him. She had frequently described him, and he was the man in charge of the smithy.

Geire looked pensively at Holme, but couldn't remember where he had seen him before. Perhaps from some bartering when his brothers were alive.

Holme recognized the burned sword as soon as he took hold of it. He had forged it at the cleft in the rocks when he was still a thrall. It was the first time he had held any of his old work, and he examined it closely without saying anything. He caught a glimpse of the boy's eyes, filled with wonder and terror, and he felt some bitter memory move in his depths.

Holme said nothing, merely offered the warrior a new sword in exchange for the burned one. Geire accepted his offer in surprise, and the terror in Svein's eyes disappeared behind his happiness over the new sword. The smiths laughed and watched his strange movements. He turned his whole body where he wanted to look. On the thong over his shoulder, he still carried the alien winged cap.

After they left, Holme walked to the door and watched them, still scouring his memory, marvelling over what they had brought to life. At the same time, Svein turned his upper body and looked back; instantly everything became clear to Holme. He gave a start as if to follow them, and Svein clutched Geire in terror. Soon they turned a corner and were gone. All day long, Holme kept thinking about the time he had fled with Ausi and their baby, and he remembered the day at the edge of the forest when he had marked the chieftain's son forever with a stone.

Something must have happened at the old settlement. He'd go back there again someday and see it all again—the cleft in the rocks, his old smithy; the dogs, if they were still alive, that were his friends; and the cave in the forest, their former home. He didn't care about the people.

He noticed the streets were pretty lively, the way they always were when the king was in town. Just as he started to go back into the smithy, two strange figures walked by on the opposite street, two men neither warriors, merchants, nor craftsmen. They were more dangerous than most though they didn't often carry weapons. There could be no doubt what their mission was if you remembered the one who had once wanted to build a church, the one who finally hung, eyes shut, in the tree outside the huge temple housing the wooden gods.

When Holme went inside, the smiths could tell something was wrong, but they knew nothing yet about the two Christians who had arrived that morning.

By the time the ground was bare again, there were many Christians in town who had already raised a small church by the courtyard outside the chieftain's quarters. Across the yard, one of the heathens had donated space for a shrine to house a lofty wooden god. Twice as tall as a man, it stood there looking grimly toward the church. Neither god seemed able to drive the other away; both stood fast there although the shrine's sacrificial smoke occasionally encircled the church, and the smell of burning flesh forced its way to the Christian altar. And the wooden god's servant, who had lit the fire, could hear songs and calls to Christ rising from the glistening gold and silver church.

An open area separated the shrine and the church, perhaps intended by the heathens as a place for the gods to fight. One day, after sacrificing fruitlessly to the wooden god, an enraged heathen walked insolently across to see if Christ had more power to help. Once they saw that the wooden god was unmoved and that nothing bad had befallen the blasphemer, several others followed. One of the strangers in the Christian church received them joyfully and promised that Christ would soon help them out of all their difficulties and troubles. They stood apprehensively in front of His altar, stealing occasional furtive glances through the door where they could see the gigantic, grayish-red wooden god searching for them with rigid, menacing eyes.

At the autumn assembly, the foreign monks obtained permission to preach wherever and whenever they wanted. Immediately, they began marching around, fearlessly talking about their god's remarkable qualities. Holme saw them frequently, and once they came into the smithy. One started to talk, already having learned enough of the Norse tongue to be understood. Holme's face was hard as wood, and he walked toward them, sledgehammer raised. They cowered out of the dark figure's way, and the one in front said his time had not yet come.

When they were outside, Holme told them in his gruff voice that they wouldn't have any better luck than their fellow countryman had many years before, but they just looked at him in surprise and didn't respond. Maybe they didn't know about their countryman. Behind Holme, his smiths watched, laughing scornfully. Curious, derisive faces peered out from the other smithies and craftsmen's sheds, and the strangers felt death closing in on them. They left the craftsmen's quarter where the work would be hard and dangerous and walked back toward town again.

Rumors about their work soon started making the rounds. The town's chieftain, who was the most powerful man next to the king, had joined them, and the Christains lived securely in his court and held their meetings there.[4] Many attended them to gain favor with the chieftain, and others attended out of curiosity. Numerous merchants freed the thralls they had captured in Christian lands.

All the while, Ausi floated around in uneasy excitement, and Holme looked at her now and then with a stern warning in his eye. The past had returned, and she felt often that the Christian stranger's teaching, filled with peace, had brought her only strife and unpleasantness. Still she couldn't stop thinking about

---

[4] This chieftain is likely modeled after the chieftain named Herigar described by Rimbert. See *Anskar*, chapter 11, p. 49.

everything the new god had promised his followers, and besides she was still bound to him because of her baptism. She wished that Christ would tell the strangers about it. Holme would never allow her to approach them.

But a rumor about the wooden gods had sprung up too, making it clear that they had no intention of letting Christ come to power. In a private shrine the battle god had stretched forth his arm toward the Christian buildings and yard during a sacrifice. Both the warrior who owned the shrine and the people who lived in his house had seen it, and now the heathens were eagerly waiting to see what would happen to the Christians. Others had noticed countless sails on the horizon gradually changing into clouds. That had to portend impending evil.

Although it was late in the year and the days were short, no snow fell and the lakes had not frozen over. One day, a light blazed across the half-dark town, and a powerful boom shook the buildings. Everyone who had heard the rumors ran outside and looked toward the Christian buildings and yard, thinking that perhaps the wooden god had spoken. Many of those who had joined the Christians decided to leave them because of the clear warning from the most powerful of gods.

While the heavens still rumbled, Holme opened the door of the smithy and stuck his head out. He too hoped that the god had struck the Christians, but there was no smoke to be seen. He shook his head, thinking that he'd probably have to do it himself to get rid of the Christians and the destruction they brought. Privately he had always felt that the motionless, wooden gods weren't worth much, but there had been some years of peace for Ausi and him. Now she was being torn again by the old uneasiness, and those causing it had to go.

The day before the midwinter sacrifice, Ausi ran into one of the monks, who gestured amiably for her to stop. He said she should come to the Christians' house early the next morning to see and hear what the new god had to offer those who came to him. She should bring her family along, too.

While he talked, he looked wonderingly at the beautiful woman, whom he knew was the master smith's wife. Her eyes sparkled, her lips quivered, and she looked around timidly. Then she told him briefly, excitedly, that she had been baptized. A long time ago, over there. She pointed with a supple arm toward the shore.

This wasn't the first time the monk had heard about his predecessor, but it had the same unpleasant effect every time. It must have been a false teacher. He himself was the one God had chosen to be the light in the north. Ausi saw his face darken as she described the stranger who had baptized her, but he didn't respond; he merely repeated that the true and perfect Christ awaited her the next morning. Then he walked on, and Ausi saw him stop a thrall farther down the street.

So it wasn't the stranger who had sent the new monks, she thought with disappointment. But she still wanted to join the Christians; maybe Christ Himself would recognize her. The stranger had once said that not so much as a bird fell to earth without His knowing it, and she was much bigger than a bird. Sometimes she believed Christ had helped them, since everything was going so well, but she didn't dare say so to Holme.

In any case, she had talked with one of the new men now, and even if they weren't like the stranger, they still must know a lot about Christ. She had to know more or she'd never have any peace. If Holme wouldn't let her, she'd have to go behind his back. Maybe she could gradually win Tora over to her side. But the new god and his monks would never get the best of Holme.

Ausi had lain awake since midnight, and when she got up to light the fire, she could still see stars shining through the smoke vent. After a long, uneasy wait, she heard a door slam and steps tramping outside on the hard frozen ground. She knew it was the Christian family from down the street, and she got up and dressed in the feeble light from the fire. She remembered how difficult that would have been to do back when they were thralls, but now that no danger threatened, Holme slept more soundly.

As she sneaked out, she pushed back the thought of what would happen when she returned. Maybe she'd think of something to say before then, or maybe Christ would help since she was doing this for His sake. He could make Holme and Tora keep sleeping.

The houses were still quiet as she walked through the streets; but the smoke was rising denser from the vents where the Christians lived. They were awake. It was cold, and the narrow crescent of the moon hung at an angle above the mainland forest. A dog was barking somewhere on the outskirts of town, and the ice around the island roared as it contracted from the cold.

The Christians' door stood ajar, and it was lighted inside; in the heathen temple, a fire was burning, and there was a smell of burnt meat. Some people entered, and Ausi hesitated a moment between the house of Christ and the shrine of the wooden god. If she went into the temple, Holme would be surprised but not enraged; their life would continue peacefully. But strife and danger attended the new god, and everything would be as it had been before.

She was still hesitating between the gates when the Christians' door opened wide, and a voice asked her to come in. She saw the heathens streaming into the temple; then she entered the Christians' house, and the bolt was thrown behind her. Anxious but happy, she was led into the light, and everyone, including the chieftain, recognized her and welcomed her with friendly faces.

The hall was more beautiful than the one the stranger had used a long time ago, but most of the things inside belonged to the chieftain. The most distinguished of the monks said that things would be coming on ships in the spring to enable them to serve their God in a way more worthy of Him. Not that it meant so much; He looked most at the heart. Ausi remembered some Christians returning in surprise with gifts and sacrifices they had tried to offer Christ in return for his help. The monk had told them that He would help them for nothing. Many of them were glad; others didn't believe it and turned back to the wooden gods with their gifts.

She understood more of the monk's words than she had hoped, but it was still strange that He who ruled all things and was the strongest of all gods had sent His servants on foot and unarmed. She had heard that they would cry frequently and abuse themselves. That was partly why Holme and many others despised them. They should be like Holme, powerful and manly, and everything would be easier to understand.

Sporadic shouts and murmurs came through the smoke vent, and Ausi realized that the main sacrifice had begun across the yard. Once they heard a loud scornful laugh, and many of the Christians stopped listening to what the monk was saying and turned in terror to the door. The monk seemed not to notice until the uproar threatened to drown him out, at which point his voice raised, his face grew lighter, and he almost looked happy about what was going on outside. The chieftain, however, looked sternly toward the door, wrinkling his forehead and twitching his beard.

Not many could join in the singing once the monk had stopped talking. The song to the wooden gods consisted mostly of loud yells intermingled with prayers for help in danger or for a good harvest. The tumult outside kept mounting, and suddenly there was a loud crash against the door. Ausi trembled, thinking of Holme. He was probably out there; the rock had probably flown from his hand.

When the service was over and the monk had held his hands over them, the chieftain opened the door. The space separating the houses of the gods was packed with people who grew quiet as they saw the door open. The chieftain angrily spoke to them and ordered them all to make room for the Christians. He took the lead himself, clearing a path between two ranks of heathens who were more threatening now with their silence than with the noise they had made before.

Ausi walked with downcast eyes but sensed someone step out of the crowd and walk behind her. When she turned onto a side street, the heavy steps followed, but neither spoke. Once again she realized that all gods were powerless against Holme, both the old ones and the new one.

From the church door the monk watched his little congregation disperse and disappear. They were nothing compared to the remaining mob of heathens. Everywhere, pillars of smoke from the sacrificial feast jutted into the cold green sky. The sun would soon rise and the pagans would take this as a sign of the wooden gods' victory over Christ. Here nature itself was against Him.

The heathens stared at the monk silently, a sea of clear eyes and long beards. Their anger was gone, and he marvelled at this strange people in their wintery land. They could seize and kill him, but instead they went their ways, finally leaving the yard empty. Only a few figures continued to move around the crude idol on the other side.

A moment later, the monk saw the hills filled with people facing east. The blood-red sliver of the sun rose through the cold haze on the horizon, and a strange shout erupted from a thousand throats. As he walked away, he could hear the sun worshippers' loud, monotonous songs.

The chieftain had warned the foreigners not to show themselves that day or night. The tumultuous morning was nothing compared to what could happen during the evening's raucous eating and drinking. Many would surely vow to kill the foreigners during the year that would begin after the midwinter sacrifice. But the monks refused to shut themselves in; their lives were in someone else's hands.

After the people had greeted the sun, they disappeared into their homes, and the town fell silent. On the far side of the island, smoke rose from the king's farmstead. It was a cold, quiet, and hard land, and the people were just like it. The monk's work had scarcely begun. For a moment, as though in a vision, he saw the hundreds of years that it would take, the infinitesimal impact he would have. The ancient empire of the wooden gods was standing against him.

In the spring when the ice would neither support you nor break up, the store of grain ran out, and the townspeople had to live on fish and meat for several days. But the same day the bluish-white, glittering ice floes heaved splashing and roaring against the shore, numerous sails approached at a good clip before a heavy wind.

Ausi and her daughter heard feet running, and looking outside, they saw people, old, young, and children, rushing to the harbor. They also saw the king's familiar black and yellow sail on the lake.

Mother and daughter quickly closed up their house and ran after the others. They raced past the smithies, lifting their skirts high, and saw Holme with his smiths gathered around him. He yelled angrily at them for their curiosity, and the smiths laughed. The daughter smiled back at them, her black hair flying in the wind. She passed her mother and reached the harbor before her. Holme watched them, his anger turning to pride when the smiths praised them both.

The Christian priests stood a short distance behind the mass of people in the harbor, so Ausi could get a better look at them. They tensely watched the first ship with its golden dragon head and talked softly in their mother tongue. You could already make out the king standing among his warriors. He nodded and smiled, and the crowd buzzed animatedly in response.

Behind the war ships came a row of boats loaded with grain. The barricade was raised and the boats tied up at the dock, one beside the other. While the king talked with the town leaders, hundreds of inhabitants with baskets crowded around the boats, and the sale began. By the time Ausi returned with her bushel, the hand mills were already clattering in many houses. The king's men stood up to their knees in the yellow grain they were measuring out from the boats.

After the king, the chieftain, and both monks had walked back to town, Ausi and her daughter stood looking at the ships. Ausi noticed a young man or boy on one of them, staring at her and Tora. He had wicked, blue eyes, and his head was bent forward as if a weight sat on his neck. He was almost as tall as the men, but he seemed more like an overgrown child. He stared at Tora with intense, scornful interest. Uneasy, Ausi picked up her basket and left, holding her daughter by the hand. She looked back a couple of times and saw the strange figure silhouetted against the sky.

For several days she thought about the peculiar boy and his stare. He must presage some evil that would befall her or her daughter. Nothing could happen to Holme — hardened to misfortune, he was always the strongest.

Ausi was concerned about Holme for another reason. He hadn't said a word about her attending the Christians' worship service; he just cautioned her not to do it again. But she could tell he was up to something against the Christians, and many people supported him, the thralls most of all. They would walk through fire and water for him if they had to. He associated with them as equals, and he didn't hide the fact that he had once been a thrall himself. He constantly worked to make things better for them. No one in town any longer dared whip a thrall in front of Holme. This had happened on two occasions and both times, the consequences had been grave.

The most distinguished of the two monks walked among the thousands of green burial mounds, while the spring sun shone on his gray cape and drawn face. It was totally silent; only an occasional puff of wind moved through the grass on the sides of the mounds and softly rustled delicate birch leaves. The monk looked out over the mounds and thought with sorrow about the thousands of heathen souls burning in the eternal fires while their bodies rested in this idyllic place. For a moment, he thought their punishment for ignorance was too severe, but he pushed the thought away, putting it in God's hands. Perhaps on the Day of Judgement, He would be moved by mercy, and walk among the mounds, calling up the stern, bearded men, the self-assured women, and the guiltless children from the graves. Perhaps He would give them a chance to enter His kingdom.

From one of the tallest mounds, he looked down at the town and the water glistening brightly beyond it. Many disappointments had been prepared for him; still, his work had begun. Soon a ship would come with everything they needed to hold more worthy and dignified worship services. The heathens were like children; they believed only in demonstrations of power, wanted to see glitter and hear songs and music. They didn't believe in empty hands and meek promises.

Through the silence came distant, melodic sounds from town. Ringing blows from the smithies, tapping and scraping from the craftsmen's sheds, songs and shouting from the harbor. The distance refined the sounds, blending them together with the soft whispering wind and the songs of birds. God had given the pagans a beautiful land; someday they would realize that and be filled with gratitude.

The monk noticed there were more ships in the harbor than usual; that meant a business journey to a foreign land. He knew what kind of business the heathens conducted on their journeys—he had run into them himself. That's why he had come to the heathen land empty-handed, and that's why his work had been obstructed. They were thieves, not merchants.

Perhaps resistance would lessen after enough of the most headstrong warriors had sailed away. It would be good if a storm destroyed their ships or enemies defeated them. Then the heathens would be enraged at the wooden gods and turn to Christ—on the other hand, they might think that Christ had provoked their gods into sending misfortune upon their people.

Still mulling that over, he left the mounds and walked to the city gate. He had to step aside for a line of people carrying a corpse toward the mounds. It was an old man, and the sun lit up his silver beard against the yellow skin. His head rocked slightly from the motion of the pall-bearers. Behind him came a man carrying his tools and the food he would need for the journey. The Christian monk watched the procession and prayed silently for the old heathen's soul; then he walked through the gate.

Between the defense works and town lay an untouched meadow where the children could play. The monk passed a group of children sitting on the ground, and he stopped, marvelling at their play. They sat in rows, and the biggest boy stood in front of them, holding something in his hand. Meadow blossoms and cowslips danced around him in the gentle breeze. The monk stared at what the boy was holding and thought the devil was playing a trick on him. He rubbed his eyes and looked again. What the heathen boy had, and what the northern sun was shining on, was a book, perhaps one he had lost on the journey.[5]

The monk walked over and stretched out his hand; the boy gave him the book. The children watched him silently as he examined it and asked them where they had gotten it. It was in bad shape, but it was one of his, stolen by pirates. Over fathomless roads, it had found him after a winter and spring.

Clutching the book to his chest, he told the children to visit him at the chieftain's house for a reward; the boy nodded sullenly. He surely couldn't think the foreign plaything was worth much. But how could the children pretend to hold a Christian worship service—where had they seen one? It had to be the first Bible ever in town, perhaps in the whole heathen land. The book's inherent power had probably taken hold of the children and given them the idea.

---

[5] Rimbert reports that Ansgar and Witmar were plundered 'of nearly forty books which they had accumulated for the service of god' (*Anskar*, chapter 10, pp. 47–48), but not that they retrieved any of them.

The monk felt infused with new strength when he saw God's printed word. He didn't need to know how it had reached him; he could see the hand behind it and that gave him new powers. Soon he would have other books, but this one would always be dearest. It had been returned to him by the hand of God.

The sunshine was dazzling, and the various sounds from town contained light and hope. That evening he would call his little congregation together and share some of the extraordinary news. Everything could move forward more quickly now.

A dark, powerful figure like a fragment of the night walked past on the cross street in front of him, and a vague sense of danger emanated from it. For a moment, he felt his new joy subdued. The silent master smith was his and the congregation's most dangerous enemy, a Saul of the North, but a miracle could happen, even with him. His wife hadn't returned since the mid-winter sacrifice, but the work had begun in her; you could see that in her restless look. Surely she must have been mistaken when she spoke indignantly about having been baptized a long time ago.

Summer was coming to the heathen land, and before it was over, the church must be well established. Then he could return to his homeland and witness before God and king that he had completed his task.

A few days later the monk went to the harbor to watch the ships sail. The entire town was there, the warriors' families standing closest to the dock. Many of them would never see their husbands, fathers, or sons again. The warriors ranged in age from adolescents with sparsely haired chins to grim, gray-bearded adults. The sacrificial fires had burned all night so the gods would favor the journey, but the Christian monk beseeched Christ to bring down storm and devastation. The weather was still favorable though, with sun and a fresh breeze.

Work had stopped throughout town; no sounds came from the smithies or sheds. The monk observed a weeping wife hang a small cross around her husband's neck to protect him on the perilous journey. But he had seen many such crosses, and they didn't fool him anymore. They didn't represent the Cross of Christ but a hammer, the weapon of the most powerful wooden god.

The monk stood there until the ships were far away, their golden dragons glowing against the blue waves capped with white. When he finally returned to town, the families were still standing there. The smell of the sacrifices was everywhere, and once again the monk petitioned Christ to send a ruinous storm against the Viking fleet to demonstrate His superiority over the wooden gods. Many of His staunchest opponents were gone, and the work could accelerate. But the black-haired Saul was still standing in the way; maybe the hand of God would strike him down.

Even as he thought, the first blows resounded from the smithies. Black smoke and sparks rose from the roof vents, and the bellows creaked. He took the road past Holme's house and looked at the snake-adorned door fittings. Once he had asked the chieftain to drive Holme from town, but the chieftain, the town's most powerful man besides the king, didn't dare. He was afraid that the smiths, the craftsmen, and the masses of thralls would riot if he laid hands on the master smith. They all considered Holme their chieftain and protector, and they did everything he asked.

The monk had stopped in front of the ornamented door, but when he saw two female figures coming up the street, he walked on. He had wanted to talk with the smith's wife, but should Holme happen to come home no one knew what might happen. Smiling, he shook his head at that thought—was he afraid of the smith now, too? Yes. He didn't want to die yet, but once the work had a firm foundation, he wouldn't back down.

A group of women, old men, and children were standing on the point, watching the ships. The breeze played in the women's clothes and the old men's beards. The wooden god stood in the shrine, the corners of his mouth drawn up as if he smiled scornfully at the servant of Christ.

The chieftain's wife labored with other women thralls in the foreign land, digging up the ground for their master. Her face was gray and angry; no one would guess that she had once been a chieftain's wife and had herself ruled over thralls.

Two days had passed since they had first seen smoke rising beyond the forest; the day before it had come closer, and today the smell of it was riding on the wind. The first survivors arrived that afternoon, saying the invaders spared no one. Those who valued their lives had to flee to the woods or to town for protection within its walls.

With inner glee, the chieftain's wife had watched the smoke drawing closer and closer. She hoped her countrymen were on their way. She had once heard two men speaking her language when they visited the master, but she had been locked away and couldn't be heard herself. Perhaps her liberation was moving through the forest from the west. In the confusion, she would try to stay behind when the others left.

But in the late afternoon when the smoke began to rise from the neighboring farmstead across the woods, no one thought about forcing her to leave with them. There was a wave and a shout from the yard, and the women rushed back, all except the two kidnapped women. The nearly grown daughter had already raced off, a young thrall clutching her hand. When she saw her mother remaining behind, she turned back a few steps, waving and calling, but the older woman stood peacefully by her former mistress's side. The girl hesitated, looked around for the young thrall who was frantically waving for her, and then gave up her mother and ran toward safety with him.

Shouting and commotion came from the farmstead; a wagon was wheeled up and loaded with the most valuable possessions. The thralls had chased off the cows and pigs as they fled. Smoke billowed in waves above the forest, and an indeterminate clamor rose from it. The thrall girl's mother suddenly had a change of heart and began running after the fleeing people.

They were still in sight when the thieves came swarming out of the forest on horseback and on foot. They stopped at the forest's edge, looking suspiciously at the silent farmstead that blocked the fleeing people from view. They saw the woman standing fearlessly in the middle of the field, and they looked about in all directions as if they expected an ambush.

"Bring the witch here," the chieftain ordered, and two men walked toward the farmstead. The woman came forward to meet them, and they brought her back, surprised she spoke their language. The chieftain sat down on a rock, gestured toward another for the woman, and listened as she told her story, energetically pointing and gesticulating in her happiness.

A tall, grizzled warrior paid closer, more eager attention to her than the others did. As she described the attack, the burning, and the kidnapping, he nodded as if he knew all about it and was invigorated by what she said. But he said nothing.

After the chieftain had heard the woman out, he went to the farmstead with his army. They searched the buildings, but everything of value was gone. Some provisions were carried out and laid at a distance from the buildings. When all was ready, Geire walked up to the chieftain and asked if he could light the fire.

"Why?"

"He burned my farmstead."

"So burn his," the chieftain said without further ado.

The woman sat down in the grass, and her eyes shone with happiness when the farmstead began to burn. The warriors sat down, too. Some fetched water for the bread they had found. The youngest of them, a deformed boy, moved as close he could get to the fire as he ate his bread. His head was bowed under an invisible burden. Suddenly the woman caught sight of him through the smoke and hurried toward him.

"Svein!" she screamed shrilly, but the youth didn't look at her. She rushed up, grabbed him, and spun him around. The rows of seated warriors looked up in surprise as they ate.

The woman hugged the youth, scrutinizing his eyes, nose, and hands. Then, as she felt his neck, Svein shoved her violently away, screaming in rage, "What do you want from me, you old hag?"

The warriors began laughing but stopped abruptly when Geire walked up to the pair, put his hand out to the woman, and murmured something that made the boy stare at her in surprise from beneath a lowered forehead. Then the three of them sat apart from the others while the farmstead burned. Geire happened upon a tool in the field and threw that into the fire too so everything would be consumed. They had been avenged by fire now; maybe they could catch the survivors and complete their revenge with the sword.

At midsummer, the families in the island town vainly watched and waited for their marauding ships to return. Some approached Christ, asking Him to bring the ships home; others sacrificed almost everything they had to the wooden gods. Autumn came, but they still continued to hope. Wintering in a foreign, conquered land was not unusual.

The Christian congregation hadn't grown as much as the monks had hoped. They had the things they needed now for a worship service. Two bells, a big one and a small one, rang out crisply over the island and surrounding water. The blackened smiths stood in the doorway, listening and laughing at the new gimmick. In the summer night, a heathen fisherman rested on his oars as he listened in half-terror to the strange clear tones bounding across the water. But no one heeded their call to come to Christ.

The monks had to admit that the Christianity of the pagans they had managed to convert wasn't worth much. All they wanted were the advantages; their hearts were cold and indifferent before the blood of the Cross. To them the Cross was a simple, carved god, and they saw blood much too often for it to make any impression. Without daily guidance, they would soon slide back into darkness. Many of them would leave the worship service and go to their household god, sacrificing to him for help with what Christ couldn't or wouldn't do. The monks sensed the boundlessness of their field of labor.

They could see clearly how small their congregation was one spring day when they left for their homeland.[6] The lake had just opened, and the last thin ice floes were clanking against the rocks on shore. A big ship had come for them, and many realized then that the priests must be men of high station in their homeland. But no one cared about that here.

The Christians clustered at the front of the small harbor gathering; behind stood the crowds of heathens, come to see the departure. Holme watched with his smiths from the hill where he had once torn down the church. The foundation stones were still there, half sunk into the ground. The smiths could view the whole harbor. Holme knew his wife and daughter were down there and thought he could see them next to the Christians. The whole time the bells clanged anxious, hasty peals.

Before the vessel was rowed out, the most distinguished monk stood on the prow, lifted his hands into the air, and in a loud clear voice, delivered his followers into God's hands. The heathens were totally silent, and the smiths could hear some of his words. Holme smiled grimly, confident that when they were gone, everyone would return to his old ways.

From the vessel, the departing monk, tears streaming down his face, watched his congregation on the shore. Some of the women cried; others waved; the men

---

[6] Ansgar and Witmar spent a total of a year and a half on this mission (*Anskar*, chapter 12, p. 49).

raised their arms in a gesture of farewell. The children played obliviously, clambering over the pilings. The old chieftain, whom they had to thank for whatever success they had achieved, was standing in front. As the vessel moved farther out, the monk could see the entire town. The sun was shining on the yellowish-green sod roofs, and the wind was driving the smoke eastward. A few figures, black against the yellow-green background, were standing on a rise. When he saw them he had a sudden premonition that his work was not secure; he thought of the powerful enemies he had in town. The monks had felt Holme's hostility in various ways. Many agreed with him.

No doubt many in the congregation would fall back into paganism. As soon as something went wrong, Christ would take the blame, and they would return to their wooden idols. Christ faced an ancient army of blood-smeared wooden gods in these northern heathen lands.

Thin, dirty cows and goats were grazing on the shores. Once a few horn blasts blared from the woods. The town was still visible, and the monk could distinguish the bell tower and the bells. When he got to his homeland, he would continue to send the chieftain items for the worship service until the new monks arrived to carry on the good work.

He had been the first of God's messengers to come to this luminous and beautiful, but difficult, land. They had probably had Christian thralls there for a long time, and he had heard vague rumors about a man who supposedly had come through the woods on foot, spoken God's words, and baptized people by the shore. But there was no further trace of him, and once those heathens who still remembered him had gone, he would never be mentioned again. He undoubtedly was one of the many deluded souls who had been wrong about God's call. Most of them never reached their destination; instead God allowed the heathens to kill them en route so they'd be spared an even worse fate. His own unmistakable sign had been God's saving him from the hands of the pirates and guiding him to his goal — the remote heathen town on the island.

A cloud had risen quickly in the west, and when he caught his last glimpse of the town, it was in shadow. In that instant, the distant bells rang irregularly, anxiously, and then fell silent. Did that mean the wooden gods would reclaim their town entirely? The wind mounted and large, wet flakes of snow flew along on it. The Frisians' vessel picked up speed, white water foaming around the prow. Had heathens been on board, they would have believed their gods were blowing the Christians away from their land, and their faith in the gods would have grown still stronger.

Islets and isthmuses that moments before had been bathing in the spring light on the blue water, turned sullen and dark, and the swirling spring snow colored their northern sides a gray-white. The ship soon entered an area where a current flowed on both sides of an islet. On the north end, a long gravel ridge thrust up, its slopes covered with woods, its crown bare; on the south side the water slammed against lofty, precipitous gray cliffs. Some fishermen were busy on the shores, and some boats lay tied to a log landing on the sides sheltered from the wind. But the monk's God did not allow him to see the powerful Christian town and many churches that one day would stand there.[7]

The sleet turned to a cold rain, and he sought shelter, his heart troubled and heavy because of his departure.

The ship was still in sight and the people were still standing in the harbor when Holme and the smiths walked up toward the Christian buildings and yard. No one was there except the free thrall ringing the bells. The thrall looked as though he felt important and satisfied with the sound he was creating, and the bells swung on their pole.

But as the dark group approached, the sound quickened, becoming more anxious than before. The bell-ringer knew perfectly well what the master smith and the others thought of the Christians, and he was alone. A distance away, they started picking up stones, and when the first came whizzing, the bell-ringer let go the rope and ran toward the town gate. The smiths' laughter pursued him, and he heard the smaller bell ring out a shrill cry when a stone hit it.

The smiths walked up to the bell-tower and shook it, but didn't tear it down. The mass of people in the harbor began dispersing, and the chieftain might come any minute. Violence toward the Christians and their possessions wouldn't go over well in broad daylight; the king and the chieftain protected them. But the opportunity would come soon enough.

From the heathen shrine, a couple of the wooden god's servants delighted in watching the smiths. The wooden god himself peered rigidly ahead with his crooked, scornful smile. Stripes of darkened blood from the spring sacrifice stained him. The smiths looked at him respectfully, but Holme cared as little about him as he did about Christ. Holme had never sacrificed to any god, and no god had ever helped him either. He had made his own way, and that's what he would always do.

When the chieftain appeared, provoked by the bell-ringer's story, the smiths were already gone and everything was still. He didn't dare go to the smithies to make them answer for this. The smiths had their own understanding of law and justice. It wasn't far to their sledgehammers and axes when they needed them, and it did no good to talk with their grim leader. He was born a thrall, and a thrall he remained—a difficult and dangerous thrall chieftain.

When Geire, Svein, and his mother stepped ashore below their burned settlement one day in the late summer, they saw a couple of gray-haired figures stumbling and hobbling toward the forest through the open area. The new arrivals moved cautiously up the slope, keeping their weapons ready, but all they

---

[7] i.e., Stockholm.

found were two half-grown pigs that let out a terrified guttural squeal, wheeled around, and fled in a waddling gallop.

The mounds of ashes had been nearly leveled by the year's rain and wind, and were almost overgrown with grass and shrubs, but among the trees stood a little hut made of sticks and mud. The old men had fled from it. Barley was growing in a couple of small fields, and a narrow path had been worn between them and the buildings. The charred wooden god, turned a shimmering gray by wind and weather, stood on the slope. The woman recognized him but paid no attention. He hadn't been able to stop the misfortune that befell the settlement and its people.

The three sat resting at the settlement after checking the hut. There were no valuables inside; everything had probably burned. The old men who had fled to the forest were surely nearby, but they didn't look dangerous.

From where they sat, they had a view of the three large mounds in the burial grounds, and they talked nostalgically about the last man who had been put there and about the good years they had when he was alive. They talked about Holme and Ausi too, but the woman's face contorted with hate and rage, and she admonished her brother and son to take revenge if they ever found those two alive. She suspected Holme had shown the invaders to the farmstead. When it came to sorcery, he knew more than most people did.

Geire listened, and as she talked, he began to call the thrall back to mind. He remembered him now as the master of the largest smithy in town, who had given Svein a new sword to replace the burned one. He also remembered Svein's strange fear of the smith. Soon everything was clear to him.

If his sister was right, the worst of the revenge remained to be exacted. The gods had helped them find the invaders' farmsteads in the unknown land; many had fallen in the battle, some had been taken prisoner, and he had cut some down with his sword when they defiantly affirmed they had burned and harried where he was now sitting. If the black-haired smith was behind it all, he would answer for it with his life.

When they walked on, they saw a little mound of earth where the grass had not yet taken root. They didn't know that the old woman thrall was resting there — Stor and Tan had buried her early that summer. She had her spindle-whorl with her, a couple of needles, a pair of scissors, and a clay bowl with meat and bread in it. Since then, the old men talked about their greatest worry — who would prepare them for their final journey?

They hadn't recognized the three visitors. As they had many times before, they hid among the trees, anxiously and fearfully sticking their bristly gray snouts out. No one stayed at the burned settlement long; the menacing wooden god stood on his stone, ruling over the solitude and desolation, and the place just usually wasn't as fit for human habitation as it should be.

After stopping at the edge and looking back at what had once been their home, the three proceeded into the woods. They agreed they would rebuild it

when the time came, and it wouldn't hurt anything for a couple of old outlaws to
keep up parts of the fields. There were good forest meadows in the area, and the
chieftain's wife wanted to rest a while beside her first husband. She didn't care
about the second one with the spindly legs. He probably had never been buried.
No doubt wild animals had eaten him once they dared brave the heat after the
invaders had dragged her off and Svein had run into the forest.

Late in the summer, a rumor went around town that the two Christians who
had gone home in the spring had sent two replacements. The new ones had
received permission to do whatever they wanted to spread the teaching of the
new god.[8]

But another rumor came from the fields and meadows, from the large farmsteads and the small clearings in the forest, that the wooden gods were more
incensed than ever before. The fertility god had loosed a disease on the grain, a
black blight that rode the wind, devouring the grain in its path. Instead of loaded
grain boats, famine would sweep grinning down on the town from the forests
and flatlands. The heathens scornfully asked each other what Christ could do
about that.

In autumn the townspeople looked vainly toward the mainland for the boats,
as their storehouses quickly ran dry. Soon people spoke openly, claiming that the
misery had to be caused by the new god. Some people could see clear signs of the
wooden gods' wrath. Many took their boats to distant farmsteads seeking grain,
but there was none to be found. The farmers held onto whatever they could of
the miserable harvest. A royal decree to sell the extra grain was received with
scorn, axes, and swords. Then one day, a large ship loaded with grain came to the
Christians from their homeland.

The smithies and craftsmen's sheds gradually fell silent. No one was willing to
exchange grain and meat for tools or weapons. Many had left the town for the
farmsteads of relatives or for foreign lands, trying to find something to sustain
them. The pigs no longer grubbed in the streets; the dogs ran around emaciated
and half-crazed, and their famished howls rose loudly toward the sky at night.
Many had sacrificed the last of their household animals to the wooden gods, but
they stared ahead grimly, unmoved. Among the heathens a murmur of hate was
born and grew—the Christians had to go or everyone would perish. Those who
owned thralls drove them off so they wouldn't deplete the already sparse provisions. Starving thralls were slinking everywhere; panting, they crawled into the
forest, stuffing berries in their mouths with cupped hands, digging up roots and

---

[8] Louis the Pious arranged for Ansgar to become the first archbishop of Hamburg,
with all of Scandinavia under his jurisdiction, and Ansgar in turn consecrated his nephew
Gautbert as bishop of Sweden. Gautbert then went to Sweden with his companion, Nithard, to carry on the mission work. (*Anskar*, chapter 16, p. 57).

picking bitter acorns. During the frosty nights, they would make their way to town and hunch close to the building walls to keep warm.

But everyone knew the Christians had grain.

When Holme could no longer stand the silent pleas in his wife's and daughter's eyes, he walked to town. Their drawn faces followed him beseechingly; they were used to his always finding a way. Holme couldn't live on roots and berries anymore; he had a wild craving for a loaf of bread or a piece of meat.

For several nights he had searched near the Christians' building trying to find something from their storeroom, but it was well protected and there was always a guard. He wasn't alone on his nightly prowls; dark figures sneaked around him, looking hungrily at the stout building that held the grain.

After Holme had given all he could give, he preferred spending the days inside. When the starving thralls saw him, they hurried up with hope-filled eyes, but he drove them away in despair. Why did they think he could do more than anyone else? He felt more and more responsible for them, even though his look was threatening and his words hard. When the Christian bells rang, he shook his fist at them, remembering Ausi's timidly asking him if she could go to the Christians for a little grain.

This time he hadn't gone far before a couple of homeless thralls started following him, refusing to be put off by his stern demeanor. A group on a street corner noticed and joined them. Holme could hear them tramping along behind him, and their numbers swelled. He felt their trust weighing him down, and he didn't know what to do.

The larger church bell struck hesitantly, and the smaller bell started tinkling along with it. Without knowing why, Holme walked toward the sound, and the silent, plodding group followed him. Others came running up the roads and streets to join them.

Dozens of heathens were already standing outside the Christian yard where the large church building had been begun. They had assorted goods with them and begged the Christians to trade them grain. Holme and the group of thralls stood like a large shadow in the open area, but the Christians could see they were unarmed and paid them no attention.

One of the new Christians told the pagans that anyone who accepted the new teaching would get grain and whatever else he needed. That was the only condition—they weren't selling or bartering anything. The Christians claimed that Christ had sent this misfortune on the heathens to save them and bring them to Himself.

As Holme listened to their words, he noticed a stone font where they would baptize those coming to Christ. There was water in it, and one of the monks stood ready beside it. Holme felt the old defiance and rage, dormant for several years, begin to waken. He looked at the Christians' full cheeks and clear eyes and then at the thralls, standing there, looking like starving dogs, chewing on nothing. He had to get them something to eat, even if it meant risking his security or his life. There he stood with the unarmed thralls, shaking with hunger, while the Christians were well-fed and armed. They would fight for their grain.

Holme watched a woman walk hesitantly over to the Christians, holding her child by the hand. He knew that Ausi would do the same if she dared. Maybe in the end she would anyway. It would be better if the Christians were killed and their buildings burned, even if the chieftain himself was one of them and the buildings belonged to him. Lives were at stake here—he realized that soon his body would no longer obey his will.

The Christians, beginning to get a little nervous about the threatening band of thralls, saw its well-known leader give an order to the thralls, who all disappeared with him toward the smithies. The Christians breathed easier and their voices, offering a bushel of grain per soul, became more relaxed.

Some of the thralls were hoping Holme had bread in his smithy, but what he took out of the chests and down from the walls was nothing to chew on—axes, swords, knives, and sledgehammers. He passed the weapons out among them, thinking that this time someone would be fighting by his side; he had always been alone before.

But, when he stood before the Christian buildings and yard again with his armed thralls, he was reluctant to attack. The Christians kept luring people with their grain, while a dull chanting voice from the pagan shrine warned of the wooden gods' further wrath.

While the thralls had gone to get weapons, more women had approached the Christians, among them Holme's wife and daughter. Ausi was chewing greedily, waving for him to come over though she was terrified by what she had done. Tora, eating peacefully and looking out across the open area, didn't seem to understand the price she would have to pay for the bread.

Having taken in all this, Holme ran without a sound toward the Christians; before anyone knew what had happened, he had smashed the baptismal font to bits with his sledgehammer. Water splashed everywhere, and the Christians fled, shrieking in confusion. The thralls gave chase, and then there was chaos. The chieftain was gone, but the Christians ran to his house for protection while the heathens searched for the grain. When everyone was safe inside and the bar was thrown, a window opened, and a voice threatened the thralls with eternal damnation.

Two men stood guard at the storeroom, and one made a valiant effort to defend himself against the thralls. A stick struck the spear from his hand, and another landed on his skull. By then, the other was already at the chieftain's house banging on the door to get in. At the same time, the hatch of the storeroom gave way before Holme's sledgehammer, revealing the golden grain in a huge bin. The thralls leaped into it, stuffing themselves with their hands. The throng outside grew and with it, the cries of hunger from the children with their mothers. People streamed in from town; everyone wanted to be there. No one cared how all this had happened.

Holme tossed the closest thralls aside when he saw the mass of people, and a while later, the Christians could see the pagans coming with bushels and tankards. The master smith stood measuring out equal portions of the grain. Men, women, and children hurried back to their homes, cramming grain into their mouths. It wasn't long before the hand mills and millstones in every hut began clattering. Some of the newly converted Christians had remained outside, and Holme gave them a share even though their hair was still dripping with Christian baptismal water.

Once everything had been handed out, the area was deserted; only a few children were left crawling around, picking up the spilled grain. The larder was empty, and Holme had neglected himself. The Christians saw him stop, looking around with a sledgehammer in one hand and the empty measuring pail in the other. His daughter wanted to run to him, but some of the others restrained her. Ausi stood in silent dread, not knowing what to do. Holme turned his head like a bear and looked up at them before he walked down the street and disappeared.

Ausi heard the Christians around her growling that Holme had forfeited his life by doing what he had done. As soon as the chieftain returned, he'd complain to the king. The hater of Christ—now a murderer and a thief too—would get his punishment from both earthly and heavenly powers.

She saw her daughter glare with raging eyes at those charging her father with these things, and Ausi wished she had stayed home and not come to the Christians. Then Holme would not have forgotten to take his share of the grain for his wife and daughter. But she also wanted to stay with the Christians and learn more about them. If Christ was who they said He was, then, of course, He could forgive Holme for what he had done for the hungry thralls.

The Christians weren't going to starve to death; the monks were already talking about another ship coming from their homeland. Maybe she could hide some food for Holme if she found out where he was. The Christians would become more and more powerful, and Holme would understand someday why she had gone to them.

The Christians' threats that Holme would be punished soon meant nothing to her. Only people who didn't know Holme talked that way. Yet she constantly avoided the anger and accusation in her daughter's eyes.

At a worship service one day, it became clear to Ausi that Christ could have defended Himself against those who hanged Him on the Cross if He had chosen to, and she became very happy. She understood why the stranger had let himself be slaughtered at the spring sacrificial feast so long ago: he wanted to be Christlike. If she had known that before, she could have explained it to Holme though he could never be that way himself. No matter how many men attacked him, he'd fight as long as he could move, and they'd be able to hang him up on a cross only if he were almost dead.

Both the new monks took more interest than their predecessors had in her story about the stranger who had baptized her by the shore many years before. They listened attentively to her description, from the thralldom at the settlement to the great sacrifice when the stranger was hanged in the sacrificial grove together with animals of every size. They shook their heads at Holme's wickedness and said that now he would truly be lost for all time. Christ would strike him down wherever he was hiding. Ausi heard that with a heavy heart, thinking that she had been deceived. A wife should be at her husband's side to the end.

The monks said she should be baptized again; no one could be sure if the stranger had the right to baptize. They had also heard that the master smith had plenty of earthly possessions—she should give some of them for building the church and for her and her daughter's eternal happiness. She thought about the bound chest containing the silver and expensive weapons, the pearls and glass items that Holme had bartered from foreign merchants. Holme should decide all such things, but he was gone and had taken only his weapons with him. The monks would have to wait until she heard from him.

As Ausi saw the gray baptismal font under her bowed head and felt the water dripping in her hair, she wasn't thinking about Christ as she should have been. She was thinking first that the font was smaller than the one Holme had smashed to bits, and she felt some pride over the violence of the sledgehammer blow. Holme always struck hard and straight; no one else was like him.

Then she thought about the summer day when she was first baptized. It was much more beautiful when the stranger stood in the sparkling water, stretching his hand out toward her with a friendly smile. He must have been closer to Christ than those who came after him. She remembered the Cross on his chest glittering in the water, but this time she saw only the gray bottom of the font and heard the monk's words repeated over and over again.

But now she could be sure she'd be one of those called up out of the ground when Christ returned. Tora would be baptized too and become one of them. The Christians said that no heathen would be raised, but Holme wasn't aware of that. If he wanted to, he'd get up with or without Christ's help or water on his head.

Tora had watched the baptismal rites with mounting surprise, and Ausi realized she was becoming more and more like her father. Ausi had been ashamed to look Tora in the eye when her turn had come, and when she stood before her daughter with dripping hair, telling her it was her turn, she was asking more than ordering her.

She saw then that Tora was Holme's daughter. Silent but with black, angry disdain in her eyes she looked at both her mother and the monks, who gently called for her.

When coaxing didn't work, a couple of the baptized women grabbed her and dragged her to the font. She fought them fiercely, and one of them screamed out in pain, then displayed a deep bite in her arm, blood oozing from it.

But they couldn't have a heathen in their midst; you had to force a child who didn't understand what was for her own good. Strong arms dragged the panting, furious girl up and held her fast while the water dropped into her black hair. Ausi thought that if Holme had been around, their lives wouldn't have been worth much. When he came back, he would exact hard revenge. With a pang in her heart, she felt that Christ had come between her and her loved ones. Both of them would soon come to loathe her.

After Tora had been baptized, she raced through the door toward their house. Ausi hurried after her, but Tora was already leaving with her few belongings when she arrived. She ignored her mother's plea and ran toward the harbor. She probably intended to go to the mainland to find her father, Ausi thought with great anxiety. It could mean her death; how could she defend herself against wild animals and evil people?

But the harbor was deserted, and the oarsman hadn't seen her daughter. He laughed and said she might have taken a side street to fool her mother. She'd probably come back.

Ausi spent the whole day crying and walking back and forth between harbor and home to see if Tora had returned. She felt great bitterness for Christ and His servants, who had stolen everything dear to her. Why should she rise from the grave on the last day if neither Tora nor Holme could be with her? No, she would rather stay in the earth with them and sleep until the end of time.

The oarsman tried to console her and turned his head in every direction to look for her daughter. A boat had crossed from the other harbor; maybe she was in it. He had rowed Holme across a few days before. When he told her that, his voice took on an admiring tone. A free, rich, and powerful man had never endangered his life, family, and possessions before for the sake of thralls. Holme had saved many from starvation; the grain he had taken from the Christians was still holding out, and it was rumored that several more ships were on the way. No one else would die of hunger now. It was no hardship for the Christians—they had probably hidden grain in several places.

But what the oarsman said did not make Ausi happy. His words reminded her that Holme always thought of himself last; the weak and down-trodden had a powerful protector in him. She had always known that but only thought it natural. Everyone looked to him for help when something went wrong, and he always had advice. But when he had taken that perilous last resort of attacking the Christians and stealing their grain for her, Tora, and the starving thralls, she had turned away from him and stood by the Christians—the Christians who, through their speeches and their invisible white god, had only caused her trouble.

After Holme had paid the oarsman, he headed for the woods the same way he had as a runaway thrall. He wasn't quite sure what to do; he mostly wanted to be by himself to look at the old paths, the old haunts. He wasn't worried about his wife and daughter; no one would harm them, and the Christians would give them whatever they might need. He suspected they had more grain than he had divided up among the starving, homeless thralls.

He was still bitter because Ausi hadn't waited before going to the Christians. That was the first time she hadn't trusted him, and she wasn't the only one who was hungry. It wasn't so bad for Tora—they had hidden away a little food and persuaded her to eat it. This was all because of the Christians and their temptations. Someday he would return and take his revenge, even if he didn't know right now how he would do it.

Toward evening he reached the cave, approaching it cautiously. Someone or something might be living there, a robber or a wolf. The entrance was too small for a bear.

Everything was quiet; the stillness of the summer ruled in the forest. The marshland still lay below the ridge as before, and a mist hung brooding over it. Stenulf's burial mound had sunk and shrank. Before Holme left the next day, he'd put a stone on the mound so everyone would know it was a grave. He shuddered at the thought of spending the night so close to the warrior he had killed and put in the mound himself. Stenulf probably wasn't there anymore; he had doubtlessly moved on. He hadn't had any provisions for the journey, but a warrior like Stenulf would get along well enough without them.

Holme's legs were shaking from the day's journey, and he realized how long he had survived on berries and roots. He remembered that wild strawberries grew on the mossy pile of rocks, and he climbed up to look. They were still there, large forest strawberries so ripe they were almost black. They had vanished from the glades and along the roads a long time ago.

The cave hadn't changed except for the old moss bed where he had slept with Ausi, and where she had later born the child who froze to death in the forest. The bed had almost moldered away, so he carried in fresh moss before lying down.

Through the door, he could hear an evening wind in the forest, and he thought about how strange it all was. Everything was just like it had been before; all the years he had spent as a smith in town seemed unreal. Perhaps he had been asleep in the cave conjuring them in a dream. Though everything seemed dark to him, he felt more secure in the cave than any place else. He'd be an outlaw now after what he had done to the Christians, and the cave was the best place of refuge and defence for him.

For a moment he thought about Christ and His servants. Anyone could see now how weak He was; He couldn't even protect His own grain. At least you could see the wooden gods. There they stood—stock still, staring. Since you couldn't see Christ, He must not exist. How could a non-existent god help or punish anyone? Ausi and all the others who had gone to the Christians must be simple-minded.

He'd go back someday, and then there'd be trouble. The first Christian stranger had tried to burn the temple of the wooden gods at the great festival of sacrifice, but he had failed and ended up hanging in a tree. Perhaps the Christian buildings would burn a little easier.

His last sensation was an intense longing for home. He thought about his daughter and the harm that might befall her, and his breathing deepened with rage. He decided to slip back one night soon to check things out. Anyone who had hurt her wouldn't live to see the sun rise.

Then Holme calmed down a little, realizing that the smiths and thralls would protect her. He knew too, now that his fatigue wasn't so great, that Tora wouldn't stay with the Christians long. She probably hadn't even realized where her mother was taking her. Maybe he should have taken her with him.

It was quiet outside; only the occasional, hoarse bark of a fox broke the silence. There was no sound from either of the ones he had killed near the cave—no heavy steps from Stenulf, no crying from the baby who had frozen to death in the woods. Holme put his weapons within reach and fell asleep, the darkness erasing the entrance to the cave.

The marsh land had firmed up quite a bit in the years he had been away. He didn't have to venture on rocking tufts any more, but the shovel-winged birds were still either flying around him with nervous shrieks or skittering between the tufts.

He headed out at first light to reach the settlement before anyone was up. He wanted to look it over in the open. He didn't know what else he wanted to do yet. He might run across something to eat near the settlement, and then he would find a way out. He felt dizzy from hunger now and then, and the green tufts shifted in front of his feet.

Numerous memories followed him on the road or called to him from the forest. For a long time, Ausi and he had talked of returning to the settlement now that they were safe and secure, to freshen their memories about all that had happened there. Neither had expected they'd be separated; now he came alone, hunted, and on foot, and everything seemed to be in the distant past. The life of an outlaw was all that was left for him.

He reached the settlement just before sunrise. Even before he got there, he knew things had changed; he had noticed that the cow trail to the settlement hadn't been used in years. Animals never gave up their trails. But these were all grown over, and there were no animal smells in the air.

He froze in bewilderment, staring across the empty space where grass and shrubs had covered the ashes of the buildings. He sensed a building nearby, but he couldn't see it from the edge of the forest.

An almost imperceptible path ran past the mounds of ashes to the lake. But there was no boat, and the path was little used. He followed it cautiously a ways, then stopped and saw with surprise the crude and charred wooden god on the stone. He recognized it despite the great change. Who had put it there? What was it guarding?

He also saw fresh pig tracks on the slope, and hunger screamed inside him. Maybe he could find an animal to kill and eat. There were probably some wild ones around that had once lived at the settlement.

He looked toward the old pigsty and saw the sod roof was still there with its grass and tall flowers. Curious, he walked closer and heard muffled grunts. When he opened the door he heard a louder barking sound, and three skinny pigs, a big one and two small ones, blinked at him with terrified white eyes.

Over the years a clump of trees had grown up on three sides of the little hut that Stor and Tan had built and almost hid it completely, much to the old thralls' satisfaction. They thought the wooden god on the stone was helping them, so they offered him thanks by putting food on the stone. As soon as they were out of sight, the forest birds diligently plucked up the offering.

Many forest wanderers, wild and dangerous with hunger, had passed close by, but most of them had moved on without catching sight of the hut. One day at dusk, a famished woodsman had grabbed one of the smaller pigs, but the old men had heard the squeals and rushed over. The thief didn't look dangerous, so they attacked him with their sticks, knocking him unconscious. After a while, he crawled away, moaning. This time, they hadn't been awakened by the pigs' squeals. But when Stor woke up and looked at the blue sky through the vent, he saw what appeared to be a light smoke passing over it. They hadn't had a fire since last night, and those were no morning clouds; it was smoke gliding just over their roof.

He woke up Tan, and the old men cautiously opened the door. They could smell smoke but couldn't see a fire. A soft breeze was passing over the settlement. They sneaked through the grove to get a better look at the yard and slope.

They almost fell over each other in their first terror. A vision from their worst nightmares was standing before them. A little fire was burning in the yard, and beside it stood a mighty, dark figure—the man they feared more than anyone else and who meant certain death for them. One of the small pigs lay slaughtered and skewered next to him, and he seemed to be cooking part of it. He didn't hear them and didn't move. The old thralls withdrew their quivering faces from the foliage, sneaked back to their hut, and barred the door as quietly as they could.

Eyes filled with terror, they squinted at each other in total silence all morning long, hoping the hut wouldn't be discovered. Maybe the god on the stone would help them. They heard the pigs squeal when it was time for them to root in the forest, and several times they heard their enemy coughing and grumbling. They couldn't see the smoke anymore, and soon the sun shone through the smoke vent. The old men stared at the encouraging ray of light and hoped that everything would be all right. Finally, they dared to open the door and listen; they couldn't hear anything except the grunting of pigs, the slow whispering of the forest, and the lapping of the waves.

When they sneaked out among the young trees again, the yard was empty and the fire had gone out. They stood there a long time, poking their beards through the leaves, then inching forward, constantly on the alert. The pig was gone, but a pool of blood showed where it had lost its life. They mumbled to each other that only Holme could have done that without making the pigs squeal. Their peace and safety was gone now. He'd come back as long as there was something to eat. They knew about the famine even though they'd gotten along well themselves because of their stinginess.

In any case, they had seen their deadly enemy again and were still alive. That cheered them, and, grinning, they let the pigs into the forest, then turned to find something to eat themselves. Suddenly they froze like the wooden god on the stone. Among the young trees between them and the hut stood Holme, holding a long-handled ax and looking at them. They realized in terror that he had been watching them all along.

When the ominous figure approached, Tan started to run but Holme said something so surprising that it stopped him in his tracks. In a soft voice he said that he had no intention of killing them or doing them any harm, and he set the ax against a stone to prove it. The old thralls looked fearful and dubious and didn't answer him. Why had he come if not to hurt them?

But he spoke strange, grave words about how things had changed, and he asked them what had happened to the settlement and its inhabitants. The old men gradually stopped trembling and mumbled to each other, not understanding a thing. Was Holme toying with them, enjoying their agony, or was he going to let them live?

But Holme wasn't remembering the contempt he once had felt for the two fawning, spineless thralls. They were alone and old now and had a right to stay and fend for themselves. But the settlement was big and well-situated; more than just a couple of old men should make use of it.

He had always longed to come back even though he had lived a wretched life as a thrall here. Everything was different; he could stay and rebuild the settlement. The old thralls wouldn't have it any better now, no matter where they might go. Maybe he could bring Tora and Ausi here, that is, if the Christians hadn't won them completely over. Since the relatives' farmstead was deserted and burned too, surely no one would come to claim this land.

He could tell that Stor and Tan didn't like him and would much rather see him go. When he talked with them, they exchanged terrified and angry glances. After so many years, they felt like they owned the settlement. But most of the fields lay fallow, and they had only the two pigs. A strong man with a wife and children should come here—someone who could carve wood and forge new tools and weapons. For a start, he could fix some of the things he had seen lying in a ravine.

He got up from the rock and walked to the cleft where he had once had his smithy. The sod-covered, birch-bark roof had caved in, but the support, red with rust, poked out of the debris. He would clean the place up so the sledgehammer could resound once more.

Stor and Tan, still sitting on the slope, had moved closer to each other; he could see their beards flapping as they mumbled and whispered. They weren't too pleased with the visitor, but that didn't matter. Things would be no worse for them; they would still have their freedom and their harvest. Once the settlement came to life again, everyone there, both men and women, would be free. Holme had been a thrall himself and didn't want to see other thralls around him.

He was out in the forest the same day searching out suitable trees. Stor and Tan could hear his ax, and they rolled their eyes treacherously, clutching the handles of theirs with veined fists. The wooden god on the stone received offerings all day, and they mumbled a prayer for help in their undertaking. He had once been protector of the whole settlement; maybe he'd help them against its (and their) greatest enemy.

The old dead woman's bench was empty so Holme lay down on it. All three of them ate pork that evening, and the old men fetched salt from its hiding place whining all the while about how little they had left and how close they had come to starving several times.

Later they were in an extremely good mood; they vied with each other in complimenting Holme and trying to be his friend. They had hated the old masters as much as he had and thought he had done the right thing by throwing a rock at their son. Now he'd spend his whole life peering at the ground as if he were searching for a rock to throw back.

The old men laughed and snorted through their blackened teeth and filthy beards, exchanging glances as long as there was light. Holme finally told them to be quiet and go to sleep. He listened to the whispering forest for a while through the smoke vent and felt as if he had come home.

In the first gray daylight, a thud woke him up and he opened his eyes to find an ax blade sticking in the wall just above his head. He heard labored breathing, as a pair of hands pulled the ax out and raised it quiveringly again. But it didn't fall a second time.

With a frightened little cry Tan slid back the bar as he saw Stor first in Holme's grip, then slammed to the floor with a crash. He heard an unpleasant cracking, and then he was outside, running toward the forest, then changing direction again for the lake. Halfway down the slope he heard his pursuer's steps behind him and his legs went stiff; he floated as though in a dream. Maybe the water would save him; he had always been the best swimmer at the settlement.

From Holme's silence Tan knew he should expect no mercy. He was old enough to know that a yelling, shouting man wasn't the most dangerous. And he remembered Holme's silent rage from before. He shed his clothes when he reached the landing, ran straight into the water, and started swimming without looking back.

His pursuer didn't rush out into the lake; instead, he returned to the beach and picked up some rocks the size of his fist. The first one flew too far; Tan saw it fall in front of him and turned around. The other fell close in front of him, and when he lifted his hands either to defend himself or ask for mercy the third one hit him right in the head. He saw a brilliant star of sun and water before he sank.

Holme waited a moment but nothing surfaced; the waves rolled peacefully toward the beach as before. When he walked away after a moment, he spied the old men's fishing gear hidden under the logs. It would come in handy. He examined it closely before he returned to the hut.

Stor lay where Holme had left him and would probably never move again. He couldn't take much. Holme dragged him out thinking that if the waves spit Tan onto the shore, the two old men would have each other's company on their journey. They could have lived and lived well if they hadn't tried to ax him in his sleep. In his anxiety, Stor hadn't considered the height of the ceiling. The ax had caromed off the roof and stuck in the wall. Otherwise Holme would be the one lying there now, and the old men would be laughing about their cleverness.

Holme was alone. He went out and sat on a rock on the sunny slope. The wind was wafting over the tall, shimmering grass and he recognized all the smells. The smells of summer from the dry flowers on the slope and from the shore's reeds and seaweed. A sea bird followed by a column of peeping chicks waddled out of the reeds in exactly the same place where, one summer morning half a lifetime ago, he had emerged from the forest to get weapons for himself and food for Ausi and the newborn baby in the cave.

He let the pigs out, drank water from the spring, and sat down again on the rock. Images from the past meandered across the slope; he saw the chieftain and his family, the buildings, and his fellow thralls. Ausi and he were probably the only ones left alive, now that Stor and Tan were dead.

He felt an intense longing for Ausi and was less angry about her going to the Christians. Someday he would bring her and Tora here; they would rebuild the place and everything would be as before, here where no Christians could lead her astray. They didn't need a wooden god either; he would roll the scorched clump of wood down the slope so it would never bother anyone again.

He heard a powerful snorting from the pigs and saw one of them with its back up standing next to Stor's body. He got up and drove it away thinking that the time had come to dig a grave. Stor lay there, his mouth agape, the wind slowly rustling his beard. His fingers looked as if they were clutching something, although he had dropped the ax when the smith's hands closed around his old body.

The digging was easy between the burial grove and the shore, and there Stor would rest. The next day Holme saw Tan's bumpy back outside the reeds, the waves rocking and washing over him. The anxious thralls, who had been friends their whole lives, had each other's company on the final journey, but they had neither weapons nor provisions. Thralls were used to getting along without either.

They had worried about how the last one of them to die would get buried. They should have been glad they were able to depart and hobble along together wherever they were now.

After visiting a relative's distant farmstead, Geire, Svein, and his mother traveled the same forest road that, a little farther away, led down to the ferry crossing. Geire was thinking of offering his arm and his weapon to some chieftain needing a warrior. Svein and his mother would probably get by in town somehow.

They ran into Tora at a bend in the road, and both parties stopped in surprise. Tora's black eyes passed from one to another, from the woman and the lanky boy, with their hard eyes and faces, to the graying warrior. She looked at him almost with trust and asked to pass by.

The chieftain's wife felt like she recognized the girl but couldn't remember from where. Svein remembered her from the harbor in town, and to him the road, the forest, and everything else immediately lit up, becoming joyful and more pleasant. His only fear was that she would disappear into the forest, never to be seen again.

Geire looked at the girl in wonder too, thinking at first that she was a forest being. The road she was on led into the wasteland, and many things could happen to her there. There was something strange about her, and he asked where she was going and why.

She didn't answer his questions, just asked if they had seen her father, the smith. You don't run into many people in the forest; those wandering around in there preferred getting out of each other's way if they were equally matched. If not, the stronger would strike down the weaker and at the very least would rob him of everything he owned. Geire explained all this to the girl and urged her to turn around and return with them before night fell. She was well-dressed, but her face was thin and her bare legs were covered with scratches. Her fingers were stained blue from berries; she must have been on the road for days.

It wasn't until Geire said he was sure her father was already back in town that she turned around and reluctantly followed them. Svein walked sideways the whole time so he could look at her, and his eyes were happy and gentle. But his mother felt a vague dislike for the girl and would have preferred to see her continue into the forest. What did she have to do with them? She with her black eyes and troll-like hair would probably bring them nothing but trouble.

They reached the shore the same evening. The boatman smiled happily when he saw Tora; he said she was like her father, and should have been a boy instead when she ran away. He said too that her mother had come down to look for her every time a boat came in. She was going to be so happy.

There still had been no sign of Holme, but he'd show up. Probably very soon, the boatman said, trying to console Tora when he saw the tears on her cheeks. Clenching her teeth, she said nothing, and she wouldn't look at anyone in the boat.

But the hunger crisis had been averted for the moment; several boats had brought grain and livestock from the other side of the sea. So said the boatman, turning his head to look toward the town. Some figures were standing by the landing, but only a practiced eye could distinguish them from the pilings in the harbor.

Tora sat alone in the prow, and Svein leaned to one side so he could see her from behind the oarsman. It didn't bother him that she didn't look back. He wished there were enemies on the shore so he could show her how he could wield a sword. When he got bigger, he'd search her out and take care of her.

But his mother grimly pondered the memories and feelings the girl had awakened in her. Not even in front of the ashes of her burned home had she felt as strongly about the past as now. With longing and grief she thought of that time when her first husband had been alive, when they had had more than enough warriors and thralls. She had been young and beautiful then, but the long period of thralldom in a foreign land had made her old and ugly.

Among those waiting on the shore, she saw a beautiful middle-aged woman whose troubled face lit up at the sight of the girl in the boat. The bitter woman had a flash of intuition when she saw the familiar shape. The woman had to be the thrall Ausi, who had done her so much harm. The boatman willingly answered her questions and told her that the woman's husband and the girl's father was called Holme and was the best smith in town.

Her first thought was to scream out her discovery and demand justice and revenge. But that would accomplish nothing here where no one knew her or her past. She must wait and consult with Geire. The boatman had spoken in a respectful tone about Holme and his family, and many might be on their side here in town.

Sick with anger, she watched the mother and daughter walk onto a street, but the daughter walked ahead without turning around or acknowledging what her mother said. She seemed like her father even in that regard. All three of them were still her thralls, and when the time was right she would demand to have them back. Or else they'd have to pay a heavy ransom. She was glad they'd brought the girl back with them.

Svein watched Tora for a long time, then slowly followed the same road. From the street corner, he saw the mother vainly try to get her daughter to come into the house. She walked on and the mother followed, crying. Svein smiled to himself, thinking that she was doing the right thing. He could see in her eyes that she was enraged at her mother. Then his own mother called to him, and he fixed in his mind where the girl had gone. He'd come back later and look for her.

Geire was surprised by his sister's impassioned report, impressed that this strange smith, time after time, kept crossing his path. If he was guilty of everything he was accused of, then his end couldn't be far off. Here in town, justice was administered at the assembly, and each accused man had the right to defend himself. The law of the forest was different. However, his sister would go to the assembly to demand her rights. No one had bought the thrall family's freedom; they belonged to her as long as they lived.

They would go to the town's chieftain, lay their case before him, and ask for help. He would surely advise them what to do, and the fugitive thralls would be punished and returned to their owner.

I n Holme's smithy, the work went on without him. He had told the smiths more than once that the smithy belonged to all of them. If he or someone else left, the others should carry on. But the work didn't have the same life in it; it would stop for long stretches while the smiths sat talking about everything that had happened and what was likely to come. Holme had fled for his life, but they were sure they'd hear from him somehow. They talked bitterly about Ausi, who had gone back to the Christians again even though they were her husband's enemies. They hoped that Tora had found her father on the mainland; they knew the dangers that awaited a child by herself in the forest.

White eyes and teeth gleamed in the happy blackened faces when Holme's daughter walked into the smithy. All of them liked her although she was generally as quiet and stern as her father. They knew too that, like Holme, she had a good heart and was enraged by all injustice and cruelty perpetrated against the defenseless.

She walked in and sat down with them, answering their eager questions with tearful eyes. Ausi stood outside the door, not daring to go in, ignored by them all. With sorrow and bitterness she heard the blackened smiths comforting her daughter, the oldest one stroking her hair, saying she could stay with them until either they heard from Holme or he came back. Ausi felt bitterness again toward Christ, the one who supposedly was the god of love, but who had taken Holme and Tora's love from her. The Christians had promised her that everything would be all right if she was patient and trusted in Christ, but that was a little hard to believe now.

She hesitantly called her daughter's name and was ready to give the Christians up, but no one answered her or came out. She lingered awkwardly there until she heard the bell ringing from the tower. She walked toward it, thinking that Christ still might help if He had a little time. She had given half of all the silver they owned to the church when the Christian priests suggested she should, but things were none the better for it. The other half had to be there when Holme came back.

From the doors of the smithies and the craftsmen's sheds, people watched her, and she could sense that they weren't friendly looks. Everyone knew what had happened and most of them were on Holme's side. Only the rich merchants were partial to Christ and held a grudge against Holme. They secretly considered him just another thrall because he got along so well with them and was always thinking of their welfare.

Ausi was upset by the idleness that had beset her since Holme and Tora had left. The Christians had told her that she should be walking among the heathens, witnessing about Christ and all He could do, but she had refused. Holme would be even more provoked, and she still wasn't so sure that Christ could do so much more than the wooden gods could. If the first stranger who had talked about Christ were still alive, everything would be different. He believed in a different Christ. The summer day she was given to Him at the baptism on the shore was filled with sunshine and promise. But that priest had been tortured to death just like Christ himself.

Suddenly she stopped. Something was lighting up and expanding inside her, and she was breathing heavily. She saw everything now. The stranger had been Christ Himself, come to earth once more. He was as gentle and good as the sun; he tolerated everything without complaint, and he wanted nothing for himself. He endured death without fear. He was Christ, and he had come back for her sake.

She felt her head spin with happiness, and she could clearly see the image of the stranger in front of her after many years of darkness. Next to him, the monks in town now seemed like dark, insignificant human beings. They thought about themselves like everyone else; they calculated and apportioned just like everyone else. They behaved as if Christ were an invisible, powerful wooden god, but she alone knew Him as He was. Only she knew how fine, gentle, and strong. He was both within her and walking beside her. He would take care of everything that troubled her, and she would talk with Him about Holme and Tora.

That was what the stranger had meant when he said that he'd either return or send someone else in his place. And she also knew then why no one had claimed that he was a powerful man in his homeland as people had said about his imitators. He didn't want to be one. She alone knew where he came from and where he had gone.

The two Christian priests stared in surprise at her beaming face as they listened to her story. On the way to the church, she had become more and more convinced that some voice had clarified everything for her, and she told the priests that. But they weren't happy with her; instead, their eyes narrowed and repudiated her. They told her that she had heard the voice of the devil and that she should be on guard. How could a heathen woman like herself presume to think that Christ would reveal Himself to her? The stranger had been sent by the devil to deceive the heathens before Christ's true heralds got there.

But she didn't believe them; they couldn't put out the light she had so recently felt lit inside her. She reminded them of the numerous similarities between Christ and the stranger, of everything they had said about what Christ had experienced and suffered. Why hadn't any of those who had followed him been sacrificed like him or Christ, she asked, looking at them with penetrating eyes?

But they gave their usual answer that their time hadn't come yet and that Christ alone decided over life and death. That the stranger was killed was his own doing because he was a false teacher, not sent by Christ.

Still Ausi wouldn't give in. Instead she pondered what other evidence there might be for the stranger's being Christ. She remembered what the priests had said about Christ's never having been near a woman. She triumphantly told the men standing before her about the still summer day when the stranger had come to her from town while Holme was away. That her breasts had been exposed, and that she wouldn't have resisted him that warm, lonely day. But he hadn't stayed with her; no one would have stopped him, but he fled from her and disappeared into the forest. Wasn't that doing what Christ Himself would have done?

Again the priests felt her eagerly questioning eyes directed at them. They exchanged looks several times during her story but didn't interrupt her. They realized that the heathens didn't fight very hard against the claims of the flesh if they felt attracted to each other. They understood too that the temptation had been considerable for their unknown predecessor. There was something intensely alluring about the woman before them, and she was still in her prime.

In her stubborn, luminous look they saw such a staunch belief in the experience she had imagined that they refrained from admonishing her any further. With time, she'd forget all this and become like the others. The dead monk's words and deeds would fade away before the preaching of the living.

In truth the woman's faith unnerved them, and each secretly wished that his own were as strong and joyous although not as sinful as hers. They told each other that if Christ were to come, she'd open her arms and want to give Him everything. Oblivious of her soul, she would offer Him her body.

And they cursed themselves for the strange feelings these thoughts aroused—a vague jealousy of the stranger who had been sacrificed, but not before carving indelible marks in this beautiful, warm, heathen woman. It was perfectly clear to them that they would never be looked at with such eyes, hers or anyone else's. The heathens who had come to them had other reasons for coming. One was greedy and wondered if Christ could improve his business; another wanted a cure for some disease, refused to believe before he felt completely well, and afterwards thought he didn't need any god at all. And all of them still secretly worshipped the ancient wooden gods. The moment God's word stopped being preached, it would be forgotten and the wooden gods would reclaim their dark empire. But for years, this woman had carried an image of Christ in her heart, a false image because it hadn't come from them.

When Ausi was taken to the assembly, she thought it was because of what Holme had done. They wanted to find out what she knew and perhaps let her hear him condemned as an outlaw. She didn't recognize the hard-faced woman standing nearby with a boy and a grizzled warrior.

Without understanding at first what this was all about, Ausi heard parts of her past, from her period of thralldom forward, dragged into the light of day. She saw the warrior pointing at her before he showed the judges that the lanky boy couldn't turn his head. She had seen the boy before and again felt a vague apprehension.

Everything they said was true, and when the gray-haired chieftain who was the judge asked her, she confirmed it. She saw a smug twinkling in the unfamiliar woman's stony face, and then it all became clear to her. They were her old masters intruding into her life again—now when Holme wasn't around to help. Before she fully understood her misfortune, she felt some satisfaction over the chieftain's wife having grown so old and ugly.

The people round about sat listening in silent surprise about her past. That the respected smith and his wife were runaway thralls. A number of them nodded their heads, recollecting Holme's always being with the thralls, protecting them. Now they knew why.

Ausi heard herself and Tora condemned to return to their masters and Holme condemned as an outlaw. He wasn't there and they didn't want him back as a thrall. After taxes and other costs had been subtracted, everything they owned would go to the masters—the son and the mother—to compensate for what the masters had lost while the thralls were on the loose for so many years.

She looked around for someone to help, but everyone averted his eyes. The chieftain wouldn't look at her, and the two monks standing nearby conversed quietly and did nothing for her. After the judgment had fallen, the old chieftain's wife came up and, hissing a few words dripping with hate, grabbed her violently by the arm. There was nothing but silence as she was dragged off to be a thrall in her own house.

The two women, Geire, and Svein, walked between the heathen temple and the Christian church, but everything was quiet and still there too. The church was closed, but in the door of the shrine she saw the wooden god stare rigidly at her. Neither Christ nor the wooden god wanted to help her. Only Holme would, the one she had harmed, but he was far away and knew nothing about this.

The chieftain's wife looked Holme's house over with satisfaction and decided where everyone's place would be. Geire's cheekbones were red under his beard, and he mumbled that he'd be on his way soon. He wanted neither to have any part of the thralls' possessions nor to live in their house. All he had wanted was justice for his sister. Svein too looked angrily at his mother and wouldn't respond to her words, tender though they became whenever she turned to him.

Ausi took her place by the door, once the keys to the lock Holme had forged were taken from her. The chieftain's wife rifled greedily through the family's possessions, clothes, jewelry, and ornaments that Holme had made or bartered for. She let the silver nuggets and foreign coins run between her fingers while Geire, clearing his throat in disgust, got up, and left. Svein was keenly interested in some swords and spears of unusual shape hanging on the low wall above the master's place.

Then came Ausi's turn. Her mistress took her own raggedy clothes off and ordered Ausi to trade with her. Ausi obeyed, thinking that her years as a respected and free housewife had been just a dream. Everything was as before—worse than before—without Holme, Tora, and her thrall companions.

Ausi's new-found joy couldn't fully compensate for what had befallen her that day, but as she lay on the floor listening to the other three breathing quietly on the sleeping benches, some of it returned. When her lot was this hard, she was almost like Christ and the stranger. They would probably notice and send help. He would come himself or send someone in his place, but not one of the priests. The best thing would be if He found Holme and let him know how things stood. Happily she imagined how terrified her owner, Geire, and the boy would be if Holme suddenly appeared in the doorway, huge, silent, and deadly. No judges or swords would help them then.

She also found it strange that neither Christ nor the wooden gods had destroyed Holme, since he had despised and persecuted both them and their servants. Could it be that they liked Holme despite all that, just as the most powerful warriors did, eyeing him with a certain respect, not daring to treat him as they did the other thralls? That was probably the case, and it was to the benefit of all three of them—Holme, Ausi, and Tora.

Perhaps things were not as the priests had told her. They could have misunderstood things despite their being priests. Christ really should go straight to Holme and talk with him frankly, man to man. No crying, ringing bells, or sacrifices. They could be friends, and with Holme on his side, Christ could feel secure about His church and followers.

The chieftain's wife had locked up all the weapons and had gone to sleep with the keys still on her. She was probably afraid that Ausi would try to kill them in their sleep. But it would be better if Ausi herself were dead and gone. As long as she, Holme, or Tora were alive, their old masters would hate them and hurt them whenever they could. The woman had growled at Ausi that the settlement had been ravaged and burned by thieves, she'd been taken into thralldom in a foreign land, and had recently been saved by a raid there. She said further that Holme's evil power had been the cause of all that misfortune. But he had no evil power, he who was so good to all thralls and all the oppressed.

Ausi was also thinking that there was an end now to her going to the Christian buildings and yard for the worship services. That didn't feel so bad now that she knew more about Christ than the monks did. He would come straight to her once more, but this time she'd be able to recognize Him and not look at Him as she would an ordinary man. Then He'd hear all about her, Holme, and Tora. She wouldn't even keep quiet about the thing called sin. He'd listen with the gentle smile she remembered so well and then destroy all their enemies and reunite her with Holme and Tora. Later on, when they had been dead and buried for a while, He would raise all three of them and ascend with them into heaven.

In her heart, she was thankful that Holme hadn't been at the assembly. Many would have fallen before his rage, but in the end, he would have fallen before the swords of the many warriors. The chieftain's wife would have been even happier if she could have seen him dead. She couldn't really feel safe from him now; she spent the whole first day in his house listening and trembling whenever anyone passed by outside. You could also hear in her voice that she was uneasy, even though several times she assured them that he had received his just punishment and was no longer walking among the living.

But Ausi paid no attention to her; she knew Holme was alive and would come back. She felt it in her heart and so could endure her new thralldom. With Christ and Holme living peacefully together within her, who could do her harm?

She could hear the wind outside among the buildings, moving heavily the way it did just before a rain. A cold draft blew in under the door, and once a pig came right up to it, rooting and snorting. She was in an uncomfortable position and had to turn over, but maybe Holme had it even worse. Christ, of course, had once had to sleep with a stone or a clump of grass for a pillow. And she was weaker and more sinful than He or Holme; why should she have it any better?

But Holme wouldn't be very nice when he learned that she was sleeping as a thrall by her own door.

She had been without a man for many days now and was feeling an unquenchable longing. Finally she fell asleep, imagining alternately her dark-complected Holme and the light-complected stranger next to her breast. After a while Geire woke up, raised his head, and listened to her regular breathing. Then he looked toward his sister's bed, sighed, and laid his head down again. For a long time, he visualized the thrall's beautiful face and ripe body. But she wouldn't be receptive to him because he had done her harm. Besides, she was the kind who'd only give herself to the man who had claimed her heart.

A couple of days later one of the Christian priests came to her. He told her solemnly that what had happened was punishment for her grave sin of calling a false teacher, sent by the devil, Christ. She should bear her punishment with humility and gratitude because it came at such an early stage of the sin. That was a sign that she hadn't been cast away from the face of God for eternity.

But something inside Ausi told her that his words were empty and that he was talking about some other Christ. The real one would come to her, not send someone like him. She felt almost happy when the chieftain's wife interrupted the priest and started loudly telling the story of all the evil Holme and his family had inflicted upon her.

Svein wandered down among the smithies looking for Tora. He had seen her go that way and thought she might still be there. He finally caught a glimpse of her walking into the biggest smithy, a wooden bucket in hand. Soon afterward the sledgehammers stopped clanging.

He sneaked up to the door and looked in. A number of big smiths were sitting around a table eating. Tora was standing by the hearth looking into the fire, blowing on it occasionally with a hand bellows. Before he knew it, Svein was standing there inside the smithy, all the smiths' eyes directed at him.

The judgment against Ausi was already known throughout the town, but even if the smiths thought she deserved it, they couldn't stand Holme's former owner moving into his house and taking everything he owned. They laughed scornfully at Svein's message that the daughter should join her mother to begin her thralldom. No one would lay a hand on her as long as they could lift a hammer or an ax.

They recognized the stiff-necked youth and looked at him in surprise. How did he dare come here? He paid them no heed but instead stared at Tora, his blue eyes twinkling with admiration. The smiths stopped eating, waiting to see what was going to happen.

When Tora first caught sight of him, she looked away immediately, her mouth drawing into a scornful smile. Then she dropped the bellows, picked up a handful of soot, and walked up to the boy who was standing there motionless, following her with his eyes. He didn't even try to protect himself when she threw the soot in his face; he just kept staring at her as if he were under a spell.

The smiths' roaring laughter brought him out of it, and he wiped the soot from his eyes. He looked at his dirty hand, and his face became hard and angry. He took a step or two toward Tora, who had returned to the firepit, but one of the smiths stuck his foot out, and Svein fell flat on his face on the black floor. When he came to again, he was lying outside the smithy with a sooty and bloody face.

Sobbing with rage he got up and shook his fists defiantly at the smiths even though he felt great fear of their strength. When he grew up, he'd come back and take the girl by force if she wouldn't come of her own free will. He had a right to her; she belonged to him and his mother.

Ausi was pleased when he came home and his mother pried out of him how he had been treated at the smithy. She remembered the uneasiness she had felt when she had seen the stiff-necked boy a number of years ago. Now she was glad that Tora had mighty defenders when she herself was powerless and Holme was gone. Holme could take credit for this; without the respect and friendship the smiths felt for him, they wouldn't have cared what happened to his daughter.

But Ausi's owner could see she was gloating. She yanked her by the hair and listed the things she'd do to Tora once she had her in her clutches. Next year they would go back and rebuild the settlement; her son would be the chieftain and the thralls would be closely watched so they couldn't escape anymore to pretend they were freemen and as good as their masters.

Ausi was thinking, however, that Holme would soon come to her rescue and avenge all these wrongs. Christ would give him the message soon. As she watched her owner pluck her blonde hair from her fingers, she fantasized about the moment when Holme would appear in the door. Everything would change in that instant and peaceful, happy years would return. Holme and Tora would learn to know the real Christ and they wouldn't scorn Him because He was as good and true as they were.

She hoped Holme wouldn't take long. There was a great deal of malice in the mother's and son's eyes and it was flashing at her and Tora.

A number of starving vagabonds had come to Holme during the winter and spring; he had given them what he could and seen them on their way. A couple had stayed for a few days to help with the construction, and a younger woman had chosen not to go on but instead had stayed and shared his bed until a man came and got her. The man wasn't angry; he talked calmly with Holme about the woman. He hadn't been able to keep her from leaving when there was no more food in his house. But things were better now and he had searched the area for her for a long time. He said too that if he had found another woman, Holme could have kept the first one.

But Holme let them go their way and was relieved when they disappeared down the path. The woman looked back frequently, crying into her arm. She had worked hard and willingly, perhaps believing it was for her own benefit. Her husband was no bigger than she was and had a scraggly beard. There weren't many women around; that's why he had travelled so far looking for her. He had gotten her back in more supple and beautiful condition than when she had left. Holme thought as he watched them go that if she had gone to any man other than himself, the two men would have had to fight over her.

That evening he paced restlessly around the empty house. He missed the woman's shy smile when he came in the door and now and then he wished he had held onto her.

He had doubled the size of his house and had weather-proofed it with mud. He had also sown larger areas than the thralls had, thinking that there should be grain enough for several during the winter. Before the woman had shown up, his longing for Ausi and Tora had been so great that he had geared up to return but had controlled himself because everything had to be ready first. They would buy cows, pigs, and iron for tools with the silver in the chest.

One day, when the golden grain was swaying on the slope, he saw a small boat approaching shore. He walked down the path, ax in hand, and the man in the boat rested hesitantly on his oars a little ways out. Then he let out a surprised yell and rowed eagerly in. He called Holme by name and ran up to him, his face glowing with happiness.

It was one of the starving thralls from town who had helped divide up the Christian grain. Holme couldn't quite recognize the emaciated man but was glad that he might get some news about his family now anyway. The thrall hadn't been on his journey for very many days. He immediately told Holme how he had taken the boat from a farmstead where rather than giving him something to eat they had set dogs on him.

He ate the whole time he talked. Holme was relieved his daughter was in good hands, but when the thrall told about Ausi's new enslavement, he got up and walked to the door so the thrall couldn't see his face. When he turned around again, he began taking stock of weapons, and the thrall got uneasy at the signs of imminent departure. He certainly would have preferred to stay there where there was both food and safety.

The thrall talked on about how peaceful the town had been during the winter and spring once the king had sent grain and meat. But the black blight had come back again on the wind and settled on the ripening barley. It had to be the fertility god who had sent this misfortune, and everywhere people were beginning to see that he must be appeased if they didn't want famine to ravage the entire land.

The thrall also told Holme that the Christians had gained many followers among the wealthy merchants. But everyone else, craftsmen and thralls, were convinced that the Christians were responsible for the blight. If they were killed or driven off, the blight would vanish with them and everything would be like it was before. But the monks were under the king's protection, and no one dared lift a hand against them.

Holme said nothing, but when his weapons were ready, he found an ax and spear for the thrall. He hid the leftover grain and let the pigs out. The two men walked around carefully examining the grain swaying and whispering in the wind, but there was no sign of blight. The thrall looked at the crude god on the stone and said he'd guard the grain and everything else at the settlement. No Christians were provoking him out here in the woods.

They left the next morning after Holme refused to let the thrall stay and keep an eye on things until Holme could return with his family. Deep behind the thrall's bushy eyebrows, Holme sensed a hope lurking that Holme would not come back at all. He knew that Holme's life was worthless among the freemen, and he could be the new owner of this beautiful and peaceful place beyond the forests. Going to town could mean his life too.

But Holme was adamant, causing him to fall silent and give up the hope that had momentarily sprung up. Like most people, he felt a fear inside that Holme could do more than other men. It was rumored that no weapon could harm him. But he could kill a man with his bare hands.

Thin and scraggly, the thrall plodded along through the marshy ground, over the ridge by the cave, and then up to the pathless woods. Silent and huge, Holme walked beside him, answering his ingratiating words with a grumble. They walked toward town and perhaps toward death.

The last night Geire spent in Holme's house, he could no longer restrain his craving for the thrall woman lying on the floor by the door. Day after day he had watched her tantalizing face and gentle movements and couldn't get her out of his mind. He thought about how long it had been since he had had a woman and now he was leaving on another long journey.

He listened to her even breathing, thinking that if he sneaked up on her, she couldn't wake up to defend herself until it was too late. His sister was sleeping too, and if she woke up it would be awkward, but not dangerous. She wouldn't say a word about it.

He hesitated a long time, but the night was drawing to a close. Through the vent in the ceiling he had just heard the town guard challenge an early visitor. He himself would be gone soon after the sun had come up.

Ausi was asleep and was unaware of it when the bearded warrior sat down on the floor beside her. She was lying on her side and had her garment on top of her like a blanket. For a moment Geire thought this act was beneath him, but through the darkness he saw a bare white shoulder and couldn't force himself to get up again.

He had imagined her sleeping on her back; now she might wake up too quickly and be harder to handle. He slowly put his hand on her hip and carefully pushed her over on her back. Her breathing stopped for a moment, and he thought she'd wake up. But then she turned her head to the side and slept more deeply in her new position. Geire carefully pulled the clothes away from her, the clasps softly jingling. Someone was walking by outside, although it was still night. The footsteps stopped and Geire hesitated, waiting until he heard them continue down the street.

It had never been any use for a thrall woman to scream for help when a man took her, but Ausi fought with silent fury. She couldn't throw the weight off her, but she could heave it back and forth. Panting heavily, the warrior grumbled in bitter disappointment.

The struggle woke the chieftain's wife, and when it became clear to her what was happening, she whispered an angry order in the midst of everything for Ausi to stop resisting. As the woman drew closer, Ausi could hear her whispering harsh, scornful words that she should be glad to have a man other than her black-haired thrall. The warrior said nothing, but Ausi could feel his coarse beard on her neck, and he was panting more and more heavily. On the other hand, she still had some strength left and began to hope she might save herself.

But then she felt a pair of hard hands on her arms; they yanked her hands back, away from the rapist's chest, so she couldn't fend him off any longer. Her arms were pulled back over her head and pinned to the floor by the chieftain's wife, who kept hissing insults. The warrior finally vanquished her weakening legs, and the battle was over. The sky had begun to turn gray through the smoke vent, and the table and benches emerged from the darkness. On one of them lay Svein, his eyes closed and breathing deeply.

When the struggle on the floor had wakened the chieftain's wife and she had seen Geire's empty bed, she was angry that he had lowered himself to seek the loathsome thrall. But when she heard the fierce resistance and realized that Ausi was doing all she could to get free, she quickly changed her mind. Did that thrall still dare oppose her masters?

And when Geire and she together had subdued her, she had gleefully listened to Ausi's sobbing, rhythmically broken by the man's thrusts. She felt Ausi's arms relax, and when the man got up, averting his face, Ausi had turned toward the door and lay still. The chieftain's wife whispered a few scornful remarks and returned to her bed, but Geire put on his clothes in the first light of day shining through the smoke vent. After getting his weapons, he walked to the door and pulled back the bar, stepped over Ausi, and disappeared.

Svein had awakened because something in the room was moving. He sensed immediately that it had nothing to do with him, but a curious excitement took hold of him, sending warm waves through his body. He looked toward the two figures he could hear breathing on the floor and listened excitedly.

He could make out something white emerging from the darkness, and for an instant he could see the entire female body. Then it was hidden by something dark and the fight began. He heard his mother wake up and join in and he sat up on his bed to see better. He could see the white legs flailing and hands grabbing at them to hold them still. All three were panting and no one noticed him. When the battle was over and only weak sounds could be heard, he sank back on his bed, terrified by the new things he felt inside. It wasn't what had happened on the floor that had kindled the fire within him — he had imagined himself and the woman's daughter in the same position. That's how it should be someday, otherwise he didn't want to go on living. Instantly he thought that it was shameful for such old people to do what they had done — that belonged to the young. He didn't want to look at them, so he shut his eyes and kept breathing deeply when they got up. But it would be fun to see how the thrall looked — to see if she had been changed much by all this. Geire left and that was for the best; he didn't want to look at him anymore.

But now he and his mother had to find a way to get the girl. She belonged to them, and he yearned for her so much his whole body ached. His mother had always tried to get him whatever he wanted; and he wanted the girl from the smithy.

Several farmsteads lined the road leading out of the forest toward town. Once they had housed large herds of animals, but now there were only solitary cows or pigs. Most of the animals had died during the year of famine.

The grain fields were swaying in the warm breeze, but the thrall triumphantly showed Holme that the black blight, which had come on the wind, was

clinging to the ears. It had consumed the insides so that the empty ears rat-
tled delicately. A dour man there predicted that those who survived the winter
wouldn't see another summer since there were no animals for them. He shook his
fist at the town and cursed the Christians. Then he took Holme and the thrall to
a stone, full of small hollows, to show them he had never stopped smearing those
hollows with fat. But the fertility god must be angrier than ever before; nothing
seemed to help.

He offered them some of his bread, light and dry with bran, but they had
their own provisions. When he heard that they were going to town and were
embittered about the Christians, he picked up his weapons to go along. His wife
and child looked mutely at him when he turned around to tell them what they
ought to do while he was gone.

Holme was thinking that what he wanted to do in town he would do alone
as always, but he couldn't keep anyone else from going there. There was no grain
to gather, no animals to tend; there was nothing else for a farmer to do than take
his weapons from the wall.

The new man asked them to take a detour with him to his relatives' farmstead. It was a day's journey, and there they found three grim men and blight
on the grain. Then there were six men walking toward town, and the group
increased little by little. They all considered Holme the leader although no one
had chosen him and he didn't say much himself. Several knew him from town
and a few had bartered with him.

Before dawn of the third day, the group was standing on the shore, and the
oarsman, who had been sleeping in the boat, stared at them in consternation. If
all of them wanted to go across, he'd be rowing all morning. But there were several boats by the shore, and most of them would have to row themselves across.
He didn't often see so many silent, well-armed men showing up at once during
peace time.

When he caught sight of Holme and noticed that all the others turned to
him, he knew that danger was in the offing and he'd have to proceed cautiously
when he reached town with the first group.

Holme was among those taking a seat in his boat; the rest manned the other
boats and followed them. In the middle of the lake, the oarsman was ordered
to change course to the shore west of town. He was thinking that when they
reached shore he'd run to town with the news. They wouldn't be able to catch
him in the short stretch to the nearest town gate.

But that changed too. Holme said a few words and the oarsman found himself surrounded by stern men while the boat was rowed back to fetch those on
the opposite shore. Holme himself disappeared into the darkness toward town.
The guard at the gate peered sleepily and disagreeably at him but didn't stop him
from passing through.

Holme walked past his house and listened for a moment. Inside a man sat
on the floor beside the sleeping Ausi, listening to the steps outside. Had Holme

returned a short time later, he would have heard the panting and struggling that began on the other side of the door as soon as his steps had died away. Then many things would have been different for many people.

The smithies were silent but he greedily breathed in the smell of soot and iron. He walked to the oldest smith's house and knocked on the door. It took a while for the smith to appear, ax in hand. He immediately recognized the massive figure standing in the darkness and let out a happy yell, put his ax down and opened the door wide.

Holme looked around eagerly when he entered, and with a smile the smith laid a few sticks on the fire so that it came to life. Tora was sleeping on a bench, and her father sat beside her, watching her silently. A moment later the smith saw Holme's cheeks glisten with moisture he brushed off on the sleeve of his shirt. Then Holme softly told the smith what was going on and asked him to wake the others.

While Holme waited and the smith's wife busied herself by the fire, Tora woke up and saw her father in the firelight. However, she had seen the vision in her dreams several times, and so was afraid to move. But then he turned toward her, and the two pairs of dark eyes met. She leaped up with a scream and threw her arms around his neck. She clung to him, just as she had as a child when he had found her in the garbage pile with the dogs and pigs. Her eyes twinkled with joy and pride as she looked at her father and complained about how the Christians had treated her. Neither of them mentioned Ausi.

Holme sent the smiths all over town to call thralls and craftsmen together who wanted to join them. It would be daylight soon, and before then they had to assemble so quietly and inconspicuously that no one sounded the alarm or closed the gates. Holme went back to the shore with the smith and Tora.

The last of the boats were out on the lake, and the shore was swarming with men. When they were all there, they discussed what to do, and it was decided that the guards at the gate would have to be struck down if they wouldn't take their side against the Christians.

Dawn was just beginning to break when the group approached the rampart near the shore. Men kept coming, wild, emaciated men in rags who had been sleeping in the surrounding areas—thralls who had been driven off when the famine came. They crowded happily around Holme, and his face softened for an instant.

The guard saw a couple of men approaching and took position by the bar to get a better look at them. He had no idea that long files of additional men were sneaking along the rampart. At the same time that he challenged those directly in front of him, he found himself surrounded by silent, armed men who immediately disarmed him. But the other guard ran along the rampart gangway, yelling for someone to sound the alarm.

Meanwhile, the intruders kept heading toward the smithies. Many windows opened up a crack, and surprised faces peeked out as they passed. Such a strange troop had never moved through the town at that time of the day before. Heading the group was the huge master smith and his daughter, followed by many nameless, well-armed men, and finally by ragged, emaciated thralls armed with clubs and axes. Many of the townspeople began gathering the things together they'd need when they fled to the fortress, although no alarm had been sounded and no order had come from the chieftain.

But people were hurrying toward the smithies from everywhere, and when some of them met some others, they'd talk in low, excited voices, then join the others. A message was sent to the heathen priest across from the Christian church to light the sacrificial fire at once. The underside of a long cloud bank in the east gradually reddened—the time was near.

In the smithies, the thralls were handing out axes and spears, and rage and greed flashed from their eyes. The farmers watched them calmly and without disdain; working in the fields, on the lake, and in the forest had brought lord and thrall closer together than they could ever be with merchants and townspeople. The farmers wanted to strike down the enemy so that the fertility god would look on them again with favor, and then they wanted to go home. But the thralls were fighting for something to eat, for revenge for countless wrongs, and because they were miserable. Holme wanted to fight because he recognized the great injustice and abuse looming over anyone held in servitude.

Meanwhile, he was getting uneasy about what to do with all these men once their job was done. The farmers would surely return to their farmsteads, believing that there'd be a good crop then free of blight, but there were dozens of thralls. It would be just like the year before when they were starving and homeless, following him like dogs, waiting silently for him to do whatever he could do for them. But he couldn't do anything, and many of them would go back to their owners, if they survived the famine, and be whipped or even killed; others would disappear in the forests. Their skulls and bones would lie there turning white in the moss under some branch.

Then a thought hit him like a punch. They'd all do as he had—go back to the mainland and live on their own. He had broken free of thralldom; why couldn't they all do that? Land was everywhere, even some burned out, abandoned farmsteads where the fields were still in good shape. They could take thrall women with them as wives or get them later. But no one who had once been a thrall would ever have a thrall himself.

He was very happy about all this; it seemed so simple and right. All the thralls could walk the same road he had walked to freedom. Many of them were too feeble to make their way themselves, but the others could lend them a hand.

His chest expanded as he envisioned a land and people free of masters and thralls. Everyone was happy there, no one had to fight for his possessions or his life. The vision clouded over and disappeared, but he never forgot it. The thralls, who were brandishing their axes, clubs, and spears in the air around him as they were waiting to leave, saw his face soften toward them, but didn't know why.

He had no plan in mind when they marched up toward the Christian buildings and yard; he was used to letting the moment dictate its own terms. The merchants and maybe the town guard from the fortress would stand against them and the battle might be hard. When it was over, he would show the thralls the land he had just seen; then they'd fight to attain it even if he were gone.

From the chieftain's buildings and yard, the Christians saw the smoke billowing from the heathen shrine early that morning. Shortly, there was a loud knock on the door, and anxious men told them that Holme had come back with armed men to throw the town into chaos. Everything had been so peaceful and had gone so well for the Christians during the year he had been away.

But the chieftain wasn't concerned that some masterless thralls had gathered together at the smithies. Starved as they were, they'd be quickly defeated. Little unpleasantries like this came with hard times. But their leader would be captured and punished because he had dared come back to town. He would have been better off if he had never shown his face again. He always had been a troublemaker, unlike the others, both masters and thralls.

The rumor spread quickly in the early morning, and many people closed up their houses and sought protection with the chieftain. Among them were Ausi's mistress and her son, and they took their thrall along so she wouldn't escape. She wasn't aware yet that Holme had returned, but she had already decided to run away and find Holme on the mainland, even if she got lost on the way. She kept imagining the stranger there with her, Christ there with her, and kept asking him for help. The outrage perpetrated on her was now affecting her innermost being; for a long time she had belonged only to Holme and Christ, although He didn't care about women in that way.

But the chieftain's wife gave her no opportunity to escape. She was carefully guarded on the way. The streets were almost deserted, but from the smithies you could hear muffled voices and activity. A skinny, ragged thrall, his eyes glistening, came running toward them, rushed by, and kept going down toward the smithies. In front of them a richly clad merchant's family was hurrying toward the Christian yard.

When the chieftain's scout returned and told him how many thralls, farmers, and craftsmen were gathered together at the smithies, the chieftain sent a message to the town guard inside the fortress. They were powerful, seasoned warriors, and their presence would terrify the pack of thralls into submission or flight. It would never have to come to a fight.

The Christians were called together by ringing the bell, and a fisherman, out on the lake, rested on his oars, looking toward town as the peal rolled out over the reeds and water. He had never heard the Christian bells so early before. A ship was getting ready to leave the harbor, but that was all the life he saw. Maybe the priests were sailing home on it and were being honored by the bells.

The monotonous ringing was also a signal to Holme and his band. Several of the mainland farmers listened in surprise to the strange sound they were hearing for the first time. A couple of thralls had found some big horns, which they would try out. They looked each other in the eye, puffed out their cheeks, and played a tune they usually called each other with in the forests. Between the shrill blasts on the horn, the Christian bells tinkled out full, but thin, notes.

Holme had never imagined he'd return like this. He had thought he'd be alone as always when he had his showdown with his enemies. But when this band with him realized they'd have to drive out the Christians in order to survive, you couldn't stop them. In the end, they'd probably be condemned as outlaws, but the forests on the mainland were large and could protect as many as poured into them.

The horn blasts, when they rose shrill from the woods, answering each other morning and evening made him recall his days as a thrall. It was the song of the thralls, and so he let the two with the horns take the lead to the Christian yard. Over and over again, they sounded the song of the forest, used to call for help when wild animals attacked their cows or pigs.

The chieftain, the Christian priests, and a group of armed merchants were standing outside the Christian yard when the blaring horns approached from the side street, drowning out the bells. They saw Holme's band swarming, crowding together in front of the shrine of the wooden god, where the sacrificial smoke was constantly billowing, and where the smell of burnt flesh hung above the courtyard. The open area between the shrine and the church soon filled, and the thralls lowered the horns, panting from the strain of blowing them. At the same time the bells also stopped — the large one with a tentative, final clang — and all was quiet. Only the murmuring of praying voices inside the Christian church blended with the crackling of the heathen sacrificial fire.

For a moment, Holme had doubts about what to do. He had never been able to attack before he had been provoked. Nor could he assail with words. But from the silence behind him, one of the farmers from the blighted farmsteads came forward. He had talked at the assembly before, and he began speaking in a relaxed but powerful voice.

He levelled sharp words at the chieftain, who was clinging to the Christians and protecting them. The Christians and their followers had brought calamity on the land and the people by angering the ancient gods. For the second year, the blight had ravished the entire land, and it was being said everywhere that the Christians were at fault. They insisted that the Christians return to their home-land before something worse happened, and that their temple be torn down. Otherwise it would come to a fight and the farmers might just as well die that way as return to their farmsteads and starve to death with their families.

When he had finished, the others demonstrated he had spoken for them. Those with shields beat on them, as they would at the assembly; the others shouted and roared. The thralls stood silent, feeling as usual that no one had spoken for them. They all knew that Holme spoke best with his sledgehammer and fists.

When it grew quiet again, the chieftain came forward to show he wasn't afraid of them. In an angry voice he called them foolish heathens and ordered each and every one of them to go home. He would, however, answer the farmers' charges if the thralls were driven away and Holme was captured. How could freemen from the mainland allow themselves to be led by an outlaw and runaway thrall, he scornfully asked.

It was apparent that he had said the right things. The farmers seemed to wake up and look at each other and the thralls solemnly and awkwardly. They had always thought the smith was a respected man; they knew nothing about either his being a thrall or what he was guilty of. They had seen the noblest people in town doing business in Holme's smithy.

Holme sensed their hesitation and mounting disdain, and he felt a sense of relief. He hadn't known how he would relate to them; they had farmsteads and land; he couldn't plead their case. They were no part of him or the thralls. If they pulled out now, his hands would be free. Then it only concerned him and the thralls, and no one would even talk to thralls.

Just as before, not knowing what he should do made him furious. The thralls stood close behind him waiting for a word or action from him. The farmers were standing to one side, conferring amongst themselves. The chieftain turned directly to him, scornfully ordering him to give himself up and the thralls to disperse and return to their masters.

Holme felt his hesitation transform into a rage, which flowed out into his arms. His sledgehammer rose up and fell with a mighty blow against the nearest leg of the bell tower. It snapped like a straw, and the bells groaned, but the tower remained standing on its two other legs. Then the sledgehammer fell again, and the tower teetered to one side while the chieftain and those close by leaped out of the way. It quickly toppled over and the bells hit the ground with a muffled clang. The thralls laughed and began hacking wildly with their axes at the prostrate tower.

At the chieftain's signal, some Christian warriors advanced toward the thralls but soon had to retreat before the dense, wild group of axes, clubs, and spears. Seeing this, the chieftain gave a new order for someone to get the warriors who hadn't arrived yet from the fortress. The Christian priests hurried into the temple, followed by women and children; the doors were shut and the bar thrown before the thralls could stop it. While some of them followed the retreating warriors, deriding them, Holme's sledgehammer resounded against the church door and soon smashed it to bits. The thralls pressed in after him and the heathen priests urged them on with loud yells from the shrine.

One of the Christian priests headed straight down the aisle for Holme, carrying a cross in front of him while he called on his god in a loud voice. He barred the way, and Holme lowered his sledgehammer before the unarmed man. But one of the thralls stepped forward and hacked the priest down with his ax. He fell in the aisle, his cross beneath him, gasped a few more words to his god, and then lay still.[9]

When the other priest saw that their lives were in danger, he opened a small door behind the altar and let the terrified women and children crawl out. He waited until last, and no one cut him down, although he witnessed the thralls' axes smash savagely into the benches and Holme's sledgehammer fall on the altar with a deafening crash. The holy relics bounced high into the air and landed in the hands of thralls, who fondled them curiously. Then they were on top of him, the point of a spear thrusting through the door as he made his escape.

After the thralls had demolished everything in the church, they gathered again in the open area outside the shrine. It was almost deserted; most of the Christians had run for shelter with the chieftain. The farmers stood to the side, ignoring the victorious thralls' taunting yells. The warriors from the fortress came at a run, and the chieftain opened the gate as they approached. There weren't as many of them as there were thralls, but they were well-armed, seasoned men.

The chieftain talked with them a moment and pointed toward the band of thralls. The warriors turned around and looked at the emaciated, wild throng that stood mutely waiting. First there was Holme, whom they knew well and respected for his strength and skill; around him, the other smiths, who were nothing to play with; then the dense ranks of thralls, starving and mistreated. They would fight like wolves because they had nothing to lose and everything to gain. They were leaning on their axes, spears, and sledgehammers. The whole dismal band awaited the attack and wouldn't be scared off. If it came to a fight, it would cost many warriors their lives.

Many of the warriors secretly approved what had just happened at the Christian yard. They would gladly see Christ and his servants driven off or killed so that all would be as before. Holme and his men had done a good deed and the wooden gods would approve it.

The highest ranking warrior spoke with the chieftain and said that it was their duty to defend the town against foreign invaders, but they would have nothing to do with what they saw standing before them. Why had the thralls

---

[9] Rimbert reports Nithard's death as follows: "It happened, too, at this time, at the instigation of the devil, that the Swedish people were inflamed with zeal and fury, and began by insidious means to persecute Bishop Gautbert. Thus it came about that some people, moved by a common impulse, made a sudden attack upon the house in which he was staying, with the object of destroying it; and in their hatred of the Christian name they killed Nithard, and made him, in our opinion, a true martyr" (*Anskar*, chapter 17, p. 59). The second revolt led by Holme, then, has some historical validity, although Rimbert does not mention thralls or hunger as a motivating force. The revolt of the previous year, however, is Fridegård's fabrication.

been allowed through the gates and given the chance to arm themselves? And they hadn't attacked the town or anything attached to it, just the temple of the foreigners. The shrine stood there untouched. They would answer to the king for refusing to attack the thralls and craftsmen.

Meanwhile, everyone who had run for cover with the chieftain came out into the open again. A few of them picked up the dead Christian priest and carried him across the open area while the surviving monk followed along with head bowed. The chieftain's wife was at the front, her eyes full of hatred for Holme. She had expected to see him captured and cut down and couldn't understand why he was still standing there like a free and significant man. Svein stared at him too, unable to control a shudder before the figure of terror from his childhood. Ausi and the other thrall women were locked in a room so they couldn't join their husbands and brothers among the thralls.

For the second time, the chieftain ordered his warriors to clear the thralls from the building, but they pretended not to hear and assumed indifferent expressions. They looked around, yawned hugely, and talked softly among themselves. The sun was high over the lake, and the two bells lying in the grass between the two groups of people glistened in the sunlight. The heathen priests had moved the wooden god forward, and he stood, freshly smeared with blood, looking out over the open area with his angular face. But the Christian church was empty and gutted, and Christ hadn't struck down any of His enemies.[10] The warriors couldn't hide their delight over all that had happened without their help.

Rumor of the disturbance soon reached the harbor, and the ship that Geire had already boarded postponed its departure. Many of the warriors on board had relatives in town and didn't want to leave until they knew the final outcome.

Geire passed by Holme's closed house and walked toward the Christian buildings and yard. Everywhere he saw people going in the same direction, many of them carrying their valuables. In the distance, he could see the warriors racing down the slope by the fortress, fixing their clothes and weapons as they went. Something serious must have happened.

He was glad to see Holme at the head of the thralls. He wouldn't escape his punishment this time, and Geire's sister would finally be revenged. He stood listening to the exchange between the chieftain and the leader of the warriors and became afraid that the dangerous smith would get away. He walked up to the chieftain, explained briefly what had happened at his sister's farmstead, and asked if he could take revenge on Holme. He shrugged his shoulders at the warnings that came from several directions around him. But the chieftain was

---

[10] Contrary to Fridegård's account, Rimbert tells us that almost all involved in the attack on the Christians were soon punished (*Anskar*, chapter 18, p. 59).

glad for this solution—no one would deny an unimpeachable warrior his right to cut down an outlaw.

Geire took an ax in hand and walked across the open area as if he were going to chop down a dry tree. He drew his sword only against his equals. But he had forgotten that for thralls there were no rules of battle. They sensed what he wanted, and his disdainful bearing angered them. A threatening murmur rose from their ranks. The thralls knew that without Holme they were lost, and this warrior was coming at him with an ax. They forced their way past Holme, and Geire soon found himself surrounded. Hard, emaciated faces were all around him and he begrudgingly looked for help. But the warriors stood by indifferently, and the chieftain's threatening shout had no effect.

Geire raised his ax but it never touched a single thrall. A club struck him from behind, knocking him to the ground. A woman screamed shrilly, following that with a flood of insults for men who didn't dare take on thralls. Holme recognized the voice and soon, even the woman with her hard face. She was the one who had forced Ausi back into thralldom.

Through the brief silence that descended once Geire had been struck down came another shout, a woman's voice, distant but still strangely near. There was both hope and despair in the shout.

"Holme!"

The shout sounded twice, and the second time Holme distinctly heard it come from a small building at the back of the chieftain's property. Those standing closest to him got out of the way before he had even moved, and many scurried toward the doors to seek shelter from the silent smith, whom they had seen in their town for so many peaceful years. A path opened before him as he rushed toward the building, and the thralls clamored after him, trampling Geire under their bare feet.

But Holme didn't touch anyone fleeing from him, paying no attention to friend or foe. When he got to the building, he heard the shout once more, weaker this time, as if someone were trying to force Ausi to shut up. There was no back door and the front door was already barred from the inside. He was aware that the warriors had left the open area, but the farmers were still there, uncertain what to do.

For a moment he hesitated to smash open a building that belonged to the chieftain. But it was his woman who was screaming, and he wasn't concerned anymore about her having gone to the Christians. This was his beautiful Ausi, who shared his life with him and would to the end. They had made her into a thrall again, but there wouldn't be a third time. Behind him stood the mass of thralls, panting, expectant.

Indistinct sounds came in the window near Ausi and the other thrall women. They changed to wild shrieks and crashing when the thralls burst into the Christian building and smashed it. Ausi suddenly felt in her heart that Holme was nearby. So the new Christ had finally heard her voice and had told him. She laughed out loud with happiness and gratitude. The other women looked at her in terror and tried to quiet her down.

The uproar died away again, and the fear that Holme would leave without saving her seized her. She didn't consider for a moment that he might get killed. He was Holme, whom no one could vanquish, and now Christ was with him too, the real Christ. That was why she hadn't gotten any help when Geire raped her; Christ was with Holme and He couldn't be in two places at once, even though they said He could. Geire would answer for his actions when the time came.

The silence scared her; she listened but could hear only a weak murmuring and then a woman's scream. Ausi yelled as loud as she could twice. The other women thralls jumped on her and dragged her from the window, covering her mouth. In their stupidity, they believed that only inside the building were they safe from the dangerous man, who now laid in wait outside.

At the first resounding blow, she knew that Holme had come. It echoed exquisitely in her ears because she knew it was him. Christ was gentle, but when He wanted something like this put to rights, He had to use Holme.

Another door was smashed apart before the one trapping her caved in under a single blow. There was soon a huge hole in it, and an ax chopped wildly at the edges. The thrall women cowered in a corner, frightened to death, even though Ausi kept explaining to them that the man who had come wasn't dangerous for thralls. She stood in the middle of the floor, and when the last piece of the door fell, she rushed out and threw her arms around Holme, who looked at her, astounded and out-of-breath. The thralls around them laughed good-naturedly but were still jealous. Most of them didn't have a family.

Ausi's eyes searched apprehensively until she saw Tora standing among the thralls. She met her daughter's eyes, no longer hateful but not yet gentle either. It was difficult for Tora to forget the baptism that she had been subjected to, but now she might have her revenge. Holme stood with sledgehammer in hand; that surely meant that the enemies had been struck to the ground and all would be well. Holme and Tora hadn't spoken a word to her, but she felt they wanted her back. Otherwise, why had they come and rescued her?

During all the chaos, Holme hadn't once forgotten his responsibility for the crazed band following him wherever he went. There were many men, but few women. Numerous women thralls were crouching here, pressing themselves against the wall while they looked at him in terror. Most of them were young or middle-aged. It would be good if they followed along to the mainland. They'd be needed there.

He quickly explained to Ausi what he was thinking, and she was willing to talk with the women at once. Many of them didn't understand, but some of them came over reluctantly, once they heard about the impending freedom at their own farmstead. No one would violate them; they'd get their pick of the men who didn't have women.

Loaded down with valuables and provisions, and most of them chewing some kind of food, the band of thralls returned to the open area. The surviving priest stood alone outside his devastated church. He said in a loud, trembling voice that they would get their just reward for what they had perpetrated against Christ and His servants. Their days were numbered. A gust of wind passed over the shrine, engulfing him with sacrificial smoke. The heathens were pleased with that response from the ancient gods, who were not afraid of Christ. Many axes and spears were raised against the priest, but Holme said a few words and the band, still eating, filed past the priest on both sides, but he didn't budge from the spot.

Ausi turned around and watched him walk into his church through the broken door. He didn't fear for himself, but he still knew nothing about the real Christ—the one who felt like fire in your chest and made you run instead of walk.

No guard stood at the gate, and the thralls streamed out and down to the boats. The women and the feeblest men got to row across first. The chieftain might be in town gathering everyone together to stop the crossing. But two women, mother and daughter, refused to go without the dark, silent leader, whom they watched with love and admiration in their eyes.

But there wasn't a sound from town; it stood there in the quiet, late morning sun, and no trace of what had happened in the morning hours could be seen from the shore. A few figures were standing in the town gate, watching the thralls' departure. A group of warriors was standing on the rocks by the fortress, but they often stood there, looking in every direction. Maybe they were watching the thralls, happy they were leaving now that their work was done.

The first thing Geire noticed when he came to was a pair of bare, gray feet. He gradually remembered what had happened and figured out that he was lying between the feet of the thralls. They probably thought he was dead. If they knew he was still alive, they'd surely beat him to death like a dog with their clubs. His foggy brain tried to follow what was happening, but suddenly, all the gray feet around him took to flight, all rushing in the same direction, stomping and making an uproar, violently trampling him. Thralls! He had challenged them with an ax in his hand to exact revenge on their leader and scare the others away, but that's not how things had turned out.

Geire was used to punishing thralls and dogs with a stick. You didn't use a sword or a spear against them. But that smith had put a will in them along with the dangerous idea that they were just as good as their masters. That could do a lot of harm and cause a lot of unrest.

He saw the feet disappear behind the building after knocking the wind out of him, trampling heavily on his stomach and chest. Why didn't anyone drive the thralls from the chieftain's yard? Where would it all end if everyone yielded before them? It was like a bad dream, an impossibility—the thralls had taken up weapons and could harry wherever they wanted. If their leader at least were cut down, it would be easy enough to scare them into submission.

He tried struggling to his feet, but was still too exhausted. He could see the thralls returning, and walking beside the smith was his wife, the thrall Geire had raped that very morning. She still aroused that desire in him, despite his being half-dead. But she didn't see him and that probably saved his life. He wanted to stay alive so that someday he could get the upper hand in battle with the thralls and especially the dangerous smith.

When he finally got to his feet, his face covered with dried blood, the door to the chieftain's house was opened for him, but he walked by in disdain. He wanted to show them that he wasn't afraid of the thralls no matter what. He limped past those standing in the town gate and approached the shore. The last boats had just set out, but he yelled a threat across the water and then saw the smith rest on his oars. His wife talked animatedly to him and soon he rowed on without answering.

Before long half the town was on shore, talking about what had happened and what ought to be done. Thralls had never dared act this way before. What were things coming to? It wouldn't be pleasant for anyone running into them on the mainland after they arrived, flushed with victory.

Most of the smiths and craftsmen stayed in town rather than follow Holme and the thralls toward an uncertain fate on the mainland. They weren't afraid of the consequences; they weren't defenseless, and the town needed them, both for its own sake and for the sake of business. They would gladly have seen Holme stay and take over the largest smithy, but that could no longer happen after the morning's events. Maybe another time, when there was a new chieftain in the town.

A couple of the new women thralls were wary of the whistling, unfamiliar forest that they'd be hidden in, perhaps forever. They were allowed to turn back; no one tried to stop them, though numerous jealous and disappointed eyes watched them go. Even Ausi felt for a moment the old fear of disappearing into the woods for good. To that point, she had kept reminding herself about the new Christ who'd be there to help them with everything, He who understood Holme and worked along with him, although Holme still didn't realize it. He'd be there in the forests, and for her sake, He'd probably help the thralls, whom every man now had a right to kill. Holme had been in the same position ever since robbing the Christian storehouse and distributing the grain, but there was a difference—no man would dare try killing him.

Ausi could sense the hesitancy of the two women once they had almost reached the shore. Some of the men sensed it too and encouraged them to come back. But they couldn't make up their minds and sat down where they were while the group continued down the forest road. No boats were coming after them from town yet. Probably nothing would be done before the king's order had been received.

That evening, they passed one of the farmsteads where a farmer had joined them to fight the Christians. The people there were standing outside silently and anxiously, aware that their master hadn't returned. A question to the dark figure at the front went unanswered. The thralls were emaciated and almost naked, but they looked happy as they talked or sang. They might have killed the free farmers who had joined them and then stolen their weapons, provisions, and possessions.

At sunset they stopped for the night. Holme had been looking for a good place for a long time, and he finally saw a sparkling vein of water running out from under a low-hanging rock and disappearing in a meadow of green, tender grass. He had passed by here once in the middle of the summer, and the meadow had been full of white, wooly balls on every stem. The water was fresh and cold there. The thralls stood in rows with their pails while Tora slurped from her hand on the rock above them.

Farther up, it was dry under the branches, and they lay down on the twigs in rows with their few tattered clothes on top of them. They were all happy and talked about the future when they'd walk as free men on their own land. They would rather fight and die in battle against their old masters than return to thralldom. They had weapons, and Holme knew how to do everything.

Ausi found a place for herself and her family away from the thralls' camp. All day she had been thinking about evening and night when she would tell Holme what had happened to her that morning. He would understand that she had done everything she could to get away, and when she lay pinned to the floor, unable to defend herself further, she had repressed those feelings that had built up so long inside her and had wanted to come out with the rapist's movements. She had been able to, too, but she still felt uneasy all day. Holme would have all the warmth she could give him now.

The thrall women went off by themselves to sleep, and she suggested quietly to Holme that the men should leave them alone. They'd choose among the men for themselves soon; she had already noticed some of them looking at each other warmly. If someone else stepped in there would be discontent and fighting among the men. Holme thought it good advice, and none of the thralls objected when he said they should let the women sleep by themselves. Holme didn't order them to do anything, but instead he talked with them as equals, and so they wanted to do as he asked. But they turned their heads often to the women's camp, and many of them lay awake hoping to see one of the women go off somewhere so a man would follow her.

When a younger woman finally got up, several heads popped up among the men, but she took only a couple of steps, and then came a hissing noise when she squatted in the moss. They envied Holme and strained to hear, but he was too far away. The only sound was from a gentle breeze passing through the great forest.

Once Tora had fallen asleep and the time had come, Ausi felt she should keep quiet about what had happened to her that morning. It seemed meaningless at that point; she hadn't let go at all. Holme was so calm and his eyes so gentle. She didn't want to see them turn stern and threatening again.

He didn't ask anything about her life while they had been apart and didn't say much about his own. Ausi had managed to place a clump of trees between them and the thralls, but still she listened in that direction before pulling Holme to her. Her body quivered, and she smiled more tenderly at him than ever before. They both turned their heads, listened to Tora's breathing and peered at her face through the darkness. Then all that could be heard was the rivulet gently rippling on the rocks and the soft rustling of leaves under Ausi's body.

After Holme gently freed himself from the arms of the sleeping Ausi, he lay for a long time listening to the sounds of the night in the woods—the murmur of the spring, which always sounded the same, the forest's almost imperceptible sigh, the whispering which never quite died away but inhered in the silence itself, and now another ordinary sound from the thralls. He tried to plan what he would do for them so they might all have a roof over their heads and something to live on. The first winter would be the hardest to survive. He didn't have many pigs—they wouldn't last long. He had an uneasy feeling that they might have to resort to robbing and plundering. And that would bring more pursuers, more dangers. Only merchants and farmers could plunder and steal without consequences. It meant death for thralls to commit the same crimes freemen did.

They could probably get meat in the woods but not bread. Everyone would look to him when they lacked anything. He was like a father to them. He had wanted to live alone with his family where they had once been thralls, but it wasn't going to work out that way. The thralls would offer sacrifices to the wooden gods and Ausi would call on Christ, but when danger was at hand, they would all come to him. And he would have to help as best he could; he couldn't say no to a thrall when he remembered his own thralldom.

Once during the night he heard a powerful snorting in the forest and then a lumbering run. It might be a bear, but it probably wouldn't attack so many. It could be a moose, too, that was just about to walk out there and suddenly caught the scent. Wild boars were the most dangerous of all; they attacked blindly and viciously, whether there was one or a whole herd. During the winter all those animals would be needed as game. Many hungry men would eat their flesh.

Giere's hatred was smoldering inside as he watched the thralls disappear toward the mainland. He no longer wanted to sail with the ship, preparing instead to stay until he had gotten even with the smith. The Vikings would have to find another warrior to take his place. He would never forget that the thralls had beaten him to the ground with their clubs and trampled on him with their bare feet.

Later, he sat with his sister and her son in Holme's house, and they talked about what had happened. They criticized both the chieftain, who couldn't control a pack of thralls, and the warriors, who had refused to obey him. At the same time, Geire couldn't help feeling a certain admiration for the thralls' courage. He had always considered them whimpering, crawling dogs, but these hadn't retreated for anything. However, it was Holme who held them together; without him they'd be the same helpless herd as before.

They also considered the possibility of Holme's returning alone during the night. They had recently seen his sledgehammer open doors, so they couldn't sleep easily in his house anymore. Geire wasn't afraid for himself, but the smith wouldn't spare the woman or the boy if Geire fell under the sledgehammer's blows. Then there'd be no one left to avenge them.

He had seen Svein's terror of the smith and that disturbed him. It had to have come from the mother's endless stories and warnings when he was a child. He'd be full grown soon and strong for his age. He could handle a weapon, too, and one of them had to kill the smith.

His sister, the thralls' former owner, wallowed in her own terrible, bitter thoughts. She had been so sure she was going to see her hated enemy, Holme, hacked down and his wife delivered into her hands again, this time along with their daughter. But they had been able to row away, right in front of her eyes, and there wasn't a judge at the assembly who could do a thing about it. What had the country come to when thralls could do exactly as they pleased? She also felt like she was homeless even though she owned her enemy's house. As long as he was alive and free, they wouldn't have one single peaceful night's sleep, afraid every minute of a thunderous blow against the door.

Everything had turned sour on her after her first husband had died and was buried at the settlement. She hadn't made sacrifices to any god since then; maybe that was the reason for all this. The scorched god on the slope at the settlement might be taking revenge on her. That had to be it; she should have realized it before. She should at least have made an offering to him when she passed by the settlement after escaping thralldom in the foreign land. But instead she had despised him for his helplessness.

Now, though, she couldn't get back there to set things right. Besides, there was so little to sacrifice in these times of adversity. Half of Holme's silver had already been used up, and it was going to be a rough winter. The blackened god would keep standing on the stone, conjuring new problems for her. There was no god in Holme's house, and if there had been, she wouldn't have dared turn to him.

With an aching heart that afternoon when Geire and Svein were out, she took a fist full of silver, tied it in a piece of cloth, and walked to the shrine opposite the Christian church. Maybe the huge god there was the most powerful of gods and could keep the one at the settlement from visiting misfortunes on her. She would talk with his servant in the temple about it.

The Christian church was quiet and deserted. The bell tower that Holme had chopped to the ground was still lying there, but the bells were gone. Curiosity prompted her to walk up to the door and look in after glancing furtively at the wooden god. Everything was smashed to bits inside and the valuables had disappeared. A strange sound echoed in the empty hall, and presently she saw the Christian priest on his knees among the debris. His face was turned upward — he was probably calling down his god's punishment on Holme and the thralls. She hoped his god would have the power to destroy them.

The priest seemed to sense someone in the doorway and got up to look. She started to pull back, but he was beside her in an instant, showing her the destruction with a sorrowful smile. He didn't know this heathen woman with the hard face, but he showed her the disaster that had befallen him anyway. His companion lay dead in the chieftain's courtyard, and he was no doubt feeling threatened and forsaken in this pagan country.

The woman expected him to blame his god for what it couldn't or chose not to stop, but instead he spoke even warmer and more appreciative words about him. She suddenly remembered something that had happened while her squat, powerful husband was still alive. A hailstorm had come and struck down his beautiful grain, even though sacrificial smoke had floated around the fertility god in veils. Moments later the chieftain, consumed with rage, chopped the god to bits, railing against him for his worthlessness as he did so. But after he had calmed down, he had gone looking for a suitable tree to carve a new god out of. He had looked so high up the trunks that his beard had stood straight out.

She didn't pay much attention to what the priest was saying, but she did listen to his soft voice with surprise and pleasure. She had never heard such gentleness in a man's voice, had not even known that it could exist. And after all he had lost! It wasn't easy to understand him.

She didn't see anyone moving in the shrine of the wooden god, and she needed to talk with someone who could advise and help her. When the foreign priest asked why she was at the ravaged church, she told him everything in her own abrupt way — about the blackened god standing on the stone far away at the settlement and sending evil into her life. About Holme and Ausi and all they had inflicted upon her. She was going to offer a sacrifice to the god in the other temple so that he might divert the misfortune from her and let it fall on her enemies instead.

When she had finished, the priest started in about the powerless wooden gods and the living Christ. But the woman could see His demolished church; no one could make her believe in His power when He couldn't even drive away a pack of thralls. How could he save her from the revenge of the settlement's god? The priest assured her that Christ would do that without asking anything in return, but that made her even more suspicious. Who would do something for nothing?

She listened silently to the priest's words, but they were like water on a duck's back. She was looking toward the temple the whole time, and finally one of the attendants came out of the shrine, yawned, looked up at the wooden god, and began cleaning him up after the morning sacrifice. The heathen woman was getting restless. She looked once more at the devastation of the Christian church, and then walked toward the untouched shrine of the wooden god. He was obviously the strongest one; he and his house were still standing there undamaged.

The priest watched her go, thinking again that the work was lost. It wasn't his work, but the one who had started it had said that it was standing firm on its foundation; it was just a matter of moving it along. But now Christ surely wasn't left in a single heathen heart, not with the church and all the sparkling things in it gone. No one had understood or wished to understand the inner meaning of the message. As far as he was concerned, the heathens could keep their wooden gods until the end of time. He'd go back home before he too was cut down. The one who had kindled the light in the north could return himself to keep it burning.

With the first ship he would send a report of what had happened and request a replacement. Then his companion, who now wore the crown of martyrdom, would be buried with as much dignity as possible among enemies and nominal Christians. The chieftain would still help, even if he hadn't been able to protect the church or the priest's life. The thralls had defied him, and the warriors had refused to follow his orders and strike them down. This strange people had kings and chieftains, but ignored their orders and did as they pleased. He had heard stories that the people had more than once seized a king or chieftain and sacrificed him when some great misfortune had come on the land;[11] he wondered if such a people would ever become Christian.

He felt like a tiny, flickering candle in an endless night. Could he get himself out of this? He didn't want to die here and lie waiting for the Day of Judgment among heathen burial mounds. Maybe Christ wouldn't even bother with this place, and the everlasting silence would settle over it. An eternal oblivion was already whispering across the burial mounds outside the town; he had sensed that as a threat and as challenging the power of Christ. Maybe God never intended this land to see the light. And so He had let thralls destroy His church and turn His disciple into a martyr.

The heathen woman was coming out of the temple with a smug look on her face. She had probably been promised help by the servant of the wooden god. She folded up the piece of cloth she had brought the silver in, looked respectfully up at the lofty wooden god, and walked away without giving the Christian church a single glance.

The smith's wife, Ausi, had once told a story about a Christian priest who had labored there in town but had ultimately been sacrificed when he had tried to burn down the heathens' greatest temple on the mainland. The monk hadn't believed the story, but it was beginning to seem plausible. There certainly had

---

[11] E. O. G. Turville-Petre, *Myth and Religion of the North* (New York: Holt, Rinehart, & Winston, 1964), p. 253, points out that the king represented the relevant Norse god, even incorporated the god within him. He may therefore have been sacrificed in the autumn so that he could revive again in the spring.

been many men during the course of time who had believed they were called as apostles to the heathens, but had been lost forever in the forests and at the heathens' sacrificial altars.

He didn't want to become one of them; he would request a replacement as fast as possible. He yearned for Christ to return him to his homeland so he could convince everyone that his mission was hopeless.[12]

When Holme and the band of thralls started getting close to the cave, he took a detour so they wouldn't discover it. He had a vague feeling that someday he might need it again as a hiding place for himself and his family. There were many dangerous enemies who would never give him any peace as long as he was still alive.

With great expectation and happiness, Ausi saw again the place where she had spent her childhood and lived in servitude. The whole band stopped at the edge of the forest to look down on the yellow grain swaying in Holme's fields. Ausi saw lush grass and shrubs with red berries now where the buildings had once stood. The mill stone that she had ground grain with so often was still standing in the same place, and a shower had left a little water in the indentation.

The thralls wandered happily around the slope and looked expertly at the grain where it was still unaffected by the blight. They picked up handfuls of earth and let it run between their fingers, grunting appreciatively. While there were a lot of things unusable here, a good number of people could still have bread. A couple of men were already trying their luck with Holme's fishing gear at the shore. Others stood looking at the mounds in the burial grove while they exchanged opinions about them. Muddy, black paths had been worn by the hooves of the pigs under the alder bushes by the shore.

Farther up the hillside, the blackened wooden god was standing on his rock, and someone had already placed a couple of tiny morsels from the last meal in front of him. Birds flew back and forth between the trees and the god, carrying the small bits of food in their beaks.

The thralls were prancing around like carefree children, but Holme looked at them with concern. There were just too many of them for one spot. He had seen a building at the other farmstead that was about ready to cave in, and wild grain was flourishing in the old fields; some of them would have to go there. They could fish and hunt, and when the grain was harvested, it would be divided up equally among all of them. He'd go along himself and help them get started.

The women had stopped on the slope, talking or lying on their backs with their eyes closed. A few of them would go with the men to the other farmstead.

---

[12] Gautbert was driven from Sweden in about 845 and was not replaced until 851 (*Anskar*, chapter 19, p. 61).

A new building would soon be built for them, and the men could live in the old one for a while.

When the time had come, Holme walked down to the shore and looked for an equal number of white and gray stones to put in a wooden bowl. He called the men together and said that those who picked gray stones would move on, those with white stones would stay. The same would be true for the women. Ausi's suggestion that she be allowed to keep one of the younger girls she had grown fond of was turned down.

But when their turn came, the women indicated that several of them had already made their choice. They walked self-consciously over to stand near the man they had secretly had an eye on. They were full of anxiety about not being able to go where their men went. Some even went without bothering with the drawing of lots, thinking that life would probably be about the same in both places. Only the youngest, almost a child like Tora, looked anxiously at the bearded men and stood next to Ausi for protection. No one ordered her to come along to the other farmstead, and Ausi gladly took her to her house.

Early the next morning, Holme walked on with the men, women, and tools. He walked alone at the head of the group, followed by the women and then the men, who were laughing and singing and ringing the little Christian bell. From the settlement Ausi could hear the ringing grow weaker and finally die away in the forest. Holme would probably be back again the next day.

Tora and the young girl were asleep in the house, the men were out in the woods cutting down trees for the new building, and the women were wandering here and there. Ausi went off by herself, looking at everything and recalling things that had happened in different places.

She hadn't felt this happy and safe for a long time. The old uneasiness that the stranger had infused in her was gone, now that she knew he was Christ Himself. There was nothing more she had to know; no matter how bad things might look, he would eventually fix them all. That's why she was there with her loved ones. The Christ she knew would never stand between her and Holme.

She stopped by the pile of ashes that had once been the two thrall huts. She had given birth in one of them to Tora, whom Stor and Tan had carried off into the forest. She had still been afraid of Holme back then and bitter too because he had done nothing to stop them. Instead, he did what no man had ever done before for his woman and baby. Stor and Tan were dead now; Holme had told her during the night that they had tried to ax him in his sleep, even though he had meant them no harm. They shared a grave here at the settlement where they had lived all their lives. But that was all right; they wouldn't dare come back to do any mischief as long as Holme was around.

She also stopped by the wooden god, and a little gray bird flew off with a crumb of bread in its beak. She wouldn't offer him anything, although the settlement was hers now. He could do nothing against Christ and Holme. Anyway, she would ask Holme to lift him down from the rock and take him away. Otherwise, the people living here now might give him food they could make better use of themselves. She looked for a moment at the blackened clump of wood that still had the human shape, and she remembered when the chieftain had called in a skillful craftsman to carve and paint him. That was just before Tora was born.

There was no sign of the pigs yet, but they would probably come back at night. The flies buzzing around the tracks in the warm mud indicated they had been home the last few nights. Holme had let them out before going to town to rescue her. The pigs would come home in the evening; she knew their habits well and knew they'd stop at the edge of the forest, blinking mistrustfully at the new life in the settlement. They probably couldn't be called in before Holme, whom they knew, came back.

The three largest burial mounds all looked alike now since thick grass had grown on even the newest of them. She thought about the stocky chieftain lying in his; he had condemned her baby to be abandoned in the woods. He had hated Holme and hadn't wanted to let the baby live because it was his. Even so, thrall children had been needed at the settlement. Now he lay there in a mound and Holme was in charge. It was amusing when what happened was the opposite of what the powerful wanted. He certainly wouldn't be able to rise up and do them any harm; she had seen the fire consume all but his largest bones.

It was quiet and beautiful down among the mounds, and the wild strawberries growing on their sides were blooming for the second time. Adjacent to the mounds were several smaller graves of women, and farther away there were numerous tiny, uneven mounds. There lay all the thralls who had died or been killed at the settlement. The chieftain in the mound had many warriors so he could attack and plunder passing ships. The mightiest of them, Stenulf, had been killed by Holme with an ax and now lay under a high mound of round stones near the cave.

Ausi had seen all that was left from her days as a thrall. The landing was falling apart and the logs turning white. The little boat the thrall had stolen still lay there, its bottom filled with warm rain water. Big round rocks that used to be underwater were now up on land, whitening in the sun. She climbed on them and they almost burned her bare feet. A spry, ice-gray bird with a long, fluttering tail landed on a log and looked at her with cocked head before resuming its airy hunt among the warm logs and stones.

There was one more place she wanted to see again. She looked around self-consciously and walked along the shore a ways. Between a few alder bushes was a small chamber-like area where the grass was green far into the autumn. She stopped, looked at the place, and smiled. Holme had dragged her in there one autumn. Then winter came, and in the summer, Tora was born. She had fought him off as long as she could, but two of her friends had seen them through an opening in the bushes, and they said she had finally thrown her arms around his neck. She didn't remember that but didn't think it impossible.

There she stood now, glad it was Holme and no one else who had taken her. She leaned over and caressed the grass before returning to the settlement. It was damp and she remembered that her skirt had clung to her back that time after she had broken loose and stood up.

After a mild winter when the lake didn't freeze over, a summer came with a good harvest. The people at the farmsteads didn't see strangers too often and they heard nothing from the outside. Then one day a man came by Holme's place and said that the blight had attacked the grain again, for the third straight year, and that many people had starved to death during the winter and spring. There had also been much less seed to be sown, so the harvest would have an even smaller yield than during the last two years of famine.

The man looked in surprise at the dazzling grain swaying in Holme's fields. He recognized Holme and knew what had happened in town, but he kept it to himself; instead, he praised all he saw as he ate their food. But he took careful note of everything he could tell about it when he got back. He could see how it all fit together now and looked with terror-stricken eyes at the blackened god that Holme hadn't bothered to take off the rock. It was clear to him that the blight had swept across the land directly from that grimy god and that Holme was responsible. Everyone knew or believed that Holme knew more than other people did. This was a great discovery, and once the man had eaten his fill, he turned back toward town instead of continuing his journey.

Holme watched him and for an instant felt a dark sense of foreboding. But he couldn't do anything against a man seeking hospitality. A whole year had passed since they had settled down here, and he had begun to hope that all would be forgotten. The chieftain surely wouldn't want to waste time and warriors hunting thralls in the woods. He might even be expecting them to come to town sooner or later to barter for things they couldn't get any place else. Many of the thralls at both farmsteads were running short of clothes and shoes. A couple of the least recognized men might be able to travel to town and trade for cloth and skins without risking anything happening to them. But Holme couldn't go to town. Everyone knew him.

The chieftain listened pensively to the man's animated story. The chieftain still believed in Christ, even though the last priest had lost heart and gone home. Replacements would come as soon as they felt called to this difficult mission—at least that's what a message said from the monk directing everything from his cloister in the far-off land.[13] He asked the chieftain and the few others

---

[13] i.e., Ansgar.

still clinging to Christ to keep faith. The reward would be great and glorious in its time, and they would triumph over their adversaries.

But even though Christ might be the most powerful, the chieftain didn't take lightly the wooden gods' abilities to be revenged. He had seen all too much proof of what they could do. He could well imagine the evil smith using the charred god on the stone to send disease on the grain throughout the land. It had to be true. Blight from a black god, a black god for a dark man like Holme. That man had to be destroyed, along with his god, if starvation was to be stopped from ultimately laying waste to the entire land. The blight had spread more and more each year.

The same day the chieftain himself was rowed to the king's farmstead to make the situation clear to him. The king was walking around his grain fields, looking with dismay at the pitiful stalks where the blight had taken hold. He had ordered the fertility god moved out into the middle of the fields, where it stood, gazing across the lake with the stalks brushing against its base. It had been there since the grain had sprouted, but it either couldn't or wouldn't stop the blight.

The king listened to his chieftain's story and soon became convinced that they had finally discovered where the blight came from. He too remembered the smith, having once been provoked by his indifference and defiance. The smith was also an outlaw from many years before; even so, the king still suggested that the chieftain take him alive and bring him before the assembly. He might have things to say that would be useful to know. The king ordered that Holme and everyone with him be brought to town—and as fast as possible, if any of the harvest was to be saved. He also mentioned a reward for the man who had made this important discovery.

As had happened many years before when the short-legged chieftain fell in battle, a man came running through the forest, panting, a terrible message in his mouth. Coughing and wheezing, he rushed to Holme and told his story. He had been in an outlying field at the other farmstead and had seen it suddenly surrounded by warriors, all on horseback, and he recognized some of them. They were the king's guard, and the chieftain himself was riding at their head. The thrall had seen his gray beard under the golden helmet. He said that no one else had gotten out alive.

Holme listened with apprehension and anger and realized there'd be no more peace. It would be pointless to try to fight the warrior troop with axes and spears. They had probably gone to the other farmstead first by mistake, or perhaps they had been confident that no one would escape to spread the news.

Holme rang the bell to call the people together for a brief meeting. The enemies were many and strong; everyone agreed that there was no point in fighting them in the open. But some of the people looked sad and some enraged because of the year they had spent at the settlement living a good and peaceful life, and because of the whispering, golden grain that would soon be ripe.

Soon the last of them disappeared into the forest, loaded down with their possessions, and the settlement was empty. The door of the pigsty stood open. The pigs had been driven into the forest, and the fire pit was still hissing softly from the water it had been doused with. Holme turned around and looked back at the settlement as he had so often done before. He had lost count of the number of times he had run away from it and then returned. But he didn't feel at home anywhere else.

Holme came back alone after taking his people a good distance into the woods. Ausi calmly watched him arrive; she had been convinced that Christ, in the shape of the stranger, would be walking beside him and protecting him. But the men were dour and irritable; one of them suddenly growled that they should have stayed and fought. The forest was whispering and the birds were singing around the band of thralls sitting there on the ground, but a powerful enemy was threatening the freedom in the forest they had fought for and enjoyed for a year.

Holme had to wait in his hiding place for a while before he heard them coming. A horse whinnied, probably catching the settlement's scent. Then Holme heard more than saw the horsemen fan out and surround the settlement so no one could escape.

He could hear horses snorting and twigs cracking in several places at once, and then the horses flashed into sight and disappeared. At a loud yell, they all thundered toward the settlement, many of them riding straight through the fields of golden grain. Holme laughed sardonically as he watched them whirling around amongst the empty buildings, searching for victims. The troop of warriors they had sent against him and his thralls was large, but as always, the forest sheltered the fugitive and the outlaw.

Holme stayed put until the warriors got off their horses and gathered around the chieftain to confer with him. It was moving toward evening; they would probably spend the night there. But he had to get back to his people. He had already planned to double back to the farmstead the horsemen had just left and see how much damage they had done. Surely they'd take another route home.

Just then, he heard men coming from the same direction, so he took cover again. Five or six horsemen rode up with thralls tied behind their horses, both men and women. He was close enough to hear their labored breathing and see their bulging eyes. One of the women was carrying her baby and was trying to nurse it as she ran. The thralls' legs were bleeding from cuts and scratches they had gotten on branches and stones in the forest.

Holme ground his teeth and then ran through the forest as he had run only once before in his life. He still didn't know exactly what he was going to do, but he knew he'd act that night. They were dragging his people behind their horses, people whose only crime was choosing to fend for themselves and live in peace.

Ausi heard him coming before she could see him, and she too remembered the night he had raced three times between the cave and the settlement. The thralls were waiting in a place not very far from the cave, but no one but she and Holme knew about it. When she caught sight of him, she could see he was running as fast as the last time, though he was much older now. He glided like a shadow across the ground. Most of the others had settled down to rest while they waited for him, and some were already asleep.

The other men, having been free only for the past year, were just glad their companions were still alive. They felt no outrage at having been dragged behind horses; their own thralldom was still too fresh in their minds. But Ausi was aware that it had been a long time since she had seen Holme's face so hard and bitter. Even so, he could expect nothing but death for the people from the other farmstead.

The man who had brought Holme the news was allowed to lead the women and children to the other farmstead; the men went with Holme. He had no idea what they were going to do; attacking the horsemen would be insane. But the coming night would be the thralls' and outlaws' ally, made for quiet steps, silent shadows, and the flight of spears.

There was still a little daylight left when they reached the edge of the forest. Holme scouted ahead while the men waited just inside the forest. Surely, the warriors had posted a guard.

When he got close enough to the settlement, he could see that something was going on. Horses were neighing, a couple of warriors were coming up the path from the lake, talking, and a couple of others were standing by the fields of grain. Something was missing, and it took a moment for Holme to figure out what it was. The wooden god on the rock was gone. The warriors had probably knocked him down, angry because their prey had flown.

He could discern a larger group of horses and people near the grove by the house. It was the thralls and their women—still bound to the horses—sitting on the ground. They kept turning toward the forest, as if looking for help. In all likelihood, they knew Holme and the others were still free. Occasionally, he could hear a baby cry. Two or three warriors stood in front of the horses.

In the woods behind him, Holme heard sounds—a stifled cough, a breaking twig, a whisper. Dark figures scampered from tree to tree, and soon he was surrounded. The thralls just couldn't wait, and he smiled in the darkness at their zeal. The warriors had posted no guard, either by the forest or by the lake, probably because they felt nothing but disdain for the thralls who had escaped their grasp.

Moments later, Holme and the thralls heard the chieftain come out and give the warriors their orders. He said they'd sleep until daybreak and then begin tracking Holme and the thralls. They couldn't afford to return to town without the smith, the most dangerous man in the land. Holme heard the familiar voice say something about Christ being with them on their journey so it had to succeed. Besides, this mission was to save the whole land from famine. He finished by asking for Christ's protection during the night.

The statement about famine surprised Holme. How could capturing and killing him and the thralls save the land from the blight? As usual, the Christians were going to involve Christ in everything and then blame the heathens or the wooden gods if anything went wrong.

The warriors disappeared into the buildings, and soon the chewing and snorting of the horses were the only sounds that could be heard. The guard standing in front of the horses would move now and then, stopping and looking out over the lake or turning toward the forest and listening. The captured thralls had lain down, and every once in a while you could hear the sound of women sobbing. The sweet smell of ripened grain grew stronger in the humid night air, reaching the men hiding behind the trees.

The guard never went behind the horses to check on the prisoners. Perhaps he didn't like the silent weeping of the women, or perhaps the darkness of the night and the silence made him fearful that one of the men might break free and sneak up on him with a knife. Once he took out some food, smacking his lips as he ate. The thralls who hadn't had anything to eat or drink since morning could hear him, and their own hunger pangs increased.

Once he reached the grove it wasn't too far for Holme to crawl. A horse turned its head and looked indifferently at him through the darkness as he emerged from the foliage and crawled stealthily through the grass. His biggest concern was that the thralls in their surprise would give him away. Even so, he might still be able to get them loose and into the woods before the warriors could get to their feet and attack.

The first thrall to catch sight of him gasped, and for a moment Holme stopped in his tracks. A whisper moved quickly among the people lying on the ground; the women stopped crying, and heads slowly bent forward straining to see. A knife appeared passing from hand to hand, and as it moved the straps fell away from raw, swollen wrists.

Once they were free, the prisoners had a single thought — the woods. Some leaped up and fled on wobbly legs; others, unable to stay on their feet, fell and crawled toward the forest. The mother's hurried movements woke the baby and it started screaming. The horses grew restless, and suddenly the guard gave a loud yell and, before Holme could stop him, ran toward the buildings. The four horses that had been cut loose sensed they had and started galloping across the slope.

Holme was last to leave. He watched as the warriors came tumbling out of the buildings, fumbling with their clothes and weapons. The horses that were still tied had spooked — several of them yanked loose and galloped wildly around. The thralls had enough time to get to the edge of the forest, and those who couldn't run fast enough were held up or dragged along by the others. The baby kept screaming, and that meant they had to get out of hearing range fast.

A chase couldn't easily begin before dawn, so, after he made certain that everyone would meet at the other farmstead, Holme turned back again. He wanted to find out what the warriors were up to so he'd know how to respond. If they decided to ride to the other farmstead again, he'd have to get there before them somehow.

Once he was alone, walking back through the forest, he felt a great sense of relief and happiness at having been able to set the thralls free. The danger wasn't over yet, but they had bought valuable time. Maybe the enemy would finally tire of the hunt and let them live as they pleased in the forest. They would never bother anybody but, instead, would help all the outlawed, wretched people who happened along the roads.

Soon he was back at the edge of the forest and could see the commotion in the darkness among the buildings. Some of the horses had not been caught yet and were running scared, crazed with fear, rearing up when the men got near them and pawing violently at the air. Voices raised excitedly, and Holme could hear the guard defending himself as best he could. He told them that the blackened wooden god they had toppled from the stone had come sneaking up in the darkness to free the prisoners. Then it had charged him—he had only narrowly escaped.

Holme heard his own name mentioned when the chieftain said that the black god hadn't budged. The one who had freed the prisoners was Holme, whom most of them knew from town. In the darkness, he might look like the black wooden god. But Christ was stronger than all the other gods, and when daylight came He would help them. Until then, they must stay alert. No one knew what the smith would do next. He was undoubtedly in league with the evil powers living there in the forest, and the chieftain blamed himself for not putting a stronger guard over the thralls.

A moment later, about half the warriors went back into the buildings, while the other half stayed outside, talking quietly and looking around. A soft light was shining above the fields, and fireflies danced in silent swarms. An occasional chirping from the young sea birds drifted up from the reeds below.

Countless thoughts passed through Holme's mind as he sat there at the forest's edge. They came out of the long ago, and he wasn't sure sometimes what had really happened. Many dreams and old plans had become mixed with his memories. He had been greatly mistreated and hunted, but he had fought back too. Many men had never gotten up again, but he had acted wrongfully only once. That was when the man had moved into the house outside town where Ausi and he had lived before. He had had a perfect right to move into the empty house, as much right as they had had. But Holme's ax had spoken before his mind could.

More than anything else, he would have chosen to live in the forest all his life and have a little farmstead with a smithy. But he hadn't been able to do that;

instead he had been forced into violence. If everyone were free, there would be no need to fight and kill each other. No one had any idea how big the country was; there was enough for everybody. But no one was going to free a thrall, so they had had to fight for freedom as he had done. Then the chase was on, and it had been a freedom without peace.

But most of those who had been free for a while would rather fight and die than return to thralldom. And if anyone did return, he would never be the same; he would carry his freedom in his heart and search for the chance to reach it again. Their lords would never be able to sleep peacefully with thralls around who'd had a taste of freedom. When enough thralls had tasted, they would shove away everything that stood in the path of freedom.

If this thrall hunt failed, they might be left in peace for a while. But they'd always have to live with one eye on the forest and the other on the lake. If the freemen could understand, then the thralls could approach them calmly and suggest a truce. If the free men would let the thralls live in the forest and come to town to barter occasionally, they would in turn never cause anybody any trouble. That way, all thralls would finally be free, and no difference would separate freemen and thralls. They were basically the same from the beginning anyway. A thrall was just as strong, sometimes stronger, than a freeman. One didn't dare do more than the other, and you couldn't tell the difference between a lord and a thrall once they took their clothes off.

Before dawn, Holme understood that freemen could never be reasoned with. There was only one way — to unite all the thralls in the land and kill every freeman who opposed the thralls' freedom. Many thralls, perhaps himself included, would fall in that struggle, but others could live on freely and happily on their farmsteads and in small forest clearings.

When the warriors gathered together again, Holme could hear the chieftain telling them that if they could just get Holme, the others didn't matter. With him out of the way, they'd make short work of the thralls. He also told them he would send men back to these farmsteads to harvest the crop for the king. As they could see, it was plentiful and untouched by the blight. But they wouldn't send anybody for the bell the thralls had hung up on the gable of the building to call each other with. They'd take it with them immediately.

The warriors ate their breakfast standing by their horses and drank water from the wooden tankards hanging on the saddles. They were in a good mood, kidding and cackling in their beards over the various ideas they kept coming up with for capturing Holme and the thralls. But the chieftain warned them to be careful; there wasn't a man among them who could take Holme alone, and the thralls would fight like wolves for their freedom. Those who had escaped from this farmstead were surely armed, and they knew what was waiting for them in town.

The chieftain turned down a warrior's suggestion that they destroy the charred wooden god. The clump of wood could do no harm by itself; Holme was calling forth the blight through it. If they could capture him, everything would go back to normal.

When they left, a man was sent ahead of them on foot to track the thralls through the moss and brush. After a while Holme recognized him and knew at once who was behind everything that was happening—the man who had come through the forest, eaten his food, and taken stock of everything on the farmsteads—he who afterwards had gone back the same way he had come.

Holme watched him as closely as he could through the branches. He had a new goal now to add to all the others. He had to get even with that man when the time was right.

After the horsemen had disappeared into the forest, he crouched and ran down to the shore, took the small boat from the landing, and began rowing. Just outside the reeds, he put his back into it and the boat sped silently forward. It was closer by water than by land; even if the warriors rode straight to the other farmstead, he'd get there at the same time or ahead of them. But it should take them a while to find the thralls' tracks.

He soon rowed past the place where he and Ausi had stopped to rest during their escape from thralldom, and again everything seemed like a recurrent dream. But he couldn't help it; everything he did seemed inevitable—whether it meant striking a man down, or stepping to the side so he didn't trample an insect on the forest path.

But he didn't give any thought as to who was in control of all these things. The heathens said it was the wooden gods, the sun, or the stars; the Christians said it was their god. He didn't care about any of it; when the time came for him to do something, he always knew it.

The chieftain allowed the younger, more zealous warriors to ride in front through the forest, just behind the tracker, while he rode last. He was old and sure the thralls wouldn't attack; they would only defend themselves once they were caught.

He let his head hang so that his beard lay on his chest while the horse picked its own way through the rocks and thickets. He thought about the strange mission he was out on. Some inner sense had whispered to him the whole time that no mortal could send the blight, but he didn't mention it to the others. If the warriors believed otherwise, everything was easier. The thralls were guilty enough anyway. Never before had they tried fighting for freedom and then begin living like farmers. What would happen if they did that all through the country? But it was probably Holme's fault that they had done the things they had. Once he was gone, everything would fall back into the old familiar order.

The longer the chieftain thought about their gall, the more he began to boil. Thralls living like lords! They should be whipped so they'd never pull a stunt like that again. It might be best to kill them all so they couldn't entice others to repeat what they had done. However, the king would decide in this matter.

If only Christ would help them with the capture. The day was clear and blue; He could see them all from heaven—the thralls fleeing and the warriors tracking through the forest. The priests said that He was omnipresent, so He could surely give them a hint about which way to ride. The tracker lost the track again and again, and the horsemen had to stand by until he sniffed it out. Sometimes he'd kneel down, groping in the grass and moss. A couple of times, he even put his nose down and sniffed like a dog. He should have used a dog instead; then tracking a pack of thralls would have been easy.

But Christ didn't help, maybe because so many of the warriors were still heathens. A few had been baptized before riding out on the thrall hunt, just in case, but not all of them. If the newly baptized fell, at least they could ascend to heaven, where Christ would help their souls. But the unbaptized would sleep forever. The wooden gods had no power to awaken their followers.

It was hard to understand how the thralls could escape in the dark of night with women and children. But their leader was friendly with the powers of darkness, and they probably helped him in the forest. That meant the chieftain and his men would have to catch the thralls while it was still day when Christ and all the gods of light held sway.

In a glade, the tracker triumphantly picked up some loose berries that indicated the thralls had passed there. But a lot of animals like bears and birds ate berries so they meant little. The chieftain had been convinced for a long time they were going the wrong way, and decided to take the lead himself—with Christ's help, of course.

He gathered his warriors around him in the next glade and told them his misgivings about the route they were taking. He pointed out too that Christ could see them and probably wanted to give them a sign. The warriors looked silently at him.

He bent his head back, making his beard stand out from his chin, looked up into the blue above the treetops, and prayed in a loud voice for Christ to show them the way. Afterwards, he would show his gratitude with gifts to the Church.

It was absolutely quiet for a moment, and the warriors sat motionless on their horses in anxious expectation. Then the clear, drawn-out cry of a bird emerged from deep in the forest to the right of the glade. A glow of triumph passed over the chieftain's face when he asked if everyone had heard it.

Most of the warriors' faces lit up with surprise or happiness, but a couple of the men were skeptical.

"It was just a bird," one of them said.

But the chieftain turned his horse toward the sound, and his voice expressed unshakable certainty when he said that Christ could respond in whatever tongue He wanted to. He was that powerful in comparison to the wooden idols. He was in all things and knew about everything before it happened.

It was already midday, and they hadn't gotten far following the crawling, hunched-over tracker. Now they moved quickly with the gray-haired chieftain riding proudly at the head of the troop. Christ had answered him and everything would be fine. He could approach the king with Holme and the thralls in tow, and then they'd get what was coming to them.

In the first daylight, the thralls saw again the farmstead they were sure they had left forever the day before when they had been dragged away behind horses. Nothing had been burned or stolen because the chieftain had planned to send people back here too to take charge of the fine grain, the most beautiful he had seen in many years. The grain had convinced him more than anything else that Holme and the thralls were in league with the powers of evil.

Ausi and Tora sat down with a view of the forest road to wait for Holme. Ausi prayed silently for Christ to accompany and protect him through the forest. She concentrated so hard that she conjured them in a vision. Holme was walking down the path with that gliding stride he always used in the forest. The stranger was walking among the bushes lining both sides of the path. He was only one man, but Ausi somehow saw him among the trees and stones on both sides of Holme.

She was certain everything would be fine. The chieftain was Christian, but not like the stranger and herself. He was like the last priests, those who had to make offerings and promises to get any help. Her Christ sat like a clear, joyous light in her chest. He wasn't austere and demanding like the last priests, but mild, and He understood everything, even whatever was called sin. She alone knew what He was like, but there was no one to tell. Not yet.

Most of the thralls lay down to rest after tending their wounds. A couple of the strongest men had walked down to the landing with fishing gear. A big, almost new boat was tied at the landing, and the men were pleased to see no one had touched it while they had been away.

Tora lay down on the ground and was soon asleep. Ausi kept waiting for Holme to come out of the forest; Christ would be standing there at the edge, smiling as if to say, "Here you are." But even Ausi felt the weight and the fatigue after the night in the woods and all the tension. The edge of the forest grew dark and shimmered in a pleasant twilight.

Just as she was about to fall asleep, a shout came from the lake, and opening her eyes, she saw one of the men on the landing, pointing toward the east. Her first thought was that other enemies were approaching by water now that Holme wasn't home. But before she could get to her feet a boat glided out of the swath of fire in front of the sun, and she recognized instantly the figure bent over the oars. She had expected him to come through the forest! As always, he knew what was best—he and Christ.

Ausi quietly left the sleeping girl and ran down the slope to meet Holme. They could rest now, all three of them, after the hard night. Then they'd get up and get something to eat.

But even at a distance, she could tell there'd be no rest. Holme wasn't moving any faster than usual, but from his crouched position she could see that the danger wasn't over.

Holme had rowed about half way when it occurred to him that his calculations were wrong. The warriors would track the people all the way to the farmstead. He had thought they'd give up and return to town, but he could see more clearly now. During the day, they'd have plenty of time to reach the farmstead even if they lost the track several times.

It angered him that his fatigue had kept him from seeing that. He was no old man and was responsible for a lot of people. Now there had to be either a fight or another escape into the woods with the horsemen on their heels. He'd let the men decide for themselves if they wanted to stay and fight. As for him, he was tired of fleeing like a wolf through the forest.

He was relieved to see the men on the landing when he approached. Everything seemed to be all right. The farmstead was close to a cove, and a short distance out was an islet with a grassy meadow and some trees. An idea struck him and he rested on his oars as he turned his head to look at the islet. His face lit up even more when he began rowing again.

The farmstead lay in the early morning sun, calm as could be. Why couldn't they be left in peace when they weren't bothering anybody? But someplace in the forest, deadly trackers they had never done any harm were coming after them. The farmstead was off the beaten track, and the old owners were gone now. What did it matter if a few thralls whose owners had driven them off because of the famine settled down here?

He got mad again, thinking that if the men stayed with him, they might make it through a fight. The women, children, and the feeblest men could row over to the islet during the battle, but they would have to hurry. No one knew how soon the horsemen might get there.

Ausi greeted him with warm, troubled eyes, and he thought longingly about their past year of freedom at the settlement. Who knew if it would ever be that way again—sunny days with an impending harvest, peaceful nights in Ausi's arms?

But there wasn't time to think about such things. The people were awakened, and Holme briefly explained the situation to everybody. He had already given up the notion of fighting. There were just too many horsemen; not a single thrall would be left alive.

The boats set out soon with their first load. Holme stayed behind with the strongest men to detain the warriors if they arrived before the women and children were safe. But the boats came back and left with a new cargo, and still nothing moved at the edge of the forest. Some of the thralls hurriedly cut a boat-load of the ripe grain and rowed across with it. Holme and his men came down the slope last, looking constantly toward the forest. It couldn't be long before the warriors would get there.

One of the thralls ran back to the building and returned with the little wooden god under his arm. Holme looked at him but didn't say anything. The men pulled back their legs so there'd be room for the god in the boat. Tiny ants crept in and out of the cracks furrowing his grinning wooden face. The farmstead and log landing moved farther and farther away, but everything remained quiet there. Maybe the warriors had given up and gone home.

After the chieftain and his warriors had pursued the bird's cry for a long time, he stopped at a well-worn path. Triumphantly he asked his men if they believed in Christ's sign now. He rode on, the horsemen following in single file, happy to abandon the rough ride in the woods with its low branches threatening to knock them off their horses. No one considered that, since they now had the sun in their faces, they had changed directions.

The chieftain quickened the pace, eager for the climax he was sure would be triumphant. The path began descending and soon they glimpsed an open field with water glittering below it. The field lay peaceful and quiet in the sun; a skinny pig, rooting alone by the shore, lifted its head and listened. The riders, their horses snorting, stopped at the edge of the forest and peered in bewilderment down at the settlement they had left at daybreak. Some of the men stifled their belly laughs in their beards.

The chieftain sat dumbfounded for a moment; then he assured them that Christ must have had some reason for bringing them back. He had doubtlessly seen some danger from heaven and had thus rescued them from it.

But he could see that the warriors were beginning to tire of the thankless hunt for thralls. It didn't matter much to them if the thralls got away; they'd much rather go back to town. The charred, wicked god no longer stood on the stone, so the blight would probably stop soon if he had sent it. Inside the chieftain was bitter at Christ's having deceived him. He remembered the successes he had had when he was still a heathen. Maybe the powerful wooden battle-god would help him one more time. Christ wouldn't like that, but if He wasn't going to help, what could He expect?

And so mumbling in his beard, he promised rich gifts and sacrifices to the ancient god of his fathers if he'd deliver the thralls into his hands quickly. He conjured up the biggest image he could of the god, remembering he had been there long before Christ had. He surely knew the forest better and could give them the right directions.

The chieftain heard the warriors scorning Christ and His bird cry, but he kept quiet. He'd learn more about how to get help from Christ when a new priest showed up. For now, it couldn't hurt to be on the ancient gods' good side.

He ordered his men to dismount, rest, and get something to eat while they tried to decide what to do. They couldn't go home until they carried out the king's order. He tried to enrage the warriors by taunting them, telling them that thralls, women, and children had led them around by the nose for two days. They could burn the farmsteads but that wouldn't do anything. The thralls would just rebuild them again. They could destroy their grain, but the thralls wouldn't starve to death; they'd find some way to keep going. They had shown they could by robbing the Christians of grain.

The chieftain managed to provoke the warriors into giving it another try. The thralls couldn't have gone far. Many of the warriors approved of the chieftain's promise of gifts to the wooden gods if they would come to their aid.

Surely the thralls must have stayed near the farmsteads, probably waiting to return until the danger had passed.

Holme kept guard alone that night so the others could get some sleep. The thralls had spread out long beds of branches and grass under the densest trees they could find on the islet. Now they were all sleeping and the only sound to be heard was the lapping of the waves on the side of the islet facing into the wind.

The horsemen hadn't shown up all day. They might have gotten lost in the woods, but then again, it might be a trick. Or maybe they got tired and went home. A chieftain couldn't always get his warriors to do what he wanted.

Down on the shore in front of Holme stood the wooden god, looking across the water. He was supposed to be protecting the grain fields. A bundle of grain lay in front of him to remind him of his duties.

They could probably return after a few days. First Holme and a few of the men would check to see if the horsemen were waiting in the woods. If they had gone back to town, either he or someone else would find out if danger was on its way or if they'd be safe for a while.

He heard whispering from the people behind him. One of the younger couples had awakened and were playing with or caressing each other; he could hear the woman giggle. He got up and left quietly so as not to disturb them. Hearing them made him long for Ausi, but she was asleep beside Tora. It would be kind of fun anyway to see how she'd manage for them to be alone for a while. She always pretended it just happened. When she was younger she had always responded to him but, she had never made the overtures as she did now.

When it became too cool to sit still, he walked around the islet a couple of times. The dew had settled on the grass and a cool gust of wind came in from the lake before the sun rose. A pair of sea birds swimming outside the reeds turned their triangular faces toward him before diving and surfacing farther away.

When he came back, the man who had been whispering with the woman raised his head and quietly offered to relieve him. The man couldn't sleep anyway. Holme accepted and they talked quietly about whether the warriors really had returned to town after failing in their hunt. Before going out on watch, the man covered the sleeping woman, and Holme lay down beside Ausi, who snuggled closer to him without waking.

Half asleep, he was aware of Ausi getting up and laying something over him; he let his eyes focus on the area around him but found no danger. He could see sunshine on green branches and could hear calm voices. Being awake for two nights heavily weighted his eyelids and he allowed himself to sleep a while longer. They could decide on the best thing to do when he woke up.

But the next time he woke someone was yelling his name. The call was an anxious one coming from the shore. He was alone in the sleeping area when he leaped up; the grass and twig beds lay there empty in the sunlight and shadow.

A number of voices were shouting from the shore now, and he was there in a flash. One of the boats was gone—it was tied at the log landing on the other side of the water. He saw three women running down the slope from the settlement toward the boat with horsemen galloping after them. The women would never make it to the boat. Holme looked hastily around, but neither Ausi nor Tora was anywhere to be seen.

As he untied the boat, anxious voices explained that the women had rowed over for the fishing gear. They needed fish and discovered that the gear was still at the landing. Although no one thought their pursuers were still around, the women had promised not to go up to the farmstead. But they had anyway and now they were all seeing the consequences.

The women were surrounded and disappeared among the horses. Before Holme shoved the boat out, a younger man hopped in with an ax in his hand. It was the one who had stood guard that morning. Holme looked toward the people on the shore again but couldn't see the man's wife. She was obviously the third one on the other side.

Holme knew there would be no sense in fighting this time. There were only two of them and arrows and spears might get them before they even reached land. The thrall told him that the horsemen had their weapons ready, but Holme rowed on without turning around. The people on the islet retreated into the distance, and he remembered they didn't have a boat. Maybe they could cross on logs and fetch the boats once the horsemen were gone.

The chieftain began admonishing Holme to give up even before he reached the landing, pointing out how hopeless it would be to resist. They had the dangerous man in a trap, and the chieftain felt glad and grateful to the wooden god who had helped them when Christ either wouldn't or couldn't. It might be a valuable thing to remember in the future.

The women had already been bound, and Ausi was in despair since she had never seen Holme give up without a fight before. She had put them in a bad situation again, even though she had meant well. Holme stepped out of the boat and stood before the warriors who approached cautiously, prepared for anything in spite of his being unarmed. The younger thrall had grabbed his ax but, looking at his captured woman, laid it hesitantly down and walked ashore behind Holme. The warriors tied them carefully without insults or scorn and their faces showed relief that the hunt was over.

The chieftain looked toward the islet and decided that the people over there could just as well stay for the time being. They couldn't escape and they weren't that important anyway. Holme and his family had been captured; that was the important thing. Their mission had been accomplished and the king would be pleased.

The chieftain ordered them to break camp. Hands bound, the prisoners followed along behind the last horses. The horsemen looked back frequently, having heard that Holme had knowledge exceeding other men's. They rode at a walk through the forest, and the thralls had no difficulty keeping up.

Ausi cried and chastised herself, but Holme was silent. He seemed deep in thought but not angry. Ausi knew he was planning their escape, and in her heart she called incessantly on Christ. If He could help them now, Holme would see and begin to believe in Him, too.

Toward evening, they reached the other farmstead. They were thralls again and worse off now than ever before. The chieftain decided they would spend the night there and warned that the thralls weren't going to deceive them again. They'd keep watch two at a time and not let Holme out of their sight for a single moment.

The night was as peaceful and clear as the one before. Holme could see no way out for him and his family; two warriors sat armed and ready on the grass beside him. The women slept intermittently in their discomfort, crying and moaning in their sleep.

In the middle of the night, Holme heard a strange distant sound that seemed to come from the sea—an almost imperceptible murmur and muffled yell. The guards were talking quietly and didn't seem to notice. The sound lasted a moment then disappeared. Holme wondered what it could be. It came again at regular intervals, rising and falling. He had heard such sounds once from a fleet of big ships. They had many oars with one man at each oar, and the men shouted rhythmically so everyone would pull together. A large Viking fleet might be out there now. The wind was too calm to hoist a sail.

As the sound died away his thoughts returned. He knew they were headed for certain death; at least he and the younger thrall were. The women would probably be kept living in slavery. And yet he still wondered what the place where he had been both thrall and lord, and where he was now bound as a prisoner, would look like the next time he saw it. He was considered the most dangerous man in the land, even though all he had done was to try to help others. He had gotten grain for the starving thralls where there was grain to get, but that was regarded a criminal act. He was despised by the merchants for remaining with the thralls when he didn't have to. Had he forgotten his own slavery instead and begun living like the merchants, everything would have been all right and he would always have been the respected master smith. Ausi had wanted that more than once, but he had been born a thrall and as long as there were thralls anywhere, he had to be among them, working for their freedom. He had broken free himself, so he knew it could be done.

If the women hadn't decided to row across that morning, they all would have gotten away. But he didn't blame them; he shouldn't have slept so long. You couldn't give women responsibilities; he had found that out during the many years Ausi had been his wife. She would vacillate and do things she'd bitter regret later. It couldn't be helped. She had been lured to the Christians several times and had accepted their baptism, but she never said a word anymore about Christ or his priests. She had reverted to her old self in the forest.

He thought, too, that if they did manage to escape and could gather the free thralls together again, they'd move so far north that no one could find them. They'd settle by some lake deep in the forest. They would break the ground and raise buildings, sow grain they'd take with them, forge weapons and tools. They'd erect walls around the farmstead too in case their enemies should come after all.

He'd gather all the outlaws and the oppressed there; everyone would be free to earn a living. They'd never show themselves around the town again, where the population was dense. They'd have their own nation far away. Maybe they could still get some women to join them; most of the men would join in the forests. There might be so many women in those districts that each man could have his own.

He heard Ausi wake up and whisper something to Christ. If that comforted her, let her do it. Tora had been calm the whole day, looking as though she thought her father could save them whenever he wanted to, that it amused him to let the enemy be in control for a while. Toward evening, they'd probably be at the shore opposite the town. A hard day lay ahead of them.

Some black, powerful figures came into his thoughts, and he smiled in the darkness. He had friends in town who shouldn't be messed with. In one way or another the smiths would intervene once they heard he was a condemned prisoner.

Ausi edged closer to him, and the guards turned around suspiciously. After they had checked to make sure none of the straps were loose, they returned to their places. It had grown lighter and the couple could begin to see each other. Holme saw that all the anxiety had left Ausi's face, and she whispered to him that she wasn't afraid anymore. They would get help. And she rubbed against him affectionately.

She saw a rare smile light up the bitter features of his face, and she felt a strong surge of happiness at being his. Nothing would come between them, now that she knew Christ was with people like Holme. He was a lot like Christ; he too wanted everyone to be free and to live well. Christ must like him, even though he was heathen.

Early in the morning, the chieftain detailed some of the horsemen to follow behind with the thralls. He rode at the front with the bulk of the troop. They had been away longer than he had thought they would be, and he was impatient to get home and report to the king. A stately man with a short-clipped beard was put in charge of the small detail. The chieftain reminded him how important it was for the prisoners to be closely watched. If they got away, they'd both suffer for it.

Then the chieftain disappeared into the forest with most of the warriors, and those left behind prepared to break camp. Ausi looked at the new leader, wondering half-afraid who he was. His gaze and build seemed familiar. He looked back at her a moment and it came to her. It was Geire, the man who had raped her. He had grown thin, the bridge of his nose was caved in, and he had cut his beard, but it was still him.

At first, she thought of saying something to Holme, who surely wouldn't recognize him. She also thought of telling him about the rape but restrained herself; it was so hard for Holme anyway. If he got angry enough, he might break loose and attack the men, but there were several of them and they were armed—they'd cut him down. If they were going to die—Holme, she, and Tora—it was best to keep quiet about what had happened. If they managed to escape, she could tell Holme about it later when he was free and could take revenge.

Geire's gaze, which before had been open and resolute, now seemed grave and treacherous. There was also something in it that made her remember the battle on the floor in front of the door. She sensed that he would rape her again if he got the chance. But Holme was there and would protect her even if he was tied up. At the right time, Christ would allow Holme to do whatever was best for all of them.

Six horsemen would escort them to town, and Ausi could see that Holme's face was brighter than it had been the day before. He could take six men if he were free and had a weapon. Maybe during the day his chance would come.

The thralls were allowed to have their legs untied, and they staggered among the horses a while before the journey began. Two men rode at the front with the younger thrall and his woman; then came three others with Holme, Ausi, and Tora tied behind the horses. Geire rode last so he could watch all of them constantly.

Back in town, Geire, hearing that Holme and his thralls would be tracked down and captured, had immediately sought the chieftain out to ask permission to go along. One of the two farmsteads the thralls had taken over belonged to him and the other to his sister. When the chieftain heard that, he decided it might be a good idea to have a warrior along who both knew the area and hated Holme and the thralls.

It was, in fact, because of Geire that they had finally managed to capture Holme and the others. He had ridden off to his farmstead by himself and discovered the thralls fleeing to the islet. It had then only been a matter of setting up an ambush for them since the horsemen didn't have boats to get to the islet.

The chieftain had no qualms about leaving the prisoners in Geire's custody after he'd heard the things he had against Holme. But despite everything, Holme was a known and, in his way, a respected man; it wouldn't go over well to kill him like a dog in the woods as Geire wanted. Undoubtedly, the king wanted to make him responsible for the blight, and so he would also want to mete out his punishment himself. The wife and daughter would surely be returned to their former owner once Holme was dead.

Geire was riding behind the prisoners and was, on the whole, satisfied. Over a year ago, the thralls had beaten him to the ground with their sticks, but he had begun to settle accounts.

Never in all his life had he imagined that someday he would have to join an army against thralls. He had always considered them necessities on a farmstead, nothing you had to deal with like ordinary people. But the smith walking in front of him had made himself a free man and had given many others the notion that they too could be free to fend for themselves. It was dangerous to let such a thought spread. Slaves far outnumbered freemen, and if they got hold of weapons, things could end disastrously.

With Holme captured however, the danger was past. Geire's sister would get Ausi and the daughter back as thralls, as was only right. And then everyone could sleep without worrying about hearing the resounding blow of a sledgehammer on the door at night.

The thralls in front of him had had their arms freed so they could move faster. They were secured only with leather straps around their waists, but the straps were so strong that ten smiths couldn't break them. The women had taken off their jackets and were walking with their shoulders bare. It was a clear, warm autumn day, and they had to trudge through dense thickets.

That whole year, Geire had been unable to forget the thrall woman he had raped on the floor. She walked ahead of him now; he could see her bare shoulders and the battle raged in his memory — her alabaster body, struggling and panting; the final surrender and his victory. It was shameful that his sister had awakened and pinned her arms, but at the time all he'd been able to do was accept the help.

Geire didn't just want to rape her again; he wanted to live with the woman. The thought that she might someday come to him of her own free will seemed to him an idea worth living and striving for. Her husband was going to die; someday, after a little time had passed, he might be able to get along with her all right. Svein could have the daughter; it was small recompense for the deformity her father had bestowed upon him.

Sometimes he believed that Ausi had cast a spell on him to avenge the rape. Before, he had given no thought to women after his farmstead had burned. There had been a woman thrall there he had visited regularly. But this last year he had had no peace. He had tried others, only to realize an even stronger desire for the woman walking before him now with supple, fluid hips.

At midday, he decided they would stop and rest. They were in a little glade with mixed forest around it. The horses began grazing, and the thralls sat down behind them, sliding themselves along behind whenever the horses moved and made the straps too tight.

Geire had come to a decision during the last hour. He felt shame, but his lust was too intense and he couldn't help it. Softly he talked with the other men and their eyes began twinkling and roving around. They could have the young girl and the thrall woman; Holme's wife he reserved for himself. No one would know; besides, no one would care. Both men were going to die, and the women would return to slavery.

Quivering with excitement, the warriors approached the thralls and suddenly threw themselves on the men, who still didn't quite grasp what was happening. They managed to throw a strap around Holme's wrists and pull it tight. The young thrall was tied the same way, and then all the warriors worked together tying their legs with another strap. Having done that, they freed the women from the horses.

The thralls finally understood what the men were up to. The women struggled, kicking and biting as they were dragged toward the edge of the forest by the panting men. Holme and the thrall rolled on the ground, roaring and yanking on the straps. The horses, getting restless, neighed and tossed their heads.

Hearing his daughter's screams from the bushes, Holme pulled his legs up with a powerful yank and caught the strap with his bound hands. With a violent jerk, he snapped the strap and leaped to his feet. The horses spooked, broke loose, and took off toward the woods. Holme threw his body backwards with all his might and the straps tying him to the horse snapped, too. But his friend, dragged bouncing along behind his horse, disappeared into the brush.

His hands still tied, Holme ran toward the fighting and screaming. He met one of the men who had come out to see what was disturbing the horses. The man stared at Holme and reached for his weapon, but Holme gave him a tremendous kick. He fell to the ground and lay there while the others, letting go of the women, rushed over. A quick glance assured Holme that all three women remained untouched.

But five men surrounded him with weapons drawn while he was alone with his hands tied. Geire soon calmed down and stopped the others from cutting the prisoner down. He must be handed over to the chieftain alive, or it could mean their lives too. As he watched the women getting up triumphantly and rearranging their clothes, he shot a dark, hate-filled look at Holme. The smith had upset his plans this time, too, but never again.

Geire guarded the prisoners himself while the others searched for the horses snorting nearby. They found them soon enough and the bloody, torn thrall came stumbling along behind them after they had untied his legs. His woman cried out with joy, then answered the question in his eyes, explaining eagerly that nothing had happened to her or the others. Holme, who still hadn't caught his breath, was surprised and relieved to see that the thrall was still alive in spite of being dragged behind the horse. He was glaring with hatred at the horsemen as he spit out dirt and grass.

But the man Holme had kicked in the stomach wasn't moving. The others turned him over and tried to sit him up, but blood was running down his beard and he fell limply to the ground. Geire decided they should rest a while longer so he'd have a chance to come to. Already he regretted what had just happened and wished somehow it could be undone. He turned away from the hatred and disdain in the thralls' eyes. After this, he would never be able to woo Ausi once she was alone and independent.

It was midday and the group of people, so recently violent, now was quiet and still. The leaves of the young aspen trees rustled slowly, and the dragonflies flew back and forth over the clearing with a slow beating of wings. The young thrall woman tore chunks of moss and wiped the blood from her man's face and hands.

Holme's legs were still free and he sat between Ausi and Tora. He was thinking about the things that had just happened, how close they had come to freedom. If his hands had been free, he would have taken on those five men. But the day wasn't over yet. He thought with distaste of the town, and something from the fathomless forests tugged at him with a magnetic force.

Again he heard the strange sound he had heard the night before. Barely audible but rhythmic. Sometimes more distinct, then dying completely away. He glanced around, but none of the others appeared to hear anything.

He knew approximately how far it was to town; they had long stretches of the lake to the west of them. The sound came from there. An almost inaudible, yet roaring and rhythmical, yell. It seemed to come from the very sunshine and silence themselves. Perhaps it was from the land beyond the dead, and that was why he alone heard it. That didn't scare him, but he was uneasy at the thought of what they would do to Ausi and Tora when he was gone. He had just had a glimpse of what they could expect.

He pushed the thoughts aside and listened again. He heard the sound retreating farther to the west then dying away in the rustling of the aspen leaves. The still motionless man lay at the foot of the trees, his cheeks ashen beneath his beard.

It was a quiet, angry Geire who gave the order to break camp a short time later. Finally he had realized that the man was dead, so they tied him securely onto his horse. He hung across the saddle, blood dripping on the ground as the horse walked.

For the moment, Geire's lust for the woman had been dampened by the violent and unpredictable events, and he was thinking that the most important thing now was to complete their mission. He began to believe himself that Holme was in league with the powers beyond, and it would be a relief to leave him in the chieftain's hands. Geire examined the straps Holme had ripped apart, convinced that no ordinary human being could have done that. Not five ordinary men. And he had never heard of a single kick being enough to kill a man without his even making a sound.

But he still felt bitter disappointment at not getting a chance to rape the women. Everything had been so well planned; none of them had thought anything could stop them. The opportunity would come round again after Holme's death, though, and then there'd be no one who'd be able to stop him. He could still sense the smell of leaves and damp moss from the ground where he'd wrestled briefly with Ausi. Then he had heard the horses breaking loose and the girl screaming for her father. That despairing shriek had only further incited Holme to violence. It would have served Holme right to have to lie there, tied up, hearing everything, but he had won again, for the last time.

Geire saw the fear and anger in the other men's eyes whenever they turned toward Holme. What was it about him that was so ominous and threatening, in spite of his customary silence? Geire scrutinized him closely for the first time. He was taller than he looked; his shoulders were broad and full, his hands large and well-formed. But there was something else; there were many men who looked like they'd be just as strong. He couldn't pinpoint it exactly, but no one could meet him and not be impressed. You had to be either his enemy or his friend. But his only friends were among the thralls, even though freemen had treated him as their equal. And he still held his head high, thinking himself as good as anyone else. It was high time that such a mysterious being got his just punishment—death.

They'd have to travel faster now to arrive on time. The prisoners had the straps tied around their waists again, but their arms had been left free so they could run behind the horses. They'd soon reach a wider road that was bumpy and winding but at least it wouldn't have boulders and bushes to slow them down.

Embittered, Geire sat on his horse behind the prisoners. The man tied up in front of him might have frustrated his plans, but Geire was the leader and would have some kind of revenge while he still could. He could at least run the obstinacy out of the prisoners by nightfall. Both thralls had pretended they were freemen, and their women considered themselves too good to be taken by free warriors.

When they emerged onto the road, he told the his men what he had in mind and they agreed at once. The thralls had won in the glade back there, but now they'd teach them.

Holme had already guessed what was coming, and his threatening, disdainful look provoked Geire even more. From his position behind the prisoners, he could soon see them start running as the straps began tightening around their waists. The women lifted their skirts with one hand, and he could see their bare legs. That intensified his excitement, and he yelled to the horsemen to go faster. In the meantime, he wondered what had come over him, a quiet, good-tempered warrior and farmer. That woman had probably cast a spell on him so he was no longer himself.

The legs in front of him moved faster and faster, and the thralls began panting more and more heavily. He saw Holme turn his head and look first at his wife and then at his daughter to see how long they could hold out. Suddenly Ausi tripped, but before she could fall, Holme's arm shot out and grabbed her. He ran on as she clung panting to his arm. Grudgingly, Geire marvelled again at the smith's strength and quickness, which had to exceed that of any normal man.

Holme soon got his wife back on her feet again and supported her until she could follow along. At the same time he snatched up his daughter with the other arm, and she flung her arms around his neck. As far back as Geire was he could hear the thralls' wheezing, so finally he ordered the horsemen to slow to a walk. Maybe the thralls had mellowed by now.

Holme put Tora down and shot a look back at Geire. Holme's face was swollen and shiny with the sweat running down it. Geire was not a timid man, but it was clear to him that Holme's impending death would be his own salvation. The smith before him was not to be taken lightly. His enemies would forever be in mortal danger. The fact remained that, despite his being tied up during the whole journey, a dead warrior dangled across his own horse.

But they'd be in town before nightfall. Though Geire had failed with the woman in the woods, soon no one would be able to stop him from doing whatever he pleased with her and her daughter.

The third time, Holme wasn't the only one who heard the strange, rhythmical sounds. From deep in the woods they could hear the sounds as they neared the landing and Geire called for silence: the shout of multitudes blended with the distinct roar of churning water. Geire galloped up a hill near the road but couldn't see anything. The eery sounds created an atmosphere of their own, but for Geire it was nothing new. The wind was completely down and he realized that many large battleships had come out onto the lake. What they heard was the rhythmical yell of the oarsmen rowing in unison; the churning water came from the prows and the plunging oars.

Soon it was clear to Holme, too, where the sound was coming from. They had had a long way to go in the silent night and peaceful day, but now only a rim of forest stood between them and the town. Geire ordered them to approach cautiously so they could take a look without being discovered from the lake. They could see hoof prints the whole way where the road passed through swampy areas.

Even before they had reached the forest's edge, they could catch glimpses of the cheery colors among the trees. Geire ordered the horsemen to stop, and they watched a large Viking fleet rowing slowly by on the lake. The shout sounded hard and rhythmic and hundredfold. The long oars glistened in the evening sunlight as the water ran off them, and the golden dragons, their red maws gaping widely toward the town, glared rigidly at it.

Geire and his men stared in astonishment and disappointment at the ships, but Holme once again contemplated escape. The chieftain and the king had something else to think about now. He could see people swarming into the harbor, and a narrow file of people streaming toward the fortress. Enemies were on their way to plunder and burn.

Geire conferred with his men a moment, then decided to leave the horses on the mainland. The oarsman was nowhere to be seen and the ferry was on the other side, but a few small boats were at the shore. They might have time to get over and into the town before it was surrounded. Surely the dragon ships wouldn't bother chasing the small boats when they were so close to the town.

Holme didn't want to jeopardize his and his family's lives by starting a fight on the shore. It would be better to cross peacefully to the other side. In the great confusion that would engulf the town a better opportunity for escape might come along.

People came running from farmsteads to the shore to watch the Vikings. The owners of the small boats stood there guarding them, but by threatening the chieftain's disfavor, Geire finally managed to borrow two of the boats. The horses had to be left as collateral.

When they lifted the dead man from his horse to put him into a boat, they found that his body had stiffened in the shape of a bow. They couldn't straighten him out so had to drape him over the prow, exchanging vexed words about his having to walk doubled over through the land of the dead. It wouldn't be easy for him to use his weapons or get around.

A ways from shore, they could see the harbor guards on the run, trying to organize the defense; frenetic horn blasts sailed across the water. But not a group of warriors was ready for battle, and people kept fleeing to the fortress. On the nearby lookout hill stood a group of men, looking down at the advancing enemy. Boats of all sizes had taken off from shore, but a couple of the dragons broke out of the fleet and would soon block their path to the coves and all their hiding places. The rest of the fleet headed straight for the harbor, but the shout of the oarsmen had fallen silent and the boats were changing formation as they approached.

Geire and his men rowed with their prisoners between the fleeing and the pursuing boats. Cold wakes from the big ships came rolling into them, rocking them violently, and they could see long rows of shields along the sides of the ships. But no one would bother chasing two little boats from the mainland. The ones from town, on the other hand, would have valuables on board.

They managed to reach the jutting edge of land and get ashore out of sight of the ships. The younger thrall looked questioningly at Holme and signalled with his wounded head; he thought they should make their move, even though their hands were still tied, but Holme shook his head. He knew better than to think he could kick to death five men who were armed and wary of him. There'd be better opportunities. They could hear the tumult from the lake but couldn't see anything from where they stood. The dragons had probably caught their prey.

With this new situation threatening ruin for the whole town, the warriors forgot that the thralls were dangerous too. They dragged them hurriedly along, scarcely looking back at all. They were afraid they might not make it to the fortress before the enemy landed and laid siege to it. It wouldn't be a good idea to be outside once that happened. No one knew what the advancing enemy would do—demand ransom from the town and sail off, or plunder and burn and kill everything in their path.

Holme knew there'd be no battle. Too many enemy warriors were arriving and there didn't seem to be anyone to stop them in the harbor. Perhaps the king and most of his men were gone. In that case the men on the hill might be the chieftain and the warriors who had been with him on the thrall hunt, and another hunt would soon begin.

The warriors and thralls jogged through the grove and across the meadow. The prisoners didn't resist so the straps dangled loose all the way. Soon they were below the hill, looking up at the warriors on the top, who quickly turned toward the strange little group that had just broken out of the forest. When the group reached the top, the chieftain's face was deeply troubled, and he barely listened to Geire's report of the journey. He said the king was gone; they were just too few of them to fight, but they'd lock themselves in the fortress and defend themselves as long as they could. Maybe Christ would come to their aid.

From the hill, Holme could see that many people were hurrying toward the forest, not the fortress, and he thought bitterly to himself that they were undoubtedly the thralls who weren't allowed to take up valuable space and therefore had to seek shelter wherever they could find it. A few men were walking toward the harbor to meet the enemy. Holme had known for a long time that some young thralls would go over to the enemy in order to get new lords in another land. But they might just as easily be cut down or driven off. So they walked hesitantly, always on the alert.

The chieftain considered a moment what to do with the prisoners. He would have liked to kill the men and drive off the women, but the king's order was still in effect, so he finally decided to take them into the fortress. The men would have to be kept under constant guard, but the women could help with the work if need be.

As he was being led into the fortress, Holme saw the enemy breaking through the barriers in the harbor and swarming onto shore. The town defenders came running toward the fortress in the mounting dusk.

The fortress was teeming with people of all ages. Many of them had spread their animal skins and clothes on the ground for their children and had set their store chests down beside them. Some had ponderous, iron-clad chests that weighed more than a man; others had simple wooden ones. The richest merchants and their wives wore expensive clothes with gold and pearls hanging down the arms.

A lot of people recognized Holme in the dim light, and a surprised murmur arose as the prisoners were brought forward. Some of the townspeople grumbled out loud about thralls and outlaws taking up precious space. But other voices anxiously countered that it was all the same since they'd probably all fall victim to the enemies' weapons, and all the women would be enslaved. Everywhere, women and children were moaning and crying.

Holme listened for the smiths' voices, but couldn't hear them anywhere. It would hardly have been possible to keep them out of the fortress if they had wanted to come in. His hands were still bound, and although the women had been untied, they were forbidden to move freely within the fortress. They rubbed their swollen wrists and tried in any way they could to make things easier for their men. All the while, they kept staring at the expensively dressed women glittering in the dim light.

It was nearly dark when the gate opened for one last group of men. Holme didn't see them, but he couldn't mistake their voices. They reported that the enemy had the whole town in their hands now and would soon reach the fortress. But they hadn't killed anyone or burned any buildings.

The smiths' news quickened the atmosphere in the fortress, and many of the people began to hope they'd escape with their lives. The warriors had taken up positions along the wall, ready to fight if the enemy suddenly stormed the fortress. But it was more likely that they would wait for daylight so the defenders couldn't see them outlined against the sky as they rushed up the slope.

The smiths moved to the far side of the fortress and their voices were lost in the noise. Holme and Ausi talked softly about how surprised the smiths would be when dawn broke and they could all see each other. The guards weren't staying so close anymore, probably figuring that there were enough guards outside the fortress. No one in his right mind would want to leave the protection of the fortress to be cut down.

They finally laid down to try to sleep. It had been a rough, exhausting day, but they hadn't been hurt. They were still alive, and Ausi was convinced that Christ had sent the enemies for their deliverance. The chieftain was a baptized Christian, but enemies were still threatening his town and himself—proof that his wasn't the real Christ.

The noise died away as night fell, replaced occasionally by heavy breathing and snores. Ausi lay on her back, watching the dark clouds above her. A star sparkled through now and then where the clouds thinned out or dispersed. Once a bright circle of stars took shape over her face. It remained fixed for a moment, and she thought that Christ had parted the clouds to see what was happening to His wards. She was filled with joy and began guessing how He was going to save them.

Holme and Tora were asleep next to her. She thought how she and her daughter had been rescued in the forest and was grateful. The men had planned to rape Tora, a mere child who had never even looked at a man. But they had underestimated Holme; though he was bound hand and foot, he had struggled to her aid and saved all three women from the rapists. A few minutes later and it would have been too late. Holme had kicked one rapist to death, the one who now lay bent double at the shore. They hadn't had time to carry him with them. They had lain his weapon beside him, thrown some branches over him, and said they'd be back after the battle.

She could hear the chieftain's voice in the distance as he conferred with the town leaders. They speculated about how big a ransom they would have to pay to keep life and town intact. They also considered the gods and what they should sacrifice to them. The chieftain raised his voice when he affirmed that only Christ could help them now and that this would never have happened if everyone had lived a good Christian life like he did.

In the middle of the night fresh warriors relieved those standing guard. The ones going off duty said that the fortress had been surrounded since dusk. They had heard muffled voices and rattling weapons. The enemy would probably attack at daybreak.

People would wake up now and then, yawn, and try to keep their voices calm when they spoke. Occasionally a baby would whimper or someone would call out in his sleep. The young thrall and his woman slept in a close embrace near Ausi.

After midnight the whistling wind rose among the trees around the fortress and Ausi felt raindrops on her face. She put her own garment over Holme and Tora, then lay down herself without any covering. Joyfully she felt how cold and wet she was getting. She had finally found something she could do for them. But the rain shower got heavier and soon water was running under the sleeping people. Holme woke up first, and those near them soon started moving and getting up. A roof jutted out from inside the fortress wall, so they woke Tora and hurried there for shelter.

After the rain, the ground was too wet to lie on. Everyone walked around miserably, trying to keep warm. The thralls' guards were walking around too, and no one noticed in the darkness that two of the thralls had their hands tied. Holme had hoped that during the night they might get a knife or something to cut the straps with, but they hadn't been able to yet. He also realized that the tense, irritable crowd would welcome a chance to attack a couple of bound thralls. At dawn he'd probably run into the smiths and get free. Then no matter what happened, at least they wouldn't die with their hands tied, and with his hands free, he wouldn't die alone.

The straps had cut into their wrists until their arms went numb. The women rubbed and caressed them to ease the pain and to show their affection. But Tora still looked at her father in bewilderment; she couldn't believe he was going along with all this. When he had kicked the man to death in the forest, she had laughed delightedly but nothing had changed. But since he was going along with everything, he must be waiting for something. He was the strongest man of all.

The gray light of dawn began to spread in the east over the lake, and inside the fortress they were finally able to see. A number of people began loosening their clothes and walking toward a fenced-off area. The chieftain climbed up on the barricade to survey the surrounding enemy. Everyone inside the fortress could hear them; they were talking loudly and occasionally laughing. They probably had no respect for their victims. The chieftain, who had travelled widely and could tell where they came from by their speech, told his men they were Danes and that it was a good sign they hadn't attacked yet. Maybe they'd be satisfied with a ransom.

The smiths shook their heads in disbelief when a man told them that Holme was a prisoner in the fortress. He had been gone a long time, and they hadn't heard anything about his coming back. And he wasn't easy to capture and hold prisoner.

But the man persisted, and the smiths finally went searching among the wet, miserable crowd. Holme saw them coming, and the surprised smiths soon surrounded the prisoners. Without a word the oldest smith drew his knife and cut the straps, first Holme's and then the younger thrall's. Both men gratefully stretched their arms, smiling with relief.

The smiths' short-lived surprise turned quickly to happiness at the reunion. A number of the wealthy merchant families glared at the smiths and thralls who belonged in the forest, not taking up room here. Ever since Holme had come to town, the smiths and craftsmen had been insubordinate and too sure of themselves. But that wasn't all — he had even managed to make ordinary thralls think they were just as good as freemen. Look at them standing there now, talking openly and happily as if they were the most important people in town.

There were three people who regarded them with even greater disdain. Geire had found his sister and Svein, who were glad to hear that Holme was a prisoner and would soon die. The chieftain's wife would get Ausi and Tora back again — it was her due. She had already given her brother permission to do whatever he wanted to with Ausi. And she was pleased to see that Svein had prowled like an aroused animal all night after discovering that the girl was in the fortress.

As soon as day broke they had started looking for the thralls so they could gloat over their misery. But the smiths were there first and the prisoners were free. Once again the chieftain's wife had to endure seeing Ausi as beautiful as ever, unaffected by all she'd been through. Tora was almost grown, and though she wasn't beautiful, she still caught your eye. She'd probably become a sorcerer like her father.

She gleefully noticed that Holme's hair was graying at the temples and that his face had grown thin. His cheek bones were more prominent than before and his eyes deeper set. He'd be dead soon and then she would get even with the slave woman and her daughter. It had been a long time since she had offered silver to the wooden god in order to get hold of them, but he had finally lived up to his part of the bargain.

Ausi's eyes caught the spiteful look in those of her former owner and she moved a few steps closer to Holme even though the smiths stood protectively in a ring around them. She knew what was in store for her and Tora if those three ever got their hands on them again. Geire was looking angrily at the smiths but no doubt realized how hard they would be to handle. She recognized Svein by the steely way his eyes stared at Tora, seldom blinking. He had grown as tall as Geire and was armed like a warrior. She hoped he would never get his hands on Tora.

Suddenly a loud horn blast came from outside the fortress, bringing immediate silence inside. A clear voice in their own tongue warned them that the enemy was strong enough to storm the fortress and kill everyone in it. They could raze the town too if they wanted. They would spare the town, though, since their chieftain had once been king in this land but had been driven away. He wanted to make peace with his former people despite the indignity he had suffered.[14]

When the townspeople heard the former king's name, they looked at each other and remembered. He was a man of his word, but he had been driven away for trying to force his own will above that of the people at the assembly. Now, he was back with an army.

The voice spoke again, promising that those inside would be allowed to live and keep their town but for a price. And the voice stopped when it told them how big the price would be. They demanded a quick answer; otherwise they would attack.

The chieftain gathered the merchants around him, and a lively exchange began. Everyone seemed relieved; they'd be left alive and the ransom wasn't as much as they had feared. Holme watched this chain of events uneasily. If the enemy withdrew, the danger for them was just as great as before. He and the smiths couldn't hope to fight the whole town even if the smiths were fully armed.

When the meeting was over, the chieftain stepped up on the rampart so that his gray head could be seen from every direction. He answered that, though it was a great burden, they would pay the ransom in silver demanded of them. Even as he spoke, the silver was being measured into a chest and would be set outside one of the gates. He hoped that the enemy wouldn't change their minds and would sail away as promised.

From where they stood, the prisoners could see the chieftain taking silver from the merchants and weighing it before putting it in the chest. There were masses of tiny white coins, long silver bars, and rings of all sizes. Even the poor had to contribute what they could to ransom their lives. The sum demanded was finally in the chest, and the chieftain had it dragged to one of the gates. Warriors were ordered to stand on both sides of the gate with swords drawn in case anyone tried sneaking into the fortress.

---

[14] The king's name, according to Rimbert (*Anskar*, chapter 19, p. 65), is Anoundus, and the raid described on the following pages occurred after Gautbert's replacement, Ardgar, arrived in Sweden (i.e., seven years later, not one year).

Once the gate was closed again, the atmosphere among the people was buoyant. They sighed in relief and began thinking about their everyday concerns again. All they had to do was wait until the enemy sailed away and then they could go back to town.

They gathered round the prisoners, looking at them with curiosity or malice while they repeated to each other the crimes the thralls had committed. Geire took this opportunity to approach the chieftain and remind him about the prisoners. He asked that his sister be permitted to take Ausi and Tora with her—as had been decided at the assembly—when she left the fortress. Soon Holme saw the chieftain approaching, surrounded by merchants and warriors. They stopped in front of the group of thralls and silent smiths, who stood waiting to one side.

The chieftain spoke and reminded everybody about Holme's past, how he had escaped from his owners and passed himself off as a freeman in town. How he then plundered the Christians' storehouse and handed out the grain to his fellow thralls while the rest of the towns' populace lived on the brink of starvation. Then he described the attack on the Christian church and the murder of the priest. Holme had been condemned as an outlaw long ago, but time after time he had returned to town. No one until now had managed to strike him down, but his time had come.

The chieftain talked too about the charred god on the rock far away in the forest. Holme had used his sorcery to make the god spread the blight over the grain: everyone knew that. Many people had starved to death and still more might starve during the winter. The chieftain concluded by telling of the thrall hunt and the capture. As proof that all he said was true, he pointed out that the grain at the thrall farmsteads was free from the blight that was ravaging everywhere else.

Ausi listened to the chieftain's speech more and more anxiously, wondering how all the good Holme had done could be construed as a criminal outrage. If a thrall had told the story, the truth would have come to light. He would have told how Holme had fixed his tools for nothing, had taken him into his house and given him food and drink, had risked his own life and liberty to obtain food for the thralls when they were near death from hunger, and had forgotten himself. He had shared their troubles and in the end had tried to make them free and happy. If Holme was a criminal, so was Christ, who also went around helping the poor and downtrodden. And now they were going to kill Holme for the good he had done.

Holme's face was unaffected by the chieftain's story, but the smiths looked surprised and troubled. They had known Holme for many years, but they couldn't get away from the fact that he had done what the chieftain accused him of. Even so, they had no intention of letting him be killed in front of their eyes. He had been good to them and fair; when the time came they'd be on his side.

They soon heard the chieftain say, however, that the prisoners would be held in safekeeping until the king returned. He'd stand judge over them himself. The smiths calmed down, resolved not to sit idly by in the meantime. Sledgehammers and axes could sink into most doors.

Before the chieftain could issue his final order, the lookout shouted to him and he climbed back up on the barricade. The sun had come up and was shining on his gray hair and horned helmet.[15] Down in the meadow between the town and the fortress the enemy was crowded around the silver chest, and a roar of agitated voices was rising. The chieftain could see that they didn't think there was enough ransom. A huge warrior kicked the chest in disdain and looked around defiantly.

The chieftain realized they had celebrated too soon; the danger still hadn't passed. The invaders probably hadn't appreciated their chieftain asking for so little from so rich a town. The noise grew louder, and the chieftain came down to talk with his closest advisors. The crowd surrounding the prisoners thinned out again with the advent of the bad news, and everyone crowded around the chieftain, terror on their faces. A number of them loudly promised their gods great gifts and sacrifices if they would help them out of this new peril.

But the chieftain had gone back to Christ even though the wooden god had done him a good turn when he was hunting thralls in the forest. He spoke now, advising the merchants to promise Christ their gifts because the wooden gods had only deceived them. The ransom was lost, and it looked as if the enemy would plunder, burn, and kill despite their promise to sail away. The chieftains probably couldn't control the warriors.

The chieftain graphically described how they would storm the fortress, kill all the men, and rape or steal the women. All because his people didn't believe in Christ. It did not occur to him that the same fate would befall him.

He spoke in an ominous voice, and the merchants began turning hesitantly away from the image of the battle god that stood in the fortress to put their fate into the chieftain's hands. He finally relented and turned his face upwards to put their case before Christ. He pointed out that he had been a good Christian from the start, emphasizing the services he had done the priests and finishing by listing the gifts the merchants were willing to give. In addition, the people wouldn't eat meat for a prescribed number of days.

The people around him watched timidly and attentively, and many of them peered up into the swirling white clouds after the new god's face. The noise from the enemy mounted, threatening to crash down from the sky onto the beleaguered fortress.

---

[15] The popular notion that Vikings wore horned helmets cannot be supported by archeological evidence, all of which suggests that the Viking helmet was conical. Horned helmets may have been worn for ceremonial purposes during the Bronze Age and pre-Viking period, but the evidence for that is slight as well. See James Graham-Campbell, *The Viking World* (New Haven: Ticknor & Fields, 1980), p. 24, and Almgren, *The Viking*, p. 221.

The thralls left on the islet watched with sorrow and anger as the horsemen captured Holme, the young thrall, and the women. When they had disappeared into the forest and everything was quiet, the thralls felt like a flock of abandoned children. What would they do without Holme?

They knew their pursuers wanted Holme, not them, but the boats were at the opposite shore, too far away to swim. Their provisions would give out soon, and the wild berries wouldn't last for long. They could see their barley fields across the water—large patches of gold beside the gray buildings. The grain was ready to be harvested; it would fall from the stalks soon and lie useless on the ground.

The men started chopping down trees the same day. They stripped the trunks and dragged them to shore, made ropes out of everybody's clothes, and tied the logs together into a raft. By evening it was in the water, and it could hold about half of them. They had split big pieces of wood for oars.

The clumsy raft inched across the still water while a group of thralls sat waiting mutely on the islet. Occasionally they heard a strange, rhythmical sound that seemed to come from an endless distance, a sound no one had ever heard before. It floated across the water from where the lake opened into the sea. The women shivered, fearing sorcery and bad omens. What could it mean? Maybe the horsemen were still in the woods and would attack the men once they got across.

When the raft bumped into the landing, one of the younger men hopped up on shore while the others shoved off again to safety. They still suspected a trap. The younger man was single, without wife and child, and he had volunteered to go ashore and reconnoiter. He could run away from the horsemen and hide in the woods. And why would they want to catch him anyway? He couldn't possibly be worth more than Holme.

The other men agreed to let him have his way. They watched him as he walked past the grainfield; he tore off an ear, rubbed it between his hands, and blew away the bran before stuffing the grain in his mouth. He was probably trying to show how calm he was. He circled the building to see if anyone was hiding there. Finally he ventured into the forest, and the men could hear him heaping scorn and defiance on the horsemen. But there was no response, and he soon came back down the slope. The others went ashore too, except for those going back for the rest of the thralls.

By midnight everyone was across, and the hoof prints were still visible in the mire on the shore. It was warmer at the forest's edge than on the islet, where the wind never really stopped blowing. The smell of ripe barley permeated the night, and the damp grass felt cool against their ankles. But Holme was gone, and none of them felt safe there anymore even though it had been their home for a year. A couple of the men stood guard outside while the others went inside to try to get some sleep.

One of the women complained bitterly about the way life had been since they gained their freedom. It had been good, but what would it be like now?

No peace, night or day; who could stand that? She was sorry she hadn't stayed in town as a thrall. Her mistress might have beaten her black and blue when she was in a bad mood, but that was still better than life on the run in the woods. They could never return to town and see people; they could never even get any new clothes.

The others sitting or lying on the benches and floor began to mull over what she had said, and soon they were murmuring in the corners. But in the end, it was only the complaining woman who had spoken who really wanted to go back to slavery. The rest searched for the right words to express their feelings, but it was hard. Had Holme heard them, he would have been glad that the thralls had freedom lodged so deeply in their hearts after just one year. They would never forget it and would tell the story of their year of freedom as long as they lived.

One of the older men reminded them what Holme had said, that everyone should be free and live their lives the way they wanted to. In a weak but steady voice he asked, weren't thralls as strong as freemen and just as skillful workers and warriors? Didn't a thrall hurt as much when he was beaten and suffering as a freeman did? Weren't slave women just as beautiful as free women? Oh, the freemen obviously thought so too since they always took the most beautiful slave women by fair means or foul, he concluded bitterly and scornfully.

But the woman didn't back down; instead, she asked when they'd be able to enjoy their freedom if they were never left alone. When would they dare walk the roads and paths as other people did? Where would they get the goods they needed when they couldn't barter with and buy things from anybody? They could never show themselves at the great sacrificial feasts. The freemen would kill them if they did, so they'd have to hide in the woods. And so would their children. What good would their freedom be then? the woman demanded bitterly, and her question was answered with a heavy silence. Most of them thought she was right; looked at from her point of view, freedom was more burdensome and dangerous than anything else could be.

The woman sat triumphantly in the darkness and dared the older man to respond. He finally said that he wasn't the one who had discovered freedom and given it to them; Holme was and he probably would have been able to answer her. Hadn't they lived well during the past year? And when Holme came back he'd probably know how to get even with the enemy again. He might marshal all the thralls in the land together, mount an army against the freemen, and make them all slaves. But no, that's not how it would be; thralls shouldn't exist at all. Better just to kill the freemen.

The thrall's thoughts were leading him nowhere, and he soon tired of the effort. Holme would have all the answers for everything when he returned. If they could only stay at the farmsteads, they'd have nothing to complain about. The old man told the woman that and then lay back down to sleep hoping that Holme would be back when he woke up. Then no one else would have to think or worry, just work and be glad about the day, the grain, and freedom.

But the disagreement lingered in the hall, dividing the thralls into two opposing camps. One feared the dangerous freedom that the woman had so aptly described. The other, comprised of the strongest men, wanted to fight and live in peace rather than give up. But all of them longed for the massive figure who could calm the waters and guide them with few words and little trouble.

The sun rose from the sea into a clear sky, and they started working the grain early. Men were sharpening their scythes on pieces of slate, sending a ringing, grinding sound out over the shore and lake, and two of them were already out fishing.

The women tied the grain in sheaves and stood them in the field to dry. The grain was rich and heavy, but there was no happiness in the harvest. Uncertainty affected everyone, and they turned toward the forest again and again. The horsemen might burst out again at any moment and surround them. Some had galloped straight through the field, trampling down the stalks. The harvesters tried to reassure each other that the enemy was far, far away and didn't give a damn about them anyway after capturing Holme and his family. But it didn't help.

Around midday, they saw a man standing at the edge of the forest watching them. He was an older man, who probably meant them no harm, but they were edgy and suspicious. They thought he might be a spy, who would lead the enemy to them, so they threw down their scythes for their axes and spears. The man saw what they did and ran into the forest. The men chased him, whooping and yelling, but soon returned. He had either gotten away or was a forest creature. You saw them every once in a while at abandoned farmsteads. They had seen this one flutter amongst the thickets and then vanish.

The men laughed raucously about the brief hunt and the mood lightened. They had agreed from the beginning that when the grain was cut and ready here, they'd move on to Holme's settlement and harvest the crop there. Otherwise, someone else might at any minute. During hard times, there were a lot of people — individuals and families — lurking at the forest's edge.

No one mentioned what they were going to do after all the work was finished, but it hung in the air around them. They didn't want to live with this apprehension and uncertainty; they had to know what was going on in town once the horsemen arrived with their prisoners. Maybe they could be of some help to Holme and the others. At the very least they could find out what dangers to expect from town.

When they peered out from the edge of the forest at the settlement all was peaceful. Everybody — both women and men — had walked there. They felt like a group of fatherless brothers and sisters without Holme. They had seen hoof prints all along the soft forest road and knew that the horsemen had spent the night at the settlement. Part of the grain had been reaped, and the millstone showed signs of recent use. Either the horsemen or the forest dwellers might be responsible.

Something was missing from the slope, and it took a while before they realized that the charred god was no longer standing on its rock. The men went searching through the dense brush down below and soon found the blackened clump of wood. The horsemen had knocked it off its perch but had forgotten—or decided not—to destroy it. The thralls put it back in place, thinking that it would probably take their and Holme's side. They would sacrifice some of their goods to him before evening.

The next day everything was ready. The grain was drying, and the women could take care of whatever was still left to do by themselves. A couple of the older men would stay behind too. The men still hadn't said anything, but the women looked at them anxiously. They sensed that they were going to be left unprotected, perhaps for good, becoming prey to outlaws and other men from the woods.

The men gathered by the smithy in the cleft, and soon you could hear the clanging and rasping sounds as they repaired and sharpened their weapons. A couple of them sat fixing their shoes in the sunshine on the slope. The women cleaned and ground grain so the men could have bread for the journey, and there was still some fish left from the previous day.

They spent all day in preparation and then retired at dusk. They weren't sure exactly what to do, but they had to do something. Without Holme, the forest no longer felt safe. They had to know what was in store for them. The skeptical woman jeered again at this oppressive thing they called freedom, but grew silent when no one responded.

They rose at first light to be on their way, a curious, silent band who, shivering in the morning cold, gathered outside the building and strapped on their weapons. The grass under their feet felt stiff from the frost but was almost warm at the edge of the forest. As Holme had done many times before, the thralls turned around and looked down over the settlement. They doubtless wondered if this could be the last time they would see it, if they were going off to pay for their year of freedom with their lives.

When the men were completely out of sight, the women withdrew into the building and barred the door. A few of them were crying; others were criticizing the men who had just abandoned them. The two older men who had remained behind were silent; they were aware that the women didn't think they counted for much.

After a while the sun came up, and a pale red glow fell on the buildings and the edge of the forest. A ray of light touched the blackened god and shone on a cooked fish lying on the stone before him. Beside it lay a piece of last night's bread, bran and charcoal baked into it.

From the fortress, the chieftain watched the enemy gathering in the open area, preparing to cast lots. Their behavior and talk told him that a great deal was at stake.

He was able to pick up a few indistinct voices asking the god if this town was theirs to plunder and burn. There was complete silence when the dice fell; then he heard a disappointed howl from a hundred throats. But the chieftain brightened, hoping again for salvation. Surely Christ had heard his plea for help and had directed the roll of the dice.

A few more questions were settled by lot, and then there was a meeting, which ended with most of the warriors withdrawing from the fortress and walking toward the ships. The chieftain yelled out the miracle triumphantly, and a roar of surprise and joy answered him. Christ was still the mightiest of gods. As many people as could find room ran up onto the barricade to see the departing enemy for themselves.

The land's former king stood with his men, the smallest part of the enemy army. The others were hastily tending to their ships; the wind was good and all the other signs favorable for the journey. Their god had promised them another, richer town if they left this one alone. It wasn't long before two-thirds of the ships were on their way, and their rhythmical chants could be heard clear up to the fortress.

But the fortress gates did not open. No one knew what those staying behind had in mind. If they attacked, there was hope of defending the fortress for a while. A message had been sent to the king to come back soon with his men.

A horn blast sounded outside, and the fortress fell completely silent. The former king began talking in a friendly voice, offering them friendship and alliance. He was their countryman and didn't want to destroy their town. That was why he had suggested casting of the lots that had ended so fortunately. The Danish chieftain was at that moment on his way to the town the gods had set aside for him to plunder and burn.

The chieftain in the fortress got up on the barricade and said that they had listened with joy to the king's words about friendship and alliance. As far as he was concerned, the king was a man of his word, but the people inside the fortress were frightened and feared treachery; therefore, they wanted warriors from both camps to meet outside first and start the alliance before their eyes. Then everyone would come out and return to his home.

The king agreed, and soon the warriors came down from the barricade. A moment later the gate was opened, and both groups of warriors met in the field while people swarmed above them, eager to see what would happen. It was just as the king had said; no one raised sword or spear against the resident warriors. The alien fleet was sailing east in front of a good wind and soon would be out of sight.[16]

---

[16] Rimbert offers the following description of the Danish raid: 'It happened that a certain Swedish king named Anoundus had been driven from his kingdom, and was in exile amongst the Danes. Desiring to regain what had once been his kingdom, he sought

In their great joy, the people forgot all about the prisoners. Only Geire was on his guard. While the people streamed out of the fortress, buzzing with happiness, he approached the chieftain and reminded him about the prisoners. The chieftain knit his brow in irritation and said that they'd be shut in the fortress until he had time to consider the matter. A heavy guard would be posted there so they couldn't escape. Geire himself was the most reliable; he could take as many men as he wanted and take charge of the prisoners. Having said that, the chieftain walked toward town with the foreign king.

The smiths, the last ones to leave the fortress, promised the prisoners they would be hearing from them. The guards angrily shut the gate behind them and didn't respond to their threats that they had better treat the prisoners well.

The grass was yellow and trampled down in the fortress. Pieces of coal, bread, and other scrap lay on the ground, and some of the heavy chests were still there. Inside the atmosphere was oppressive now that everyone was gone, and the joyous noise of the people grew distant and died away in town. The blue sky was clear, and the wind whispered across the blades of grass on the barricade.

Holme's heart ached for freedom. Stone walls rose above him, stifling him, making it impossible for him to see the woods and the lake. He could hear the whispering birch trees on the ramparts and the splashing of the waves against the rocks below. The smiths had gone, the gate had been barred behind them,

---

aid of them and promised that if they would follow him they would be able to secure much treasure. He offerd the Birka . . . they filled twenty-one ships . . . he had eleven of his own ships . . . It so happened that the king of the town was absent . . . Only Herigar, the prefect of this place, was present with the merchants and people who remained there . . . The king before mentioned commanded them to pay a hundred pounds of silver in order to redeem Birka and obtain peace. They forthwith sent the amount asked and it was received by the king. The Danes resented this agreement, because it was not in accord with their arrangement and they wanted to make a sudden attack upon them and to pillage and burn the place . . . As they were discussing this and were preparing to destroy the town to which the others had fled [i.e., Stigtuna, north of Birka], their design became known to those in the town . . . [who] exhorted one another to make vows and to offer greater sacrifice to their own gods. [Birka's chieftan] Herigar, the faithful servant of the Lord, was angry with them . . . Meanwhile the king proposed to the Danes that they should enquire by the casting of lots whether it was the will of the gods that this place should be ravaged by them . . . As his words were in accord with their custom they could not refuse to adopt the suggestion . . . and that [instead] they ought to go to a certain town which was situated at a distance on the borders of the lands belonging to the Slavonians. The Danes then, believing that this order had come to them from heaven, retired from this place and hastened to go by a direct route to that town . . . . Moreover the king who had come with the object of plundering the Swedes, made peace with them and restored the money that he had recently received from them. He remained also for some time with them as he wished to become reconciled to their nation' (*Anskar*, chapter 19, pp. 65–68.)

and their promise to return seemed empty now. Holme had detected a touch of uncertainty in their voices, so he would have to depend on himself alone.

He had talked with the smiths that morning about freedom for the thralls, but they hadn't understood him. There'd always been thralls and always would be. It was good that he considered thralls people and his equals, but how could he think others would ever do so? Chieftains, merchants, and farmers needed thralls, so there would always be thralls. He said he didn't know much more than they did, and it was true that there were countless thralls. But there was also land and forest as far as the eye could see. And the merchants could work for themselves or hire freemen. He had always known in his heart that freedom belonged to everyone, even if he didn't know how it could be attained.

He noticed that the guards were searching for straps to tie them up again. Their wrists still ached. Ausi looked at him with deepening despair and Tora with surprise. The thrall looked at him too, his eyes seeming to ask whether they shouldn't fight instead of getting tied up again. There were five men, including Geire, against them, and Holme and his friend were unarmed.

But when that gate shut, Holme knew he'd fight. He'd been a prisoner for days, had run behind horses, and had lain bound and scorned, waiting for his chance. He'd waited for the smiths too, but as usual, he was alone. Not completely—the young man by his side could handle at least one of his opponents, maybe two. He was strong and knew what to do. The forest and freedom were outside beckoning with a magnetic force, and Holme probably wasn't the only one feeling that.

Maybe Geire thought that the prisoners weren't dangerous in their new surroundings, that once they were in town, they had resigned themselves to their fate. And his men hadn't been along hunting the thralls down; all they knew was that the master smith, whom they had seen in town before, was guilty of a major crime and would be sentenced. They approached the thralls, arranging the straps as if they were going to bridle horses. Geire stopped a few steps away to watch everything with a furrowed brow. He was still furious that something always came between Holme's sentence and his death.

Holme knew he couldn't delay. The guards were still standing with the straps in their hands when he charged them. But they weren't the ones he had to get to first; Geire, who was standing beside their weapons, was the most dangerous. He could see the sword sliding out of the sheath at the same instant he got him in his grip . . .

The prisoners had been subdued and compliant in the fortress, so the chieftain would have let them keep their hands untied; he might not even have thought about the fact that the smiths had cut the straps. But when Geire was alone with them and the guards, he ordered them tied up again. He hadn't thought that they were dangerous once they were inside the fortress, but it was important that they not try to escape. They wouldn't be able to climb up the barricade with their hands tied.

While the guards were getting the straps he was thinking about Ausi. He'd soon have a right to her, and no one could stop him once her husband was dead. After days and nights of captivity, this strange woman was still beautiful and enticing. But she kept her eyes affectionately directed the whole time at the dark, silent man by her side.

If Geire had been wholly on his guard, he might have had a chance. He realized he was being charged and started to draw his sword. But he wasn't able to get it into the air before he felt a pair of hands grab him. These were no ordinary hands; he could feel death in their incredible power. He felt himself rise into the air, saw the sky and the stone walls flash before his eyes, and then everything was dark and quiet.

The astonished guards stood stock still when they saw what had happened to their leader. They weren't ready for an attack; no one had warned them. When Holme seized Geire, the young thrall was instantly on top of one of the guards, grabbing him by the throat and slamming him to the ground. Pinning him there, he took the guard's own short sword and stabbed him where he lay.

The three other guards fled toward the gate as Holme, unarmed, rushed them. The rage emanating from him made them forget about their weapons, but they didn't have time to open the heavy gate before Holme and the thrall were there. After a brief scuffle, five silent men lay inside the fortress, with two men and three women just as silently looking down at them.

Immediately, the five figures walked cautiously out through the gate facing town. The men had taken the guards' weapons, but Holme wasn't happy about the deaths. They hadn't had any choice, of course, but the hunt for them now would be more intense than ever.

There was still no danger from town; most of the inhabitants had either forgotten about the prisoners or thought that they were in safe custody. The boats were still where they had left them, and the doubled-up warrior was lying in the same spot under the bushes. They couldn't see him, but nothing had been disturbed, and big flies were buzzing around the area or sitting almost pensively on the leaves.

You could see the great, silent happiness in the faces of the young thrall and his woman, and you could hear it in their whispers. Even Holme looked relieved, though he alone understood how dangerous their situation was after what had happened at the fortress. Five men were dead; now the enraged king would order the thralls eradicated once and for all. Warriors would ride to the farmsteads once again, and they wouldn't return empty-handed. Holme and the other four had to be gone long before that.

But for now they were still free and had a good head start. Maybe they'd have time to pick up the others from the islet and then go north through unknown, endless forest. It was their only hope and it made Holme's face pensive and subdued even as the others rejoiced about going home. The young man talked the whole time about the fight. He had helped Holme by killing two of the guards; he was proud of that and happy.

In the early afternoon they came to where the path forked toward the separate farmsteads. They stopped to think a moment, then decided to go to the relatives' farmstead first to see if the others were still on the islet. Holme sensed that the men, once they realized that the horsemen had taken the prisoners away, wouldn't still be walking around there wondering what to do. There were trees there, and they had axes.

The fork was quiet for a while after they left it, but then the sound of footsteps and voices came down the other path from the settlement and the band of thralls came into view. If anyone from either group had yelled, the other group would have heard him. But they were all quiet, and the thralls went on toward town to see what had happened to Holme and, if possible, to find out what was going to happen to them.

Svein reluctantly followed along when everyone was cleared out of the fortress. He had kept close to the prisoners, staring so much at Tora that, tired and angry, she would occasionally crawl behind her father. Svein had hoped they could take the mother and daughter home with them, but the fortress was closed behind them with the prisoners inside. Still the thralls couldn't get away; Geire was there with several men to watch them.

The crowd streamed down toward the harbor to look at the foreign ships. But Svein stayed behind. The ships would be there a while; he could see them any time. When everyone had passed by, he turned slowly around and walked across the empty meadow. He looked around frequently, expecting his mother to come running after him any minute, anxiety etched in her gray face. She had to stop that; he'd be full grown soon and would have to go his own way.

He thought he heard something from the fortress and stopped to listen. But all was quiet, so he kept going. Somewhere inside he was afraid that one of the young warriors would look at Tora even though Geire was there with her. She was his alone, and he wouldn't tolerate anyone else even looking at her. He couldn't control his terror of her father—that he knew—but Holme would be dead soon, and then they'd see, the girl and her mother.

The fortress rose mute and lofty above him, and he clambered up the rampart. There were openings in the wooden barrier to shoot arrows through against attackers, and he looked in through one. He saw a warrior lying by the wall, blood running from his beard; another one lay in the middle of the fortress and three more in different positions by the big gate. None of them moved, and the wind passed through the opening beside him. He crouched quickly down, emitted a hoarse sound, and rolled down the rampart. At the bottom, he got up, looked around in terror for Holme, and then dashed toward town, his head lowered like a bull's.

He saw his mother looking for him among the buildings at the edge of town. Breathlessly he told her of the horror he had witnessed, and she began howling and crying in sorrow and rage. So Holme had taken Geire from her too, and now she was alone with her son who was marked for life. That thrall had taken everything from her, and he always got away.

Oblivious to everything else, she rushed toward the harbor. She ran straight to the chieftain and the foreign king, who were standing by the largest dragon ship, and sobbed out what had happened. She demanded revenge. The people crowded around her, listening in surprise to the raging woman before they understood what she was saying. Then some of them started running toward the fortress; several others followed, and soon half the town was on its way back to see what had happened.

The chieftain ordered the island searched and boats sent out to keep the thralls from fleeing to the mainland. No one noticed that a boat had already glided along into the shadow of the mainland forest and that some people were jumping out of it and running into the woods.

The chieftain's wife watched her brother Geire, eyes shut and beard bloody, rocking back and forth on a bier being carried from the fortress. So the smith had finally defeated him. She had only Svein now, and he was still too young to do battle with the deadliest of thralls. She no longer dared hope that the chieftain and his warriors would put an end to her enemy.

Inside the fortress the chieftain told the thrall smith's story to the foreign king—about his many deeds of violence, his thinking the thralls could be free, and his power. They were surprised to see that Geire had only a head wound, and they could figure out what had happened. Blood was running from two of the men, but the other two just seemed to be asleep. The people standing there murmured with fear and reluctant admiration that Holme had crushed them to death with his bare hands.

The foreign king marvelled and said that he'd like very much to see such a man. He asked why they hadn't made him a warrior long ago and tried to win his good will. It would be worthwhile making a man like that your friend. He had heard and could see what it was like to have him for an enemy.

But the chieftain refused to listen to such talk. No freeman would lower himself to seek the good will of a runaway slave, and this was the last straw. The next time they got hold of him, he would be cut down on the spot; taking him prisoner was foolhardy. And his fellow thralls would be rooted out to the last man. The smith's dangerous longing for freedom would disappear with them and order would be restored in the land.

Holme and his companions were pleased to see the grain drying and everything in order. The raft was tied at the landing, waves washing over it. The boats hadn't been touched. There was no life at the farmstead, but it wasn't difficult to figure out where the people were. Holme was pleased to think that the thralls could get along without his leadership and help.

They would spend the night here and follow them the next morning. The women were soon busy cleaning the grain, and the men went fishing by the landing. They might have time to clean most of the grain to take along before their enemies caught up with them.

The days were growing shorter, and the darkness would help them escape to the north. They would keep someone constantly on guard at the farmsteads so they wouldn't have to flee until the last minute. Something might delay the pursuit.

The next morning they took the little boat to the settlement. The young thrall and his woman rowed, joking and laughing. Ausi and Holme watched the shore from which they had once fled the settlement—the stones, the reeds, the dark forest that reached all the way down to the water. But even before Holme caught sight of the settlement, he knew something was wrong. It was quiet and deserted; the grain stood drying here too, but there were no happy voices or other human sounds. It was with great relief that he finally saw one of the older men by the shore.

The women came running to the boat when it pulled up, but their excitement soon turned to despair when they saw that their men hadn't come back with them. Holme listened quietly to their story, fatigue enveloping his face. He had looked forward to a couple of quiet days before the great flight north, but now he had to return to town. If the men got there first, it would be their death because of what had happened. The people's revenge would destroy the first ones to appear. It might already be too late. But they had known it would be dangerous; maybe he could still catch them.

Both the older men wanted to go along, but he refused. Ausi and Tora also wanted to go with him, but he refused them, too. He had travelled between settlement and town many times, but this trip would be the roughest and most dangerous. And before he had understood what freedom was and had had so many people to answer for, he had always managed best by himself. If the enemy came, he would probably be aware of it in plenty of time.

As he prepared for the return trip, the women became petulant. They said straight out that things had been better for them before. They hadn't had to live in constant danger then. And why should they get husbands if they were only to be taken away from them? They looked askance at Holme and his family. Ausi snapped back at them, but Holme was quiet, seeming not to hear them. The important thing now was the men who had gone to town. What to do afterwards they would decide together—if they were ever together again. Besides, the women were anxious about their husbands; it was best to pay no attention to them.

He told the men what to do while they waited. With the women's help, they should clean as much grain as possible. They might have to break camp quickly when he returned with the other men. But he noticed that even the two older men looked at him differently now that things weren't going so well. Perhaps they missed their slavery too and despised freedom when it meant they had to do something for it. They were probably afraid, like Stor and Tan. Those journeying to town, however, had shown that they understood what he had meant by freedom.

The boat was gone by the time he reached the shore opposite the island, and he knew his men were in it. A hermit who lived just inside the forest told him that a lot had been happening in town the last few days. And Holme heard a skewed account about what he had done and about the cancelled attack on the town. In answer to his question, the hermit said that some badly dressed men had come down out of the forest and had taken the boat. They had waited for dusk before daring to venture across.

Holme traded some provisions for the hermit's boat, which lay hidden in the reeds. The hermit walked in front of him, whining about what a great burden it would be for him if he didn't get his boat back. He'd starve to death because he subsisted on fish. Without a word, Holme took out the silver he still had left and put it in the hermit's outstretched hand. He skirted the reeds a good ways before setting course for the wooded side of the island.

A small ship from inside the coves crossed his path and the oarsmen saw him but nothing happened. He had seen the alien vessels in the harbor, but now the mountain blocked them from view. It was a clear autumn day with a cool breeze that intensified the farther out you rowed. He could see horses and people by the ferry in the distance. An occasional shout or other sound wafted across the water.

Holme didn't know how he was going to save his men, but he hoped they were still loose and hiding in the island forests. All he had to do was find them and get back to the farmsteads before their enemies did. Everyone knew where the thralls' hideaway was and would ride right to it.

He scoured the shore and finally saw their boat. It was floating in the reeds, and he tied the hermit's boat beside it and went ashore. He couldn't see or hear anything except some cows ambling around in the forest on the shore, snorting and rustling in the thickets.

Holme began to search but found no trace of his men. After circling round, he happened onto the countless burial mounds. One or two other people were walking around there, visible on a mound for a moment, or disappearing between them. Holme watched them closely without getting any nearer but they weren't out after him. He decided to walk to the woods on the other side of the graveyard and search there. The wind was whistling across the mounds, and the leaves on a lone aspen tree were dancing and twinkling.

He walked out in the open; no one would suspect him of being up here. The woods began where the mounds grew sparser, and many men were moving about there; he could hear spades clanging against stone. He crouched down, crept along a mound, and looked cautiously through the tall blades of grass on the top. The autumn sun was shining brightly, making it difficult to see into the trees.

When Holme finally figured out what was going on, he just stopped, maybe because the activity reflected a kind of peace, the end of a battle. For the first time he felt defeat and despair. Some men were digging in the darkness of the forest, and others lay in a silent, motionless row, waiting for their graves. Holme couldn't recognize them from that distance, but he didn't have to. He knew he had come too late this time.

He could feel, stronger than ever before, the power of the freemen levelled against him. He had no intention of attacking and killing any of the grave diggers; that wouldn't gain him anything. And he remembered the men and women at the settlement, who still needed him.

He didn't know how the men had died, but they had probably been taken while the townsfolk were still in a fury over the siege and the killings in the fortress. No one would bother bringing a pack of thralls before the assembly. They would just kill them, and there they lay all in a row. The branches swayed, causing sun and shadow to flicker on their tattered clothes. A few men and women stood in silence to one side. They might have known the dead men or maybe they had just followed along out of curiosity.

Before the men had finished burying the thralls, Holme had slid down and sneaked away among the mounds. He reached the boat and rowed across as though in a dream. The hermit chattered happily about getting his boat back again, but the hard face neither looked at him nor answered his words. Holme cast a final look at the town before disappearing into the forest.

Two joyous shouts greeted him when he emerged from the forest. His wife and daughter ran to him and told him they were alone. The older men and the rest of the women had taken the large boat and as much grain as they could carry. The younger couple had gone to the other farmstead to harvest as much grain as they could. They probably hoped it would be theirs someday after the pursuit had ended and the danger had passed.

Holme felt somehow relieved. Now he didn't have to tell what he had seen under the spruce trees on the island. No one would bother taking revenge on the two old men and the women, even if it was discovered they had belonged to the free thralls.

But what about themselves? They could stay at the settlement for one night, but no more. They would mill grain all night and take as much as possible with them. Holme could hide the rest in the forest. The cave would be their home, just like the old days.

As at every other great change in his life, Holme lay awake the first night in the cave, thinking everything over. They weren't sleeping on moss as they had before; this time they had animal skins and clothes. Sixteen summers had passed since they hid in the cave with their newborn baby. The coarse pine trees on the gravel ridge were the same, but the pine forest in the marshland had grown taller and denser.

Tora had fallen asleep at once, but Ausi had only recently dozed off. She had insisted on staying awake and coming to him the first night in the cave, remembering all that had happened there. She didn't grieve over what they had just lost, and Holme was grateful to her for that.

He was alone again now with his freedom. Those who had understood it and shared it with him had died for it, but the others hadn't been strong enough to bear the burden. He hoped the dead men had attained freedom in the land they inhabited now. No one else here would know what freedom was after he was gone. Somehow he had to teach others about it while he still lived. He owed it to those dead men to keep freedom alive.

He thought a moment about the provisions those men would need on their journey to the other land. He could have dug them up and put the provisions in. They had their weapons; he had seen them lying beside their owners, waiting. No one would rob even his enemy of weapons on the unknown journey.

Holme missed nothing he had lost, not the smithy in town, not the house, not the settlement they had just left. The safest hiding place they could find was here; the forest whispered outside the cave, they had grain, and he could get meat with his weapons. There was water in the spring below. But he wouldn't be able to stay in the forest and live out his life. He had the burden of freedom to carry, and he had to go out with it to the countless thralls who were suffering pain, who were being whipped and killed whenever it pleased their masters. He must try to explain freedom to them; then they could do as they pleased.

The last time had been hard, and he felt depleted. His wife and daughter lay sleeping beside him, and he hoped he could stay alive to protect them. He was the only one; neither Christ nor the wooden gods could or would. He'd had enough proof of that.

In town he had longed for the whistling of the forest; now it was coming to him again. As he listened, he immediately felt how insignificant what happened outside the forest was. It was pleasant to sleep in the whispering woods; maybe they could tell him how to help his fellow thralls gain their freedom.

Ausi woke up at dawn and saw the jagged rock hanging just above her face. She smiled with a sense of well-being when she remembered where she was. They were together. They had grain and water; Christ and Holme would take care of the rest. It was too bad about the men who had been killed in town, but the most important thing was that Holme was still alive. Anybody could see now that Christ walked with and protected him. He Himself had been beaten and persecuted; that was why He was on the side of Holme and the thralls. And He had doubtlessly taken charge of the dead thralls and given them freedom and everything they wanted in heaven.

Ausi was back in her first home, and it felt good, although Holme would have to make some changes before winter. Their enemies might be searching for them in the forest that very day, but that didn't bother her. There was One standing by their side protecting them. And if they were captured, she and Tora would follow Holme in death. They must be together on the last journey so she could explain everything to Christ. No, as far as she could see, there was nothing to fear.

They were like a dream, those sixteen years since she had lain there with her newborn, Tora, with Holme standing naked outside the cave. It smelled of earth and moss as it had then, and the forest whispered now too. When Holme and Tora woke up, it would be nice to talk about the future.

She felt great affection for her husband and daughter and gently caressed them. She could hear the morning caw of the crows outside and imagined them flying over the marshy ground, searching for food.

But in town the same morning, a powerful division of warriors was being outfitted to capture and kill the man who dared say that freedom belonged to all mankind.

SACRIFICIAL SMOKE

Just before sunrise, Holme crawled out of the cave. Ausi and Tora were still sleeping on the moss bed inside, but before they had fallen asleep, he had forbidden them to leave the cave until he returned. He suspected that the forest would be scoured during the next few days and that this time his enemies wouldn't give up before he was captured or dead.

The gray dew was shimmering on the grassy slope and the spring down below was murmuring just as it had before. The air was cool, the sky clear. By midday, it would be like summer—warm with air so clear you could see the woods and hills in the endless distance. That's how the two days before had been.

He closed up the cave with some dry branches before leaving. As he did so, he thought it strange that no wolf, fox, or badger had taken over the cave during his long absences. But maybe the smell of man had lingered on and scared them away.

He had never before walked through the forest without knowing exactly where he was going or what he was doing. He had fought for slaves' rights for a long time, but everything had turned sour. Hardly a single thrall had been freed—or stayed free; many of them had been slaughtered like dogs or hunted through the forest like wild boars as he had been. Whoever finally killed him would be famous.

From old habit, Holme walked toward the settlement where he had spent his youth as a thrall. He had been overseer there, too, for a short time. The men chasing him couldn't have gotten there so early in the morning. He could expect them first around midday. Maybe he could find something at the settlement that could be useful to him either in the cave or during his escape. Everyone in the area knew him and his family. He could never again hunt openly in the woods, or fish in the coves, or exchange goods without being recognized, then captured or killed by the chieftain's men. Like an outlaw or an animal, he would be forced to keep hidden during the days and seek food for himself and his family during the dark of night.

At sunrise, he was standing and looking out over the abandoned settlement. Some shocks of grain were still lying where they had been blown over, and the yellowish-gray stubble was glowing among them. The air was awash with dew and crystal clear—from where he stood at the forest's edge he could see a small rat scampering here and there among the sheaves. A light morning mist hung above the cool autumn water in the cove down below, and a couple of coots were gliding like black dots through it.

A few days earlier the settlement had been full of life and laughter, but now it was silent and deserted. A number of slaves who had believed in freedom and the future were now lying beneath the earth outside town, killed and then buried without provisions for their journey, without tools or weapons for the life after death. No one would avenge them, no one would be punished or ordered to pay compensation to their relatives. Thralls lived without the benefit of the law, beyond the provenance of the assembly, which protected free men.

Though he fought it, Holme felt the old bitterness rising. But there was nothing to do now but run or keep hidden. He still wasn't sure which he would do. The great unknown forests were still beckoning to him. They were unpopulated, and if there were any people in them at all, they were being hunted too, just like him. But the old problem was still there: Ausi could not tolerate the solitude for long. She was different from him and his daughter. She would pine and dream with a sickness her Christ couldn't even cure. On the contrary, He and his appointed priest had given it to her.

Holme walked past the smithy in the rocks and picked up a little birch bark box with various kinds of tools in its compartments. He would need the tools if he was going to build a house in some isolated place.

The sheaves of grain were swarming with tiny gray sparrows that looked like rats peeping out here and there in the yellow straw. In the chieftain's day the children thralls had always guarded the grain and scared the birds away from the fields. They had been forced to get up with the sun and run around the fields, waving their arms, yelling and throwing stones. But now the sparrows were unmolested. They flew away with a roar of wings when Holme approached the field while the field rats moved fitfully and constantly among the shocks.

The wooden god's stone was empty, but there was a dark clump of wood lying on the slope. Someone had knocked the harvest god over, and Holme wasn't sure who. It couldn't have been him. He walked down to examine the god more closely. The rain had washed most of the soot from the fire off, so gray wood was peeping through now. The god lay on his back, a spider web, gray with fine dewdrops, over his face.

Holme stood there looking at him for a long time, and for the first time he was moved by a wooden god. This one had been at the settlement long before he had; it had seen a great deal and had survived the ravages of the fire, just like him. There might be something to the god after all.

But who had knocked him off his stone, he wondered again. He remembered that the thralls had put him up there before starting to harvest the grain. Maybe a moose or a wild boar was scratching itself against the stone and pushed it over. He didn't think that any Christian, who would be provoked by the god, had passed by there recently.

Holme picked up the heavy clump of wood and put it back in place, wondering why as he did so. It might be that he felt it belonged there and that its absence would be noticed. Or maybe he did it to annoy the Christian chieftain, who would surely come after him with his riders that day. Another possibility occurred to him. He had never been in a worse situation, and maybe he should ask the charred wooden god for help. He might still be able to do something for an old acquaintance.

The little hut stood in the clump of trees, the first yellow aspen leaves lying on the sod roof around the smoke vent. The men following him would surely completely destroy the settlement this time when they couldn't find him there. And later, anyone spotting him in the forest would hurry off toward town with the news and they would take up the hunt again. It would probably be just as well to flee north with his wife and daughter the same day.

The millstone was standing where it had always stood with a little rainwater in it. It would be handy to have but was too heavy to carry. He could probably manage to grind a new one once they got to a safe place. And it would be a while before he could exchange goods for grain to mill anyway.

He picked up some other things he found too — a small sledgehammer with a broken handle, a rusty spindle whorl, a little pot with a handle for hanging above the fire, a couple of whetstones. The sun was hanging above the cove, and the trees were glimmering yellow and red. It was all so calm and peaceful — maybe they could stay in the cave until the worst was over. During the winter they would at least be left in peace, although their footprints in the fresh snow could be dangerous.

Relieved, Holme headed back toward the cave. He never retraced his own steps, so as not to wear a path through the grass. When he looked back, the field rat was still scampering among the yellow stubble and the chirping sparrows were fluttering from sheave to sheave. The mist, gliding now in light veils across the surface of the water, would soon completely dissipate in the sun. He sensed somehow that he had known all this from the beginning of time. He wasn't sure just how old he was, but Ausi had notched a short piece of wood every summer since Tora was born.

He walked back through the still and somewhat pungent autumn forest. Gorgeous mushrooms were glowing, leaves constantly falling. Near his path grew a number of hazel trees, and he walked over to see if the nuts were ready. A young bird flew off with a shriek from under the bushes suffused with sunlight.

The nuts were brown and lying on the ground. He picked up a few and put them into the iron pot. Tora would be glad, of course. If they didn't have to run, they could come back and gather a big store for the winter.

In town the chieftain's wife, Svein's mother, fought bitterly for what she thought were her rights. After the town's Christian chieftain had tired of her complaint and had driven her away, she managed to get permission to meet the king at his farmstead a couple of hours away by boat.[1]

---

[1] In this final volume of the trilogy, Fridegård continues to rely for the outlines of the historical narrative on Bishop Rimbert's ninth-century life of Saint Ansgar. He is not as heavily dependent on Rimbert in *Sacrificial Smoke* as he is in volumes one and two of

Blight had not touched the king's crop, perhaps because he was living on an island, but he construed it as a blessing from the gods. And so he was cheerful when the middle-aged woman with the hard face came seeking justice from him. Svein walked behind her, and the thrall they had paid to do the rowing stayed behind in the boat. He looked with curiosity and admiration at the king's dragon ship lying outside the blockade.

Against the wall of the main building stood some chairs in the sunshine, and the king invited the woman and her son to join him there. He listened quietly to the woman's long history of suffering. As she spoke, one of his most trusted men came and stood by in silence. When the woman began telling about Holme's throwing a rock that injured her son, she got up and showed the king her angry and glaring son's stiff neck.

The king was perfectly familiar with Holme's history in town, so he was more interested in hearing about his past life as a slave. He thought briefly of the Danish king's advice to make a man like Holme his friend and warrior, but he knew he couldn't. His men would never acknowledge him as their equal, and strife and discontent would follow. They would withdraw from Holme, not because he had committed a crime, but because he had been a thrall. The town merchants were different; they had accepted him because of his skill and strength, but the warriors had always kept their distance.

The woman finished her tale of woe by demanding her rights. Holme should be put to death and his wife and daughter returned to her. She should have help, too, with rebuilding the old settlement—Svein, soon grown, would need a farmstead like his father's. That one was in a good place and produced good harvests. In addition, she would need three or four men and a couple of women thralls.

The king replied that he had already sent out a number of riders that very day to capture Holme. They were under strict orders to capture and kill him and then bring his body to town. She wasn't the only one who wanted some peace. He also agreed that she should get Holme's wife and daughter back since they were only runaway thralls. But she would have to get any other thralls she needed on her own. There had to be a number of them wandering around who'd be willing to follow her to the settlement.

---

the trilogy, however. It seems, for example, that he still intends the chieftain in *Sacrificial Smoke* to be the chieftain from the previous volume, although that chieftain was modeled on a man named Herigar who died in 851, a couple of years before the events described here. Fridegård likewise does not seem to relinquish Björn, a king mentioned in Rimbert and depicted in *People of the Dawn*, although Olaf, perhaps Björn's son, replaced Björn by about 852—before the events of *Sacrifical Smoke*. Fridegård increases the ambiguity about the kings by mentioning the two of them toward the end of *Sacrificial Smoke*, but the whole problem may ultimately derive from Rimbert, who also introduces the second king in chapter 26 without having explained what happened to the first. For a detailed chronology based on Rimbert, see note 6, p. 278.

After some food and drink, the mother and son returned to their boat where the thrall was asleep on the seat. The woman, feeling satisfied with what she had gained, scolded him sternly. It was just a matter of time now before she could gaze on Holme's corpse and reclaim his wife and daughter. Finally, after all these years, she would be happy. She sat in the boat enjoying the thought of what she was going to do to them. And she fantasized about building the family settlement bigger and more beautiful than ever. She and Svein would be in command, and everything would be like it was in bygone, happier days.

A little shadow now and then clouded her dreams. The chieftain had called her "heathen" when he drove her out of town. Many of the most important people there—both men and women—had been baptized. Maybe in the long run only the people of lowest rank and the slaves would stick to the ancient wooden gods. She didn't want to be one of them; her husband had been a great chieftain. Maybe she should accept baptism, and then the chieftain and many others would be on her side. Besides, for all she knew, Christ just may be the most powerful of the gods.

She tried to discuss the future with Svein, but he either answered curtly or not at all as he gazed out over the water. He only really listened when she talked about the search for Holme that now was in full swing. Sacrifices to the gods had already begun over this matter, but now she didn't exactly know what she wanted. Once ashore, they walked across the field separating the Christian church from the heathen temple, and she looked from side to side, not knowing who could bring success to the warriors hunting Holme. She turned finally to Christ. If any of these gods were protecting Holme, it would have to be one of the ancient wooden ones.

The church was empty and she walked all the way up to the altar in her curiosity. A gold and red picture was hanging there, brought by the Christians from their homeland. A cloth with some beautiful vessels on it was lying on the altar.

She looked around for a priest to talk with. Svein yelled something to her through the open door and kept going. She could hear various sounds from the heathen temple, including the regular bleating of a sheep or a goat that would surely be sacrificed. The woman wondered what she could offer Christ to make Him take her side against Holme. Maybe just a promise. Then if Christ failed, she wouldn't have to keep it.

Something was moving in the little room behind the altar, and a man soon emerged. After hearing the woman's story, he told her that there were no priests in town but one or two were on their way. In the meantime, the chieftain was leading the church services. The man was positive Christ would help her if she made a donation to the church. He'd also heard that the new priests would erect a bigger church—one bigger and taller than the heathen temple. Two bells would ring out from it and render the wooden gods powerless.

And as she glanced furtively out the door toward the hall of the wooden gods, the woman promised Christ a gift for the new church. In exchange He should arrange for Holme to die and his wife and daughter to be returned to her, just like the king had promised.

But she kept wondering how that tiny picture with the drooping head could be stronger than the ancient and stern wooden gods. She'd wait and see, though. Once He had fulfilled his part of the bargain, the gift would be on its way.

She passed between both temples again as she departed, again feeling great distrust for Christ. His temple was desolate and empty except when the Christians gathered and sang their tedious songs. But the heathen temple was always bustling and full of laughter. It would smell of roasted meat and the offerings of beer would sizzle on the hot stones. The rejuvenated settlement would seem bleak without a little heathen shrine and a god in it looking out over the fields. You could make sacrifices to him at various times and keep yourself happy all the while with food and drink. So had her forefathers done from time immemorial.

But she could still do what many others had—cling to Christ sometimes without relinquishing the ancient gods. It would all depend on who gave her the most help during the next few days.

I t was a group of sullen, tired warriors who, on the king's orders, armed themselves again to hunt Holme through the mainland forests. They mumbled in their beards that they had taken him back to town already but someone had let him escape. They weren't going to spend their whole lives searching for some thrall in the woods, no matter how criminal and dangerous he might be. Their duty was to defend the town.

Their anger erupted when they gathered around the chieftain. Angry words were flying from every direction, and the warriors insisted again that they should be fighting for their king, not forever engaging in this manhunt.

"Let the thrall go," a voice called out and several other voices rose in agreement. Though too proud to admit it, the men knew that some of them would never come back alive if they ever caught Holme. But if they left him alone, they'd probably seen the last of him on the island. Why hunt him?

The chieftain concurred but he had his orders. He tried reasoning with the warriors again, this time threatening them with the king's wrath. But they laughed scornfully and repeated that they were warriors, not thrall overseers. Some said that if the gods really wanted Holme dead, he wouldn't have gotten away so many times.

With that the chieftain's ears perked up and he saw a possible way out. They'd cast lots to see if the gods wanted them to keep hunting Holme. If the lot went against him, the warriors would abide by it. If not, the king would retract his order and not thwart the will of the gods.

He surveyed the warriors again before making his suggestion, and he could see that his hesitation had helped increase their resolve. Nothing but the will of the gods could get them into the forest now.

A little while later, they were all gathered at the place of council outside town, their horses wandering loose and snorting among the burial mounds a short distance away. Children, women, merchants, craftsmen—everyone had come to see what was going on. Svein and his mother had come too, and her face contorted with anger when she heard why they were casting lots. She sensed that most of them would just as well let Holme go. But she and her son would never have a day's rest as long as he was alive and free.

She saw one of the heathen priests cutting twigs off the apple tree standing nearby, small red fruit glistening among the yellow foliage. He put a different mark on each twig, and the chieftain stood there examining the marks one after another. The warriors' faces had grown yet more sullen and angry; they knew they'd have to bow to the will of the gods, regardless of how the lot fell.

The priests spread a large, pastel yellow cloth on the ground and secured the corners with stones so the wind wouldn't catch them. Tiny black autumn flies immediately lit on the cloth, and a spider numb from the frost crept slowly across one of the corners. The temple attendants emerged from the temple carrying an image of a god between them. They set it down next to the cloth. An unpleasant smell of stale blood wafted on the wind from it. The warriors and other people looked at it with respect, but the Christian chieftain turned away in displeasure and disgust. He would rather have washed his hands of all this.

A whisper passed through the crowd when everything was ready, and then there was complete silence. A gust of wind urged the yellow leaves still on the tree into a rustling dance, then died away as a stillness settled over everything in the clear autumn day.

Everyone took the stillness as a sign, so the priest cast the twigs down on the cloth. When they came to rest, he got on his knees to decipher the will of the gods. The warriors were mistrustful and huddled around him to see for themselves. They depended on no one, neither the priest nor the chieftain, because they had been deceived too many times before. The chieftain was standing up behind them in disdain.

The priest loudly counted the twigs, and when he was done it had all turned out as the warriors had hoped. They should not hunt the thrall, but should stay home instead. The priest interpreted the sign and said that an enemy fleet lying in wait would have attacked if the warriors had left the town defenseless. Now they wouldn't dare.

The warriors rose in satisfaction, looking triumphantly at their chieftain. But he was just as glad as they were although he didn't show it. He would much rather stay in town because he was expecting a ship from the Christian lands, and he too had had his fill of Holme. Besides, he knew that most of his people would follow what they believed was the will of the gods even in this case.

But there was one observer who would not tolerate the outcome. Svein's mother had followed the casting of lots with mounting anxiety and rage. When the satisfied warriors started back to the fortress, she began hurling insults at them in her shrill voice. They were lazy and had cowered before a single thrall. Then she turned on the chieftain and threatened him with the king's ire. She had talked with him the same day and he had promised that a company of warriors would hunt Holme down and bring his body back to town. And his family would be returned to their rightful owner.

The men listened to her but didn't bother to respond. They looked the other way and talked softly among themselves while they gathered their horses and walked toward the fortress. Then the chieftain ordered his thralls to man one of the smaller boats, probably so he could report to the king.

The council place was soon empty. The gods were put back in place and the cloth was removed. The apple tree twigs, perhaps having saved Holme's life, were lying discarded in the grass. You could still hear the woman's distant angry yelping as she and her son retreated to their home at the far end of town.

Holme stuck to the ridge all day so he could keep an eye on the dried marshland dotted by the dwarf pines growing on tall lingonberry tufts. His enemies would have to show up there or in the dense woods on the opposite slope. The ridge was too bumpy and rocky for their horses.

Ausi and Tora were trying to make the cave more comfortable for the next night. They were chattering away like a couple of young girls, seemingly unaware of the danger threatening them. The cave's mossy ceiling was covered with dark red clumps of lingonberries, and Tora would occasionally grab a handful and stuff them into her mouth.

Holme, his mind still not made up, paced heavily back and forth on the ridge, anxious as a bear. It was so peaceful up there that it was hard to grasp the immensity of the danger. But his enemies would probably gallop in every direction through the forest that day. Not alone—they wouldn't dare—but in groups, and if they discovered the cave while he, Ausi, and Tora were inside, that would be the end of them all.

Holme was also thinking that they ought to have some meat or fish. The bread that Ausi had baked on the hot stone early in the morning would get tiresome. He might still have time, and there ought to be a domestic pig or two still at the settlement. He should have thought of that when he was there at sunrise. It hadn't been too many days before when he had seen two of them looking down on the settlement from the edge of the forest. They were already half wild so they spooked suddenly and disappeared in a waddling gallop through the underbrush.

A smiling mother and daughter greeted him when he walked back to the cave. They hadn't worried too much about his deciding to return to the settlement—they knew he was better off alone than when he had them or others to look after. They had promised to keep hidden and to be on the lookout while he was away.

For the second time that day Holme was looking at the settlement, but this time it was more dangerous. He turned an ear toward the forest, but all was quiet. A noise now and then from the lake made his face tense for a moment. A pig's muffled grunting came from an alder grove to the left of the jetty.

He listened again before venturing down the slope. If his enemies showed up, he could probably hide in the grove and then slip off into the forest farther away along the shore. The ridge near the cave branched down to the cove farther off, and he could make it home that way in just about any degree of darkness.

A lot depended on how wild the pig had become. Holme should have taken his bow with him, but he had always relied more on his ax and knife. The pig was probably still a little tame since it had stuck so close to the settlement.

The grunting stopped while he was still a ways from the grove, and he knew he'd been discovered. As softly as he had walked, the pig had still picked up his steps in its funnel-like ears. But he knew pigs well; instead of trying to slip away, it would stand stock still until he was right next to it.

Holme carefully parted the alder bushes, then stepped into the darkness that smelled of mire. Right in front of him were some fresh tracks with yellow leaves trampled down into them. He stood still, letting his eyes grow accustomed to the dark inside. A few treetops rose high above the grove, and the leaves still clinging to them glowed a gaudy yellow in the afternoon sun.

It took a while before anything happened. He had begun to fear he hadn't really heard anything, but the tracks didn't lie. A single fly was buzzing somewhere outside the foliage where the sun was shining. Just as Holme was about to take a few steps forward, the white of an eye flashed and the pig's gray silhouette soon appeared against the thicket and mud.

But then came the hard part. If the half-wild pig ran away, he wouldn't be able to catch it, and he wasn't close enough yet to use his ax. For a moment he thought about throwing the ax, but the chances of his hitting the pig hard enough to penetrate it were slight. Besides, the pig would probably take off as soon as he raised his weapon.

Holme had always had a way with animals more than with people, and it struck him that he might be able to calm the pig. He began talking gently to it and saw the eye flash again. But the pig stayed completely still, and Holme carefully moved one foot forward. If he could get three or four steps closer, he could dive on the pig, which was only half-grown. It had to be one born during the spring and so must have seen people the entire summer.

Holme took another step and nothing happened. He kept talking calmly, receiving at least one weak grunt in response. That gave him confidence and he kept moving forward. When he was only four or five steps away, the pig started backing away grunting, blinking, sniffing, and stretching its snout toward him. For a moment, he felt compassion for it and considered sparing its life. Pigs were somehow the animals of thralls, kindred spirits.

Many years before, he had maliciously and gleefully plunged his knife into one of the master's young pigs in the forest swamp while the swineherds napped. He had just needed food for his wife and child then too, but he hadn't felt what he did now. Since that time he had tasted freedom, and the pig before him now resembled himself—free but pursued.

The pig, friendly and curious, kept moving out of his way, grunting. Suddenly it came out through the farthest thicket, and the sun shone on its bristly back, caked with dried mud. In the same instant, it let go a terrified, indistinct scolding sound and rushed away. But Holme was tight on its heels, blocking its retreat into the grove.

The pig dashed back and forth on the few feet of shoreline, Holme between it and safety. Holme's compassion was gone now. He concentrated only on the blow he had to strike. But landing it wasn't easy, and he twice struck only the air. When the pig could find no way back into the grove, it ran into a space under the logs and stones. It got stuck in there, and Holme managed to grab a hind leg. The pig had time to let out a few long cries of distress before it was pulled out and stunned with the butt of the ax.

Holme got up looking tensely toward the edge of the forest by the settlement, but there was nothing there and he heard no riders. The pig was still kicking in the gravel, so he stabbed it in the throat and lifted it into the air until all the blood drained out. Then he rinsed it clean by the shore. For a moment the water among the stones turned pink, but more waves rolled in, washing away every trace.

Holme carried the carcass to the grove so he couldn't be seen from the settlement. There he chopped a strong stick, slit the pig's hind legs with his knife, then shoved the stick under the tendons to make it easier to carry the load. The sun would set soon, and it was time to return to the cave. He had long had a store of salt there for preserving meat.

He had forgotten his pursuers for a while but on the way back it struck him again what danger he was in. The first day was almost over and nothing had happened, but that didn't mean he could feel safe. Besides, he didn't know what was happening at the cave, a thought that made him quicken his pace. He passed the old master's burial mound where two small aspen trees had started growing on the south side. They had already lost all their leaves, which now lay like a yellow rug around their feet. Many years had passed since the chieftain's bones and ashes had been laid in the mound, and many things had happened at his settlement.

He knew he had to reach a decision. He could flee into the unknown with its dangers and hardships or stay here, forever sneaking around like a night animal. He had no other choice. Or did he? A thought came like a flash, stopping him dead in his tracks. Then he shook his head and walked on.

But the thought stuck with him, whispering in his ear. He had seen the king on more than one occasion, and there was something about him he liked. His simple clothes, his grave, friendly look. Rumor had it that he treated his thralls well. He might understand. But Holme had to talk with him alone. That was impossible in town, but maybe at his farmstead, a long boat ride away. Holme knew he'd try anyway before disappearing into the forests forever. As long as nothing had happened at the cave, that is.

He walked faster as he got closer, the pig swinging from his shoulder. But all was quiet, the sun was down, and the grass was stiffening again with the frost. The hunt probably wouldn't begin before the next day.

Mother and daughter crawled happily out of the cave and caressed him lovingly until his eyes took on a friendly luster. They were delighted with the meat and praised him for his hunting. Now they dared build a fire to cook the meat together with some broth and roots, and Holme quickly constructed a tripod for suspending the pot over the fire. The three of them were soon hungrily eating the meal, their eyes and teeth glistening. Mother and daughter, enjoying the moment, had no fears. They had food, a roof over their heads, and protection.

Holme, however, was thinking that weathering a winter in the cave would be hard even without pursuers. He had heard of people long ago living in caves all year round, but the winters were probably milder then, and people were used to cold and hunger. It wouldn't be easy to get food when the snow was deep in the forest and thick ice covered the lakes. He had to do something and quickly. But not tomorrow, the day after. If his pursuers hadn't come by then, something had probably happened in town. He thought that foreign vessels might have sailed in, friendly or hostile, and he had to find out. Not knowing was worse than anything else because he could never feel at ease about his wife and daughter in the cave, could never go far without stopping and listening. Things just couldn't go on that way.

At midnight Holme left the cave, followed by Ausi's anxious warnings. Tora was confident as usual; she always thought there wasn't a man alive who could get the better of her father.

Holme walked for hours while the autumn moon sank toward the forest's crest. He wanted to reach a spot just about directly opposite the king's farmstead, so he wouldn't have far to row. He had always felt more comfortable in the woods than on the open lake.

The night forest was alive everywhere he walked, and he kept his ax constantly ready. Wolves and wild boars didn't concern him much, but the invisible, evil powers you can't defend yourself against did. The older he grew the more he believed in them, and he was certain that all the magicians in the area were hard at work casting spells in his path. When he heard the sound of paws moving softly in the moss, when he saw a pair of cold, green eyes glowing through a thicket, or when an owl let out a shrill hoot, he couldn't stop the chill running up and down his spine. This had never happened to him before, and he wished he was in a fury or a bad mood. Then no kind of danger frightened him, neither visible nor invisible.

Much of this probably also had to do with the mission he was on. He was an outlaw and anyone at all had the right to kill him. And now he was on his way to visit the king who had given that order. Nothing like this had ever happened before, so this journey might be his last. But he had had to do something, and the danger he faced would be equally great no matter what. With wife and daughter, he couldn't live the life of an outlaw this close to town. If his talk with the king did no good, he'd return to the cave, and then it would be time to leave.

Holme finally happened upon a scarcely noticeable path and followed it to the shore. Walking was easier here, although the occasional boulder jutting into the water forced him back into the forest. He saw a boat by a little jetty and moved closer for a better look. It wasn't well secured, so he probably could have gotten it loose, but the farmstead was still too far away. Then he saw a sharply pitched roof outlined against the blue-green night sky and walked closer. Everything was quiet, but a trace of smoke was still rising shadow-like from the smoke vent, and the withered grass at the peak of the sod roof whispered in the night wind.

The moon was sinking fast, growing larger and redder as it neared the treetops. Once it disappeared, the night would be dark for a good while, making it more difficult for him to find his way in the forest and bogs. Sometimes the forest reached all the way to the water, its huge trees leaning hesitantly over it. In a couple of places forest streams rippled past, and several times cold water seeped through his goatskin shoes as he hopped the streams or slogged through their sedge-covered banks.

The shore soon became more even and he could move faster. Then it changed direction and the moon wandered from woods to lake. An endless red stream shot across the water, broken here and there by dark flecks that were probably belts of reeds. He'd be directly opposite the king's farmstead soon. He knew some fishermen lived in the area, and he'd borrow a boat from them.

Several boats of various sizes lay at the shore, but the fishing village was still asleep. Holme walked down to a jetty where two boats were tied and stepped into the smaller one. He figured the fisherman could get along with one until he returned. It wouldn't take long. He'd either have to flee or reach an agreement with the king and would have to return this way in either case.

The thin layer of ice that forms at night clanged against the side of the boat as it cut a furrow into the high reeds. The sea birds, chattering in astonishment, raced farther back into the reeds. Massive and red now, the moon finally sank in the endless distance, and he somehow felt more alone after it was gone. It had followed him all night long. For a long time afterwards, the horizon stayed a shimmering red where it had sunk.

The boat creaked with every tug of the oars, but it didn't matter. No one would be waiting for him. They wouldn't dream he'd come this way, much less try to find the king. He didn't even know himself why he was doing this. He knew what might happen, but he was tired of hiding in a hole like a wolf or fox.

The king's forest was soon before him and Holme rowed cautiously to land. He had guessed the time right since the sun was just beginning to rise, and now he'd have time to search the surrounding area before anyone woke up. He had to know the best escape route into the forest in case he needed it. He had decided not to fight the king's men if he could avoid it. It was enough that the whole town was after him.

In the distance far across the water he could barely make out the island where the town was and wondered if he'd ever return. Then he hid the boat in the bushes by the shore and walked toward the king's farmstead.

At the king's farmstead, they had already started brewing the beer that was to last the whole winter. Everyone was in a congenial mood after a good harvest of barley and hops. With his own hands the king laid crossed sticks of mountain ash in the brewing vats, and placed a flint ax in the vat of brewer's malt. He and his people believed that the ax, a bolt from the Thundergod, would protect the malt. If you didn't have a thunderbolt you'd put a silver object of some kind into the vat or you could almost be sure that magic would destroy the brew.

When the beer was ready and tasted it would be left standing until the mid-winter sacrifice. Then everybody got their share, both people and animals. The king himself would soak a piece of bread in the beer and give it to his horses and cows. They would snort and sniff at it awhile but soon begin to eat it. When it was gone, they would lick their chops and whinny and moo wildly for more, and that was a good sign for the coming year.

When the morning light shone through the openings in the building where the king was brewing his beer, it fell on what looked very much like a troll. For many generations it had been the custom that the ugliest man around would brew the beer to insure success. If it wouldn't ferment, you could see him running around the brewing chamber, yelling and conjuring wildly. The whole time he would pull his hair or beat himself with his fists. If nothing else helped, he would calm down, fetch a big piece of meat, and lay it under the brewing vat. But he didn't often have to resort to making that sacrifice to a minor deity. They did only what their fathers had taught them. [2]

Holme sneaked up to the sleeping farmstead. It was still early so he wasn't afraid of being discovered. And if a sleepy thrall on his way to work in the king's barn should discover him in the gray dawn, he'd only hurry inside faster, thinking he had just seen a troll or maybe the spirit of one of the king's relatives. He had shown himself a few times before as a portent that something was going to happen.

---

[2] Schön, *Jan Fridegård och forntiden*, pp. 111–12, shows that the details about beer and beer brewing come from Hilding Celander's book about the pagan Nordic yule: *Nordisk jul, I. Julen i gammaldags bondesed* (Stockholm, 1928).

But there was no movement at the farmstead, no dogs barking. Holme admired the large, well-built buildings and walked closer. The hinges on the doors were shaped like dragon heads, and he became curious. He touched them, following the curves with his fingers, and then remembered: he had forged these very hinges himself. He also remembered when the farmstead's foreman had brought that assignment to the smithy.

He still didn't know how he could arrange to talk with the king, but he depended on that power in his life that had always made things happen just at the right moment. It was either good or bad, and it wasn't easy to tell. Sometimes what he thought was bad turned out to be good in the end and sometimes just the opposite. He would stick close to the farmstead and wait for something to happen.

It was growing light quickly, so he walked back to the edge of the forest. He would hide there until the people were up. It would be obvious soon if the king was there.

He hadn't seen the king's harbor on the way over; a point of land had blocked it from view. It occurred to Holme to see if the ships were there or not. The king had two ships with dragon heads and many smaller boats as well.

He sneaked around the farmstead and moved toward the lake. The first thing he saw was a man on a hill, looking across the water. He was probably the harbor guard, there both day and night. There was a birch-bark box next to the man, probably for his food. Holme felt hungry when he saw it, but he had some bread and lean pork on him. He'd find a safe place to eat soon.

He couldn't get any closer to the lake without the guard seeing him, but beyond the bushes he stood behind he could see two golden dragon heads sticking up, red mouths gaping toward land. The king had to be at his farmstead. Numerous rows of poles for drying the fishing nets stood by the harbor, and the sound of cawing crows and shrieking seagulls wafted by Holme from that direction. The cool breeze coming from lake and harbor carried the smell of water and raw fish.

The guard yawned with a howl that sounded eery through the silence, and then he looked around. When he turned to the lake again, Holme went back to the forest beyond the farmstead. He sat down on a low rock at the edge of the forest so he could keep an eye on the farmstead, and then he took out his food.

His thoughts carried him to his wife and daughter as he ate the bread and meat. As he had done many times before, he wondered now what would happen to them if he were gone. Deep inside he knew: a thrall's despicable life with all the drudgery, the beatings, the tongue lashings, the rape, and the babies left to die in the forest. Ausi and Tora would be treated even more cruelly because they had been his wife and daughter. And Tora would get the brunt of it; like him she would never bend, never give in. She would fight back as he had done. She was a girl and weak but she would still fight. Holme knew he had to live for their sake.

He sat and watched the sun come up. It flashed among the trees, and the stubble fields between the farmstead and the forest turned a sudden yellow and took on a warmer look than they had before. The rich, black earth beneath the stubble began to steam.

The farmstead was waking up and starting its day. Someone who must have been the king's foreman walked around putting all the thralls to work. Animal tenders were already at it, and from where he sat Holme could see a couple of women thralls carrying their milk pails from the barn. Smoke rose straight up through the smoke vent, and animals were mooing, neighing, grunting, and barking at the brand new day.

Holme felt once more a deep yearning for that life, for that peace and that work. Why weren't they possible for everyone? Why did he have to be hunted like an animal when all he wanted to do was work and live in peace with everyone? Defending your farmstead or village against invaders—that had to be done, but why did men fight and hunt each other?

His thoughts began to settle on the freedom that everyone ought to have, but he didn't let them stay there. Many strong, good men lay slaughtered and buried like animals, just because they had dared think of that freedom and had tried to attain it. That was why he was being hunted and had to flee from everything worth living for.

Even more powerfully than before, it struck him again how dangerous and hopeless the day ahead of him was. If he did get to talk to the king, he still wouldn't gain anything. It wasn't easy for him to talk, and the king probably wouldn't understand him, understand that he had never harmed any human being if he could have avoided it, and that all thralls were like him in this regard. Well, maybe not all; there were some who were cowardly, who would betray their friends just to get in good with their masters. On the other hand, there were plenty of bad, merciless masters, too.

But here he was. He had traveled a long way and wouldn't turn back without completing his mission. The king would probably soon make himself seen at his farmstead.

The sun shone through the windows and struck against the far wall. Various wall decorations, tapestries, and weapons hung in the crystal clear light. When the king awoke, the wall caught his eye, and he felt happy and at ease. Everything he had touched this autumn had been successful. Before returning to their land, the Christian priests had told him that he had Christ to thank for it all, and perhaps that was true. In any case, he had promised that the Christians in town would be free to hold services even without a priest. It was only about a fourth of the town's population that was in question, and when things went against them many would turn back to the old gods.

New priests were coming in the spring. They had been coming and going for years; not one of them had the courage to stay. Their lives were in constant danger, the old gods still lived a vigorous life, and the Christian priests had to walk in and out of the church constantly surrounded by sacrificial smoke. They were the ones, though, who had chosen to build their church as close to the heathen temple as possible so they could defy the wooden gods. So the Christian bells had rung out over the water for many years, but to little avail. On calm, clear days you could hear the bells all the way to the king's farmstead.

The king heard his men talking out in the hall. They were probably starting to get up and inspect their weapons. The beer would be ready that morning. Everything had gone well so the ugly brewmaster would get a princely reward. He had managed to hold all evil away from the brew, and the beer ought to have settled overnight.

The king thought too about their casting lots soon to see if the gods would give them good fortune for a spring expedition. They were running low on a number of items in town and the surrounding countryside. There wasn't enough silver but they could get some by laying seige to a town and making it pay a ransom. They could put to sea well before the new priests came with their dour faces and punishing words. On such a journey everyone had to be happy and filled with hope.

The king got up and straightened his clothes as pleasant thoughts kept buzzing in his head. Before he went out he combed his hair and beard and put on a gold-embroidered cap. His men were up and busy in the outer room and hall, and a couple of them already sat with their bearded heads bent over the chessboard. A couple of costly objects stood shining on a shelf in the morning sunlight, and everyone passing by had to glance at them. They were a couple of multi-colored Roman glasses, and there weren't many of such things in the entire country.[3]

Out in the brewery, the ugly brewmaster was watching over his work when the king came in. He sprang to his feet, an expression of either anxiety or pride on his face. He had managed to protect the beer from evil powers but it had taken its toll on him. Now all was well, the danger almost past.

After saying a few words to him, the king took a ladle of beer, pushed his beard aside, and drank, yellow pearls rolling down onto his clothes. The beer was still too fresh to drink and he quickly put down the ladle. But he smiled with satisfaction and the brewmaster's ugly face lit up. The king ordered that his men should each have a tankard of the new beer for their morning meal. Then it would be left untouched until the winter sacrifice.

---

[3] Although there is some evidence of glassmaking in Scandinavia during this period, fine glass was imported for the wealthy. See James Graham-Campbell, *The Viking World* (New Haven: Ticknor & Fields, 1980), pp. 88–91.

When he came out of the brewery, he didn't feel like returning to his house. There was a nice balance outside of warmth from the rising sun and chill from the remaining frost. He stopped for awhile in the warmth by the log wall. Then he walked toward the outlying buildings where the ground had been torn up everywhere by the pigs, where it smelled of mire and excrement when the sun shone. All that was missing was the swarms of buzzing summer flies, and he thought about that a moment.

Everything was as it should be in the outlying buildings, so he was soon outside again. He somehow felt better than he had for a long time. Everything was calm and easy that morning. The harvested barley field lay before him, and he walked out into it. There was a lot of grain left among the stalks, and he would tell the women thralls to pick it when they got the chance. He kept ambling across the field, picking up a stone now and then and tossing it into one of the little furrows that striped the field. Someone had left a sickle on a big rock over night and now it had red rust stains. Picking it up, the king muttered to himself that the guilty party was going to hear about this.

At the edge of the forest stood some aspen trees with smooth, grayish-green trunks and carpets of yellow leaves lying at their feet. The air smelled fresh but a little pungent. The king was feeling even better, but it didn't occur to him that the strong beer may have gone to his head. Since he hadn't eaten anything, he tolerated less alcohol than usual. He kept walking deeper into the forest, looking around. He saw a couple of spruce trees with dried-out trunks that would have to be felled for fire-wood. One had a hole in it and a beautiful bird popped out and flashed its head to both sides before catapulting into the air and flying away with a series of shrill cries.

The king walked a few steps further without noticing that a massive figure slowly, quietly stole behind the trees and bushes in a semi-circle around him. The figure had been sitting on a rock and had seen the king crossing the fields. He had slipped away but was now back on the rock, which lay between the king and his farmstead.

The king looked at him in surprise, and it took a moment before the contented expression in his eyes disappeared. At first, he couldn't believe the smith was sitting there on the rock. The thrall couldn't have come to the farmstead without someone seeing him and sounding the alarm. But when the king remembered everything he had heard about Holme, it didn't seem unlikely that he had once again fooled everyone out after him. But what was he doing here?

The king's and thrall's eyes met, and the feeling of terror that had already gripped the king died away. The thrall wasn't after his life — he could see that in his eyes. They were on guard and sad at one and the same time. The king took in the entire figure before him and began to understand the saga of this thrall better. There was something about him that commanded your attention. You couldn't just disdainfully walk by.

The thrall didn't move and the king sensed he was waiting for something. It was difficult to feel like a king out here; in the forest it was man against man.

"You're Holme," he said, and the figure made an affirmative gesture.

"What do you want here?"

Then the thrall began talking in his deep, gruff voice. He wasn't accustomed to talking and soon fell silent, frustrated at not being able to find the right words. The king began to think that all this was an exciting adventure. He thought again about what the Danish king had said—he had to make such a man his friend. Everyone knew what having him as an enemy meant.

The king's good mood completely revived, and he jokingly asked when it had become the custom for a king to stand and his subject to sit. Holme understood immediately and stood up. He took his ax from its leather case, and the king's face grew tense with fear. But Holme put the long-handled ax against the trunk of an aspen tree, as the king marvelled over this thrall who comported himself like a chieftain. Holme did not want to take unfair advantage of the unarmed king.

The rock had enough room for two, and the king gestured for Holme to sit beside him. He could soon tell that Holme had difficulty expressing himself, so he started asking him questions. That worked better, and the king, who was a good judge of people, could soon tell that Holme was speaking the truth.

They sat on the rock for a long time; a woman's bright voice called the king's name twice from the farmstead, but he just smiled and ignored it. To his surprise, he began to understand that the thrall smith, considered the greatest evil-doer in the kingdom, had had no choice but to do what he had done. The king would have done the same thing himself. Strange sensations were stirring deep in the king's heart. He considered himself a fair ruler, but the smith's story made him uncomfortable. He had never known or understood that a thrall could have so much substance.

But he didn't dare try to understand the thralls' battle for freedom. What would happen to the order in the land if there were no thralls? Who would work the fields, care for the animals, build boats, and erect buildings? The farmsteads would fall to ruin, and the harvests would be destroyed when the masters went on a raid or were themselves besieged.

The king pushed those thoughts away until later. Right now, he had to do something about the man sitting next to him. He had no desire to send Holme out to be killed, but his warriors would never take him into their company. There had to be another way.

The woman's voice called anxiously a third time, and there was a group of men gathered at the farmstead, obviously ready to search for the king. He got up and told Holme to follow him. He waited while Holme got his ax, then walked in front of him. Something told the king that he didn't have to fear this massive, dangerous man walking behind him, carrying a huge ax. The king felt proud and happy to think that he, alone and unarmed, was leading in the man whom it would normally take several armed men to overcome.

The queen and a group of warriors, the foreman in front, awaited them at the farmstead. The queen's lips turned white and a number of warriors grabbed their weapons, but the king waved them off. As he drew closer, he told them that Holme had come seeking protection and justice and that no harm should come to him before his case had been tried. Until then he would stay at the farmstead and no one was to bother him. As everyone knew, he could defend himself. No one had to fear him either; he never attacked unprovoked, only defended himself and his family.

When Holme had heard the king's words, he put his ax aside again, and the king smiled at his warriors in smug satisfaction. He had tamed the wild beast his way. Now everyone was curious about Holme, whom they had heard so much about. The warriors looked with reluctant admiration at the well-built body; the thralls, at a distance, looked at him with secret pride because he was one of them. The queen, who had trembled when she saw such a powerful, ominous figure with a glistening ax behind the king, looked at him now with something like gratitude. She knew that no one could have saved the king's life had Holme chosen to kill him.

The morning meal had long been ready and set out, so the queen gave the signal to go to the long tables. The brewmaster had carried out the king's order, and a few women thralls brought beer tankards from the brewery. Holme got to sit at the end of the warriors' table and he too received a foaming tankard of beer. The rumor about who he was had already spread, and the women thralls kept turning toward him in curiosity as they walked around serving the men.

Meanwhile, the king told his men what he thought of the smith's story. He told them about Holme's constantly being pursued, about his once being the master smith in town. When he said that, several heads turned to look at Holme and then back again to look meaningfully at each other. Many of them were still proudly carrying weapons of his making.

The king avoided talking about the thralls' battle for freedom, which had cost so many lives. But he did say that the Danish king had advised him to make Holme one of his warriors. He saw his men stiffen in pride and arrogance and knew they would never accept the smith as their equal. And so people from town would demand Holme's surrender as soon as it became known he was at the king's farmstead.

As he pondered, the king heard a warrior tell another in a low voice that Holme had done the metal work for the king's farmstead. He hadn't been aware of that; his foreman took care of such matters. But it gave him an idea. Holme could be the smith on the farmstead and his story would finally fall into oblivion. He would just have to stay away from town for the first few years.

The king was happy with that solution. He didn't want to let out of his sight the man most people hated or feared. A thrall had never before become so renowned, the subject of so much conversation. When foreign kings or chieftains came, they would get to hear his saga and perhaps see some proof of his powers.

The warriors sitting closest to Holme either looked at him arrogantly or ignored him. Who ever heard of a thrall sitting at the king's table? But they were used to the king's sometimes doing what struck his fancy, in direct opposition to ancient custom and practice. In the next moment he might forget about all this or turn the thrall over to the town authorities.

The king, however, was thinking constantly about what he would do when the meal was over and the thralls began running back and forth, taking away the wooden pails and tankards and cleaning up after the men. And without looking at anyone or asking anyone's advice, he took Holme with him to the silent, empty smithy and suggested he take charge of all the work that needed to be done at the farmstead. If Holme had any spare time he could make weapons he could use for bartering.

Holme had spent every moment at the table paying close attention to what was going on around him and trying to figure out what had happened. Had the king really been serious or did he invite the thrall to his table merely to amuse himself and his friends? Now he had no more doubts: the king wished to help him and Holme had done the right thing by seeking him out at the farmstead. He felt immense relief and happiness except for one thing—he still had to make arrangements for Ausi and Tora.

There were plenty of good tools lined up in rows in the king's smithy, and Holme examined them with interest. He greedily inhaled the smell of old soot, thinking how fortunate he would be to work here in peace and quiet, free from threats and persecution. Deep in his heart, something was still lodged like a thorn—he would not allow himself to forget freedom for others even if his lot were good. A number of them had sacrificed their lives, and he owed it to them to keep working for the sake of those who still lived.

But he wasn't up to that battle right then; he longed for work and quiet. There still might be something he'd be able to do, though; the king was a good master and would understand. It was better to talk than to fight. No one had ever talked to him as the king had, a man who understood a great deal at a glance.

From the smithy, Holme could see across the cove to the forest on the other side, and the town was just barely visible in the distance. The king had told Holme about a house a little ways from the farmstead where he could live. And, to Holme's relief, the king had also asked if Holme had a wife and child and where they were. In response, Holme had pointed toward the mainland forest to the east.

It wasn't long before Holme was on his way home. The boat was there where he'd left it, and he didn't have to sneak up to it. Instead he walked boldly forward, dry branches breaking under foot. He had no one to fear now. He rowed across the cove, watching the sun's dazzling rays on the water where the moon's red path had been many hours before. It was late autumn, but the day was like summer, and the surface of the water was as still as glass.

Two men and a woman stood by the jetty where he had borrowed the boat. While he was still a ways from the land, the men started threatening him for taking the boat. They yelled what would happen to him when he came ashore, and one of them picked up a heavy, dry club.

Holme rowed up, tied the boat to the jetty where he had found it, and stepped ashore. Although he had been awake all night and was tired, he stood silently before the irate men, and they stared just as silently back at him. The club sank down again, and the woman whispered his name in terror.

But nothing happened, and Holme moved on toward the edge of the forest. He didn't turn around to look back at the three people who were still standing by the jetty, staring after him, and no threats followed him. They were probably just happy to see him disappear. He didn't know them, but they had undoubtedly seen him in town and had heard the rumors about him when they were there to sell their fish.

He walked quickly through the forest, happy he hadn't been forced to strike the men down. He had fought many times, and he had killed a few men, but no one had ever won. The king, on the other hand, had come a long way with peaceful talk. Holme sensed a new way, a way where no one had to fight but where everyone could talk and come to terms. He could not see the way clearly, but the thought of it filled him with happiness. Perhaps one day the king would even understand the thoughts and feelings of thralls.

Pleasant thoughts filled Holme's head all the way back. He felt confident that nothing had happened to Ausi and Tora while he had been away. He had learned through the king that the warriors in town had refused to pursue him through the forest a second time, and that the will of the gods supported their decision. Maybe the charred god at the settlement had had a hand in this because Holme had put him back on the rock a few days ago. As he grew older, he no longer thought it completely impossible for the gods to get involved if they wanted to.

He clambered up the ridge in the dusk and walked by Stenulf's burial mound, made level by many years of pine needles settling between the stones. In a few more years the mound would be like a little hill. Stenulf had never shown himself after his death, regardless of how dark the night had been, and Holme had stopped looking toward his mound with fear. A powerful warrior like Stenulf had probably not stayed in the mound but had gone to the land of the dead.

No one came out of the cave when he approached it, but he saw that the branches covered the entrance as usual. That meant that Ausi and Tora had left of their own free will and would probably be back soon. Tonight they would all sleep in the cave, but early the next morning they would be off to the king's farmstead.

He took the branches away, crawled in, and started gathering his tools to take along. But then he remembered the good collection of tools in the king's smithy and considered the unpredictable future. He would leave his own tools hidden in the cave under branches and moss. They might be of use to him or someone else some day.

He sensed that someone was nearby and crawled out to look around. Everything was quiet, but behind a tree trunk something stuck out that didn't belong to the well-known landscape. Someone was there. He grabbed his ax and pretended to wander around haphazardly until he neared the tree. Then he pounced, his ax lifted in the air.

But it never fell. As he leaped, he heard a happy little shout and then someone came running. And there, under the ax, stood Ausi, her eyes opened wide. She and Tora had noticed that the branches were gone from the cave opening and hid to see who was there. They hadn't dared hope Holme would be back so soon.

They were overjoyed to see him in one piece and with a twinkle in his eye. They weren't used to seeing him so peaceful and happy. But they didn't ask what was going on but instead just waited until he was ready to talk. Ausi went back to the slope for some fish they had caught and started to clean them. Holme made a fire, thinking how nice it was not to be afraid that the smoke would be seen and not to have to listen all the time for his pursuers. No riders came hunting him through the forest anymore and none would be coming. For the first time in many years he felt peaceful and at ease.

The three of them sat on the ground near the fire eating their grilled fish and bread. Holme told them everything. He saw his wife's face light up with joy, his daughter's with curiosity and excitement. And he momentarily let himself feel as they did. He didn't forget for a moment what he owed his fellow thralls, both the ones who had died in the fight for freedom and those who were still alive. But he could let it be for awhile; he would see if, with the king's help, something could be done without violence and strife.

Tonight was their last night in the cave. It had protected and served them well more than once, but it looked as if they could manage without it from now on. But that was probably hoping for too much. The town, and even the king's farmstead, could be attacked and burned. Such things had happened often enough before.

After they lay down, he heard Ausi whispering in the darkness. He didn't pay much attention since he knew what she was doing. She was thanking Christ for the good fortune and asking Him for His protection in the future. It didn't do any harm any more; she could just as well keep on praying. Many years ago she would talk out loud to Christ, but Holme had tired of listening there beside her and had asked her to be quiet. After that, she whispered or talked out loud only if she was alone. But she hadn't stopped.

A hint of moonbeam settled on the sticks and grass in the cave's entrance. The night promised to be like the one before so they'd have good weather for the journey. He just hoped the king would stand by his word. Now that Holme was in the cave and it was night, his good fortune that day seemed like a dream. Nothing like it had ever happened before.

He could hear that Ausi was still awake and he told her quietly that it might be a trap, that the king might summon his warriors to kill him when they arrived. It wouldn't matter so much if he were alone. But he kept imagining his wife and daughter as thralls, beaten and scorned because of him, and that caused him more anguish than anything ever had before.

Ausi calmed him down by pointing out that the king wouldn't be so deceitful. Besides, she reminded him, he had sat among the king's warriors that very same day. If the king had wanted to, he never would have let Holme out alive. And if things still turned out as Holme feared, then she and Tora would rather die with him than live in slavery. Christ would care for all three of them and they would enjoy peace with Him.

Holme listened to what she said with only half an ear. He had calmed down but decided to watch his step. If it was a trap, he'd make sure he wasn't the only one left lying on the battlefield. The muscles in his arms and legs tightened as he imagined the battle. He wasn't young any longer, but he could still hold his own in a fight or in work.

But the happy, tranquil thoughts returned. Before falling asleep, he could see the king's smithy among the birch trees on the slope, the lake glittering down below. He would show the friendly king what he could do once left in peace with his own work.

The women were still asleep when he crawled out of the cave into the dawn. The woods were totally quiet and a mist hung over the marshland below the ridge. It rolled halfway up the slope but the ridge's uppermost part was bathed in the early morning light. The sun would melt away the mist, and it was going to be a clear day.

He wanted to go to the settlement one last time. He didn't have anything more to do there; he just wanted to see it. It might be the last time. And it might be enjoyable to go there once without having to sneak around like a troll peering out from behind tree trunks. He looked hesitatingly at his ax but let it be. Instead he picked up a heavy stick with an iron point on it. It had been in the cave since the first summer he and Ausi had lived there and the point was red with rust. He could at least defend himself with that if a wolf or wild boar decided to attack. He hesitated a moment longer then kneeled down for something a second time. It was a little grilled fish and a piece of bread. He looked almost ashamed as he hid them in his clothes.

It wasn't long before he was in the cold and raw mist. It got so thick at one point that he had to stop and feel his way forward. All he could see was an aspen branch sticking out of the mist, hung with a few yellow leaves dripping with moisture. But soon a light breeze came, revealing the treetops above him. Then the mist began glowing a yellowish-gold in the direction he was walking. The sun must be coming up.

Wet branches struck him everywhere, soon spotting his gray clothes with moisture. Beautiful, dew-laden spider webs spanned the path, and he crawled under or walked around them. A bird took off with a rush of wings, scaring a rabbit from its lair. Holme saw its bounding back legs for an instant, and then it was gone.

Nothing had changed at the settlement but he hadn't really expected it to. The fields would probably grow over again now, the buildings collapse, and that wasn't good. The ground was rich and many people could live there. But he couldn't do anything about it. The buildings would probably become a refuge for robbers and outlaws. That might be just as well, though. He knew such people better than others did and knew they often were people who didn't wish to do anyone any harm. They only had to defend themselves against injustice and mistreatment.

The charred wooden god was dimly visible through the sunlit mist, and Holme walked down to it. The god had been through quite a lot, but he was stubborn and strong. There he stood, years after the settlement had been burned and the owners were gone. Holme started to like him; they were alike somehow. He took out the fish and bread to place on the stone, but they smelled good and he was hungry. The wooden god could share with him; they could each have half. He divided the fish and the bread, laying half on the stone before him and eating the rest as he looked around. All was still. Only mild breezes came from the cove where seagulls laughed and screeched.

There wasn't anything worth taking from the settlement now. The ashes from the fire had long been overgrown with bushes and large plants, yellow and drooping now, stiff with cold, wet with dew. The mist still danced and played around the three burial mounds in the aspen grove, and Holme wondered if he would ever come back there.

He drank some water from the old spring before turning back. The spring was still gurgling, unconcerned about the settlement's desolation, and the stream from it swung left a short distance away. The hole where the water gathered was half-filled with mud.

The mist was gone; only a faint fog still hung above the surface of the water. Holme looked back from the edge of the forest with a strange feeling in his heart. The road beside him led to the farmstead where the young thrall and his woman had dared settle. He should let them know that they were in less danger than they were before, and so he decided to take that road when he and his family left later on that day. It would be good to see the man again who had stood by him through dangerous battles and whose craving for freedom was stronger than most others'. He and his woman had to know, too, that Holme wouldn't be in the cave anymore if they needed his help.

After one last look over the slope and lake, he returned to the cave where his wife and daughter joyfully awaited him.

From a distance they could hear the sound of ax blows from the farmstead, but they soon fell silent. Holme knew that the thrall had discovered them and hidden to see who was coming, friend or foe. He soon recognized them and rushed from his hiding place with child-like enthusiasm.

Everything had gone well the first few days and he proudly showed them what he had already accomplished. No enemies had shown up, and his face beamed when he heard that none would be coming from town either. He wasn't afraid of pirates and highwaymen; such men had always been around and you simply had to cope with that. And he was a free man now. The old chieftain's relatives were bound not to return, and besides, all that were left were Svein, the stiff-necked boy, and his horrible witch of a mother. They would surely stay in town forever.

Holme felt deeply satisfied seeing a thrall free and happy. He had done more work than he would ever have done as a slave. This showed again that freedom was a good that everyone should have. More work would be done and done happily, as it had been here, instead of with grumbling and a desire to cleave the master's skull with an ax.

But many thralls had lost their lives so this one could be free. They had been slaughtered like dogs. Freedom could not walk that road; there had to be another one.

Then Holme thought about the king again. Maybe he would understand all thralls as he had understood Holme and would see that they would work and fight better if they were free.

The thrall's wife hurried to get the food ready, and soon everyone was sitting around the split-log table. The thrall couple showed them the grain they had stored up and the field they had already sown. They planned to trap animals for the winter and barter for goods with their furs as people had always done. And they'd brew their own beer. If he let his beard grow, no one in the town would recognize him, and in a few winters he would get some help for the work and the hunting. The thrall laughed, clapping his wife's swelling stomach with his big hand.

Their joy refreshed Holme, and he no longer felt such deep sorrow for those who had given up their lives. Had the dead held out and stayed away from town, they too could have known freedom and happiness. But when they had no one to lead them, they soon lost their courage. A man must be able to live alone, without a leader.

Holme would much rather have stayed in the forest a free man than go to the king's farmstead as a smith. He knew that now. But he couldn't do it. If he didn't do what the king wanted, the hunt would start all over again, and then the young thrall and his family would be killed or driven away. Too many people knew that he had stood by Holme and had killed a number of free men. He had to be saved; he was the first thrall to be free and happy.

Holme soon moved on with his wife and daughter. He wanted to reach the king's farmstead while it was still daylight. The former thralls followed them on the road and both families promised to visit each other. And if either was in some kind of trouble, they would come to the other for help. Holme immediately started thinking about how he might help them out of various scrapes, since it didn't occur to him that he might ever need to call on them. He had never asked anyone to help him. Thralls couldn't and, until now, no one with power except the king had befriended him.

The families parted in the forest where sun and shadow, warmth and coolness, clashed on that clear autumn day. But Holme walked on with a lighter heart. He had seen one small consequence of his long, bitter fight. It wasn't much, but those two free, happy human beings showed how things could be. There was no limit to the land to cultivate; the woods were full of animals, and the lakes of fish. Slavery just didn't seem necessary, even though every free man said it was. He would tell the king all this when the time came.

The thrall couple's parting call rang through the forest, then died away in the direction of their farmstead. Ausi and Tora talked cheerfully, wondering what it would be like at the king's farmstead. They could see that Holme was deep in thought, so they didn't disturb him. They never took that gentle expression on his dark face for granted and were always glad to see it.

As they approached the fishing village opposite the king's farmstead, Holme remembered that they had to borrow a boat. That might present a problem. He had no desire for a confrontation; he felt calm and happy after the visit with his friends.

But he didn't have to worry. From a distance they saw people gathering by one of the jetties and someone waving to them from a boat. Holme walked closer and quickly saw his hunch was right. The king had sent a boat for them with a thrall to row it. He had been waiting there half the day.

The people in the fishing village stared at Holme and his family with excitement. They had heard so much about them, and now there they stood. It was hard for the men to believe that the powerfully built man with the calm eyes could be the dangerous, violent man whom they had heard tales about, but who was now under the king's protection. They looked too at his beautiful wife and black-eyed daughter. A few people remembered them from when they had lived in town and Holme had led the uprising against the Christians.

As they watched the boat set out with the smith family, they began chattering eagerly among themselves. Nothing like this had ever happened before: the king had taken an outlaw into his service. They'd have to wait and see what would happen now, but this probably meant that the days of peace were at an end.

The king's thrall rowed with mighty strokes to impress them, and he glowed when Holme said a few appreciative words. It was the first time the smith had been rowed in a boat like a chieftain and he wasn't really happy about it. But Ausi was and already felt that she almost belonged to the king's court. Tora looked with simultaneous curiosity and mistrust toward the king's farmstead, reminding Ausi once again that her resemblance to her father wasn't just physical. He too directed his face toward the farmstead, a threatening wrinkle lodged between his eyebrows. If this was a trick, he was ready. It would be a tough fight, but Ausi and Tora would die with Holme. That didn't frighten Ausi. Christ would meet them and understand everything. He had to know that Holme had never chosen to do any harm, that he befriended the weak just like Christ Himself did.

She stretched out her hand and caressed Holme's cheek. He looked at her and understood. Yes, if it came to a fight, it was best to do what she wanted: kill them both. If he couldn't do it, Ausi would. She and their daughter had tasted freedom; it had taken root in them and they would never again be thralls.

For the first time in his life, he reached out and returned his wife's caress. He saw her eyes gleam as never before while Tora looked wonderingly at both of them.

All three were completely calm when they stepped ashore at the king's jetty.

Svein's mother was seething with rage and despair as she walked toward her hut after the warriors had refused to go to the mainland and kill Holme. She didn't dare now go back to rebuild the settlement for her son. If Holme was on the loose in the forest, they wouldn't have a safe moment.

She still had some silver left that she had hidden for the rebuilding. The Christians wouldn't wheedle any more out of her. They said that Christ would help her for nothing, but they still came begging for His church. The priests probably kept whatever they collected, and new ones would be coming in the spring. These last monks couldn't take living among the heathens either and had gained permission to return home.

Beside her stood a large, beautiful house that she looked at enviously every time she walked outside. It belonged to a woman and her daughter, the town's richest inhabitants. While the woman's husband was alive, he had overtaken many vessels on the sea, killed their crews, and plundered them. Consequently, he was much esteemed, and people still greeted his wife and daughter with respect.

The rich woman and her daughter were Christians, and they had given a great deal to the Christian priests. The chieftain visited them often, and when the priests left, they held services there with singing and talks about Christ. Svein's mother sometimes thought about joining them, but she still resented the chieftain too much for letting Holme live. She was surprised to see Svein listening to the songs without a scoff or a frown. He had gotten more eventempered recently and seemed to have something on his mind. He went off with the warriors at the fortress every day to learn how to use weapons.

One morning Svein's mother walked down to the harbor to buy some fish. The fishermen came in early with their night catches, and many kinds of fish were flopping and splashing in the boats' bilge water. As she sorted through the catch, she heard Holme's name and her ears perked up.

Someone said that Holme had become the king's smith and lived there with his family. When she grasped what she had heard, she shrieked with rage, dropped the fish, and clutching up her skirt sped off toward town. The startled people in the harbor watched her go and isolated laughter broke out. The news spread quickly and soon people in town were talking about it everywhere.

Svein's mother ran straight to the chieftain's house, which lay close to the Christian quarters. She heard singing from the church and looked in. A handful of people were in the pews closest to the front singing a morning hymn to Christ. She was going to rush up to the chieftain anyway, who was leading the hymn, but a guard stopped her and shoved her out the door. She stood outside still sobbing with rage.

After awhile the few church-goers left and went to their work. The chieftain came out last, and the woman immediately began railing loudly about what she had just heard. The chieftain listened in surprise but didn't believe her. Some other people from the harbor, however, soon corroborated what she had said. The chieftain listened to them in silence, wondering once more how long that thrall would be allowed to live and bring unrest to the people in town. The king had to release him and he would be put on trial at the assembly.

He calmed the woman down by saying that the king could not oppose the people's will. Besides, the whole thing might be one of the king's ploys for capturing this dangerous man. In either case, she should calm down. Holme would never again return to the mainland forest and no one there would have to live in fear of him any longer. Finally he promised to visit the king that day and find out what was going on.

When Svein heard the news he snapped out of the lethargy that had engulfed him. For quite some time he had remained silent when his mother came complaining angrily and viciously about Holme and his family. But he often thought about them. He was still afraid of Holme, but he let his thoughts circumvent him and settle on Tora. He still felt he had a claim on her. He was almost a full-grown man now and needed a young woman thrall before he could get the settlement in order and find a wife.

These thoughts intensified once he heard his mother's story, and he walked up a hill to look toward the king's farmstead. So, there she was now, the slender, bad-tempered girl. If she came to town without her father, he would have her, rape her. He could lure her into the house or into the woods outside town. He had seen a great deal that time he had wandered around out there. Alien sailors, showing no respect for the family burial mounds, lay out there with women after eating and getting drunk on beer or mead. He watched it all with aching desire, but one day it would be his turn.

But winter was coming and nothing would happen. There were long days ahead in the house's darkness broken only by the firelight flickering from the hearth. The snow would be deep and the ice would roar round about the island. The mid-winter sacrifice was the only thing to look forward to. Then maybe

Holme would come to town with his daughter. If he was lucky enough not to be sentenced to death at the assembly, that is.

While he stood there looking toward the distant, royal farmstead, the view gradually faded and tiny snowflakes soon started dancing around him. This was the first snow of the autumn, and it seemed to come in response to his morose thoughts about winter. The squall rolled over the island, soon making the north sides of the burial mounds in the ancestral meadow glisten. A woman from town came walking that way. He recognized her. The whole town knew that she carried food to her husband's mound every day. She had placed a bowl in a hollow she had dug in the mound. Every day it was toppled over and empty, which made her believe that her husband had eaten the food. The Christian priests had told her that animals had, but she scoffed at them and kept up her practice.[4]

Svein watched her walk by. She was still young and looked happy. The bowl was steaming and she walked quickly, kicking up her skirt. She probably wanted to get to the mound before the soup got cold.

Driven by curiosity and some less definite feeling, Svein followed her. She didn't turn around, so from behind the closest mound, he could see her put the bowl in place as she talked in a soft, encouraging voice. When she bent forward he stared hungrily at her legs, exposed part way up the calves.

The snow squall had passed and the sun poked through the clouds. The bare limbs of the birch trees started dripping; the snowflakes were melting and the land of burial mounds glowed an autumn yellow. The woman walked home without having noticed the stiff-necked youth behind the mound. She'd come back again the next day around the same time.

Svein stood there, not knowing what to do. The idea of going home to his mother, who was always angry and railing about something or someone, wasn't very appealing. He looked around, suddenly noticing movement in some small bushes nearby. He soon saw a pair of cold eyes observing him.

He walked slowly away so that the animal would venture out. The eyes followed him as long as they could, then wandered anxiously about for a moment. With back lowered, the wild cat sneaked toward the grave and the bowl of food. Svein realized that this wasn't the first time it had dined on the dead man's food.

But the food was still too hot today. The cat snarled, pawed at the bowl gently, and sat down to wait. It turned and stared mistrustfully at Svein's motionless head behind the mound. But after a while it relaxed and tested the bowl again with its paw.

Svein was as curious as a little boy and realized that the Christian priest was right: animals had eaten the man's food. This cat was well-fed and probably came around every day.

---

[4] Schön (*Fridegård och forntiden*, pp. 148–49) reports that bowls of the type the woman uses have been found in the burial mounds at Birka.

Some magpies smelled the food too and were chattering anxiously in the nearby trees; the cat shot an occasional cold, malevolent glance at them. Finally it got up and stuck its nose into the bowl. By its movements, it seemed to be lapping up some of the broth. After awhile it extracted a piece of meat, sat down, and started chewing, its head turning from side to side.

Svein hoped the dead man would reach out and kill the cat, strangle it or something, but nothing happened. So he got bored and shouted. The cat dashed a couple of steps away but turned and retrieved the meat when it saw it was only a human being making the noise. Then it slid off between a couple of burial mounds, and the magpies moved in. When Svein looked around, there was a commotion of wings and flapping tails surrounding the bowl. It would surely be tipped over and empty for the woman the next day. He decided to hide again to watch her. Maybe her skirt would slide higher so he could see more leg.

A new snow squall came from the lake, obscuring his vision, and he began walking faster. The fortress disappeared first behind the whirling flakes and then the buildings in town. Winter had arrived—long, dark winter.

After promising Svein's mother to visit the king and bring Holme to trial, the cheiftain began to have doubts. He wasn't sure the people were behind him in this matter, and without their support he could never win.

He walked to the fortress to talk with the warriors gathered there. They showed absolutely no interest. If the king had taken the skilled smith into his service, it was nobody's business. Everyone knew that Holme was the best smith in town, perhaps even in the whole kingdom. The king obviously knew what he was doing.

The warriors yawned through their beards and talked among themselves about other things, paying no more attention to the cheiftain. This was all very odd. They hadn't been able to capture the smith—just one man—and so they gave up. It must be because he was a thrall. They surely couldn't be afraid of him.

The chieftain went back to town and talked with some of the most prominent merchants. They were indifferent, too. They talked about the days when they could get proper smith work done at a reasonable cost. If the king had taken the smith into his service, that didn't concern them. Holme had done them no harm and they didn't want to see him dead. They would not ask that he be sentenced since they didn't even know he was guilty of everything people said about him.

It was only the Christians who backed the chieftain. They thought that such a terrible criminal, and heathen besides, had to die and be lost for eternity. Hadn't he once desecrated their holy church and divided their grain among the starving heathens? Wasn't he Christ's greatest enemy in town and the surrounding district?

But there were too few Christians; they couldn't force the issue, so the chieftain postponed his trip to the king. It was autumn now and everyone was growing listless and sullen because of the approaching winter. Once winter had arrived, the atmosphere would be different.

When the angry woman came to complain, that's what he told her: she would have her justice in the spring and would be able to rebuild the settlement. During the winter, she should gather thralls to cut lumber and carry it out on crude sleds. The chieftain had seen the settlement when he had hunted Holme and knew it was in a good location and had rich fields. It was worth rebuilding. Christ would protect it from attacks and plundering if the woman would let herself and her son be baptized.

The woman promised to renounce the gods of her fathers if Christ would help her. But in her heart, she knew she would keep sacrificing to the wooden gods. No one had to know. After all, they had helped her father, her husband, and her many times before. She didn't dare turn her back on them.

The chieftain was pleased to see the woman calm down and go home. She had the law on her side and could demand her rights at the assembly. It would be a peaceful winter in the meantime, and there would be some way out come spring. New priests would arrive, and the Christian work would go forward with renewed vigor. That's the message he recently received from the Christian bishop, together with the admonition to hold out.

The king could have his smith for the winter, but the people would decide his fate in the spring. Such had always been the law of the land. The king couldn't act arbitrarily in matters affecting everybody.

Everything was ready for the winter now. Everyone had gathered stores of food, and everywhere you could hear the pigs grunting in their stalls. They would be fattened for the winter sacrifice. The chieftain had been around those winters when the food had run out, and he and his men had had to cross the snow-covered expanses of ice to find meat on the mainland. Like black dots, shivering men could be seen fishing through holes everywhere on the vast, snow-covered ice field.

At the mainland farmsteads, the chieftain bought live animals with the merchants' money—cows, sheep, goats. The next day, their new owner crossed the ice, leading the reluctant animals with him. Farmers with grain and other goods to sell followed along on their sleds, set up a market on the ice, and demanded a high price. As long as the ice was there, foreign merchants weren't.

The harvest had been bad that year because of the blight the wooden gods had visited on the grain. The heathens blamed Christ, and the priest had fled for his life. If he had stayed the winter, and the heathens had begun to starve, no one could have saved him from being sacrificed to the wooden gods, not even Christ Himself. This priest was not one to crave martyrdom. The first one had been, the one who had been slaughtered at the great spring sacrifice many years before.

The march sun beat down on the king's fields, which were almost powder dry. The only place the ground was still dark with moisture was in the indentations, and there was still a little snow water trickling in the furrows. Out in the forest, the north sides of the trees still had flecks of grainy snow on them, peppered with pine needles and dry blades of grass.

In a couple of days the spring plowing could begin, and preparations were already under way. The queen had saved a large, dry roll that had been baked for the winter sacrifice, and one of the barrels still had some beer in it. During the spring plowing, both man and beast would partake of that luck-bringing food.

The field below the birch grove where Holme lived was directly in the sun and so already dry. The ditch banks glowed with yellow flowers that would close up and disappear when the sun went down.

The smith's family had passed their calmest winter. No one chasing them, no hunger, no cold. Sometimes a rumor rippled through the farmstead about Holme's having to appear before the spring assembly, but no one mentioned it to him. The king visited the smithy almost daily, pleased about all the weapons and other barterable goods that Holme forged on the anvil. He talked with the smith frequently and became more and more convinced that he was a decent human being who didn't want to hurt anyone, who wouldn't attack unless he was forced to.

There had been some disturbances in town a couple of times during the late winter. The heathens accused the chieftain of disrespecting people's rights to the store of food. The Christians weren't suffering, and someone had seen them carrying burdens from the storehouse at night. But when the heathens confronted them about this, they answered that Christ had given them food. If you believed in Him and accepted baptism, He would supply your needs.

But the heathens would not be fooled. They kept watch and saw the chieftain dispensing grain and meat to his people, and they became enraged. Some messengers were sent across the ice to the king, saying that if justice wasn't done soon, the people would be driven into a murderous frenzy against all the Christians.

The king returned to town with the messengers and managed to restore peace. He gave whatever food he could spare from his own stores and reminded the people that as soon as the water opened, merchant ships would arrive with all kinds of goods and exchange them for the Norsemen's skins and metal work. The king wasn't very happy about the thought that new priests would be coming then, too. The heathens' bitterness against them was greater than before, and it could cost the priests their lives at any time. The ruler in the southern lands was powerful; he could forbid his people to come to Scandinavia with their goods if his missionaries got killed.

The king thought about these matters as he strolled through his fields. He was a peaceful man and would prefer seeing the Christians left in peace as long as they did the same to the wooden gods. He couldn't see much difference between them and Christ. Christ was made of wood, too, and hung above the altar in the church. There was talk in town of miracles he had done, like healing the sick, but the king hadn't seen it with his own eyes. Besides, one god had been in this land longer than human memory—a god who had healed their forefathers—and he could be just as good as Christ.[5]

Thralls were working in the field outside Holme's house now, preparing it for sowing. They had their hoods off in the sunshine and shouted light-heartedly at the work animals. The foreman stood on a ditch bank supervising, and the hammer rang in the smithy.

Everything was coming to life. The spring ice was still there, white and porous, but it had broken loose from the land, making room for the pikes to surface in the grass by the shore. In the distance, you could see a surging band of blue water. Carpenters were busy with the ships, sending the sound of frequent hammer blows from the harbor. One of them would stop for a minute now and then to fetch nails or fittings from the smithy.

The men longed for the sea when the spring winds started ruffling their hair and beards. They kept examining their weapons and visiting Holme in the smithy. And the thought the king had had the past autumn about conducting a raid across the ocean returned and grew stronger. His kingdom was poorer now than ever before, and so was he. Once the sowing and the other spring work was done, they would have to set sail.

A few days later, the ground was ready for sowing. The foreman was up early, drenching the work animals' fodder with beer before they were brought from their stalls. That would insure them health and strength for the coming year, and they would have plentiful offspring.

Meanwhile, the thralls carried a vat of beer into the field and placed it next to the seed grain. They looked expectantly toward the farmstead now and then, which was just coming to life. Some of the king's men went into his court and came out carrying a large wooden god on a pole. They took him into the field and put him down near the vat of beer. There he stood, grinning a crooked smile, his long, rough-hewn organ jutting diagonally up into the air.

More and more men and women left the farmstead to gather in the field. The thralls stood off by themselves, and Holme brought Tora and Ausi from the smithy. Ausi, wanting to distance herself from the thralls, edged closer to the freemen, but Holme yanked her back. She smiled a little shamefacedly while Holme thought that she always wanted to make herself out to be better than she was. She was a thrall, and she should stand with the others until all of them were free. Some curious children had gathered in a group, but when the foreman came, he shouted at them to go away. They reluctantly walked off just over the top of a hill. They could see everything from there.

---

[5] i.e., the Norse god, Thor.

Only the king and queen were missing. The men working on the ships stopped to watch what was happening on the field, and all grew quiet. Only the song of the lark filled the air.

Everyone watched as the king and queen approached from the farmstead. The king held a branch covered with small, fresh leaves. It had been kept in some water inside the building so it would be ready for the sowing. The king looked around and nodded in approval. Everything was right. The gods had provided good weather, so they had to be pleased with the sacrifices he had offered in the spring.

The foreman, who would sow the grain himself, walked up to the king. There were several beer tankards beside the vat, and a couple of women thralls were busy filling them. A horn belonging to the king stood there, too, but this the queen filled herself and handed it to him with a smile. The foreman and highest ranking warriors likewise had horns, which the queen or their own women filled and handed to them.

When everyone was quiet, the king dipped the branch in the beer and let it rain over the grinning wooden god, soaking it completely. The beer trickled down and was swallowed immediately by the earth, which had opened its womb to receive the offering—a good omen.

Then tankards were passed out among the hall servants and highest ranking thralls. The rest—the big crowd of thrall laborers—rushed to the vat at a signal from the queen. They filled their wooden ladles and gulped wildly, both men and women. The children on the hill had moved closer. They didn't care anymore that they could be seen. They just stared in amazement and excitement at what was going on.

After drinking from his horn, the king dipped the green birch branch in the beer again and sprinkled his smiling queen. Then it was his turn, and she sprinkled the brown liquid all over the king. The foreman was next and then each of the high ranking warriors. The thralls were standing off by themselves in a group, but a sparkle had come into their eyes because of the beer. The king walked around, smiling a friendly smile through his beard, pouring beer on all of them.

When the preliminaries were over, the king motioned for the sowing bushel to be hung around the foreman's neck. He had emptied his large horn and wasn't too steady on his feet, a fact that made everybody laugh. He soon regained his balance, though, and walked along, tossing the golden grain from side to side onto the ground. Several thralls followed him and covered the seed with rakes. As they did so, they yelled and screamed at the birds that were trying to feed on the grain as it fell.

Holme was glad to see that the king did not differentiate much between freemen and thralls. They all got beer; it was only the container—horn or tankard—that varied. And they all got sprinkled. If everyone treated their thralls like the king did, freedom might develop on its own without violence and conflict. These thralls were happy and well-fed, but the ones at other farmsteads weren't so lucky.

The foreman kept sowing but would stop occasionally for a slug of beer while the thralls refilled the basket. A butterfly, awakened too early, flew erratically along the furrow, fluttered to the vat, and landed in the sun on the sweet, moist wood.

A boat had docked at the jetty, and some men were walking toward the farmstead. The laborers looked, wondering if they could be the new Christian priests, and the king walked back toward the farmstead after leaving orders for another vat of beer for the workers. He would be back soon. When he was out of sight, some of the thralls sat down on a pile of rocks with their tankards. The rocks had been there long before they had, and the lowest layer had sunk halfway into the earth. Their fathers had probably unearthed the rocks and piled them there. When the foreman approached the pile on his next round, some of the thralls hesitantly stood up, but the more tipsy ones sat still. The foreman looked at them, but the beer had put him in a good mood so he left them alone. He knew that by dusk no one would either hear or care about anything he said. This was a day of celebration and belonged to the fertility god. That night, after the fields had been sown, it would be the women's turn. They knew it, and their eyes sparkled and their cheeks blushed when they looked at the men.

After the first field was sown, the one by the smithy, Holme tired of being out in the sun and went back inside. No one tried to stop him; they were used to his doing whatever he wanted and obeying only the king. Ausi and Tora returned to the house in the birch grove, but didn't feel like working. There was something in the air, so they soon went outside again and sat on a rock where they could watch the people in the fields. They saw the thralls dipping their ladles into the beer whenever the foreman's back was turned.

One thrall emerged from the forest driving a wagon with crude wheels and loaded with wood and dry twigs. He unloaded the wagon on a grassy area near the farmstead where a bonfire would burn that night. As he worked, a woman thrall appeared carrying a tankard that she handed to him. He drank and then grabbed hold of her, making her laugh and wriggle in his arms. Ausi knew they'd be together later that night.

In the afternoon, the work was finished. The wooden god was carried through the newly planted fields, and everyone followed in the procession. They were all tired but soon would rest. On the way back, a couple of thralls picked up the empty beer vat, and both god and vat were placed near the woodpile.

Holme started home from the smithy. All day long he had been thinking about the boat that had appeared earlier. He had been free and clear of the Christians for a while but wondered if it would start all over again. Bad things always happened when they were around, no matter what they said about peace. They divided friend from friend, wife from husband, and blood was always running wherever they went, despite their saying that they didn't offer human sacrifices.

Their boat was still there, but they would probably go back the same day. If he had figured them right, they wouldn't dare stay on a night like this. The king wouldn't want them here either. The celebration concerned only the people at the farmstead and whoever else the king invited.

It was rumored from town that many Christians had turned away from their faith during the winter. That was good, but these new monks would start gathering followers again, and the king would surely permit them to preach freely.[6] When they had come to the king's farmstead, they had thralls behind them carrying various objects. They must be gifts to this king from the king who ruled the monk's homeland.

Holme had stopped in the birch grove while he thought about all this. The scent of spring was in the air, and some downy-gray flower buds were pushing their way up near his feet. He recognized what they were and knew they would eventually open into deep blue cups with yellow specks at the bottom. When the petals were gone, they would be left standing like glittering gray spiders in the wind.

Like most people, he longed to leave there even though he had everything he could want. Something was beckoning him—the forest, his old thrall friends, the cave, the settlement. Someday he would ask the king if he could leave for a few days, and he would visit the young thrall and his woman at the relatives' farmstead. That would make it easier to stay on the island during the summer.

The large gate at the king's farmstead was suddenly opened, and a number of figures came walking out. He recognized the long gowns on two of them. It had been a long time since he had first seen such garments, and many priests had been killed or driven off. But they never gave up. The best thing now for everyone would be for those two to be chased off immediately.

Holme also recognized the town's most powerful man, the gray-bearded, Christian chieftain who, with his men, had hunted Holme through the forests. There Holme had an enemy; he could feel it in the air. In that instant of

---

[6] It is not clear which—if any—of the monks described in *Vita Anskarii* Fridegård intends these two to be, since he has not been following Rimbert closely. In 844, Gautbert, the nephew whom Ansgar had consecrated bishop, was driven from Sweden. Seven years later, Ansgar, then the archbishop of Hamburg with all of Scandinavia under his jurisdiction, sent a hermit named Ardgar to Birka (*Anskar*, chapter 19, p. 62). In that same year the chieftain Herigar died (chapter 19, p. 69) and, shortly thereafter, Ardgar left Sweden (chapter 20, p. 73). In 853 Ansgar returned for his second mission to Sweden, which then had a new king, Olaf (chapter 26, p. 89). He left a nephew of Gautbert's, Erimbert, in charge of the mission when he returned to Hamburg in 854 (chapter 28, p. 95). In 854 or 855, Gautbert sent a priest named Ansfrid to join Erimbert; they stayed for three to four years and were followed by Rimbert (chapter 33, pp. 103–4). The mission remained dormant after Ansgar's death in 865.

recognition, the chieftain turned toward Holme, possibly even seeing the dark figure among the white tree trunks.

Something told Holme that the battle wasn't over yet and he was somehow glad. He had longed for peace and work during the autumn and winter, and he had gotten what he wanted. But he was getting restless. Just like a woman, he thought, shaking his head.

Once he had tried to talk with the king about freedom for thralls, but he couldn't find the right words. Besides, the king's thralls were almost free anyway, so the king couldn't or wouldn't understand what Holme was getting at. He looked at him strangely, then changed the subject to the smithy.

It was really for the best, then, if something new happened. He couldn't walk around here his whole life while countless thralls were tormented and some even killed by their masters. It was possible that a good many of them had heard about Holme and were expecting his help. And so he felt more sharply than ever before what he had to do: help. Everything was calm and peaceful here, and that's why he had become restless. He would wait until the right time, though. Christian priests had returned and they would doubtlessly put an end to the tranquility that had lasted through the winter.

The boat set out, several pairs of oars flashing rhythmically in and out of the water. Those sending it off walked back to the farmstead, and Holme, toward his house. His wife and daughter were on a rock outside, and they looked at him with a mixture of hope and anxiety—would they get to join the festivities in the king's courtyard?

Toward evening, the whole farmstead came alive. The king and all his retinue dressed in colorful, gold-embroidered garments, the thralls who owned decent clothes put them on, and the queen and her companions made up their eyes with something from the king's physician that made them look large and lustrous.

Men and women thralls were scampering everywhere, arranging for food and drink for the feast. Squealing and grunting could be heard from the pigsty where two thralls were holding onto a medium-sized pig as they carefully scrubbed it. They talked about the upcoming feast and would slap the pig on the snout whenever it squealed too loudly. The young women kept smiling at each other as they did their chores. They had waited all winter for this night.

At dusk, a big ship sailed into the harbor, bringing friends and relatives of the royal couple. The men had donned glistening armor, and the women, richly adorned clothes. Their thralls carried the stores ashore, and the setting sun cast its last gleaming rays on the illustrious train as it moved up towards the farmstead. The thralls ogled the noble women, thinking about the lascivious chaos of the approaching night. There had been a time or two when a thrall had sneaked up to them, and they couldn't see or didn't care who was loosening their clasps because of the beer and darkness. And a powerful warrior would often secretly find a woman thrall, whose young body or beautiful face enticed him. Later, no one would see whether he had her with or without her consent. The thrall women knew all this and they glanced furtively at the warriors.

When the bonfire was lit, Holme walked out of his house with his wife and daughter. They had bathed and changed clothes. He hadn't planned on going to the feast, but he finally had to give in to the looks of two pairs of plaintive eyes. Ausi hadn't said anything. She was thinking about the sacrificial feast many years before when the frenzy had made her follow another man into a clump of pine trees. This time they would only stand to one side to watch, and she wouldn't drink anything that would make her head feel strange and cause her body to want a man who didn't belong to her.

Before they had walked to the end of the short path, the fire was already blazing high, crackling through the branches and wood. It lighted up the tables and benches, and happy faces emerged from all directions out of the darkness into the firelight. The door of the king's farmstead was standing open, revealing a big fire in the hearth in the middle of the hall, with a gigantic cauldron hanging over it. A sturdy pole had been driven into the ground just outside the door, and a steady stream of thralls carried food and drink from the building to the festival area.

The king's thralls didn't have to wait that night until their masters had finished feasting and then devour the leftovers. The king had decreed that they should have their own table. Holme thought once more that if everyone treated his thralls as the king did, it would be easy to solve a pressing problem. But no one was like him, neither heathen nor Christian.

The sight of the fire, the tables, and the happy faces, brought to mind the great sacrificial feast of long ago at the heathen temple. He looked mistrustfully at Ausi's face. As then, her eyes were glowing with expectation, and in the firelight she looked like a young girl. But she was smarter now and wouldn't run off with someone else. Besides, he wouldn't let her or Tora out of his sight. When the men got drunk, they'd grab the first woman who came along and be pleased and excited by the struggling and screaming.

The king came out and surveyed the yard. His clothes were embroidered in gold, and a short, pearl-inlaid sword hung at his belt. He walked around the courtyard to inspect the preparations, even visiting the thralls' table. Holme stood in the background, and the king approached him. He asked Holme in a friendly voice to see that the thralls were treated well and justly. All the food and drink they needed would be sent to their table. When the king saw that everything was ready, he went back into his house.

The fire blazed higher, sending a flickering light onto the wooden god standing beside the sacrificial pole. More and more people milled around waiting for the celebration to begin, while the two thralls at the pigsty kept an eye on the freshly washed pig so it wouldn't get muddy again. It had finally calmed down and was now standing there blinking patiently at the fire in the yard. People teemed and swarmed in the firelight.

The king emerged again, followed by his closest advisors. The noise died down, and everyone gathered around the pole. There were a number of bronze and iron objects lying on a bench.

The king looked toward the sty, and the thralls responded to the signal. The pig squealed protractedly as it was carried, more than led, down the slope to the place of slaughter. The thralls then lifted it up, rolled it over onto its back, and grabbed hold of its frantically kicking legs.

The king signalled the foreman, who was still dressed in his work clothes. He took one of the knives, made a calculation, then cut the pig's throat. His wife held a bronze ladle under the wound, then emptied it into a bucket while the thralls repositioned the animal so blood wouldn't spill on the ground. The pig wheezed, its kicking weakened, and its bushy white eyes gradually closed in death.

The king took the branch he had used in the morning's ceremony, dipped it in the blood, and splashed the blood all over the wooden god. As he did so, the foreman, with the thralls' help, hung the carcass on the sacrificial pole. The blood looked black in the flickering firelight, and the dogs prowled around greedily, sometimes dashing off and barking furiously at the green eyes that flashed and disappeared in the thickets. The stray cats had been enticed by the smell of blood, too.

The god had had his desires satisfied, so everyone could breathe a little easier. Now it was their turn. The king washed his hands in water a woman thrall poured over them and dried them on the towel another thrall had ready. Then in a loud voice he invited people to the table, and all kinds of figures came from various directions into the firelight. A thrall stood guard at the sacrificial pole with a big stick to keep the dogs away from the sacrifice. He looked jealously toward the thralls' table, clenching his teeth, and a younger woman thrall looked back. She would doubtlessly make sure he didn't lack anything during his watch.

Everyone sat down and picked up their horns or tankards at a signal from the king. Before lifting his horn to his lips, the king loudly promised rich offerings for the gods if they would stand by him. He named both of them, the one in the firelight beside them and the one in the darkness of the temple who gave good fortune in battle.[7] The king mentioned his plans for a raid that spring, and the rows of warriors murmured approvingly. After a quiet winter, they longed for the sea and adventure. Finally, the king named a few minor deities who watched over the harvest, the animals, house and home.[8]

Simultaneous preparations for the spring feast were going on in town as well. Svein wandered around watching but had no desire to take part. He had

---

[7] i.e., the Norse gods, Freyr and Thor.

[8] These gods are difficult to identify but are probably associated with Freyr. See H. R. Ellis Davidson, *Gods and Myths of Northern Europe* (Harmondsworth: Penguin Books, 1964), pp. 103 ff.

grown during the winter and was now half a head taller than his mother, who was a tall woman.

Svein was glad it was spring and had already decided to ask the king if he could go along on the raid he had heard rumors about in town. There'd still be plenty of time for rebuilding the old settlement, something his mother talked about daily. Or she could do it without him for that matter.

From old habit, he walked up that spring day to the burial mounds to look toward the king's farmstead. He hadn't seen any member of Holme's family during the winter, neither at the feast nor the big market on the ice. They probably still didn't dare show themselves in town. The spring assembly would meet soon, and his mother had already reminded the chieftain about her right to the smith's wife and daughter.

The year-old grass on the burial mounds had dried up, but new green shoots were sprouting on the south sides. There were yellow flowers glistening here and there, and he recognized them from previous springs at the settlement. The wind from the lake felt cooler here than it did in town.

He remembered the woman who carried food to her dead husband and walked toward the mound. There was the hollow and the overturned bowl. A few small bones looked fresh so the woman probably still came there every day. He waited a while. It was the same time of day that he had seen her the previous autumn. Some magpies were sitting in the birch trees seeming to wait, and the cat with its cold eyes might be lurking nearby, too.

Happy voices and shouts were carried on the wind from the harbor. He had heard that many of the town's most important people would go to the king's feast. He knew what went on during such occasions, and a thought came like a flash, making his face blanch then flush. The smith's daughter, Tora, was at the king's farmstead, and she was as good as grown. Someone would surely take her that night. Even her father couldn't save her if one of the king's nobles wanted her, and she might even want to be part of it all.

His blood started boiling with simultaneous rage and arousal. His clothes got tight, so he had to keep changing positions. That girl was his, and no one had a right to touch her. He imagined her struggling with another man, only finally to succumb, and he didn't know what to do. Should he ask those getting ready to go to the king's farmstead if he could go along? No, they wouldn't pay any attention to him, just drive him ignominiously away.

The cool wind passed over the mounds and rustled among the darkening flower stocks from the previous summer. A mighty stone, raised by his forefathers who had lived on the island before the town had even existed, stood atop one of the smaller mounds. It must be a powerful warrior who was buried there.

Svein calmed down but couldn't stop thinking about Tora and the sacrificial feast. He wanted to be there to see what happened. He could think about Holme now without the shudder he had once felt since he had been told many times that Holme wouldn't bother anyone unless he was attacked or provoked. Svein would have a stiff neck as long as he lived, but he didn't think about that. He only wanted revenge for it when his mother poured out her bitter hatred for the thrall's family.

Many people were walking among the burial mounds today. There were sacrificial stones in several places, and their hollows would be filled before evening. The cats, dogs, and birds would have a good day.

A woman passed through the gate, and he watched her in anticipation. It was her, so he rolled behind the mound, sneaked away, and hid behind a memorial stone. From there he could spy on her without being seen.

She approached with a bowl in her hand. From the front he could see her legs but her skirt dragged in the grass behind her. Some keys and other metal objects jingled at her waist. Watching her, Svein momentarily forgot about the king's feast. Two thralls carrying iron-tipped shovels on their shoulders passed behind him. They looked surprised but didn't dare say anything since his clothes indicated that he belonged to the ruling class.

As she exchanged bowls, the woman talked to her husband as she had last autumn. She brushed the scraps and small bones onto the ground, and Svein again felt his body grow tense and hot when her skirt slid to the side and he caught a glimpse high up her thighs. He decided to rape her, just as Geire had raped the smith's wife. But there were too many people around. She might scream and cause trouble. She was, after all, a free woman and could do as she pleased.

But he noticed a little crevice between this mound and the next one. No one would see them there, and she might not scream anyway. The smith's wife hadn't. All she had done was sob.

No one was around and the woman was sitting on the grave. She thought she was alone so she didn't seem to mind that her skirt fell open and bared her legs. Maybe she liked the cool wind caressing them. The magpies fluttered about restlessly in the nearby birch trees.

Svein could no longer control himself. In a few bounds, he was on top of the woman, grabbing her shoulders, and yanking her to the ground. They tumbled over the edge of the mound and landed in the crevice below. The woman may have been too surprised to scream, or maybe she thought it was her husband. Her eyes were expressionless and she didn't resist when the rapist threw himself on top of her.

But he was too young and too stimulated. He ejaculated before he penetrated her, and after his body had spent itself, he looked up in shame. As if in a dream, he saw two figures with spades over their heads outlined against the sky. He crawled away from the woman, who reached feebly after him, got to his feet, and ran off, without looking at the thralls who had witnessed the astonishing interlude played out between the burial mounds. From the edge of the forest, Svein saw them move on and a moment later the woman climbed up on the burial mound. She picked up the bowl and looked around before returning to town. Svein was already longing for her, realizing that she hadn't defended herself. Maybe he would have stayed if he hadn't seen the thralls and their spades outlined against the sky. Given a second chance, he probably would have fared better.

Before dusk, Svein saw the boats set out for the king's farmstead, oar blades flashing in the evening sun. He had been turned down as an oarsman and was thinking intensely again about Tora and the king's farmstead. The images kept coming back and all his power had returned. He had just spilled a little of it outside a woman's womb earlier that day.

As he looked out across the still water, he got an idea. He'd go by himself. He didn't have a boat, but there were a few whose owners were far away. He could take one and row to the farmstead. If he waited a while, no one would notice him go ashore, and if it got dark while he was rowing, there'd surely be a fire at the farmstead to guide him.

For a moment he thought about telling his mother but quickly changed his mind. She would either discourage him or insist on coming along. He often tired of her affection for him—and her hatred for others. That night she could just as well sit by herself, go to the sacrificial feast at the temple in town, or be with the Christians opposite the temple, if she wanted.

Small boats were tied up in long rows on both sides of the harbor, and soon he found one he liked. It was trim and almost new. A small boat had just come in, so he waited while the oarsman secured it and disappeared into town.

He rowed past the fortress, watching the small waves splash against the rocks below it. As always, a guard was standing on the rocks, and men's happy voices sounded from inside the guard house. The warriors were obviously having a good time. There was a smouldering pile of ashes outside that would be brought to life at sunset as a signal for seafarers. Year after year, it had burned during all of the darkest nights.

The ships from town were almost out of sight now. They were propelled by many oars, and the bows foamed from the speed. They would arrive long before he did, and that was good. Once the festival had started, no one would notice a little boat, rowed by a single man. The island soon lay behind him. Two swans whizzed overhead and landed with a crashing of wings on the water farther away. Some small dark birds in their way took to flight toward the mainland.

The dark, jagged top of a spruce tree was in front of the crest of sun that would soon slip behind the forest. For a moment, Svein hesitated about what he was getting into, but he was stubborn. The girl was his; he had a right to her. He would see to it that no one else took her this wild night when men threw down the first women they could get their hands on.

He could see when the fire flared up and could hear the distant yells when he rested on the oars. He could also see the signal fire at the fortress. His mother was out looking for him right then, he thought spitefully. That would teach her that from now on he was an adult and would go wherever he chose.

A couple of boats left the fishing village on the mainland and headed for the king's farmstead. The people had to be going to the feast. He'd try to land just behind them and follow them to the farmstead. No one would notice him in the dusk.

From the thralls' table, where Holme sat, he heard the king call his name. He got up, wiped his mouth, and walked toward him. Holme had drunk a large tankard of beer with the heavily seasoned meat, and he was happy and in a good mood.

The king was a little drunk, too, and it occurred to him to show off his famous thrall to his guests. He had just told Holme's story and had slightly exaggerated his strength and courage.

Holme was met with shining eyes everywhere as he stood awaiting the king's orders. He still didn't know what was going on and couldn't understand what all these people wanted from him. He didn't see that some of the half-drunk noble women were measuring his manly power and weight, while some of the younger men burned to match themselves against him. But he was only a thrall, even if a remarkable one, and they could hardly challenge him.

Holme stood just behind the queen, and she felt permeated by a strange sensation. Ever since the king had emerged from the forest, and the gigantic thrall had had his life in his hands, she had felt in sympathy with him. But this was something else. She wanted to lean backwards and snuggle up against him, and she was completely aghast at her desire. Maybe he was a troll capable of attracting whomever he wished.

Still, she couldn't keep herself from turning halfway around to look at him. She saw the massive body, the dark face, calm eyes, and powerful jaw. Again she felt like touching him, and a red flame shot across her cheeks at a forbidden thought. It had to be the mead's fault. She would watch herself and not drink any more.

One of the younger drunken warriors asked the king if he could wrestle with Holme after they had left the table. He would show them how much of the thrall's reputation was based on his boasting and their fear. But the king refused with a laugh, saying he wanted to keep all his warriors in one piece. He'd be needing them in the spring. But the young warrior's eyes flashed with anger, and he didn't relinquish his thought.

The king gestured cordially to Holme to return to his place. Many marvelling eyes followed him from the royal table, and still more welcomed him proudly at the thralls' table. He wasn't quite sure what had happened, or what the king had wanted, and he didn't care. He sat down and started in on the meat again. A young thrall woman brought him a full tankard of beer, accompanied by a beautiful smile. Ausi and Tora gave her an angry look as they moved closer to Holme in a gesture of ownership.

Some people had appeared in the meantime and stood near the thralls' table, watching. They were from the fishing village and Svein was with them. No one paid much attention to him, since they thought he was from the farmstead. He stared intently at the table, too, and saw a black head of hair that made a lump form in his throat. But he was relieved to see that Tora was sitting with her parents. He had seen Holme coming back from the king's table, yet he hadn't shuddered as before. Instead he felt a sense of triumph in knowing that no man would dare approach Tora against her father's will.

Before long the king noticed the fishermen with their women and children, and he sent a message to Holme that they should be entertained. Holme got up and walked toward the group, and Svein couldn't help but sneak behind the others. Maybe Holme wouldn't recognize him after all, but he sat down at the far end of the table anyway, hunched over his food as he ate. This was the first time he had eaten with thralls, and his mother would have been furious if she had known. But he didn't feel out of place and even began to enjoy his little adventure. He could keep watch over the smith's daughter all night now. Her eyes and teeth glistened in the firelight, and occasionally she would lean affectionately against her father. Svein liked that somehow.

He drank his beer and got still happier. No one paid any attention to him. He marvelled for a moment at the thralls having a table so close to the king's and getting so much food and drink. Those waiting on the king's table would come back now and then to say a few words to their friends. One young thrall looked warmly at another and ran her fingers through his hair before returning to her duties. Observing that, Svein again felt an intense longing. He wasn't contemplating rape any more, now that he had seen so many warm looks exchanged between men and women at the thralls' table. Now he wanted Tora to come to him of her own free will.

He had no idea how long they had been sitting at the table, but it was completely dark outside the circle of firelight, stars occasionally twinkling through the veil of smoke. At the royal table, the men's conduct was no longer dignified—their beards had become dishevelled, their noses were glowing red, and they gesticulated freely when they spoke. The women laughed loudly and frequently and leaned affectionately now and then against whichever man was closest. The fertility god waited rigidly for what would eventually happen. The day's seed had been sown; the night's still remained to be. Beside the wooden god hung the carcass of the pig, white in the firelight. Svein remembered that at the settlement they had always eaten the sacrificial animal after the god had been smeared with blood. But the king had many animals and gave the god the whole sacrifice.

The meal was finally over. The women started cleaning up the tables, after which the men moved them to one side of the courtyard. The beer tankards and horns stayed where they were; the drinking would continue as long as anyone could lift horn or tankard.

A figure moved into the firelight carrying a large, strange instrument with many horsehair strings on it. In his right hand, the man held something resembling a saw. Svein had never seen anything like this, but he had heard about such things.

About twenty men and women split off from the group surrounding the king and walked in couples into the open yard, the women's arms glowing, supple, and white. The musician steadied the harp against the ground, sat down, and started to play. In short, sonorous notes, he played and replayed the same melody. The dancers began their deliberate movements, passing each other, weaving in and out, and occasionally exchanging partners. All the while, they kept singing the same monotonous song. Many of the observers, who had formed a circle around the dancers, also joined in the singing.

The dance had started slowly, but the tempo gradually increased. Soon it all became a single whirl of bright, laughing faces flashing in and out of view. A skirt would fly out occasionally, revealing an upper thigh, and a strange kind of tension started spreading among the observers. They had become oblivious to everything else and even the thrall guarding the dead pig was drawn to the spectacle. The dogs were there immediately, leaping at and tearing chunks out of the carcass.

Again and again, the musician played the melody, and now and then Svein caught a word from the song and this made him listen greedily. They sang about what he had seen adults doing when they were lying together, and what he wanted to try again, too. He had failed with the woman on the burial mound that day, but he could probably do better now.

Svein looked around for Tora, finally seeing her flanked by her two parents. Wouldn't she ever be alone? Maybe later, after the dancing stopped. He didn't know what was going to happen, but he felt full of excitement and anticipation. If he didn't get to her himself, he would see that no one else did—if she ever got away from her father and mother, that is. If she wanted to be taken, then he had a right to her.

He saw many of the observers pressing in close to each other and he knew they had singled one another out. The dance went on, more and more passionately. One of the women lost her skirt, or had it ripped off her, but she kept dancing, her smile flashing into view as she whirled past.

The musician finished playing on a grating, harsh, protracted note. The dancers were dripping with sweat, and the observers applauded and cheered their efforts. Svein hoped the dance was over so the rest could begin, but the audience stood still. There was evidently going to be more.

A lot of people, not leaving their places, called for more beer, and three thrall women ran back and forth with tankards. The dancers disappeared into the building, and the woman who had lost her skirt held it in her hand. The men in the audience ogled her lasciviously, but it wasn't yet time.

The king gestured and some men picked up the wooden god and carried him into the circle. He grinned toward the fire, his penis jutting diagonally into the air. The blood that had congealed on him started loosening in the heat, bubbling and hissing softly as it trickled down.

The dancers soon returned in different clothing and gathered around the god. Svein was surprised to see that the men's organs were exposed and the women's skirts, consisting of mere dangling threads or ribbons, reached only to their knees. He saw Holme and other men pulling their young daughters away from the front of the group, and he also noticed the girls only reluctantly letting themselves be led away from the spectacle.

They started dancing in couples again, the tempo building little by little. And again they started chanting. The couples hopped around the god, and after a while the men's organs were erect just like the god's. A murmur of satisfaction passed through the crowd, since everyone interpreted this as a good omen for the next crops.

Svein stood there, mesmerized by the girations of the wild dance. The men moved more and more self-consciously as the women became all the more lithe and wild. He noticed several couples break away from the circle of observers and sneak off into the night, unable to restrain themselves any longer. One of the girls pulled away by her father climbed a tree to watch, and her face grew still, a light fleck against the dark tree. Then a child came out of the king's house, its eyes agape. One of the women from the house hurried after the child, picked it up, and carried it back inside.

Holme was alone at the front of the group, and Svein knew that his wife and daughter were somewhere behind him. Although the dance had aroused him and he wanted to see it end, Svein sneaked through the crowd to get closer to the two women. He found them about where he had thought he would. Ausi was standing on tiptoe to see, but Tora stood sullenly behind her, seeming indifferent to everything. That somehow pleased Svein, and he moved closer to try to catch her eye. It was cold there because of all the people standing between him and the fire.

He caught her eye a couple of times, but she must not have recognized him. He had grown a lot since the last time they saw each other. But he was glad she didn't remember him because that might make it a little easier for him to get near her.

The dance either stopped or the dancers did something extraordinary. An impassioned murmur rippled through the circle of observers, and several men broke away with their women and disappeared into the thickets. Single men here and there grabbed women, who sometimes resisted but usually followed apathetically along. A rowdy group of young men came laughing and staggering to where Svein stood, and they grabbed Ausi, Tora, and some other women. Svein tried fiercely to defend Tora, but he was hopelessly outnumbered. He saw her fight a young warrior hard, while her mother made only the feeblest of attempts to free herself. The teeming mass of people, panting and reeking of beer, surged and pressed all around him.

Tora suddenly screamed for her father. There was silence for a moment since many had heard the scream and were waiting to see what would happen. They didn't have to wait long. Holme plowed violently through the crowd, and Svein saw him next to him for an instant. That was the first time Svein was glad for Holme's strength. Then Svein saw Holme clutch the young warrior by the neck in a grip that made the man's arms drop from the girl's chest. He was hurled to one side, landing at the feet of the others.

Tora held her father's hand, looking up at him with a smile of gratitude. At the same time, Ausi's attacker walked past with her toward the bushes. Holme grabbed his arm, and the hand holding Ausi loosened. Then he took her by the hair and dragged her roughly away with him. Everyone made room, and the thralls gathered around to defend Holme if they had to. Soon he was beyond the firelight, and the three of them disappeared toward the smithy.

Svein followed at a distance and was full of joy. His hatred for Holme was gone now, and he felt only admiration. The girl was safe and wouldn't be allowed out again that night. He wouldn't get her, but no one else would either.

Svein also realized that the smith's wife had seemed ready to follow another man into the darkness. He had seen her give up when his uncle Geire had raped her. Holme had been right in grabbing her by the hair. He saw them now silhouetted against the dark sky as they walked on the ridge of the birch tree hill. She was walking in quiet submission, but Tora was chattering the whole time, her father occasionally grumbling a terse reply.

Svein decided to stay outside the smith's house to see what happened. Maybe Tora would come out alone after her parents had fallen asleep. He could hear the songs and the men's commotion again from the farmstead, but he would rather stay where he was.

After a while, the door opened and Svein quickly hid behind the trunk of a birch tree. Holme came out alone, looked toward the farmstead a moment, and then headed for it. He passed close to where Svein was hiding, and Svein could feel his presence. He wanted to step out and say, "I've come for Tora." But he stayed still as the massive figure walked toward the farmstead.

When Holme dragged his wife home by the hair, he was annoyed by a look he had seen in her eye when the other man had pulled her away. It was a look he knew well after many years of living together. Her eyes would close half-way, and she wouldn't blink when she sensed the moment was near. If that young man had slipped away with her in another direction, she wouldn't have been able to resist him.

She was sobbing as Holme built the fire. Tora looked angrily at her and seemed to know what was going on. Her crying annoyed Holme even more. She might be crying because she had missed her chance with the other man.

The thralls had asked Holme to come back; they understood everything. And he ought to go back because they might need his help. The beer made the young warriors boisterous, and they might decide to take a thrall's woman against her and her man's will, if she had any. The king probably wouldn't permit that, but he couldn't be every place at once.

With a few parting words to mother and daughter, Holme walked toward the door. He looked back and met Ausi's eyes. They were filled to overflowing with love and submission, but he left in silence anyway. Maybe she didn't want that other man, after all, he thought, feeling that her eyes followed him through the dark birch grove. She had always been a strange woman. There probably was none better, but she couldn't be trusted at a feast of sacrifice. If someone grabbed her, she would follow mindlessly along. She just couldn't help it.

But she was still young enough to get pregnant, and he didn't want to go through that again. He could still remember a tiny, bluish-white face that had rigidified in the moonlight one frosty night.

He hadn't felt any great desire for women during the dance, but then again he had thought that Ausi would come to him after they got home and Tora had fallen asleep. But his thoughts were busy with women now. The thralls had talked about what could happen that night. One of them had once been sought out by a noble woman, who had drawn him into the brush. She hadn't been too young, yet even so, the thrall told the story frequently and with pride. He might have just made it up.

All the way there, he could hear the commotion from the king's courtyard, and it was all about the same as it had been before. There were a lot of people hopping around laughing and yelling. The thralls welcomed Holme, and a couple of the younger women couldn't conceal their happiness at his coming back alone. They were everywhere he went, and their smiles indicated they were open to anything. But he wasn't experienced with women, and he shyly pushed them aside with a grumble. One of them soon brought him a big tankard of beer and had a look of triumph on her face when he drank it in one gulp. He was trying to make himself as happy as his thrall friends.

It was the middle of the night now. A number of people had sneaked off and then returned straightening their clothes; a man or two staggered around with his genitals totally exposed, but no one seemed to mind; and a couple of men started fighting after insulting each other. They crashed noisily to the ground, and the onlookers laughed before dispersing again. The difference between lords and thralls was nearly obliterated as the night wore on and the drunkenness took over.

The king was sitting at his table again, his horn before him. Some of the court women were sitting around him, but they no longer showed him any respect. They were fondling him and laughing and pulling his beard. Each one of them was probably hoping he'd take her when the time was right. There was no sign of the queen, so she might have gone into her house.

Holme was soon feeling the effects of the beer. He was starting to fit in, responding cordially whenever someone talked to him and fondling one of the women, who pretended to stumble and fall against him. He didn't even get angry when the young warrior from before came up to him, wanting to fight. Holme merely avoided him for a while, but the warrior pursued him, challenging him derisively. Holme finally tired of that and noticed, too, that his friends were expecting him to do something. A little ways beyond the firelight, he turned and hurled the warrior on the ground, then walked immediately away. He didn't want an incident at the king's farmstead and was also afraid of really being provoked.

The dazed warrior got up after awhile and looked around, and the group of thralls who had witnessed his defeat drew back. He knew now that he never had a chance of beating the smith, since he had found himself on the ground before he knew what happened. But no freeman had been there, so he returned dejectedly to the fire. No one had to know anything about it.

An occasional scream came out of the forest, but not even Holme cared about it now. His women were safe, and the screams could be ones of lust or of distress that night. A lot of the older people started yawning and talking about going to bed. A few of them were already asleep with their heads resting on the table.

Inside the king's house, a woman thrall reported that Holme had returned alone. Several of the court women, who were sitting inside, came to life and went back to the courtyard and feast that they had just left. Again, the queen blushed quickly, and she resentfully watched them go. She had seen their eyes following the king's smith that night and didn't want any of them to have him. She sat there restlessly for a while but soon went out after them, once she had ordered her attendants to stay inside. Darkness had enveloped the high hall, the long fire having been reduced to embers. She ran into a man and a woman, who affectionately steadied herself against him. For a moment she thought he was the king but walked on, unconcerned. A number of children running around the courtyard were his by other women. But everything was supposed to happen on the bare ground that night. No one was supposed to look for a bed to sow his seed.

When dawn first appeared like a strip of light in the east, Holme was drunker than he had ever been in his life. He sensed somehow that that was his revenge on Ausi, but he also enjoyed seeing and hearing his thrall friends talking and joking merrily all around him. Everyone wanted to be his friend and came to him with admiring words about his accomplishments. They knew most about the time he had been master smith in town.

A young woman thrall sat in his lap whispering in his ear. Just as he was about to get up to go with her, he caught an angry and hurt look from a younger thrall. In the midst of his drunkenness, he still perceived that the thrall had wanted that woman himself—she just might have been his although the drink had dazed her—and Holme decided, with great effort, to leave her alone. He wasn't going to take anything from a fellow thrall. He was going to stand by them and give them something instead. After he had said a few words to the woman, she got up obediently and approached the other man while those nearby murmured their approval.

But she left a hunger behind in Holme, a hunger that many of the others had already satisfied several times. He got up and started to roam. Many eyes watched him go, but the thrall women didn't think he'd pay any attention to them, so none followed. From the king's house, a figure sneaked off to catch him behind some shrubbery. Another, seeing that, stopped short with an angry grunt.

Holme saw a female form standing before him. Her clothing glittered in the darkness, so he knew she was from the court. He tried to give her room to pass, but she stretched out her hand and stopped him.

He couldn't see her face in the darkness, but he sensed that she was young. She was breathing heavily and said nothing. A ring of keys jingled at her waist when she turned around, indicating that she must be a housewife.

Suddenly he understood the situation: she had sought him in the brush to be taken by him. Why else would she be standing there so quietly, breathing so heavily? He was seized by a fierce lust for that free and doubtlessly noble woman. He had never been attracted to anyone except Ausi, but this woman smelled very good. He could imagine how delicate and soft her hands were.

The woman hesitantly reached out to touch him. She was probably trying to encourage him, but he already knew what she wanted and was glad. He took her hand, feeling its smallness and softness, and let his own hand glide up her arm, over and behind her shoulder. Then he put the other behind her legs and lifted her up. She averted her face, but her arms encircled his neck.

He didn't want to stay there in the nearby brush like the others did. Beyond a field rose the black edge of the forest, and he walked toward it. The woman weighed little and was no hindrance. Her keys jingled softly, rhythmically. He vaguely sensed that he was taking his revenge on freemen by carrying one of their women off to the woods. He soon found a dry place, where he laid her down, her face hidden behind one arm. He noticed that she was wearing a knee-length skirt under her long dress, one like those the dancing women had worn. He reached out and moved the keys to one side so they wouldn't do her any harm.

She was much more fragile than Ausi, and that, too, heightened his passion. She groaned and panted under his immense weight, and he twice felt her body tighten, tremble, and then go limp. But he controlled himself, true to the impulse that had made him carry her across the field: he was taking revenge on and insulting the free class through her. He felt like dirtying her face and messing up her clothes and hair so she would look more like a thrall woman.

He felt his power concentrate itself as he fantasized about her delicate limbs, soft hands, and gold-embroidered clothes. He could see a piece of jewelry glimmering at her neck, glowing a soft white in the darkness, and he soon didn't need any help from his imagination, as all conscious thought vanished. The woman stiffened for the third time and stayed that way long after him.

A moment passed before he looked around. Day had broken quickly and he could see all the way to the farmstead, which was almost quiet now. Only some dogs yelping, a bird or two chirping, and occasional voices could be heard. He freed himself, got up, and pulled the clothes over the woman who was still hiding her face. Seeing now that she had to be of the highest rank, he felt an intense sense of triumph, but something else besides. A moment like that would never come again. It had been the noble woman's whim to take him, but he was a thrall again now. For a moment, he longed for the world of the freemen, to be a powerful man among such women as the one lying on the ground at his feet.

But reality quickly returned. He was a thrall and didn't want to leave thralldom by himself. He had no right to fight for freedom and power just for his own sake.

He heard the woman move and looked down. Without uncovering her face, she motioned for him to leave, motioned with a soft, white hand, a serpentine bracelet wound round her wrist. Holme left, but he followed the edge of the forest around the field rather than walking straight across it. It was so light now that someone might see him otherwise.

He felt very pleased about what had happened. No one would ever find out about it, not even Ausi. He had done what she once had, so it wasn't too easy after all to avoid such things when they seemed destined. He understood that better now.

Some beer was still on the tables and some thralls were still on their feet. A few were asleep on the ground or sat with their heads bowed on their arms. The dogs had torn down the sacrifice, snarling and fighting over it while the early morning magpies chattered in the trees. No one paid any attention. The man guarding the sacrifice had been drunk for a long time and was released from his duty.

A couple of the younger women were still awake, too, but they bore traces of what had befallen them. One of them smiled a smile at Holme that told him she both could and would pay homage to the grinning wooden god again. But Holme had no desire to. The night was over, and he was content. He was also content with how the thralls had been treated during the festivities.

A woman came sneaking out from behind the king's house. She covered her face when she saw people were still in the courtyard. But they didn't pay any attention to her—the same thing had happened only moments before. Only Holme watched her disappear through the door. He would probably see but not recognize her the next day. She could be one of the town women, the wife of one of the most distinguished merchants. Out here, only the queen could have such a large bunch of keys. He took a swallow of the stale beer and headed for home. From a distance, he could see someone by the wall, probably some drunken man trying to lure the mother or daughter out. The person didn't move, and that surprised him. Then he saw that it was a young man, dressed like a freeman, and that one of the windows had been opened.

The young man turned toward him, and there was something strange about the way he moved, something familiar that stirred up dark memories. Holme could see Tora's face in the window, and she looked neither angry nor afraid.

For a moment Holme thought about chasing the young man off, but then he remembered the errand he had just been on himself. It probably wouldn't do too much harm if Tora talked with the boy. She'd be grown soon and didn't often get to see anyone but her parents.

The young man's face was pale in the dawn, yet he walked toward Holme, seeming to prepare himself for anything. He put out his hand with a look that was both respectful and timid. Feeling a greater sense of recognition, Holme took his hand, and Tora smiled. Without a word, Holme continued to the door, which he unlocked with his fancy key.

Ausi greeted him with a mixture of anxiety and tenderness. There were still traces of tears on her cheeks: she had dreaded what Holme might do when he came home and found a young man outside and Tora at the window. Very happy now, she thought only about what might have happened earlier that night. But it was as if she was walking in a dream when she followed the other man who drew her to him.

She had recognized the young man outside but had also seen the great change in him. The hardness and malevolence in his eyes—inherited from his mother—were gone. He was shy, and he talked respectfully to both mother and daughter, even though he was a freeman. And she was not mistaken when she saw how he looked at Tora. He meant them no harm. That was the big change, and it was probably Christ, the god of peace, who had brought it about.

She whispered all this to Holme after they had gone to bed. Tora never left the window, and occasionally she would look back into the darkness with a smile. Strange things were happening, and Holme didn't know what to think. He too had felt that the young man meant them no harm when he offered him his hand. He wouldn't have chanced that if he had had evil intentions. And he wasn't drunk.

Ausi had hoped Tora would fall asleep before Holme did. It was, after all, the night of sacrifice and her body was restless. But Holme was soon sleeping heavily, and she let her thought go. She was still glad, though, that there hadn't been any violence. Holme didn't seem bothered anymore about her weakness earlier that night. But her scalp was still tender where he had grabbed her by the hair and she smiled gently at the thought of it.

Through the open window and smoke vent she could hear a bird singing before she fell asleep. As she drifted off, she heard Tora close the window and go to bed. All was well. She had been anxious about the spring festival but it was over and Holme hadn't fought with anyone. The Christian priests who had recently come to town might have had something to do with that.

Before sleep took her completely, she whispered her thanks to Christ.

S vein eyed the ships in the king's harbor with curiosity as he rowed past them. There was no movement on board and the dragon heads gaped huge and red into the dawn. He noticed some movement on the look-out rocks and shortly after could make out two figures. The watch had a woman too that night. They had something next to them, probably a beer tankard. The woman had obviously brought the guard food and drink. Svein smiled to himself—he didn't begrudge them anything. He had talked with Tora and instead of bridling she had been calm and had even smiled a couple of times. He felt a strong and pleasant certainty that she wasn't going to care about anyone else.

All his bitterness was gone, and he no longer thought of himself as the thrall family's owner. It was hopeless anyway. Holme was alive, and no one could do anything about it. Svein, still feeling Holme's handshake, knew how insignificant he was compared to that man. But he was going to be Holme's friend, no matter what his mother might say. He would rebuild the settlement and live there with Tora. And it wouldn't do his mother any good to try to stop him.

The king's fields were newly sown and gray, striped and partitioned by narrow furrows. Beyond them, there was a large burial mound. Holme's house seemed to glide to one side, and it soon disappeared from view. Tora was asleep there. Svein felt his happiness mount again and the power rush into his arms. All thoughts of raping her were gone. He didn't want the trial at the spring assembly, which his mother talked about so often. No one could possibly gain anything by rousing Holme from the peace he was living in. He might leave with his wife and daughter, never to return.

Svein promised himself they wouldn't be requesting any trial. He would get his mother to be quiet about that matter well enough. If she didn't, he'd have to go his own way and take Holme's side.

The town was asleep when he stepped ashore after tying the boat up. A faint smoke hung above the roofs of the houses, growing denser over the heathen temple. He still didn't feel like sleeping, so he walked toward town. Maybe people were still up and about.

He heard voices from the temple. The wooden gods were enveloped by smoke, and people—both men and women—were talking behind them. Their speech was slurred, probably because they were drunk. A gust of wind scattered the smoke, momentarily allowing him a clear view: women and men in various positions, half-naked. The spectacle made him stay put until the next breeze came along. He saw even more that time, then walked on, his cheeks burning.

Svein ran into an unfamiliar, thin figure near the Christian church and knew it was one of the newly arrived priests. He got a friendly look but responded to it sullenly, not liking the Christian friendliness that thrived on nothing. Why were they so friendly to people they didn't even know?

His mother was standing in the doorway, gray in the face from anxiety and lack of sleep. He got angry, his brows knitting together. Was he a little boy who needed tending? He ignored her questions and walked past her into the house. She soon stopped asking them and put some food out for him. Something about him told her that from now on, he was a man and would be in charge. She sensed it with bitterness and relief, but above all, she was curious about what he'd been up to that night. She had searched for him everywhere around town, but no one had seen him. Some aging, tipsy men and women had settled down around a fire on the beach. Though poorly dressed, they still had beer and food. Laughing and joking coarsely, they had invited her to join them when she asked if they had seen her son, but she walked on. She had been a chieftain's wife and didn't sit down with just anyone. Besides, her body felt no need at all for a man that night. All such cravings had vanished during many years of bitterness and vindictiveness.

She was surprised to be hearing Svein himself talking about rebuilding the settlement. They'd take someone from town with them, someone who knew about building, and some thralls who could carry out his orders. The timber was already there. They should start in a few days.

He said nothing when she talked about the spring assembly, but she noticed his face harden. That pleased her since she gave her own interpretation to it. He'd have his revenge on the thrall family, revenge for his stiff neck and everything else. The king himself couldn't save his smith in the assembly. She would have justice at last.

Outside, the morning sun shone on the log walls sealed with mud, on the small, mud-plastered buildings where the twigs and grass stuck through the layer of mud. The town would keep sleeping for a couple of hours, and then life would begin again. Down by the harbor, they were still working on the ship for the raid, and the weapon-smithies clanged the whole day. When spring came the hour of the call to arms followed.

Svein's mother had heard about that and was glad she didn't have a husband. Svein was still too young and was needed at home to oversee the rebuilding of the settlement besides.

That same day, she was called to the Christians' worship service, and after a moment's hesitation, she went and was baptized. It wouldn't hurt to have the town's chieftain on her side. He helped the Christians but stood against the heathens. Holme was a heathen and there would soon be the spring assembly.

A few days later, a company approached the mainland forest. With the chieftain's help, they had gathered enough thralls to help with the rebuilding and had gotten a horse to haul the lumber. The Christian priest followed them to the harbor and raised his arms above them in a benediction. Svein and the thralls glared at him, but Svein's mother knelt as she had been taught. She had given part of her remaining silver to the Christian church. She hadn't wanted to but had been assured that it would be multiplied for her many fold. That would come in handy the first few years, before the fields began yielding real harvests.

The chieftain had also promised his help at the assembly if she came to town and made her complaint. The assimbly would meet a few days later, and she talked often with Svein about the return journey. He didn't answer, but she saw his face harden every time. His hatred for the thrall family must equal hers, and that pleased her greatly.

Svein worked all day with the others but lived with his mother in the little house Stor and Tan had built in the grove. The day before the assembly, his mother had everything prepared and told him that they'd be back from town in three days and that the thralls should have such and such done by that time. As usual, Svein said nothing. He just walked outside and shut the door. But he had fashioned a piece of lumber to bar the door from the outside. He put it in place, locking his mother inside.

He thought for a moment, then walked to the laboring thralls. He wanted to tell them what was going on so no one would let her out before the assembly was over.

As the thralls listened, grins of satisfaction spread across their faces. They didn't like the woman with the hard face. Nor did they want Holme, who was the thralls' help and refuge, to be brought before the assembly for what he had done for the thralls. They didn't say much, but Svein could tell he had them on his side.

While they were still standing there, the window in the small house banged open.

"Svein!"

The thralls grinned, and Svein pretended not to hear. The screams grew more enraged, more shrill. But the only response they received was the ax blows from the construction work.

After a moment's silence, the woman started yelling again. She turned on the thralls this time, threatening them with the most terrible punishment if they had killed her son or were keeping him from answering her. She commanded them to let her out at once. Still, only the sounds of construction work replied.

It grew quiet again and the next time she yelled, it was in a pitiful voice. Svein waved a pair of thralls up to the house to see what was wrong. The young aspen trees nearby hadn't come into leaf yet, but the buds were swelling and the house would soon be hidden until the leaves fell again in the autumn.

Unobserved, Svein too went to see what was going on and saw that his mother had tried to crawl through the window and had gotten stuck. Her upper body had made it but her middle had expanded in the past few years, so she couldn't push it through or pull it out. The stool had probably toppled over as well, leaving her dangling in the air.

He saw the thralls start pushing her back through the window without saying a word. It was unpleasant to see how they stuffed her breasts over the ledge when they got jammed. It was over quickly, although she hurled insults at them the whole time. They soon returned, smiling at the others, and started working again. Everyone knew that the hard woman was finished, that the son was going to be master of the settlement, and it made them glad.

At midday, the thrall in charge of the food called, and the work stopped. The thralls walked toward where the smoke was rising, their mouths watering as the smell of smoke and grilled meat reached them. They sat on the ground with their wooden bowls and drank water from the spring, which was gurgling constantly on the slope, its water running down over the yellowish chalk deposits.

Svein gazed across the hillside recollecting his childhood, his father, the warriors, and the thralls. The rock that came hurling from the forest to make his neck rigid for all time. But his thoughts sped past Holme without rankor, stopping at Tora. The house had to be big and roomy, so she would feel at home. She was a thrall's daughter, but Holme was no normal thrall. He was somehow superior to everyone. It wasn't easy to explain.

When he looked out over the cove, he remembered his mother's plaintive cry for him as the invaders dragged her away. And then he looked toward the little house, now completely quiet. He sent a thrall with a bowl of food, a piece of bread, and a tankard of water for his mother, which had to be passed in through the window. The door had to stay shut until the assembly was over.

The new building rose like a huge barn from the slope, only its roof missing. A couple of thralls had laid the clay floor and levelled it with their wooden spades. It had dried fast, but here and there you could see pieces of straw sticking up through the cracks where it was still drying. The hearth in the middle of the hall had been lined with stones for the long fire. Holme's old smithy in the rocks was being put to use again, and a thrall who knew something about smithing was making links, hooks, and tripods for the cauldrons.

The thrall felt the bowl of food and tankard of water being taken from his hand, and then he heard the threats repeated. If they had harmed her son, they'd all die. But if he'd open the door and let her out, he'd be granted his life and a reward to boot.

Only the wind, moving through the young aspens, answered her. She thought about the spring assembly, which would meet the next day, but she wouldn't be there. Once again, Holme, his wife, and daughter would slip through her fingers.

She started thinking about Christ, whispering promises of great gifts for Him if He'd only help her escape. But as she did so, the image of the charred black god on the stone came to mind, and so she promised him a sacrifice in turn. Maybe things would have turned out differently if she had given him something to begin with. She had seen him still standing there on the stone when they had come out of the forest but thought he couldn't help her. After all, he had witnessed the settlement burn and her being captured without doing anything. But he was still there when everything else was gone nevertheless. Maybe he did have some power. He was still the household god of her husband and his father.

She didn't know that at that moment, Svein was placing meat and bread before the god as the thralls mumbled their approval. The work had gone well, they felt happy, and it must be because of the god. He had survived a great deal but had stayed at the settlement, and that awakened their respect and reverence.

She had put the food on the floor, with no intention of eating it. But the fragrance of cooked meat and roots filled the air, and she hadn't eaten since the night before. If the thralls had killed Svein, they surely would have killed her at the same time. That would have been the easiest thing to do. But here they were giving her food, obviously wanting her to live. That had to mean that Svein was alive, too. Then what was going on? She put the thought aside for a while as she started eating. There was still a battle to be fought. She wanted to fight it, and so she had to eat the thralls' food to have the strength. Besides, she felt in her heart that Svein was still alive, perhaps just taken prisoner so the thralls could live at the settlement by themselves.

All the while, the first free thrall who had fought by Holme's side lived at the other farmstead. He had labored both day and night and had managed with the help of an old man to keep up both house and field. No one had objected, so he started thinking of the farmstead as his own. The old man had shown up begging and had been allowed to stay. He was good at mending nets and hunting up food.

One day while he was still holding his mother prisoner, Svein felt like taking a walk to the other farmstead. There probably wasn't much left of it, but he wanted to walk where he had walked as a child and see where his forefathers had settled. He remembered the day the pirates from the east burned both farmsteads and took his mother captive. Only his uncle Geire and he were alive then to seek revenge, and now Geire lay in one of the town's countless burial mounds. Holme had killed the powerful warrior with his bare hands. But Svein, of his own accord, had recently offered his hand to the killer, the man he had once hated, and he had felt death in Holme's grip. He felt neither hate nor terror any longer—he knew somehow that there was a way to be friends with the fearful man. You could walk right up to him without danger if you had good intentions in your heart.

Svein noticed how much the forest had grown during the past few years. The path vanished for long stretches, probably because the cattle weren't walking in the forest any more. But their mooing would soon be heard again in the area, and they would come down to the settlement for milking just like they did during his father's day. Men and women thralls would be there. And—this last thought stuck in his chest—Tora would come as the mistress of the house. He would convince her parents how good it would be for her. His mother's hatred for the smith's family also came to mind, but naturally, he'd keep a tight rein on her. She wasn't going to decide anything.

Svein's head swarmed with plans for the future, so his walk passed quickly. He was soon at the edge of the forest looking toward the farmstead. There was only one little building left, the one the fire had spared, but it didn't look as dilapidated as he had expected. No one was in sight, but he had the feeling that someone was nearby. A little boat lay at the shore, and the jetty bore traces of having been recently repaired. Maybe some distant relative had come and taken over the farmstead. Or maybe some outlaw had dared stay there for a while.

No matter what, though, the farmstead belonged to him and his mother. No one had a right to settle down there without permission. Then, he saw various farming implements, too—spades and plows. And the field had been sown, the new green crop carpeting the ground.

But where were the people? He'd find them and tell them who owned the farmstead. But before he had time to take a step, a muffled, twanging sound came from some bushes in front of the little building. He felt a cold puff of wind on his cheek, and when he looked around, saw an arrow quivering in a tree trunk a few feet away. It had been meant for him. He started running back on the path, not knowing how many or how dangerous his enemies might be.

After he had disappeared, the free thrall got up and looked in the direction he had gone. He didn't know who the visitor was, but he had a feeling he was an unwelcome guest. It was just as well to greet him in a way he couldn't misunderstand. He had worked day and night and was determined to defend what he had accomplished.

His woman came out and put their baby down on the ground. The child crawled to his father and reached for the bow, and then the thrall hurried them back into the building. He suspected that the young man at the edge of the forest was a spy and that at any moment, he'd have to contend with other foes, more of them and more dangerous. After a while, he walked to the edge of the forest and pulled the arrow out of the tree. It had a good point and he could use it.

He was uneasy all day long, walking around, listening and watching, too worried to work. The old man was fishing outside the belt of reeds and would glance at him occasionally with a look of surprise on his face.

For the first time the free thrall was thinking about how secure he'd feel if Holme were around. Together, it was easy to fight and defend themselves, but, alone, it was hard to know what to do. And they had vowed to help each other. But Holme lived at the king's farmstead and couldn't know if any enemies came out of the forest and killed the thrall and his family.

The thrall whittled shafts for all of his arrow heads, and he gathered a pile of stones as big as his fist to throw. He sharpened his axes with a whetstone. All the while, he knew he could expect no mercy if it was free men who were out after him. But whether Holme was alive or dead, the thrall was honor-bound to fight and kill as many free men as possible before it was his turn to fall.

The day passed without event. It might have been a forest troll that had taken a young man's form at the edge of the forest. He had seen and heard strange things before. Maybe he would have another year of peace to enjoy the farmstead as his own.

He was awake until midnight, and his last thought was to find Holme to get his advice. He was the one free thrall, and Holme was his friend. He would advise him and help him as he had done before.

He woke a few hours later, glad to see that nothing had changed. Beside him lay his wife and child, and the old man slept in the corner, his toothless mouth gaping in his beard. The singing of birds and an occasional seagull's cry from the cove floated through the smoke vent. When he cautiously peered out the door, he saw the lake glittering in the morning sunlight. Maybe the young man from the day before had been alone and had happened by accidentally.

But his old calm wouldn't return, and he decided that in the afternoon he would go to the old deserted settlement where Holme had once been a smith. If everything was as it ought to be there, he could relax. Only from there could danger threaten. The old chieftain's repulsive witch of a wife and her son were the only ones who had a right to either farmstead.

Even at a distance, he could hear the blows of hammers and axes. Like Holme many times before, he sneaked toward the edge of the forest and peered out. He saw an unfinished, rather large, new building, and several men working on it. He also saw the young man he had shot an arrow at the day before. And he understood immediately who he was and what was going on right in front of his eyes. The mother and son were rebuilding the old settlement.

Tears of sorrow and rage ran down the thrall's cheeks. His freedom would soon end, and he would get nothing for all the work he had done. All he could expect was to be run down and killed. There would surely be no mercy shown for some thrall who had dared live as a free man on his own farmstead.

He stood there watching the work for a long time. The new building wasn't where the old one had been but a little farther away instead. The old place was probably full of bad luck. He wished again that Holme was with him. Together they could attack and drive off or kill the trespassers. But alone he was powerless to stop the workers, who had axes and other weapons within reach.

As he walked back, he knew there was only one thing for him to do: he had to hide his family and go to Holme at the king's farmstead. But he might be able to take his family with him. Holme had done that more than once when he was being hunted by the free men.

On the afternoon of the last day of the assembly, Svein's mother heard the bar being drawn from the door. She waited a while, but it didn't open. She was furious but afraid at the same time of what she would see outside. She had heard the work going on the whole time and had gotten a bowl of food regularly. Why were they keeping her alive if they had killed Svein?

Finally, she pushed the door open and peered out. No one was outside threatening her. The leaves had grown bigger while she had been locked up and were obscuring the surroundings.

She sneaked anxiously through the bushes and saw the new building. The work was going on as usual, and the lumber worker was giving his instructions. The roofing had begun, and the building would be finished in a few days. But would she be allowed to live there? And where was Svein?

After a while she heard wheels squeaking, and she soon caught a glimpse of the horse's back at the edge of the forest. A thrall was driving a large load for the roof, Svein walking beside him with a spade. He looked all right, and she was deliriously happy that he was still alive. Why had he let them shut her up during those crucial days? She had yelled repeatedly through the window that she had to be at the assembly.

Svein saw her come fluttering out of the foliage and rushing toward him, and he exchanged a knowing look with the thralls. He had asked them to let her out while he was in the woods.

No one responded to her as she raged, questioned, and threatened. In the end, she sank exhausted onto a log, and then Svein spoke. He said that it had all been for the best. Everyone who had fought against or pursued Holme had lost in one way or another while he always helped his friends. From now on, Svein wanted to be friends with Holme. He was a thrall, but an extraordinary one. The king treated him better than he did his warriors.

The men around him listened while they worked more quietly, and the lumber worker nodded, as if to his stick, as he was measuring. Svein's mother berated her son, calling him a thrall and a coward, but he didn't respond, and she felt that nothing would give her words any power. They worked on, talking among themselves, not paying any more attention to her than if she had been a crow cawing or a pig grunting. But she wasn't finished yet. She would go to town and complain to the Christian chieftain. To add to his other crimes, Holme had corrupted Svein with his witchcraft. Something must have happened at the spring festival when she was looking for him all night.

She would rest a few days before going to town. Maybe the witchcraft would wear off by then, and Svein would be himself again. Just a few days ago, she had seen his face harden with loathing when she described what she would do to Holme's wife and daughter, once she got hold of them. But Holme was still alive, and not even the chieftain seemed able to cope with him.

She'd still complain to him one more time, though. Svein was walking around like a thrall among thralls and that couldn't be allowed for long. That he seemed happy doing so just showed how powerful the witchcraft was. Maybe

Christ could set him free. She had heard He could do such things better than any god before Him.

When she walked past the charred wooden god on the stone, she noticed that some meat had been placed before him. Svein or the thralls had put it there, and the god had also shown that he was on their side. But he could have helped her instead; she'd offered him sacrifices ever since she was a child. Furious, she picked up the piece of meat and hurled it down the hillside, the flies buzzing around her hands.

All day long, she kept a sulky distance from the men and didn't respond when Svein yelled for her to fix some food. They could fix their own food while they held her prisoner, so they could now too. She saw one of the older men set his ax aside and walk to the hearth, still smoking with hot ashes. She went to bed hungry, but after everyone was asleep, she got up and scavenged around in the twilight of the spring night until she found something to eat.

Because she kept away from the building again the next day, she couldn't hear what a rider from the forest had to say. He was very excited, and all of them crowded around him. Svein turned red in the face and looked around in perplexity, and his mother felt at once uneasy and curious. The man soon rode on though, and the work gradually started up again. But Svein often rested on his tool, looking either toward where the man had disappeared or out over the cove.

That evening, she managed to learn that the stranger carried the call to arms. For a moment, she worried that Svein might have to represent the farmstead in battle. But he was too young, and there was no master here. He had to stay home this time.

Svein was uneasy the whole day, not knowing what he wanted to do. He imagined the big fleet with its beautiful sails furled and the golden-red maws of its dragon heads pointing toward foreign lands, where there would be gold and silver to plunder. But he could see Tora, too, and the building; if he left, it would have to take care of itself. The settlement should be put in order first, with Tora as mistress; then would be the time for him to go raiding.

His mother grew uneasy, too, when she heard that the call had gone out. The king and the chieftain would soon set sail, and then who would insure her justice? She would have to leave the next morning before Svein and the thralls woke up. She told herself with disgust that since Svein had become friends with the thralls, she didn't have to worry about leaving him alone with them.

The free thrall didn't dare go to the ferry station, so he walked instead to where they had landed after escaping from the fortress. Several small boats were always there, and in the forest above lived their owners in little mud huts. He got there with the first light of day, and no one was awake. He was going to borrow one of the boats for the day. He ought to be back before nightfall, and the owner could have his boat back again.

He knew that old people were living there, and so he wasn't afraid. When it became completely quiet for a moment, he went down and untied the best boat. But he heard scurrying steps and some panting on the path he'd just left. He quickly untied the knotted rope in an effort to row out and away, but couldn't finish before a woman came down the path. She couldn't know that the boat didn't belong to him, so he calmed down again.

It was a middle-aged woman, and he could tell from her voice when she asked for a ride that she belonged to the free class. He wanted to chase her off, but if she raised a fuss, the boat's owner might wake up. He signalled for her to step into the boat and then shoved off.

For a moment, he heard a peculiar buzzing sound from town and couldn't figure out what it was. He had taken the boat into a cove and so had to row a good while before the town came into view. The buzzing intensified and the woman stared toward the town with uneasiness and rage. It might have been foolish to have taken her along; it would have been better had he rowed along the skirt of reeds alone until he was farther away.

The woman ordered him to row faster and he obeyed. He could tell she was used to giving orders, and he forgot for a moment that he was free. He would put her ashore a ways from town and then move on.

When they got outside the point hiding the town from view, he heard the woman cry out in dismay and turned around. He rested in total astonishment on his oars, staring at the overwhelming sight. Sail upon sail obscured the entire island, and the dragons glistened powerfully in the rising sun. A fresh morning wind had just come up and was met with great jubilation from the ships. It was a good sign. Smoke rose from countless sacrifices in the town, and a burnt smell filled the air.

He coasted on his oars, looking with constant pleasure at the long row of ships. Meanwhile, he gave half an ear to an angry stream of words from the woman in the stern. She was always late, people treated her poorly. Then he heard her let go scornful, hard words about someone, a black-haired thrall smith, a man who should have been killed a long time ago. He had done her more harm than anyone else.

The free thrall listened intently now, scrutinizing her closely. She kept telling her woeful story without even glancing at him. As she watched the ships, she said she should have come the day before. Another summer would pass by now without her getting her due.

The thrall rowed on, but with a new expression in his eyes, a watchful, sly expression. He had begun putting things together. The woman had come from the direction of the settlement, hated Holme, and talked about a son. She said she might as well go back since the king and the chieftain were both gone. But she decided to go to town and see to her house.

The woman watched the fleet of Viking ships so intently that she didn't notice the thrall changing course when he started rowing again. He headed for the woods northwest of the fortress, his thoughts racing. What would be the best thing to do? The best thing would be if the farmstead's owner were dead. That would leave only the son, and there would always be some way out with him.

His face had taken on a hard and crafty expression, but he looked down when the woman turned to castigate him for not heading toward town and answered sullenly that he wouldn't go there. She was free to go wherever she wanted on foot.

Before the free thrall knew what to do, the boat neared the shore where the rocks jutting out below the fortress blocked the town from view. The woman was still intently watching the ships when he stopped rowing, pointed an oar at her chest, and gave a sharp shove. She tumbled into the water with a scream, and he rowed quickly away. Into the belt of reeds, so no one would see the boat. He heard screams and splashing for a moment, and then excited voices on the shore by the fortress. He rowed with powerful strokes and soon had the whistling reeds enveloping him. The woman's birch-bark basket was still in the boat and he regarded it hopefully. He'd risk stopping after a while to look inside. His food was gone, and he hoped there was some there.

After following the belt of reeds for a while, he chanced rowing into the open water. He would put ashore a long way from the king's farmstead and approach through the woods. The forest afforded him safety, but out on the lake he was visible and exposed. But the king was away now with most of his men so it was less dangerous than usual.

A thought made his face darken, and he rested on his oars. The king might have taken Holme on the raid, one man who was worth several when it came to fighting or working. That depressed him, but he kept going anyway. If Holme hadn't wanted to follow along, no one could have forced him.

It was quiet after the ships had disappeared. He didn't hear a sound from the shore or from the king's farmstead. There wasn't a boat in sight, large or small. He grabbed the woman's basket, opened it, and ate the meat and bread as the boat drifted slowly with the waves. He looked around as he chewed, and when he had finished eating, he drank some lake water with the little wooden ladle that was tied to the basket with a thong.

While eating the woman's food, the free thrall felt glad about what had just happened. Even if Holme had gone with the king, he still might be able to get by and guard his farmstead. Thralls were rebuilding the other one; they would surely have no objection if their new master disappeared. An arrow could reach him from the edge of the woods or a spear come flying if he happened onto the forest path alone again. And while the warriors were away, there could be no retribution against the thralls.

Revivified, he began rowing again and soon approached the woods where he would land. He saw the fishing village across from the king's farmstead in the distance, but he saw no movement there. Some of its strongest men were probably with the king. On such a raid, they needed men who knew something about everything: smiths and other craftsmen, fishermen and hunters who could find food for the troop.

He was soon stepping ashore near where Holme had once stepped. He hid the boat and started walking toward the king's farmstead, not even bothering to move stealthily or be on guard. It was so quiet and peaceful here. No enemies, nothing to fear. And he'd soon find out whether or not Holme was at home.

At the spring assembly, the chieftain looked around in vain for Svein and his mother and was relieved at their absence. The day the king had designated for the raid was approaching, and a lot remained to be done. That stubborn woman would only have caused him trouble.

Since the new priests had arrived, the number of Christians had increased and kept growing every day. The church still stood on the piece of land he had donated, and the rich woman's gifts of silver and gold glistened on the altar. The king would issue a strict order that the Christians had the right to spread the Word freely and peacefully while the Vikings were away. And without a leader, the heathens wouldn't dare disturb or injure them. The thrall smith was in the king's service and wouldn't again begin his foolish struggle to turn the thralls into free men.

The chieftain looked with disgust at the sacrificial smoke rising for the journey and heard the heathen priests invoking their gods. The Christians stood in a silent group, doubtlessly hoping in their hearts that the enterprise would fail and the heathens would be cut down by enemies in the foreign land. As for himself, the chieftain was sure he'd return safely. The Christian priest had assured him of that and the casting of lots had indicated it, too.

When the ships were rowed up toward the wind, the heathen priests' shouts swelled into wild screams. The women waved, some of them weeping as they stretched their arms out to their husbands on the ships. Those standing closest to the king's ship heard him promise the battle god great sacrifices if he would grant their mission success. Then the king looked around at the mainland and the islands and promised sacrifices to the fertility god if he saw to it that the year's harvest was good and plentiful.

Once the fleet was out of sight, the people left behind returned to their dwellings. Many women were still crying, and the town was oppressively quiet and empty. The watch stood on the rocks as usual, and outside the fortress lived those warriors who had stayed home to defend the town. The slope was fortified with rocks and ramparts in several places.

The watch and the warriors hadn't noticed the thrall and the woman in the small boat that could be seen momentarily beyond the rocks. But they heard screams and splashing, and a couple of them ran down to the shore on the other side of the rocks. The reeds were dense from the shore outwards a couple of boat lengths, but there was a path cut through the reeds and a little boat nearby. The men rowed it out quickly and saw something sputter, gurgle, and sink. Just below the surface of the water, they could see a woman's clothes, so they grabbed hold, pulled the woman's head above the water, and towed her to shore behind the boat.

She lay for a moment snorting and hiccupping, the water streaming off her, and she looked wild and terrible with her dripping wet hair hanging over her hard face. The men were seized by fear. Where had she come from? There wasn't a boat in sight, and no one could have gotten into the water from land. They looked at each other and read each other's minds. It had to be a lake troll they had dragged up. They beat a hasty retreat, clambering hand and foot up the slope. From the top, they looked back, panting. The troll was sitting upright now, trying to get the hair out of its face. It was mumbling and hissing. The men realized they should have thrown it back into the lake, but they didn't dare get close a second time.

A little while later, all the men were standing on the hilltop, weapons in hand, looking silently at the creature on the shore. She was still fussing with her hair but had hung her garment on a bush to dry. She looked more like a normal woman now in her short jacket and bare legs. But where had she come from? The two who had dragged her up assured the others in a whisper that she had popped straight up out of the water. Maybe she'd go back where she came from soon.

The men stood there for a long time, and more and more joined them. Finally they saw the creature take its garment from the bush and feel it. It wasn't dripping any more, and she had tied her hair in a knot. After a while, she glanced up at the group of men, then began climbing toward them. They looked at each other and began pushing each other back to the fortress. The creature walked right through it and out the gate that connected to the town, the gate through which people fled into the fortress when danger threatened. The men breathed a sigh of relief and gradually returned to what they had been doing. They didn't talk about what had happened until just before nightfall.

Despite their austere silence, the Christian priests watched with inner jubilation as the sails of the heathen fleet retreated and disappeared behind the islands and islets. Their work would be easier now that the number of heathens wasn't so many times as great as their own. The most powerful and most dangerous were gone. It was probably God's will that these stubborn people of the north should finally be baptized.

The Christian chieftain was gone, too, but they had come to an agreement with him about how things should go. The rich woman gave them all the coins and silver they needed. She felt sick and asked them to pray for her soul day and night. And she paid with the silver her husband had pirated on the high seas and in distant lands. The Christian priests were constantly in attendance upon her, and their God, who didn't accept sacrifices, never seemed to get enough gifts.

In their homeland, the priests had heard a lot about the Swedes who didn't want to emerge from their heathen darkness and worship Christ. They clung tenaciously and austerely to the gods of their fathers, and hell didn't terrify them. Only great need and their own gods' disfavor could make them, for a short time, turn to Christ and pray for His help. But when the danger was past, sacrificial fires were soon burning again in the heathen temples and shrines. There must be a reason for all this. It wasn't the king, who had kindly given them permission to preach freely. But the king didn't have a great deal of power in this curious land where even the thralls were defiant enough to pitch themselves against their earthly masters.

The town was empty and quiet now. God's word should be victorious this summer. When the warriors returned, if God let them, their wives and daughters would be baptized members of the Christian congregation. Many of the men should then follow suit and the victory would be won.

The two priests talked with the rich woman about that. They also learned the story about the thrall smith, the Christians' deadliest enemy. They heard about the uprising he had led against their predecessors and about his distributing their grain among the starving thralls. The woman thought the smith was the greatest obstacle in Christ's path. If it wasn't for him, the thralls would come to Christ in droves.

The priests listened and then told about an adversary of Christ's, named Saul, who had once turned into a great man of God. That could even happen with the smith. But the woman shook her head and said that they didn't know him. And they ought to keep their distance. The priests answered as their predecessors had always done, however, that their lives lay in God's hand. Then they walked out of the rich woman's house with dignity, carrying new gifts to their church.

They saw a strange creature coming along the fortified road leading to the fortress—woman with wet hair wrapped on top of her head and dressed in wet, wrinkled clothes. She had an angry, threatening expression on her face. Since the priests considered it their duty to alleviate all that was painful and hard, they stopped the woman and gently inquired, in their broken Scandinavian, what was troubling her. They knew someone who could help in all times of need and for nothing. And they gazed kindly at her, their gifts in their hands.

Svein's mother stared back at them, her hard eyes flashing as the old thoughts returned. Everyone had deceived her; no one had helped her get revenge and justice. Maybe the Christians would.

So she followed the new priests toward the church while she repeated the story of Holme once more. As the rich woman had done, this strange creature insisted that as long as the smith was alive, the Christians would be talking in vain about their God. Holme was a great sorcerer, and the king protected him in spite of all his crimes. Therefore, he should be done away with while the king was away, and his family should be returned to her, their rightful owner.

The priests heard the woman out, then walked pensively into the church after inviting her to the evening's worship service. In a short space of time now, two women had pointed out what prevented the kingdom of Christ from expanding in this part of Scandinavia. It might be their duty to strike that barrier down. Everything seemed to say so. The king and his warriors had sailed off to the east; the smith had many enemies. The time was surely at hand to dispose of him. This black-haired man of violence was clearly no new Saul whom Christ would strike with blindness to make a Paul of him.

As their predecessors in town had often done, the priests prayed for some sign and guidance from Christ. And they soon felt the answer in their hearts. It was they who should dispose of God's enemy. How they did it didn't matter.

Fortified by the Spirit, they counted yet again the gifts of gold, coins, and silver rods the rich woman had given them in exchange for their praying for her. She was sick now and anxious despite everything that the devil would take up the struggle for her soul. She still had bountiful wealth. Her daughter, having been baptized too, humbly submitted when the priests told her how impossible it was for a rich person to enter into heaven. She hadn't laid claim to her earthly inheritance once she had understood that what those gentle-eyed men were taking from her was only a hindrance to a blessed life.

And they soon got corroboration that they were on the right track. The rich woman took a turn for the worse and became yet more anxious about her soul. She still had considerable wealth. To be assured of happiness, she wanted to do even more. She had heard that you should also give to the poor, but there weren't many poor people in town. Most people were well off and owned many thralls. She didn't think about the many homeless, oppressed people who lived off the land with no roof over their heads. They were mere thralls, and their poverty was God's just punishment. Neither did she think about setting her own or anyone else's thralls free or about giving them any other aid.[9]

When the priests thought they couldn't accept more from the woman, they advised her to send gifts to a town in the south where a number of poor Christians lived.[10] The priests there would accept the gifts and divide them among the most needy. The woman perceived immediately that Christ was speaking through them, so she called her daughter and ordered her to go to the Christian town with the gifts. A few days later, the starving, homeless thralls from the town and its environs saw the daughter with an attendant, carrying a heavy sack of silver coins, step aboard a ship that would sail to the town where poor Christians lived. Two gray-clad figures, a short one and a tall one, raised their hands over her in a blessing. The thralls stared at the departing ship, still not comprehending what was going on and unaware that they lived in a town without poverty.

---

[9] Rimbert essentially tells the same story of the wealthy woman, Frideburg, and her daughter in chapter 20 of the *Vita Anskarii* (*Anskar*, pp. 70–73). The hermit Ardgar was in charge of the mission in Birka at this time. See note 6, p. 278.

[10] The town is Dorstadt (*Anskar*, p. 72).

After the priests had seen the ship disappear, followed by their blessings, they returned to the church, their minds on their other God-ordained duty: to dispose of the man who, above all others, blocked their path. They had to proceed judiciously; there were still masses of heathens whom it wasn't wise to provoke. They could still marshal a force and run their wooden gods' bloody errands. Somewhere among the thousands of burial mounds lay one of their predecessors, a Christian priest the heathens had killed. He was awaiting redress now on the great Day of Judgment when, in pious jubilation, he would get to see the heathens burning in hell.

From the altar in the dark recess at the front of the church glittered some of the rich woman's gifts; others lay in an iron-bound box. A Christian thrall stood watch day and night. He received no earthly compensation for his faithfulness, stupidly waiting instead for what the priests had promised him beyond the portion of ground that would one day be his. But whenever he passed the heathen temple, he scurried by without responding to the abusive words the temple attendants hurled after him. He wasn't so sure yet that the wooden gods were as harmless as the Christian priests made them out to be.

After the rich woman had given away all the treasures her husband had stolen, she died with her eyes anxiously fixed on the silver cross in the priest's hands. There was only a rumor of her generosity that passed among the starving and homeless in the town and surrounding area. The heathen priests didn't get so much as a goat to sacrifice to their gods. Their eyes shot daggers at the Christian priests who passed with dignity, and they frequently asked their gods to destroy them to show everyone their power. They also took council with the merchants, who were still faithful servants of the gods, over the best way to hurt the Christians while the king and his army were away.

A dark figure occasionally passed through their minds, and they wished he were still in town. The Christians' old enemy, who had destroyed their temple and stolen their grain during the famine—he was the one who knew best how to handle them. The Christians were under the king's protection, but if the heathens could provoke his smith against them, nothing could dissuade Holme.

For now, though, the Christian priests had the upper hand. They walked around among the lonely women, who lived in constant fear for their husbands, telling them that Christ alone could bring their husbands back to them alive. And even if the men fell in foreign lands, the couples could still be reunited after death. Many pining women couldn't resist that thought, and the Christian church was soon filled for every worship service. The gifts streamed in, and coffers filled with silver and gold were sent by ship to the mother church in the priests' home parish.

The wooden gods glared threateningly out over their shrinking throngs of worshippers and diminishing sacrifices. Their priests prophesied destruction of a land and people who fell away from the gods that had granted them and their fathers good fortune and success, hoping in their hearts for misfortunes that could be blamed on Christ and his priests. Then the showdown wouldn't be far away. There might be as many Christians as heathens in town, but they were mainly women, unable to fight. They'd undoubtedly return to the wooden gods anyway if something happened to their husbands.

And so the hostility grew quietly during the warm, clear days of early summer. The Christians grew more confident, and one day, both priests walked through town carrying some object in front of them. Behind them walked a group of women and a couple of older men, two by two. They sang protractedly, staring solemnly ahead. The heathen priests stood in the hall of their temple, laughing loudly and scornfully as the crowd passed by. The rich woman's daughter had returned, and it was rumored among the Christians that Christ had sent back the silver she had given out for His sake. She was much esteemed for that and followed right behind the priests.

Svein's mother was with the women. The priests had promised her that within a short time, Christ would destroy her black-haired enemy and return his wife and daughter to her. She didn't want to return to the farmstead before she had seen a little of that, but she waited impatiently. Her old dream took on new life. Her son and everyone else would see her come back with Ausi and Tora once Holme had been killed. It had to be that way in the end. Never before had a thrall family been allowed to live after defying so many and committing so many crimes.

With that hope in her heart, she promised gifts to Christ, adding threateningly that it all had to happen quickly. She'd waited long enough. And no one knew when the king would return with the army. A message had come from the East, so everyone on the island knew that the voyage had gone well thus far. And so there were worship services in both temples again. There was mournful singing in one, loud laughter and drunken gaiety in the other. One glittered with gold and silver; the other witnessed animal carcasses roasting, blood running down the statues of the gods. Both took credit for the safe arrival of the Viking fleet at its destination.

The king stood in the smithy thinking for a long time. It might be a good idea to take the powerful smith along on the raid; he was experienced and could give sound advice. But the warriors would get upset and derisive if he took advice from a thrall in such important matters. And Holme was too good to take along only as a smith. His rightful place was at the head of the warriors, but that could never be.

They'd also need a man at home who could take responsibility for everything on the farmstead. Hostile ships could show up while they were away, and someone had to be there who could decide whether to fight or run. The queen and her companions had to be protected, and no one could do that better than Holme. He could help the foreman with the work in the fields and meadows. The thralls looked up to him and would do what he asked without complaint.

Men were working eagerly on the king's ship in the harbor, and by the distant town on the island, you could see a row of colors. It was the sails of the dragon ships that had arrived and were now waiting for the departure. They would sail early the next morning if there was a good wind. The king had directed that sacrifices be made both at the farmstead and in town to the weather spirits.

From the smithy the king could see parts of his fields, where the sprouts rose level and green. The foreman was a skillful farmer, but he knew nothing about fighting and defending himself. It was probably best to leave the smith behind. He along with the other men left at home would form the queen's guard.

Holme looked at him in silence, but a glimmer of satisfaction came into his eyes. He had wondered what would happen and felt no desire to travel to a distant land. He had never enjoyed fighting, although he had often been forced into it by his enemies. He tried to imagine what it would be like to fight people in the other town, but only felt uneasy. They had never seen him before and couldn't have done him any harm, so why should he fight and maybe kill many of them?

But now the king was telling Holme that he would stay behind to protect those still at the farmstead. The thralls could help him; they were strong men and did what he told them. And he knew what to do if the farmstead were attacked. But it was better to flee if the odds were against him. The king also said that he felt more confident putting the queen under Holme's protection than he would under anyone else's in the kingdom.

Holme said little in response, but the king knew him well. He had tested Holme many times and was no friend of words himself. A man was someone who acted instead of talked. The king said something more about what weapons should be forged while he was away. Many men would undoubtedly lose theirs in battle.

Early the next morning, all the people of the farmstead had gathered at the harbor, from the king's closest followers to the thralls who hadn't yet begun work. They formed a separate group a little ways away. The sacrificial smoke was still rising from the temples and was blown toward the harbor, which everyone interpreted as a good omen. The night had been calm, but a breeze started across the lake with the rising sun, making dark ripples on the water. It moved across the land and passed on over the swaying tree tops. The queen and some of the warriors' wives boarded the ship to accompany their husbands to town.

Holme hadn't gone with Ausi and Tora to the harbor but watched the departure from the smithy instead. A vague longing gripped him as he watched the sails and the water. But he hadn't been there for long, and a thrall should stay home to work when free men ventured out in the world. He probably still could have gone with them, but he didn't want to abandon Ausi and Tora. There was also a voice within him, one he didn't quite understand, that said he'd be needed at home. He had heard it before and knew it always had some meaning. Free men had the spirits of relatives, who showed themselves or whispered advice into their ears when danger was near. It was possible that he too had such a spirit, even though he was a mere thrall.

In any case, he should do what the king requested of him. The king was the best master in the land, but no one followed his example; they just kept on whipping their thralls, killing them, and abandoning their babies in the woods. The king was powerless to stop that, even if he tried. He was the supreme commander in battle, and the one who ruled over the kingdom's great festival of sacrifice, but otherwise his power was no greater than the leading chieftain's.

Holme felt the old sting in his chest when he thought about the thralls' misery. Here, where they were treated almost like free men, it would be so easy to forget about what was happening on other farmsteads and in town. But he couldn't do that. At the moment, it felt as if something was going to happen while the king and warriors were away. He had looked forward to a peaceful summer with his friends. The foreman wouldn't dare drive them hard, even if he wanted to.

He had to be ready day and night for what might come. He didn't know where it would come from; it might be directed at the farmstead, but it would most probably be levelled at him.

Long rows of oar blades flashed in time with a rhythmic shout, and the ships glided past the pilings, followed by the waving and shouting of the people on shore. A little ways out, the sails filled and the oars were pulled in. The dragon heads gaped toward the town, and in the stern of each ship stood a steersman. White water soon foamed at the bows; the ships would be in town in no time.

Holme's wife and daughter approached him on the narrow path along the ditch. He saw them clearly as if for the first time and consciously rejoiced in their existence. But he had a sense of foreboding at the same time. He wouldn't be able to live in peace with them much longer. In the calm, which spread across town and land after the fleet's departure, lurked an unknown danger.

It was too early to begin the day's work so they rested a while longer. The farmstead seemed deserted. Tora walked to the door several times to see how far the ships had gone. Holme noticed how much she had filled out in a very short time. Since the festival of sacrifice, she had also been more restless and uneasy than before. He knew, of course, what that meant; he had seen many people grow up and mature. But she was going to decide for herself—no one was going to rape her, as he once had her mother. He smiled at the memory and looked at her supple arm resting close to him. Rape, though, it could hardly have been called that time. He remembered well enough that arm encircling his neck once she gave up resisting.

Tora finally lay down on her bed, and soon all three of them were sleeping as the sound of the whistling birch trees made its way through the smoke vent.

When the sun reached its zenith, Holme headed home from the smithy to eat. Ausi had just called out that dinner was ready. He looked away toward town across the lake, but there was nothing to see. The queen and her companions still hadn't returned. She might stay in town until the next day.

As he walked in through the low door, he noticed something move at the edge of the forest. He stopped and could soon make out a figure sticking up out of the thicket. It motioned to him. After a moment's reflection, he picked up his ax and walked over. Mother and daughter came out and watched him in surprise. The figure disappeared as Holme started moving toward it.

The free thrall was joyfully waiting for him behind the thicket. Holme was happy too and surprised to see him. The thrall told eagerly what had happened and was happening at the old settlement, and Holme soon breathed more easily. He had expected the worst when he first saw his old battle companion.

He took his friend to his house, where both Ausi and Tora were happy to receive a visitor. At the table, he continued his story and Ausi smiled warmly and broadly at his drowning Svein's mother, her old nemesis, like a rat that morning. He suggested they should kill the stiff-necked son too; then they would be rid of anyone who could lay claim to the farmsteads. He didn't notice Ausi's reluctance, or Holme shaking his head, or Tora's eyes flashing angrily at the suggestion.

Holme felt happy again at the thought that there was a thrall who had become free and independent. He had shown himself worthy of freedom; he had worked hard and was prepared to fight for what he had gained. Maybe no one had to fight this time; maybe the matter could be settled peacably. Holme thought of the boy who was the sole owner of the farmstead and who had offered him his hand at the spring sacrifice. They would go and talk to him. Maybe he would hand the farmstead over on conditions the thrall could accept. It was worth trying anyway, now that the fierce, wicked mother was gone.

But Holme couldn't leave right away to help his old friend. He was responsible for the king's farmstead, and both the queen and the foreman had to give him permission to be away for a few days.

The thrall insisted that the easiest thing to do would be to kill the son. But his vision was limited; he was afraid of losing the farmstead, but he couldn't acquire the farmstead and land by killing its owner. That had been done many times before, of course, and would happen again, but it would always bring bloodshed and death. Neighbors had to live in peace and help each other.

And when the free thrall returned to his loved ones satisfied, he had Holme's promise to follow along soon. In return the thrall had to promise not to do anything against the other farmstead and its young owner. They'd seek a peaceful solution first; if that didn't work, they could think about other alternatives.

Holme walked with him to the hidden boat, feeling happy all the while about his friend's freedom. The others he had tried to help hadn't really understood what he had meant; they'd expected things to be done for them and complained when they hadn't had something. They were dead and buried now. They hadn't understood that they had to be strong to be free. The one walking beside him was strong and knew that you had to work and fight for freedom. Such men had to come first and then gradually teach the others. But even so, you shouldn't kill someone for his farmstead or goods; you should just defend what's yours. His friend would soon come to understand this.

The morning's premonition of hard times had passed for a moment, but when he saw the thrall row out, alone in the little boat, the feeling returned. There were only two of them, and strong, ancient powers stood against them. One day, it would be their turn to be killed and their hope would vanish as it had come. Free men didn't believe in a life without thralls and didn't want to hear it talked about.

He was puzzled about why he thought of these things when such a peaceful time lay ahead of him. The king and the warriors were gone; those who had stayed behind worked peacefully and offered sacrifices for the new harvest and the raid's success. But there was a cloud somewhere. He felt it more clearly now than ever before.

Filled with something close to certainty, he walked straight to the smithy to check his weapons. Locked inside an iron-bound chest was a stash of finished weapons, which the king kept in reserve. He opened the lid and looked at them. They might come into use sooner than anyone expected. He shook his head at the thought and locked the chest. It might be that he was just unused to going very long without fighting and being pursued.

Svein heard one of the thralls give out a yell and then point toward the edge of the forest. There stood two figures, looking down at the new building. When they noticed they had been discovered, they walked calmly down the slope.

Svein looked at them and suddenly found it hard to breathe. They were both huge men, but there was something about one of them that was hard to pin down. He had felt terror because of it before, but now he joyously threw his tool aside and hurried to meet them. All work stopped, as everyone turned toward the newcomers. They saw Svein extend his hand to the biggest man and then, after some hesitation, to the other. Svein wondered what had brought Holme to the farmstead. Could his mother have started up the old chase again? But Holme looked peaceful and his eyes were calm. It had to be something else. But he didn't ask. Instead, he showed them around the building, talking as they went. Holme greeted the thralls as he passed them. Some who had known him for a long time, beamed with happiness; the others watched him, their eyes filled with curiosity. The lumber worker started walking with them, too, talking and pointing. The house would be ready soon; they had begun putting on the finishing touches. It was a bigger house than the one the pirates had burned on the same spot.

All the while, Holme was figuring out the best way to explain why he was there. He had agreed with the free thrall that they shouldn't mention the mother's death. Neither did Svein ever need to know how it had happened, even if someone found her. No one had seen the free thrall knock her out of the boat.

When they had seen everything, Svein looked expectantly at him. Well, he naturally had to know something important brought them there. The free thrall would probably have preferred to let his ax do the talking so he could feel confident about his farmstead, but that's not the way it was going to be.

After a while, the three men sat down on the slope, and a thrall was ordered to bring beer from a container in the grove. The workers watched curiously, undoubtedly wishing they were with them to hear what was going on. Holme was pleased to see that thralls were treated well here, too; the young man talked quietly to them and worked as they did. His hands were dirty and black from the resin.

It was strange sitting there opposite the old master's son. Still stranger that this son wasn't like his parents. He had been a sulky, ill-tempered boy before, but now he had a different look and a different attitude toward his thralls. There must be something behind that change, but what?

Although the man listening to him was very young, Holme began his story far back in time so that he would understand what was going to follow. He explained how the thought of freedom had started and was the cause of everything that had happened since. Like the king before him, Svein saw that Holme had done only what he had to do. He would have done the same. Holme had defended an ideal, as well as his family and friends against violence and injustice from the free men. It pleased Svein that this was so, and he was proud that the feared Holme, Tora's father, sat beside him, talking to him man to man. And he remembered that he knew Holme wouldn't be dangerous if you approached him without guile.

Svein longed to hear Tora's name, but he asked nothing. Then he heard that the man at Holme's side had lived at his relatives' farmstead and had worked it for a year, that the man wanted to stay there, and that he was the first free thrall. All the others had been killed and were buried behind the town.

Both men's eyes were directed at Svein as Holme talked, Holme's with friendly expectation but with something else behind it, something that called forth a shudder from Svein's childhood. Something that told him that he was too little to stand in the way of this thought of freedom. The free thrall's look told him more openly that denying the request could be dangerous. But once Svein had understood what they wanted, he had no desire to say no. He was glad Holme was asking something of him, and he had no problem about the relatives' farmstead. His father's was enough for him. His thoughts settled for a moment on his mother's wrath, but only for a moment. If she made a fuss, there was still the hut in the grove. She could just sit there, locked up again.

Holme said further that they had no intention of taking anything from him. Once the free thrall had gotten on his feet and the farmstead was supporting itself, he would pay for it in a way they could agree on. That way the nay-sayers could see that neither thralls nor fighting were necessary. That was the most important thing.

And Svein shook both their hands in agreement. He didn't understand yet how all this would come about, but he felt friendship in that mighty hand. The free thrall was surely the one who had shot an arrow at him, but that didn't matter. It was easy to understand why. The thrall's face was friendly and happy now, too. He could stay at the relatives' farmstead with his wife and child. And both farmsteads would stand under Holme's protection.

Holme was surprised but also relieved that the young man was so agreeable. He sensed something behind this, but not cowardice. He remembered the morning of the spring sacrifice when he had found Svein outside his house and Tora's face in the window. His thoughts might constantly be on the girl. It was very unusual for a freeman to become attached to a thrall girl, even a girl like Tora. He remembered, too, that Tora's eyes seemed quizzical when she heard where he was going and whom he was going to see. It just might be that the children of old, deadly enemies harbored warm thoughts for each other.

Holme smiled, sensing again that a great deal in his life had taken its own course. And now the young man asked about how the mother and daughter were. Holme heard himself answer that Svein should visit the king's farmstead when the time was right and see about their well-being himself. He saw happiness in the young man's eyes and thought that too could be a stage in the fight for freedom. A young freeman was voluntarily and respectfully approaching the thrall class.

Yet again, it was clear to Holme how much had changed since he had been a thrall at the settlement under Svein's father. The short-legged chieftain lay in a burial mound down near the cove. The son didn't look like him; he was of his mother's sort, taller and lighter. But his disposition was better than his mother's; it was open and friendly. It hadn't always been so—he had been an obstinate and hard boy. But something had happened to change him. Maybe his departed relatives were looking after him, making him wiser and better than his parents.

Svein still bore the mark of the stone that hit him in the neck when he was a child. But it was less noticeable now that he'd grown up. Holme realized with surprise that he wouldn't exact revenge on a child now even if its parents had done him great harm. But he had been young then and Tora had been abandoned in the woods to die. It was more merciful to die by being hit in the head with a rock than by being eaten alive by ants, flying insects, wolves, or wild boars. Freemen always had an edge even when it came to cruelty. So what did they expect from thralls?

They soon said goodbye to the young man, who walked a short ways into the forest with them. The free thrall, full of happiness, wanted Holme to spend the night at his place, but Holme already had other plans. He'd been thinking about his old friends in town, the smiths, and thought it couldn't be too dangerous now to pass by that way to visit them. They'd be surprised, and it made him glad to think of seeing them again.

Late that night, he reached the ferry station. The same oarsman was still there, but he had grown old and gray. Twice he had ferried Holme across, fearing for his life both times, and his eyes bulged anxiously beneath his bushy eyebrows now, too. As he rowed, he tried to ingratiate himself with Holme as he talked about everything that had happened in town since the last time. But Holme didn't like his cowardice and responded only with an occasional growl, as he had before.

Not many people were moving about in the harbor and only a couple of larger ships were there—merchant vessels from foreign lands, and some fishing boats and small skiffs. Some of the older townspeople stopped and stared at the massive figure who stepped ashore and paid the oarsman. Although he was better dressed than before, they couldn't mistake who he was. And they hurried off into the quiet town to spread the big news. He walked toward the craftsmen's part of town where his smithy once had been.

Holme felt strange walking as a free man through this town where so much had happened to him. He had been the master smith and sentenced to death, had led an uprising against the Christians. He had torn down their first church. It had all happened without his wanting or planning it.

He saw that most people recognized him. The freemen kept going, puffing with excitement, but some of the thralls came up to him with pleasant words and friendly eyes. A few followed him as before, forgetting what they were supposed to be doing. Perhaps they still hoped for the freedom that he had once tried to give them. He noticed one thrall's back striped with whip marks, and he felt the old hatred moving deep inside his chest. At the same time, the feeling that he had deserted them returned. Things were going well for him, but his friends were still being whipped and tormented as before. Maybe he needed to get away from the peace and quiet of the king's farmstead after all. But not before the king came back. Holme had promised to look after his queen, children, and possessions. And the king was a good master.

There were many new smiths in the smithies, but the old ones gathered around him, buzzing with happiness. Black, powerful hands reached out to him, and voices assured him that if they had known his life was in danger in the fortress last year, they surely would have come to his aid. They talked with admiration about the time he had killed Geire and his men with his bare hands and had gotten away. The battle god, the most powerful of all the gods, had to be on his side, no matter what he thought.

Their words pleased Holme, but he realized that when the time came, the smiths might not be on his side. They were independent men not much bothered by the plight of the oppressed thralls, and while they would defend themselves, they wouldn't raise their sledgehammers for many others. They had forgotten that their independence had begun during his tenure as master smith and that they had once been mistreated thralls themselves.

But it was still fun to see them again and what they were doing. A couple of the oldest ones walked back with him and wanted to lend him a boat for the trip to the king's farmstead. The streets were livelier now than they had been moments before. Faces kept peeking out everywhere, around corners and through doorways. Mothers called their children in and slammed their doors. Having heard the news, Svein's mother positioned herself where she thought Holme would pass by. She had summoned the Christian priests, but they were nowhere to be seen.

Holme saw the woman on the street corner and felt a mixture of fear and wonder. It was the woman his friend had drowned a few days earlier. He had never before seen anyone return from the dead and felt very uncomfortable. You couldn't do anything against the dead, so, to the smiths' surprise, Holme dragged his friends across the street. When they had passed the woman, though, she sent a shrill stream of insults after them, and Holme looked back at her. She must be alive after all; the dead kept their silence and didn't insult you, and didn't show themselves in town either. The free thrall had to have been wrong, or she must have swum ashore without his noticing it. The thought made Holme breathe easier. But it would be more dangerous for the free thrall at the farmstead now since the mother wouldn't be as agreeable as the son. It would have been best for everyone if she had drowned.

While he was still talking with the smiths on shore, a number of people from town came down. Most of them stood a little ways away watching them, but some came up and said hello. They were mostly thralls, but some of them were merchants who had been there when Holme was the master smith and considered a freeman.

Many people talked at once as they tugged at his clothes. Thralls complained about their masters and asked for help. A freeman asked him to head up a fight against the Christians, who had become more and more entrenched and robbed the women while their men were out at sea. From a distance, the Christian priests themselves approached, followed by a group of women and some older men. Svein's mother was right next to the priests. They stopped a little ways away, and the woman pointed directly at Holme.

The priests looked curiously at the man who was the biggest obstacle to their progress in town. They had expected a wild animal from the primeval forest and so looked with wonder at the smiths—three powerful men. It must be the youngest of them who was Holme. The heathens crowded expectantly around him.

He was a little taller and more powerfully built than most men; otherwise there was nothing noteworthy about him. The priests said to each other that people had exaggerated his significance. That dark man would no longer stand in the way of the light. And they moved closer to show how little they feared him.

Holme was ready to step into the boat when he heard the woman's shrill, hard voice. He had heard the charges before, but now the woman was hoping for speedy justice. Indicating the priests, she said that they were more powerful than either the chieftain or the king. They and their god had promised to stand by her.

The priests hadn't intended for things to turn out this way. They had just wanted to see the feared thrall and form an opinion about him. They had done that, and now they wanted to quiet the woman down. It was clear that everyone standing with the smith was ready to protect him. It wasn't the right time yet, but a better one would present itself.

They heard him tell those around him that he had to go back to the king's farmstead, but if they needed him, if there was great danger for them, he would be there. But he didn't expect any such danger. And he shot a glance at the priests and their following of women before stepping into the boat.

Both priests felt more at ease after seeing that their enemy was an ordinary human being. He seemed almost shy as he stepped into the boat, and he didn't respond to the woman's insults. The priests walked down to the water as he rowed out, one of them observing contemptuously something about such an insignificant enemy soon being brushed aside.

Holme could only catch the tone of the priest's words, and it irritated him. Would these priests always make his life difficult? He stopped rowing and looked the priest straight in the eye. The priest thought for a moment that the ground had disappeared from under his feet, and the words he intended to add to what he had said never came out. He didn't positively know what he had seen in the smith's eyes, but it had to do with death. Holme was clearly more dangerous than he looked.

The heathens called after him to come back soon, and Holme promised more willingly to do so, now that he was irritated. Then he rowed with powerful strokes to get away from the place. He didn't want anything to happen that the king wouldn't like. When the king returned, it would be time for Holme to make his position known. If he didn't want to hear what Holme had to say about the thralls, then Holme would probably have to resort to his old ways.

His peace of mind soon began to return, though. A number of good things had still happened in his life, after all. Still better and still calmer would it have been had these gray Christian priests not, time after time, come to his land with their new god. They spread unrest among the people, and there was conflict and bloodshed wherever they went. And their god was insatiable. He wasn't satisfied with animal sacrifices but had to be appeased with silver and gold.

Holme could see the big gray buildings of the king's farmstead and his own smithy in the clump of birch trees. The lake was shimmering and everything was peaceful. Soon, Ausi and Tora would come running to meet him.

He didn't see anything he needed to be afraid of. Even so, the voice of uneasiness continued whispering inside him—this calm was foreboding. It wasn't the first time he had felt a dark premonition mixed with the sunlight itself. But this time he didn't know where the wind would be coming from.

He looked to the mainland forests and momentarily felt his old longing to walk into the depths of the woods and stay there until he died. But he had two women to answer for, and many thralls with backs torn apart by the whip were expecting his help. He couldn't think about himself. The looks the Christians gave him also told him that they hadn't forgotten what he had once done to them.

Then he saw mother and daughter running to shore, just as he had expected. Maybe a few days would pass before something happened. The queen waited every day for a call to arms from the king, and sacrificial smoke was rising into the sky now. She was in the shrine making offerings to the gods so they'd give the king good fortune on his raid. That might be necessary after all; there'd been many bad signs lately, both on the earth among the newborn animals and in the heavens. The old conflicts between Christ and the wooden gods couldn't do an undertaking like this any good.

Holme would be glad when he saw the king's sail fill the horizon. He was a good king, and as long as he was alive there was hope for the thralls. After he was gone, no one knew what was going to happen.

During the next few days, two more Christian ships came to town. The priests had frequent business to do with them, even after they had taken ashore what they needed for their work. And the two ships, which Holme had seen in the harbor, stayed there, although they'd been ready to sail for a long time.

On their way in, the newly arrived ships had heard a rumor that the Swedes had failed on their raid. First a storm had forced them ashore on the foreign coast, and then the town defenders had attacked them. There were only splinters left of the ships, and most of the men had been killed or taken prisoner.

The priests interpreted these events with thanks as Christ's doing. He had finally shown that He was the Lord. The heathens left at home would give in now and seek baptism in terror and desperation. But the Christians did not spread the news of the disaster. The heathens wouldn't believe it unless they heard it from one of their own.

The priests knew, however, that a powerful group among the heathens wouldn't give up, no matter what happened. That was why there was whispering on the Christian ships and furtive glances cast toward shore. Through trickery or violence, they would strike the heathens to the ground in the name of Christ, and their abominable temple would be burned. And without followers, the Christians' biggest enemy, the smith at the king's farmstead, would be almost harmless. The homeless thralls he could gather were both weak with hunger and unarmed.

So the plans were formulated while they waited. The new female converts, whose husbands would never return, were bound closer to Christ by the thought of a reunion in heaven. The priests were no longer saying that Christ would bring them back safely. Once news of the catastrophe reached town, many of these wives would give all they owned to save their husbands' souls from the flames of hell.

The disquiet grew, both at the king's farmstead and in town. It was midsummer, the nights were already a little longer and darker, but there was no message from the king. A smaller ship had been sent out to search, but it hadn't returned either. The heathen priests scrutinized the entrails of the sacrificial beasts but found no clear sign about what had happened or would happen.

The hostility between the Christians and heathens intensified. The Christians walked around looking scornful or self-important, as if they knew something or were certain of victory. And their numbers grew. The merchants from the foreign ships refused to deal or exchange goods with the heathens. People insulted each other's gods, and, occasionally, it came to violence.

Then one day during the harvesting of leaves, a few men appeared at the ferry on the mainland. They were thin, and their beards were long and wild. You could hardly tell if they were thralls or warriors, although a couple of them carried swords, and gold trim sometimes flashed from the tattered and torn clothes. Except for the oldest of them all—a stately, gray-bearded man—they seemed dismal and forlorn. Those who couldn't get a place in the ferry boat took boats themselves without asking the owner's permission.

You could see the three small boats from town, and many people walked down to the harbor. Everyone had been waiting with mounting excitement for news, and many had checked every boat that came across. That's how it had been for a long time. The queen was in town often, spending hours standing on the rocks by the fortress, looking across the water. But it had been barren and blue with eternally rolling waves.

Shortly after the bearded men had stepped ashore on the island, the harbor was buzzing with people. Some of the women recognized them and let out cries of joy. But most of them wept silently and disconsolately when they learned that the others were gone, probably forever. The chieftain went straight to the queen when he heard that she was in town. The king was among those who had been captured and taken away.

The chieftain's eyes were calm, and it looked like he had known all along how the raid would turn out. When the storm came up, he had encouraged the king and the men to turn to Christ, but they had refused and started offering sacrifices to their wooden gods, whose staues they had on board. Only he from his ship and then these men had been saved, after casting their wooden gods into the sea and calling on Christ. He had dragged them up on an islet after their ship had been dashed to bits on the enemy coast. After the enemies had gone inland toward their town with prisoners and goods, a merchant ship had picked up the shipwrecked warriors and put them ashore a long ways from the town. They had endured many hardships travelling home.

Everyone in town knew all this shortly after the men stepped ashore. The Christian bell summoned the people and a column of sobbing women hurried toward the church to demand their husbands back as the priests had promised. But a number of the new female converts looked toward the church with hatred. They had all the while counted on Christ's returning their husbands alive. They didn't know what heaven was, but they did know anxiety and felt compassion for their husbands, who had gone to the land of the dead unarmed and without provisions for the journey.

The heathens weren't idle either. The priests understood at once that the wooden gods had allowed this misfortune to beset their people because so many still worshipped Christ. Their patience gone, the gods would surely destroy them all if people didn't return to their fathers' faith and drive the Christians out. The muffled beating of drums was heard from the heathen temple and people streamed there, too. On the way Christians and heathens exchanged derisive words and an occasional punch or kick. Women on both sides were wailing out their accusations.

Bell and drum competed constantly, and both temples were soon filled with believers. The gray-haired chieftain came last, after taking his tale of calamity to the queen. The Christian priests received him joyously and interpreted his being spared as a sign of victory. After a thanksgiving service, they would confer together about the best way to deliver the death blow to the heathens.

In the heathen temple apprehension and suppressed rage reigned. Everyone agreed that a message had to be sent inland immediately to the main temple. The gods had to be appeased with a greater sacrifice than usual, perhaps with human offerings, if everyone wasn't to be destroyed. And the Christians in town one way or another would have to pay for what they had started by provoking the wooden gods.

Someone brought up Holme, and the name glided like a whisper through the heathen temple. Many faces brightened and the apprehension changed to confidence. Here was a man who stood in the middle between the camps of the gods, someone whom Christ had no control over and whom the wooden gods seemed to favor despite his not offering sacrifices to them. The king was gone now and it was because of the Christians. That alone would kindle Holme's wrath against them. And he wouldn't have to fight alone this time. They would send out a secret call to arms to everyone who still believed in the ancient wooden gods.

And that same day, the heathens started marshalling their forces. Boats set out in all directions with the message. The homeless in town and the surrounding areas were summoned and catered to, treated well so that when it came down to the battle, they would be on the right side. But the town's defenders at the fortress said that they intended only to do their duty—defend the town against external attack, wherever it might come from. They'd have no part in a war between the Christians and heathens.

The Christians were in full swing now, too. Everywhere among the heathens, there were those who had a foot in each camp so they could get help from either direction when danger threatened. Many of them now hurried to the Christian church with the news. When Holme was mentioned as well, the gray-bearded chieftain knew this could be serious. Would there never be an end to the smith and his actions?

And when the chieftain walked through town, he noticed that something was afoot. The heathens were standing around in groups and some of them said aloud that the old gray-bearded Christian chieftain should have been the one lost in the East instead of the good king. And thralls, who had once scurried out of his path, now dared face him and stare him in the eye. Someone must have said something to give them such courage.

The chieftain kept going toward the fortress. The shipwrecked warriors were there, with new clothes and weapons, still devouring food like wolves after a long famine. Their wives sat outside the guard house, happy the men had been spared. The chieftain encouraged them to remember who had saved their husbands—it had been Christ and no one else.

He told the warriors what the atmosphere in town was like. If the heathens attacked the Christians it was the warriors' duty to defend them and the town. The king had promised the Christians his protection, and their priests came from a powerful land. If they were killed, an army could come and destroy the town in revenge.

The shipwrecked warriors agreed with their chieftain when he said that Christ was the one who had saved them from destruction. If they hadn't been on the same ship as their Christian chieftain they would be lying on the bottom of the ocean now or in the hands of the enemy, which would be even worse. They intended to fight on the chieftain's side if the heathens wanted battle.

The town guards showed reluctance for a long time, but when the chieftain left them, he knew they'd follow his orders. They were strong men, used to battle, and the heathens were mainly merchants, craftsmen, and thralls. With Christ's help, the heathens would be quickly defeated.

The chieftain felt satisfied and gave thanks in his heart to Christ. He had forgotten Holme for a moment, but on the way back, the thought returned so fiercely that the chieftain stopped in his tracks. He had heard that the smith had been in town a few days before. Holme shouldn't have gotten out alive.

Maybe it would be safest to seek the wolf in his den. There was no one at the king's farmstead who could stand by him. A few warriors could quickly dispatch him.

But the chieftain drove the thought away and walked on. Maybe Holme would stay away. He ought to be glad to be alive after all he'd done and ought not to get mixed up in another fight. The king wasn't around to protect him now, either.

The most important thing was to protect the lives of the foreign priests. They wouldn't be allowed to show themselves in town without guards as long as there was unrest. An arrow could come silently flying from a window, or a paid thrall could be waiting around the corner of a building with an ax. They were his responsibility now until an assembly could be summoned and a king chosen. Even if Christ was big, He couldn't be everywhere to defend His followers.

Women came up to the chieftain wherever he went, wanting some word about their missing husbands or sons. He told the Christian women gently that their men were in safekeeping with Christ, but he hissed angrily in his beard at the heathen women when he told them their husbands were burning in hell. Most of them looked at him uncomprehendingly and repeated their question.

It was calmer in town now than when he had walked to the fortress before. The heathens might still think twice and wait for the assembly. He would summon it soon so that they would have something to think about besides the Christians. Meanwhile, he would confer with the Christian priests. It might be best to attack before the heathens could gather their forces.

In the church, he found the priests busy packing all the treasures to load onto the ships. They would be safer there than in town, if it should come to a fight. The rich woman was dead, and they had figured out just how many more prayers for her soul her silver would justify. Her daughter and heir looked on silently, and yet again the priests said something about the treasures she had laid up for herself in heaven.

No one working on the new building knew anything about smith work, so Svein decided to go into town to order what was needed. He was also thinking about his mother, who had been gone for several days. It would be best to take her away from town with all her hatred and rage. She couldn't do much harm at the settlement.

The lumber worker went with him since his work was done, but the others stayed to clean up. A number of them had promised to stay at the settlement when they saw that they would be treated almost like freemen. Svein wanted to pursue Holme's idea and couldn't understand how he had thought completely otherwise before. He hoped, too, to get over to the king's farmstead while he was in town. A face with a friendly, teasing smile and bordered by black hair was constantly in his mind.

The ferry man immediately told about what had happened to the king and his army. He also said that people were coming to town from every direction and pointed at a few small boats being rowed toward town. The wooden gods had commanded that the Christians be driven from town and land for all time. Otherwise, a foreign army would come and destroy everything, kill all the men, and take the women and children captive. The unrest in town was great.

Svein didn't reply but thought that Holme must be in town, and he wanted to be at his side, no matter what happened. He felt his chest expand with lust for battle. He would show them that he was no coward. And after the battle he would follow Holme to the king's farmstead and see Tora again. With a great feeling of happiness, he turned his stiff neck and looked across the water toward the king's farmstead. Svein heard the lumber worker say something about his son—he had been along on the raid in the East. He'd never see him again. He was dead or captured.

Svein knew that the gathering place was at the heathen temple and went directly there. The most prominent merchants were there and the hall was full of armed men. But the Christian church was buzzing with people outside too. Shouts of derision and threats went flying across the courtyard between the temples. Svein searched for Holme, but he was nowhere to be seen. He soon heard Holme's name, though, and understood that they had just decided to send a message to him. Full of zeal, he offered to go himself, and many men turned toward him with scrutinizing eyes.

Svein was soon chosen to go. Some said that his mother was Holme's bitterest enemy and that the son might dump Holme in the lake, but the others smiled at these words. And so, forgetting the smith work, Svein walked happily to the harbor, accompanied by two powerful oarsmen. Someone shrieked his name from the Christian church, but he neither answered nor turned around.

Holme saw the queen step ashore and walk to the farmstead, followed by the women of the court. She covered her face once as if she were crying. Her figure had gotten a little heavier. She would surely have a child this winter. A vague memory came back to him—he somehow recognized the movement when she put her arm over her face and he felt a momentary urge to caress her stomach. But the feeling soon disappeared before the others that pressed in upon him.

A while later, someone came running to the smithy with the rumor. Holme listened silently to the story and could then understand the darkness that had been blended in with the sunlight the past few days. The good king would not return, and then peace would come to an end at his farmstead, too. The wolves would remember and emerge from their dens. The man carrying the rumor walked on and Holme mechanically opened the chest to look at the masses of weapons for a moment. A row of new axes hung on the wall, and he walked along the row looking at each of them without understanding why. Howls and laughter from the king's children would occasionally press in through the open door, creating a strange atmosphere. Since none of the king's sons was grown and could take over for his father, a new king had to be chosen quickly. And probably a new smith at the king's farmstead.

Several things lay there half-finished, but his desire to work was gone with his master. Why should he forge anything when he didn't know what tomorrow would bring? If they chose a Christian king, he had to flee—the priests' looks had told him as much when he had passed through town.

He stood by the door looking out over the bay. Uneasiness gnawed at his heart, joining with a feeling resembling grief over the good king. He had never had a chance to talk with him about the thralls' misery, and now it was too late. Who would understand now? A boat appeared far in the distance, the oars glistening as they were lifted from the water. He had a feeling that this had to do with him. It was someone who needed his help or maybe someone who wanted to warn him. Anything was possible now.

The boat approached rapidly and he walked down to meet it. He sat on a beached log as the warm summer wind played in his grizzled hair. Ausi and Tora were standing outside their house with their hands shielding their eyes from the sun. It was on its way down and the water glistened. The king's children had been called in and the farmstead was completely silent. A cow's mooing came drifting across the water from some distant place.

The boat changed course when its occupants caught sight of the massive figure on shore. Holme wasn't surprised; he knew they were on their way to see him. When they laid to, he got up and walked toward them. Svein greeted him happily, and a hint of surprise finally flashed across Holme's face. He had expected someone else.

As Svein relayed his message, he kept looking up toward the two women outside Holme's house. Holme noticed that and a little smile flitted across his face, despite the gravity of the news. Followed by the three men, he walked up toward the house to inform his wife and daughter about what was going on. He had already decided to go back to town with the messengers. His master was dead, and the queen was in no danger. He could leave the farmstead for awhile.

As he talked with Ausi inside, the two young people stood outside. They didn't say much to each other. Svein mentioned something about the building work, and the girl watched him furtively. He had grown since she had seen him last, but beside Holme he had still looked like a boy as they walked up toward the house. She had turned away so her mother wouldn't see how glad she was about the visit.

Inside the house, Holme was just as taciturn. All Ausi found out was that he was going to town because the Christians were posing more and more of a threat. But surely, nothing bad would happen. He'd be back soon. Ausi and Tora ought to stay home.

The farmstead's foreman, who didn't like the king's making Holme his equal, didn't mind seeing him step into the boat. Neither did he care when they carried a chest and a bundle of axes from the smithy and loaded them into the boat. All the better if the smith never came back. The new king didn't need to know anything about him.

He saw Holme's wife and daughter saying good-bye to the men at the shore. He wasn't close enough to see the brown and blue eyes meeting hastily, parting, then meeting again. Or to see Ausi and Holme exchange a knowing smile. Ausi couldn't understand how just the sight of Svein had once made her feel uncomfortable. It must have been the painful memory of slavery at his parents' settlement. But the young man was good and reliable. Maybe sometime when she and Holme were gone . . .

And she imagined Tora as the mistress of the settlement. They wouldn't leave any thrall descendants behind, she and Holme. And she wouldn't want to live even for Tora's sake if Holme died. She had known that for a long time. She had to be there to tell Christ how good Holme was under that dour exterior. The Christians had surely lied about him, and Christ couldn't be everywhere Himself.

As the men pushed away from shore, and Ausi's heart felt heavier than it had in a long time. Things had been much worse than this many times before without her feeling this dark foreboding. It could be because they had been living in peace and safety at the farmstead. And she and Holme weren't so young anymore, either.

The thralls rowed; Holme and the young Svein waved farewell. Svein felt as if he were already part of the family. He ragarded Holme with great admiration and respect, and she and Tora had to like him just for that. He didn't have the freeman's arrogant way of looking even at ordinary thralls.

As mother and daughter returned home, some thralls yelled from the fields to find out what had happened. Ausi explained as well as she could, and they looked pensively toward town. One of them said that Holme should have taken them along. Everything was up in the air here since they had heard that the king would never return to his farmstead. No one knew how the new king would treat his underlings.

The foreman looked at the root crops, and the thralls bent down again toward the earth. But as soon as they could straighten up, they looked toward town and wondered what was going on there.

Nothing seemed unusual when Holme, Svein, and the oarsmen stepped ashore. Some of the town's heathen merchants and craftsmen met them and seemed to breathe easier at the sight of Holme. They believed that the Christians bore evil in their hearts against them, but they didn't know what they were planning on doing. The last few days, many people had gone to the side of the Christians, who had never been so strong before. And the town defenders would join them. The heathens wanted to hear what Holme intended to do — shouldn't they attack the Christians when they were off guard?

But Holme didn't want to start fighting. Defending yourself was another matter. And the Christians had the king's promise to live and hold their services as they wished. It would be better to wait and see what the Christians' intentions were. He'd stay in town until all this was over.

And that's what they did. They walked up toward the temple, a crowd of people behind them. As usual, a number of thralls came up to Holme, complaining bitterly. And he knew that if a fight broke out and the Christians were defeated, the slavery question would be taken up once more. The Christians always said that thralls meant as much as freemen to their god, but they still treated them cruelly and beat them as often as the heathens did. From them, you could expect nothing.

Many eyes, both curious and threatening, from inside the Christian church followed them to the heathen temple. Four men carried the heavy chest of weapons, and two followed with the glistening axes. The Christian chieftain thought bitterly of stepping out and ordering them to put down their weapons, but the priests stopped him, and he saw immediately that that would have been premature. The heathens would have responded with an attack, and the time wasn't right yet.

The chieftain and priests had noticed preparations going on in the heathen temple for a sacrifice. The heathens might be drunk around midnight, and that would be the time to attack and tear down their repulsive temple. They didn't dare burn it; it was too close to the church and the town buildings. If, on the other hand, they could goad the drunken heathens into an attack, that would be much better. The responsibility would then fall on them.

The priests administered the holy communion as they waited, and the whole time the kneeling Christians kept hearing the sacrificial animals at the heathen temple braying and mooing through the priests' mumbled words. They soon sensed a faint smell of smoke, too. The war between the gods had begun.

Boats kept coming from every direction on the mainland. One, two, or three men stepped out of each of them and walked toward the heathen temple. Some were armed; others came almost without clothes on their bodies. A Christian or two came as well and walked with dignity into the church. The door was immediately shut after them, but the hall of the heathen temple was swarming with people, completely visible to all. Raucous laughter came frequently from there, cutting strangely through the Christian solemnity.

Holme wasn't happy about all these preparations. He understood that the heathen merchants were friendly because they needed him. They knew that the Christians hated and feared him, and that the thralls followed him wherever he went and looked up to him. But he was uncomfortable about how everything was being built up for a battle and knew that people would expect him to fight without provocation.

The whole time, people around him were talking about the Christians' shameless ravaging after they found out that the king and his warriors wouldn't return from the raid. They didn't even balk at leading small children into the church and baptizing them. The children had gone home to their mothers with water running from their hair and told what had happened.

Holme also heard about the rich woman who had given everything she owned to the Christians, who had said there weren't any poor people in town, not even in the whole land. And he thought about all the misery he had seen, about all those who were starving and freezing. There were decrepit thralls all over the town and environs, old men and women, who had been driven away when they could no longer work. They slept under the open sky and covered themselves with whatever they could find. They searched for food in the town's garbage heaps. But the Christian woman sent her treasures to a foreign land.

Holme felt more fatigue and bitterness than anger at the thought of all this, however. Someone brought him some beer, and he drank it to get out of his bad mood. He watched the heathen priests smearing the wooden gods with sacrificial blood, but that was none of his business. Svein stayed at his side the whole time, and many old acquaintances among the thralls kept near him, talking proudly about past battles with the Christians. He couldn't desert them if it came to a fight.

Many warriors had come from the fortress and were wandering around aimlessly. They kept close to the Christian church but didn't go in. Some cast a stealthy glance at the bloody wooden god who stood at the front of the heathen temple. He had helped them in battle several times before, but now he would stand against them. His standing so far forward in the hall indicated that the heathens were expecting battle.

Both inside and outside the temple, thralls were milling about. It wasn't often they could move around so freely, and they enjoyed pretending they were freemen. They were needed now, and no one drove them away from the places they otherwise couldn't set foot on. The warriors watched them with disdain from the other side, commenting amongst themselves that they didn't need to be called away from the fortress for adversaries such as those. But inside the temple, there were well-armed merchants and craftsmen. There, too, was the man everyone was thinking about but no one was mentioning.

Holme listened to the head priest trying to incite the men to war. He listed the Christians' misdeeds and described the unrest they had caused in the town and the land. He criticized the two kings who had let them into the land.[11] Both were gone now—now the time was at hand to drive the Christians out. Everything indicated that this was the gods' will.

These words stuck in Holme's mind, and his thoughts moved back in time. The priest was right about what he said—the Christians had brought unrest and strife. And it had to be because of them that the good king and his men were dead and gone. Either the Christian god had sent the storm that destroyed them, or they had provoked the wooden gods into sending it.

Outside in the courtyard, the crowd of people was growing larger and larger. Someone said that the crews on the foreign vessels had come and joined the Christians. The church door was open now, and there was a light of some kind inside in the darkness. But in the heathen temple, the sacrificial fire was burning cheerfully, crackling and reeking, and from outside you could see everything that was going on in there.

There was some hesitation among the Christians. They were prepared for battle, but the heathens had to seem like the aggressors to everybody. The chieftain and priests conferred together on the best way to bring that about. They couldn't be certain of victory either. If they had only the heathen merchants and priests against them, they would soon overpower them. But the temple swarmed with half-wild thralls, who were excited with beer and who did whatever their dangerous leader told them to do. Without him, it would be easy to scare them off.

---

[11] i.e., Björn and Olaf.

Should they try yet again to get their hands on Holme? The merchants could be threatened with the wrath of the yet unchosen king. And the smith was, after all, already guilty and sentenced. The law had to be obeyed, justice served.

A short time later, the chieftain was standing outside the church, surrounded and protected by the town's defenders. The news moved quickly into the heathen temple, and everyone streamed from the hall into the courtyard. Many of them were hoping for a fight; others preferred to avoid one. In the middle of the hall stood Holme. The chieftain began to speak. He said that Christianity, which had been victorious in so many lands, would now be victorious among them, too. Its power could not be resisted. The new king would be a Christian, and then the era of the wooden gods would soon be through. This should have happened a long time ago, as it had in neighboring lands. No powerless wooden gods — devils, more like it — were there any longer.

The chieftain further suggested that they should try to avoid the battle that was threatening them. Many lives would be lost for no reason. The Christians didn't want any man's death, but rather each and every man's conversion and salvation. Only one man stood in the way of all that, one sent by Satan to stand against the power of the light. And the chieftain pointed at Holme, whose head and shoulders rose above the surrounding crowd.

A murmur passed through the rows of heathens, but it grew quiet again as the chieftain continued. He outlined Holme's life, and again it sounded as if Holme were the biggest criminal in the land. The heathen merchants looked pensive again. The chieftain noticed that and promised that no one would be forced to be baptized if they turned the smith over to him of their own free will. The heathen temple could stay put until it was clear that the wooden gods' power was ended.

The chieftain finished with yet another suggestion. Everyone knew Holme was a strong and dangerous thrall. To save lives, the heathens should capture him themselves and turn him over to the Christians. Afterwards, all would be peaceful and everyone could go back to their own business.

The chieftain had spoken with authority, and he was the most prominent man in town. The heathen merchants and a great many of the craftsmen looked around, not knowing what to do. They looked at Holme out of the corners of their eyes, but his face was unchanged except, perhaps, that his jaw was jutting out a little more than before the chieftain's speech.

One of the thralls who had understood the speech stepped closer to Holme and looked at him with probing eyes. The others followed suit and he was soon standing in the midst of them. The merchants' sporadic words came to him over the heads of the thralls — there was something to what the chieftain had said — he hadn't lied; maybe it would be best to come to terms with the Christians again. Fighting wouldn't do anyone any good.

Holme could smell the thralls around him and looked at their rags. Beyond them, the merchants' eyes were looking around evasively, doubtfully, partly hostile. He began to understand that the fight wouldn't be between heathens and Christians but, like before, between freemen and thralls.

His chest immediately felt lighter when that dawned on him. This wasn't a new battle; it was the same old one. He was in his place again. He saw the chief merchants walking into the courtyard and the chieftain and Christian priests meeting them. They would reach an agreement, and he'd be the prize. The head heathen priest pushed his way through the group of thralls up to him, his face full of anxiety, and he urged them to fight. The wooden gods would help them gain victory; all the signs were favorable. The priests and temple attendants would fight, too. And the message had gone out the day before to the temple inland. Help would soon be on its way.

Holme listened to the head priest as he looked around. Closest to him stood Svein, armed, and you could see by his look that he stood firm. Some of the thralls had huge sticks, some had axes, but most were unarmed. He understood better now why he had brought along the king's weapon chest. Followed by a curious group of thralls, he walked to the chest and opened it. The thralls snatched up the new swords with delight. They had never laid hands on such things before. Many of them preferred axes, the thralls' ancient tool and weapon.

The heathen merchants returned from the courtyard, and you could tell from their falsely grinning faces that they had agreed to the chieftain's conditions. Except for one thing. They didn't want, or didn't dare, to take Holme themselves. Behind them came ten men whom the chieftain had sent from the town guard, men with arrogant faces.

Holme followed all this as if it concerned someone else. He still wasn't sure what he wanted to do. He was waiting for something to happen that would clarify the situation. That's how it had been before. Something always happened when the time came.

He noticed that many of the thralls watched the approaching warriors with terror. They were used to beatings and whippings, to bending their backs and suffering. This wasn't easy for them. He himself felt that his life's toughest battle still remained to be fought and was close at hand. Maybe he would be alone—the thralls at the front looked back plaintively. He glanced out into the courtyard and saw the priests' and chieftain's faces. They were happy and already certain of victory.

That was what he needed. He felt the rage rise now, and with it, his strength. The victory might be the Christians', the thralls might die, but not alone. Some of the freemen would be carried up to where the burial mounds were at the same time as others dug holes and buried the thralls like dogs. He'd make sure of that himself.

But he still wanted to wait. The merchants, who had first called on him for help and then turned him over to the Christians, now stood at the edge of the courtyard to see what would happen. They believed the Christians' promises. One would die for all, now. He might have given himself up of his own free will if it meant saving his thrall companions. But he had never been able to believe the promises of freemen to thralls. They didn't have to be kept.

A powerfully built man forced his way through the crowd, panting. He reeked of beer, his eyes were glistening with happiness, and Holme, too, smiled with joy. It was the free thrall. A message had reached him and he had come at the last moment. Someone had described the situation to him, and so he now stood proudly by Holme's side. To those standing closest to him he boasted that this wasn't the first time he and Holme had fought together.

All the while, the temple attendants kept bringing beer for the thralls and the craftsmen who were on the heathens' side. At a call from the chieftain, the warriors had stopped outside the temple hall—the chieftain and the Christians wanted the heathens to attack so that the responsibility would fall on them. The heathen priests noticed how hesitant the thralls were and knew the beer would increase their lust for battle. Their number grew constantly and the newcomers were given swords or axes. The heathen priests started believing in victory and loudly promised their gods greater sacrifices than ever before.

From his position, Holme could see that the Christian church was filled with women. He was glad that there were no more of his enemies than the men he saw in the courtyard. The heathens' own women were nowhere to be seen. Not many of the thralls had women, and by old custom women ought not to be around when danger was threatening.

A man from town appeared now, insulting the gods of the land with a loud voice. He said they were ridiculous and weak, and challenged them triumphantly to strike him to the ground if they could. He looked defiantly at the blood-smeared wooden figures, but nothing happened, although a tense hush wafted over the courtyard. It was broken by the heathen priests' call to their gods to let something happen. From the other side rose a voice calling on Christ to demonstrate His power.

But none of the gods had any desire to listen to their children but instead left them to settle their own affairs. The old chieftain grew tired of nothing happening. He had seen the thralls retreat, and he again ordered the warriors to move in and take Holme. Cut him down if it didn't work any other way. Or were they afraid of a thrall?

When Holme heard the order, he knew the time had come. He forced his way to the front, followed by Svein and the free thrall, who laughed from the beer and his lust for battle. It was also he who started the fight because of his arrogance. He took a piece of flaming wood from the sacred pyre and hurled it at the warriors. It hit some of them, and they let out an angry roar. Sparks and smoke danced around them. The thrall laughed loudly and scornfully, and some voices joined in from the hall behind them.

But then the warriors balked, looking uneasily at the pack of stick-, sword-, and ax-swinging thralls in rags. They were good and dangerous and unworthy opponents besides. The smith was standing before them, but it was no easy matter to go up and take him, even if he were alone. The first man, and probably several more, would never see another sunrise.

Behind the ranks, the chieftain quietly gave an order to a row of archers. The heathens had attacked by throwing the burning wood, so the Christians could start defending themselves. The archers stepped up on a small rise, the strings twanged, and the arrows flew into the temple hall. Most of them flew too high, and one thumped against the chest of the battle god and fell to the ground. Screams showed that others had hit their marks. A half-naked thrall with an arrow in his shoulder pushed his way up to Holme. Groaning, the thrall looked up to him for help as a child would to his father. Behind the group of Christians, the archers drew their bows again.

When Holme attacked with the free thrall and Svein beside him, he thought vaguely that he wasn't like he had been before. Then, he would have charged on all by himself if no one would follow him, but that kind of rage hadn't come this time. It was the pitiable look from the wounded thrall that finally forced him into action and freed him from his long hesitation. Behind him, the call of the heathen priests urged them on to battle, and they had armed themselves, too. In the opposing camp, the Christian priests were unarmed. When the fighting began, they stretched their hands into the air and called aloud to their god.

The second shower of arrows hit those at the rear of the group. The number of archers had increased, and in the midst of the growing tumult, Holme understood the danger. The warriors had closed ranks when the thralls approached, but had kept their ground. If the group of thralls, unused to battle, stormed out into the courtyard the warriors could attack from the rear or take them from the side. The heathen merchants stood off to one side by themselves. They talked eagerly, waving their weapons, probably still unable to agree on which side to fight.

The warriors had silently agreed that the half-drunk band of thralls was almost harmless without its leader. If they could strike him down first, the way would be clear. But no one wanted to go up against him. Even if a number of them rushed him at once, at least a couple of them would lose their lives. That was too high a price to pay.

After a moment's consultation, the warriors had figured out the best thing to do. Someone brought out a cudgel of juniper wood almost as long as a man was tall. They would keep it hidden, and when the thralls attacked, their leader would be struck down before anyone got within reach of the thralls' axes.

The free thrall stormed past Holme in his eagerness for battle, and they were all soon out in the courtyard. The warriors stood there like a wall, but when the thralls were on top of them, they quickly opened ranks and the pole-like cudgel rose and fell. Holme saw it coming and tried to dodge it, but it hit him in the side of the head and glanced off his shoulder. He felt a hard jolt and intense pain and simultaneously saw the look on his old battle companion's face—a look both anxious and surprised.

The pain made him go berserk, and he charged straight into the warriors with his ax raised. Behind him came the thralls, yelling and roaring, and the warriors at the forefront retreated as their ranks fell into disarray. Two or three fell before Holme's and the free thrall's blows, and the others moved back, fending off the fury of the thralls. The archers couldn't shoot for fear of hitting their own men.

During all this, Holme sustained another blow against his wounded shoulder and saw the blood flow. One of the warriors had hacked him with his sword this time. He raised his sword again, but it never came down. Holme smashed his chest with his ax, then watched the man fall, his mouth wide open. An instant later, Holme saw Svein trying desperately to defend himself against one of the Christian warriors, and he rushed to his aid. The man tumbled heavily to the ground and a panting Svein looked thankfully at his rescuer.

The head priest in the heathen temple grew anxious after a while when he saw the thralls' attack slacking off and gradually stopping. They hadn't been trained to use weapons, so they were swinging them too hard and tiring themselves out. Those with axes were doing best. He saw Holme charge ahead like a wild man, bloody and torn, but the thralls didn't know enough to follow him and kept scattering more and more instead. The shouts of the Christian priests and the chieftain had the ring of victory to them, and someone soon started clanging the church bell. The thralls, confused and surprised, watched it out of the corners of their eyes as they were being driven back toward the heathen temple.

The heathen priest quickly gathered the temple attendants around him and told them his plan. If it didn't work, they'd soon all be dead. The Christians wouldn't show any of the mercy they boasted so much about if they were victorious.

The group of priests and temple attendants was soon sneaking out a back way and hurrying along the wall and past the courtyard to come out behind the Christians' quarters. Some men came running from the edge of the town to join them. From inside the Christian church came the gentle hum of female voices singing. Following the heathen priest's directions, about half the assailants sneaked to each side of the church, then with a wild howl, jumped the Christians. The archers were the closest but didn't have time to use their bows; they had to throw them down and draw their swords instead.

The retreating thralls took heart when they saw what was happening. Holme, Svein, the free thrall, and some others were still fighting in the courtyard, and now they got some relief. The heathen merchants, seeing the battle going against the Christians, took part now, too. One after another of the Christians turned and fled past the heathen priest toward the church. The chieftain yelled angrily at them to hold their ground, but to no avail.

After a while, the courtyard was in the hands of the thralls, and the Christians stood crammed together in and around their church. The warriors' ranks had thinned, but those still there were ready to fight on. But even the thralls had had enough, so the battle stopped. There were no taunting yells now; the wounded crawled toward their people for care and protection.

The heathen priests were disappointed that the fighting had stopped without the Christians being killed and their church destroyed. They tried to incite their people to attack again but the lust for battle was gone. The heathen merchants were satisfied with the Christians' being driven back despite all the talk about their god. The wooden gods stood victorious in their hall, showing that they too were not to be taken lightly.

An old priest came up to Holme and put an herb dressing on his wounded shoulder. The sword wound wasn't too deep, but he had lost a lot of blood. The Christians looked on from across the courtyard. They hadn't managed this time either to take this dangerous man's life, despite their trickery.

The heathens had won the battle, but the victory was small. Holme had wanted the fight to be for the good of the thralls, but instead it was they who had fought for the wooden gods. That's how it was, no matter how you looked at it. They had fought well, but it didn't mean anything would change for the better for them. And even so, the time should be right now, when not so many warriors were there to overpower the thralls.

He gave a hard look at the heathen merchants who had waited until they saw which way the battle would turn before taking part. They were the ones who profited from the victory. The thralls never won—whenever they worked or fought, it was for others. He was gripped by a rage greater than what he felt during the fight, and when a couple of the heathen merchants approached him smiling, he turned his back on them and walked in among the thralls.

Holme thought the heathen priests had shown greater courage than the merchants. And after the battle, they were friendly to the thralls, saw to their wounds, and gave them meat, bread, and beer—probably because they were glad that the Christians had been driven back. Had the Christians been victorious, the heathen priests and he would have been the first to be killed.

Then he saw one of the heathen priests, a scornful smile on his face, walk out into the courtyard and dip a branch into the blood of a Christian who had fallen in battle. The Christians let out angry shouts when he walked up to the wooden god and smeared it with the blood. He went back to dip the branch again, but an arrow came flying at him and he jumped quickly out of its way, raised his fist at the Christians, and ran back into the hall. There were shouts and rattling weapons on both sides, and it looked for a moment as though the battle would begin all over again.

Yet again, Holme was surrounded by thralls with their weapons and their rags. They looked happy about the victory; maybe they thought it could mean better things for them. Several had come to him, childishly but proudly telling him what they had done during the fight. He had a feeling that he himself had fought worse than ever before, but it wasn't clear to him why. But when the thralls' fight came one day, it would be different.

Svein and the free thrall stood beside him, and he praised them both. Their eyes began gleaming with happiness, and they talked about what they'd do if the battle began again. And Holme thought about those times when he had to fight alone. Now, though, many pairs of eyes looked at him with confidence, many weapons would be raised at his word.

The christian priests had watched the battle from the church steps, the women singing behind them. When the battle turned against them, they said it was because so many of them must be just nominal Christians. They secretly sacrificed to their wooden gods and made promises to them. But Christ, who saw into the heart, had allowed this setback to come to pass as a warning and punishment.

But the chieftain, who was a warrior, said that the setback was because of Holme. He had armed the thralls and led them. Without him, they could have been driven off like a flock of sheep. The heathen merchants would probably have given up without the thralls' help, and the priests then could have been overcome and killed. It was Holme alone who stood between the Christians and ultimate victory. With him gone, the setback would soon be reversed.

The chieftain withdrew with the priests into the church to discuss a new way to relieve the thralls' leader and protector of his life. Some day they were going to find him alone and unarmed. Or maybe there was a weapon he wouldn't know how to defend himself against. And the three men started whispering, their heads thrust forward.

A while later, two women came running across the courtyard toward the heathen temple. They were panting and said they were tired of the Christians, who hadn't brought their husbands back to them as they had promised. They wanted to return to the gods who had shown themselves to be the strongest in battle. They were eager to serve those in the temple in whatever way they could.

One of them was young and beautiful, but the other was older and hid her face in her kerchief. Svein watched her attentively as she followed the priests and the young woman into the temple. That the younger woman could serve the gods as women usually did in the temple, that he understood, but what could the older woman do? Well, that wasn't his concern and besides, there was a need for such women to wait on the men.

The heathen priests were elated about their success and weren't sparing with the beer. They invited Holme and those around him into the temple, and he walked in after posting a strong guard. The Christians had done the same. They probably wouldn't attack but would wait instead to see what was going to happen. Many of their women were standing outside the church now, looking toward the temple. A number of them might want to walk across the courtyard in order to serve the gods. The fertility god was standing at the front of the temple now, smiling, his organ jutting into the air.

The two women were already at work waiting on the men. The older one poured beer while the younger one served it. She smiled when they grabbed her, having completely forgotten her promises to the pure and cold Christ.

The older one kept her back to the temple entrance for the most part but stole an occasional glance under her kerchief. She started breathing more heavily when Holme came in, then busied herself a moment with a pitcher of beer. When the younger woman came back, she whispered something to her and gestured meaningfully.

Holme was the first to get some beer, then sat on a bench fastened to the wall, followed by a timid look from the woman. She came right back with beer for Svein and the free thrall who sat beside him. The thrall was still happy and suggested that they should drink to the thralls' victory and freedom.

Over the top of his tankard, the thrall saw the older woman sneaking a look back at him from under her kerchief. A wild and evil delight was flashing from her eyes as she stared at Holme, and then the thrall recognized her. He dropped his tankard to the floor, and Holme lowered his in surprise, wondering if his friend had had enough.

The thrall, speechless with terror, got up and pointed at the woman. He had drowned her, but there she stood. Holme remembered at once what had happened and understood the thrall's terror. He pulled him down on the bench and told him that she must have swum ashore or been rescued. That wasn't a dead woman he was looking at.

Many of the people standing there had followed the events and heard what Holme had said. They began staring at the older woman and noticed that she fumbled around more and more, and that her hands were shaking. The young woman was still walking around among the men, but her smile had become rigid and her hands shook too as she handed out the tankards of beer.

Holme had finally become suspicious as well. A couple of women couldn't do much harm, of course, but the Christians certainly had sent them to find out something about the heathens' plans. When the head priest came over to him, he suggested that the women should be gotten out of the temple.

The older woman thought that this might mean her life. So she took off toward the door, her clothes flapping, screaming triumphantly that Holme would soon be a dead man. What many men couldn't do, she had done alone.

Everyone was surprised at her words, but in the beginning no one understood what they meant. The woman fluttered through the hall and out into the courtyard. The younger woman tried to follow her but was seized by the thralls.

She was panting. Her terror-filled eyes were directed at Holme, and she said something about their making her do it.

The head priest questioned her while Holme stood by silently. She told him that the Christian priests and the chieftain had decided to poison Holme's beer. The older woman owned both him and his family; they had done her great harm, and she would gladly volunteer to walk to the heathen temple with the poison if she could have a younger woman to go with her.

Everyone stared in horror at Holme, and the free thrall in a rage lifted his hand against the woman. But Holme stopped him, showing his tankard. He had taken only one swallow before the thrall had dropped his tankard. It surely couldn't be enough to kill him. The thrall, Svein, and the others were jubilant. The priests smiled, too, and one of them hurried after an antidote.

The older woman had escaped, but the younger one was still there, quivering with fear in the thralls' hard grip. The head priest said that Holme should determine her fate, but he shook his head and walked away. He dumped the beer in a corner of the downtrodden dirt floor and a trickle ran out into the open. He felt a little sick and drank quickly from the tankard with the antidote in it that the priest handed him.

Meanwhile, the head priest wondered what to do with the young woman. He could see that many of the thralls were eyeing her lustfully and decided to hand her over to them. But on the condition that they take her on the fertility god's altar. The thralls slipped happily away with her, and she had an expression of relief on her face when she heard she'd be permitted to live.

For a long time, Holme sat with a severely contorted face and his hands clutching his stomach. The priest skilled in medicine didn't stop urging him to drink more beer. Svein and the thralls crowded in around him, anxiously watching his face. Svein looked away toward Freyr's Hall a few times, imagining what the thralls were doing to the woman, and that made his body tingle with excitement. He didn't want her, but he did want to watch.

The free thrall stuck close to Holme. He reproached himself bitterly for not having made sure that the witch had really drowned. Next time, he would see to it that she wouldn't cause any more trouble. Holme smiled weakly and looked at Svein standing beside him, but Svein didn't seem to care much about what happened or could happen to his mother.

The chieftain and Christian priests listened gleefully to what Svein's mother had to say. She had seen the dangerous man drinking the poisoned beer, so he would surely be dead soon. Without him the pack of thralls would be easily defeated. The warriors could see to that all by themselves.

They looked across the courtyard for a while, hoping the younger woman could manage to escape, too, but time passed and there was no sign of her. She was probably dead. The priests prayed for her soul not knowing that it was her body just then finding itself in the most peril. And they never found out that she stayed in the heathen temple of her own free will after she had taken her punishment and the men had grown tired.

Svein's mother was finally seeing her moment of justice and revenge approaching. Her son was still with the heathens, but that didn't bother her—he would probably come home to the settlement once the battle was over and the Christians had won. Out there, they could cleave to whatever gods they wanted to. But first, with the help of the Christians, she would get the smith's wife and daughter. They were going to find out that their protector was no longer there.

She could see and feel the mood brightening among the Christians. The heathens had posted a guard and withdrawn into the temple—something had to be happening inside. Almost all of the heathen merchants had gone home and surely wouldn't get involved in another fight. They had shown how fickle they were the last time. True, more and more thralls kept streaming to the temple, but what could they do without their leader? There probably weren't any weapons for them either. Their axes and clubs didn't amount to much against arrows, spears, and swords.

Far to the front above the altar, Christ hung on a cross. His head was bowed submissively, and he didn't seem to care about the battle. The warriors, who occasionally looked curiously into the church, were contemptuous of him, but some of the women looked at him with tears in their eyes. All the warriors saw was a defeated wooden god, but maybe the women felt something else for him.

The chieftain had known that Holme hadn't fought for the wooden god, but for the thralls. The strange notion that the thralls should be free men and women would disappear with him and would never be allowed to rise again. If it survived its originator, it would be struck down.

Bodies lay in the courtyard, and the chieftain gave an order for them to be carried into the church. But they should be careful not to take in a heathen along with them. The Christians laid their dead unburned in a graveyard some distance away from that of the heathens. They were buried with their faces pointing east, the direction from which Christ would be coming to awaken them. Heathens always cremated their dead, but gave them food and drink nonetheless for the journey through the land of death.

The chieftain had kept careful track of everyone leaving the heathen temple. There were only a few craftsmen and merchants left now, apart from the thralls. Their number grew constantly, but their leader had to be dead. A big, smiling thrall had fought fiercely by his side, but he probably couldn't take Holme's place and lead the others in battle.

They would wait for nightfall and see what would be best to do; the heathens would probably have a feast and make offerings to their gods for the victory, despite their losing their leader. After they had drunk a lot of beer, they would fall asleep and forget all about keeping watch.

A fleet of dragon ships, their unfamiliar sails furled, came gliding through the archipelago. It approached from the east, since a king there had heard that the wealthy town's ships and armies had left. There couldn't be many warriors left to defend the town. And as far as the king knew, no one had plundered it for many years. He had turned his ships around and sailed day and night with the dragon heads gaping toward the west.

He had known for a long time that the fortress was nearly impregnable. But if they could approach the defense works from another direction, they could surprise the handful of defenders.

The king was a Christian and had priests on every ship. They had assured him that Christ was with them in attacking the town where inhabitants still stubbornly clung to their ancient wooden gods. A number of Christians had lost their lives there, and their blood had been smeared on the terrible wooden idols. That abomination had to be stopped and the king should stop it while relieving the town's merchants of their silver and gold at the same time. Christ had brought them a favorable wind, and the water foamed around the bows.

The king knew the channel well, and he found to his surprise that the fire wasn't burning on the rocks near the fortress. Someone might have been there before him. Or the inhabitants might not fear any danger because summer was coming to an end and everyone had to be home harvesting crops. The fire might just have gone out for a short time, too, and could flame up again at any minute.

He had his men lower the sails and row carefully in on the far side of the island. They couldn't land there, but his warriors could wade quietly through meter-deep water. The town was well protected on the harbor side.

The raiders carried various objects with them from their ship—things that could help them get past the fortifications. They were soon there without being noticed. Whispering to each other, they climbed over the wall between two watch towers. No one sounded the alarm—no shout, no horn blast, nor church bell ringing. The town was quiet, except for the murmuring from the temple, and a veil of smoke rose toward the reddish-blue night sky in the west.

One after another, the Danish Vikings appeared for a moment on top of the barricades, then disappeared inside. There were no guards in the towers, none on the gangways. Something must have happened for the town to be left so unguarded. The Vikings smiled in satisfaction, happy that Christ was with them. After awhile, they stood by the hundreds inside the barricades, checking their weapons one last time.

A couple of merchants who lived nearby were on their way home, content with the day's events. The Christians had been defeated without it costing much in either blood or silver. Mostly thralls had fought and mostly thralls had fallen. That was good. No one had thought before that thralls could be used for fighting, not just for working. Now it would be nice to live in peace and quiet for a while. A king would soon be chosen, and they hoped he'd stay home and build up trade with the large kingdoms to the south.

The two merchants heard strange sounds from the craftsmen's side of town for a moment without thinking much about it. But a figure suddenly popped up on the barricades and disappeared again. No normal figure — silhouetted by the moon, which had just come up behind him, he had horns on his helmet like a bull. They whispered a few terrified words to each other and ran back toward the temple. This was going to be much more serious than the day's battle between Christians and heathens.

In the middle of the courtyard between the Christian church and the heathen temple, the merchants stood panting, yelling out the bad news. Men rushed out from both sides to hear what was happening. Some of the thralls reeled merrily about, not really grasping the problem, but the Christian chieftain walked quickly to his warriors and started organizing them for battle. They looked immediately more alive and pleased than before. They'd finally get to do their duty, something worthy of them — defend the town against invading Vikings. They had taken part in the fight with the thralls only out of necessity.

The chieftain was angry at himself for not having thought of this. The town's helplessness had to be known out on the high seas, so he should have foreseen what was happening now. He could only hope that it was a small fleet of pirates they could handle. And that the thralls and other heathens didn't throw in with the enemies. That had to be prevented.

So the chieftain ran into the middle of the courtyard. In a thundering voice he roared out the news and said that they all had to fight for the town. Otherwise, every man would undoubtedly be killed and their women raped. They knew well enough what would happen. It made no difference whether the raiders were Christian or heathen.

The heathen priests saw that the chieftain was right. Everyone's life was at stake here, Christian or not. The invaders surely wouldn't find the valuables that could be brought together in the town a sufficient ransom. So they had to fight side by side with the Christians.

Holme still wasn't himself, but he followed everything being shouted in the courtyard and hall. And the head priest soon panted up to him to explain how things had suddenly changed. For now, they had to fight; afterwards, they could settle accounts with the Christians in town.

As Holme followed him out he heard him whisper a promise of great sacrifices to the battle god if he helped them out of this fix. Dark-red Christian blood was still dripping down from the god. Outside in the courtyard, the chieftain was arranging his warriors the way he wanted them. He said they would wait for the enemy up here so they could take advantage of the slope. And if the enemy won, they had the fortified walkway to the fortress to escape through. They were closer to the gods here, too, both to Christ and to the terrible idols in the temple.

A gasp of surprise rippled through the Christian ranks when Holme stepped forth from behind the gods. The chieftain's words stuck in his throat, and his mouth hung open. But he quickly recovered himself and repeated that everyone had to fight those who had already gotten into town. He added that the thralls would not go unrewarded if they performed well. They had recently shown they could handle weapons.

Holme thought briefly about what he had been singled out for by the Christians just moments before. That was probably the reward thralls always would get. But he'd remember the chieftain's words and remind him of them after the fight. He would suggest the only proper payment—they should set the thralls free, or at least treat them well. He would also refresh their memories about how the fallen king had treated his thralls.

But first they had to defeat the enemy. If the invaders won, they'd plunder the town, kill the men, and maybe set all ablaze before moving on. Then they'd probably head for the king's farmstead. And that meant Ausi and Tora.

With that thought, Holme knew the thralls had to fight. They were already crowding around, looking at him expectantly. The chieftain observed all this from the courtyard with intense interest, maybe even anxiety. Without Holme and the thralls, or with them at their back, the Christians had no hope of defending themselves or the town.

The invaders seemed to know where the town's defenders were. A strange bull head appeared for a moment around a street corner, and an indistinct murmuring arose from down in the town. They could hear light openings being carefully opened and slammed shut by lone, frightened women. Holme thought it best to charge down the slope and attack before the enemy had a chance to regroup, but the chieftain would decide that. He was hurrying the women and children onto the pathway leading into the fortress.

But the enemy had no desire to wait. All at once, they swarmed howling and roaring up the slope. The Christian archers let their arrows fly, but there were far too few arrows to stop them. The chieftain's warriors stood like a wall against the enemy, and the street was too narrow for the attackers to force the defenders into the open courtyard. Swords flashed and clanged. The warriors seemed to launch immediately into a battle frenzy that they hadn't mustered against the thralls a few hours earlier.

To his joy, the chieftain thought they would manage to beat the attackers back. The thralls stood behind them in reserve and hadn't been needed and couldn't even take part in the battle. But things soon changed. A strong troop of invaders, who couldn't find room in the street, had gone around and now came rushing in from the other side.

Then the chieftain saw something in the midst of battle that struck him with surprise. The thralls' leader had seen the turn of events at least as quickly as he had. With a yell, he summoned the thralls and charged the new attackers. The chieftain could almost see the enemy's astonishment when they met. A

ragged, wild band with axes, swords, and clubs. Many of them were laughing and
unsteady on their feet. The chieftain couldn't follow the thralls' battle any more,
but he saw a constant stream of them rush from the temple and cast themselves
into the fray.

When Holme saw the invaders coming to attack from the rear, he knew how
great the danger was. And before he even had time to think, he had the thralls
with him charging against them.

But he could soon see that their adversaries were powerful. As soon as the
bulls recovered from their surprise, they began coldly and contemptuously hacking down the impassioned thralls. They parried the thralls' blows skillfully and
responded instantly, with dire consequences.

Holme saw his drunken companions fall bleeding on both sides of him. He
was gripped by despair and rage over their helplessness against the well-trained,
experienced enemy. Followed by Svein and the free thrall, he plowed ahead,
hacking away with his huge ax. The invaders began leaping out of the way of this
raging giant, having soon perceived that parrying did no good here. His reach
exceeded theirs, and the power in his blows made their weapons fly from their
hands. Some of the thralls regained their courage and together with Svein and
the free thrall shielded his flanks. Holme was no longer thinking about what he
was up against; he only wanted revenge on those who were killing the thralls.
More thralls rushed to his aid from the temple than those who fell, and the
enemy was slowly pushed back. A few of them could see that it was the raging
leader who gave the others courage. If he fell, the others would soon take flight.
But no one could take him from the front, and his companions protected him
on all sides.

Seeing the troop of thralls continuing to swell, the horned invaders began to
lose courage. Several of their own lay on the ground, dead or wounded by blows
from the thralls, and they began to see that victory was not certain. It was better
to flee from thralls than to fall from their blows. One after another sneaked away
from the hind ranks to run for the boats. Holme saw this and burst forward with
renewed rage. But the whole time he could feel his wounded shoulder holding
him back.

More and more enemies fled in a lumbering gait down the slope to escape
over the barricades to the safety of their ships. The thralls' howling became triumphant and their attack more wild. Their side of the courtyard was soon empty,
and the hunt raged down the slope. The last opponents to have held their ground
were fleeing now, and the thralls chased them to the edge of town. Some stopped
to relieve the fallen invaders of their weapons, clothes, and jewelry. The battle
god watched it all with a grin from his hall, his fire still burning. Some priests
who had taken part in the chase came back to the temple, panting and smiling.

Meanwhile, the main body of the invaders had pushed the town warriors
back a good distance, but they couldn't help seeing what was happening to their

comrades on the other side. They were afraid that they, too, would be attacked from the rear and withdrew as they fought. One after another broke ranks and ran for the edge of town and the ships. The Christian chieftain knew that the town had been saved and hoped that Holme, with his thralls, would know enough to stop the retreat.

But even if that was Holme's thought, he couldn't make himself heard any longer. The thralls had gone wild with success, and many of them clambered rashly over the barricades to chase the invaders on the other side. But the enemy was waiting with weapons ready, and it was an easy matter for them to skewer the thralls who came jumping or clambering down after them.

Holme could hear from the outside what was happening, but couldn't do anything about it. Nearby stood a watch tower with a gate, and he grabbed the men closest to him and rushed over there. The guard wasn't there, but they hacked at the gate with their axes and soon broke through it. Followed by some thralls, Holme rushed out. The enemy who saw the thralls' huge leader coming didn't dare wait for him but ran toward the shore instead. Below the barricades lay some wounded thralls, writhing in agony, and Holme stopped. He thought fleetingly that with more experience in battle, they would never have chased the enemy over the barricade. Many thralls were going to have to pay for the day's victory with their blood.

There was tumult again, as the main body of the enemy rolled out through the shattered gate. The town warriors were tight on their heels and Holme thought he should probably join in the chase. But that could cost more thrall blood. They had done their part in defending the town. Now the warriors would have to do what remained to be done.

Holme picked up a wounded thrall in his arms and headed toward the temple and the priests, who knew something about medicine. The others followed his example, and soon there were no thralls left at the barricades. Only a few dead remained, lying still in their blood and rags. All along the road to the temple lay the enemy dead or wounded. The thralls plundered them, hitting them in the head with clubs if they resisted. Holme watched them but said nothing. They had as much right to the enemies' possessions as the warriors did, and they needed them much more.

From the shore came shouts and the sounds of battle. The head priest smiled at Holme, pleased that he had not stayed with the chase all the way to the ships. Still more Christians would be felled by the retreating enemy, and that was good. He had noticed that the attackers were Christians, too, and they could just as well kill each other while their god sat indifferently in their church, his head hanging.

As the invaders fled, the old Christian chieftain himself led the chase. After a tough skirmish on the shore, they managed to capture two of the ships while the others were being manned and rowed out. There were many dead and wounded from both sides lying on the shore and in the water.

At first it annoyed the chieftain that Holme and his thralls weren't there for the end of the battle, but that didn't bother him after a while. Victory belonged to the Christians, now. They knew inside that they would have been lost without the thralls, but probably no one but the thralls' leader comprehended that.

The priests, who had watched the last battle from a distance, came up to the chieftain. It was clear to them Christ had a hand in the enemies' attack. What would happen now was unclear, but it would soon be revealed. Everyone, though, had seen how He even used thralls for His purposes. And His worst enemy, the leader of the thralls, had fought for His sake.

But all three thought with mortification about the same thing. Everything would have been so easy if the thralls' leader had fallen in the battle. But he lived, and he'd surely demand payment for what the thralls had done. And the thralls were strong enough to take up the fight from the temple yet again. They might get help as well from the main temple inland. The Christians knew that a message had been sent there.

The chieftain thought, too, that there was no longer any order in town. An outlaw thrall had led his fellows into battle. Such a thing had never happened before and there must be an end to it. The king was dead, so he was responsible for everything. A king would be chosen, but he had to be a Christian. The band of thralls had to be struck down before there was a vote.

As they walked up toward town, past fallen and plundered enemies, he talked with the priests. He knew that their way was the right one when they said they had to proceed with trickery. The heathens had proven too strong to strike down after they had accepted help from the thralls. Now the thralls had to be gotten rid of, and that would be an easy matter with their leader out of the way.

That said, the three Christians looked at each other. The poison hadn't affected Holme; maybe it was Christ's will that he should die violently because of the violent man he was.

And they decided that that was how it was going to be. For now, they would go along with his demands to lull him into a sense of security. The right time would come later.

The wounded were still being carried across the courtyard to both temples. They saw a priest put a poultice on Holme's shoulder and exchanged a look of satisfaction. He had been wounded and that was a good sign. They were on the right track.

A hundred thralls were standing around him, many of them wounded. When the chieftain and the priests entered the courtyard, the thralls turned toward them, and a sea of clear, childish, demanding looks washed over the chieftain. In the middle were Holme's watchful dark eyes, the hundreds of others surrounding him. The chieftain felt uneasy. What did they want from him? They had defended the town, but that was everyone's duty. Given enough warriors, he would have commanded them to drive that ragged pack from town.

The priests sensed his anger and encouraged him to have patience. There had been enough fighting; they shouldn't provoke the children of the wooden gods again. He should pretend to accept their conditions for Christ's sake. Christ would then give them into the Christians' hands.

They walked into the church to say a short prayer of thanksgiving. Across the courtyard the battle god grinned contentedly at being smeared anew with enemy blood. The thralls got more meat and beer while Holme thought silently about what he should do. The Christian chieftain would surely not go along with his idea. There was probably nothing left to do but fight yet again. All too many thralls had fallen—those who were living had to have recompense of some kind for them.

But a short while later, the chieftain was standing in the courtyard speaking. His voice was friendly and he was praising the thralls' fighting. It would not go unrewarded. For now, though, they should all keep the peace and look after the wounded on both sides. They could reach an agreement later. Those who wanted to go home could do so quietly. He wanted Holme's and the head priest's word that they wouldn't violate the peace. He was giving his.

Holme was surprised at the mild tone and reasonable words. Would they finally win something without further fighting? The head priest gave him a look of secret, mutual understanding. It meant that they knew how to make promises—but then what?

As evening approached, he decided to go to the king's farmstead for Ausi and Tora. They were probably living in dread, and it could be fun for them to visit town. He smiled at Svein's beaming look as Holme went on his way.

The head priest followed him to the edge of the courtyard and urged him to return soon. The Christians couldn't be trusted. Holme should be back early the next morning.

But many of the Christians had left the church and gone home, too. They surely weren't thinking of attacking again. They had many dead and wounded, maybe more than the heathens had.

On the other side, they tensely watched Holme leave and some hasty orders were given. Some pairs of eyes showed hesitation or terror, but finally obedience. Then several pairs of feet went running into the distance.

Dim light, flickering, fading. A shout in the distance. A memory trying to force its way to the surface and take shape.

Eventually he could hear leaves rustling in the wind and could slowly turn his head. The grass was thick in front of his face. He was on the ground, unable to get up.

After a while, he tried again and managed to roll on one side. Something stuck up out of the long blades of grass in front of him. An arm and a hand. Someone was next to him.

Ill-defined images came and went just as the light had. There was danger nearby. He strained again and got onto his hands and knees. Then he could see the whole man lying there motionless, ashen faced. He saw a pool of blood on the ground around him, still flowing from him. But he felt nothing.

He looked around from his huddled position. Was it night? In the distance the sky was red, but it hurt to look at it. He saw another man lying in the grass behind him, and a little to one side, another. Not one of them moved. Maybe they were sleeping like he had been.

He started crawling away from them through the grass. He didn't know how far he had crawled before there was another man in his path. But this man's eyes were open, and he moved. Holme had a feeling that this was the danger he had sensed. And he started crawling straight for the man.

When the wounded man saw the bloody smith crawling toward him, his eyes gaped with terror. With great effort he rolled one turn away, but his pursuer crawled after him. He managed another full turn and then half. His face was to the ground when the iron fingers clenched his neck. A moment later, he was as peaceful as the other three.

After a while, Holme crawled on. He tried getting to his feet several times, but fell down every time. Soon he saw a stone in front of him, a stone that stood among the burial mounds. It was taller than a man and he had seen it before. He clutched it, steadied himself, and managed to get up. For a long time he stood with his arms around the stone, feeling its coolness on his forehead. A fresh breeze caressed his hands on the other side of the stone.

He was headed someplace but didn't know where. The stone almost told him, but then the secret disappeared again. After a moment he could look around. The burial mounds appeared out of the darkness of the night, one after the other. Then they started rocking and turning on top of each other, and he leaned his head against the cool stone again. And after a moment, he knew where he was going. The cave opening that he wanted to crawl into. Inside, on the moss and the twigs, was deliverance.

After a while he could let go of the stone. He took a few steps, but the ground rose quickly before him, and he fell against the side of the mound. He kept crawling over a few mounds, up and down. Beyond a clump of trees on the shore the black water glistened. That's where he was headed.

He got to his feet again by the clump of trees. The trees were dense; he went from trunk to trunk, guiding himself down to the boat. It took a long time to get it away from shore, and he felt the water rising up his legs. Finally he sat by the oars, but his body burned like fire with every pull. He saw the mainland forest in jagged silhouette against the sky. He had to get there.

He rowed, his blood running off the seat and coloring the bilge water. He didn't notice. Once Ausi and Tora appeared to him, but they soon vanished. It was the cave that would save him.

The reeds were sparse and the water shallow where he reached the mainland. He toppled out of the boat and felt the cool, soothing water. He lay there a while and then crawled to shore. The boat stayed where he left it and would probably drift away, but he didn't have the strength even to think about that.

An older man, who was going out night-fishing, had watched the in-coming boat for a moment. As the huge figure crawled splashing to land, got up, fell, and got up again, the old man's hair and beard stood up, too. With a whimper, he scampered away along the shore on his skinny legs. Holme hadn't seen him. He was following something that relentlessly guided him to his goal.

The chieftain and the Christian priests waited impatiently for the four warriors to return. But the night passed, and there was no sign of them. Across the courtyard, a sacrificial feast was in progress, but all the while the heathens kept a watch outside the hall.

Toward morning, the chieftain and one of the priests, with a couple of warriors for protection, went to find out what was going on. They walked in the direction where something had to have happened. They soon found a figure lying still, face down. The warriors were angry when they saw that he was one of their own men.

The other three were not far away. But the one they longed to see wasn't there. The chieftain and the priest looked at each other in silent horror. Was there nothing that could be done against that thrall? He had to be Satan himself.

They soon found the trail of blood and followed it. Maybe he had received a fatal wound in the fight after all. The blood extended all the way to the pebbles on the shore. He must have had the strength to row, even though masses of his blood had been spilled on the ground.

The Christians turned back and began praying in their hearts that their enemy might die from his wounds. Maybe they should send boats out to look for him. He must have rowed home to the king's farmstead.

But when the chieftain and the priests talked with the warriors about that, they grimly shook their heads. They walked out instead after their dead companions. Two of them had been cut down by an ax; the other two had been crushed or beaten to death at the thrall's hand.

Before the altar, the priests prayed for their god to search out and destroy the evil creature wherever he might be. Humans were powerless against him. They also asked Christ to receive the souls of the four warriors. He should destroy the heathens across from them who wouldn't be baptized, too. As Christ knew, this land alone in the north wouldn't relinquish its heathen gods. Stubbornly and ruthlessly, they held fast to the bloody wooden idols.

Then the chieftain and priests decided to wait and see what happened. As long as the heathens didn't know about Holme, there was no danger. They would undoubtedly wait days for his return.

Svein had no peace while Holme was away. He didn't drink beer like the others, but several times he walked out and looked in a certain direction. He tried to sleep once, but the bench was hard, and the thralls were making noise around him.

At daybreak, he was out again. He was going to walk to the shore this time to look across the lake. Maybe Holme was already rowing back in the dawn with his wife and daughter. He heard some people coming toward him and hid quickly in a thicket. It wasn't so certain that peace reigned outside the temple, if they were Christians who were coming.

What he saw made him wonder at first if a battle raged on another part of the island. Several warriors came up the path carrying their dead comrades. One, two, three, four. Austerely they looked straight ahead, no one saying a word. When their steps had died away, Svein walked on.

Only upon reaching the shore did it occur to him what must have happened. He saw the trail of blood and a pair of large footprints that he knew well. He was filled with pride and joy. Four warriors had lain in wait, but Holme had killed all of them and could still continue on his way. There was a lot of blood, but he would surely be all right, just like always.

He ran back and reported everything to the heathen priests. The free thrall flew into a rage and wanted immediate revenge, but the priests calmed him down. They had to look for Holme first and find out if he was all right.

Svein immediately offered to go and took a couple of strong thralls with him to row the boat. The free thrall had to stay to take Holme's place if the Christians decided to attack. He was satisfied with that, shook his ax, and leered threateningly at the Christian church.

Ausi saw the boat in the distance. She had almost expected it; something had kept her awake all night. She felt that something was imminent, something conclusive. Maybe the end of life.

She woke Tora, and they walked to the shore. Tora, not noticing her anxiety, waited with curiosity. She soon saw, to her disappointment, that her father wasn't in the boat. But then her eyes started sparkling, and she avoided her mother's glance.

A few boat lengths from land, Svein yelled out to ask how Holme was. Mother and daughter looked with silent terror at each other; it was as if a hand had ripped at their hearts and they couldn't speak. Meanwhile, the boat landed and Svein hurried up to them. He saw at once that they knew nothing about Holme.

The women stepped silently into the boat, and the men rowed back without a word. A light-opening opened in the king's house and someone watched them go.

Ausi already knew more than anyone else, and she wasn't thinking much about Holme now. But she looked at Tora and noticed Svein, who kept looking at the girl's bowed head the whole time. His eyes were good and honest; he would surely protect her. Besides, she could protect herself better than any other woman. She was courageous, impetuous, and strong. Her father's love for freedom lived in her, and she could never be a thrall to anyone.

Svein said something about Holme's possibly returning to town, but Ausi shook her head and pointed toward the mainland forest. After some hesitation, Svein motioned for the oarsmen to row there. A calm strength streamed from Ausi, and he felt that he must do as she said. She stared constantly in one direction and seemed to have forgotten about everyone else in the boat.

When she stepped ashore, she looked at Tora and Svein for a moment. But they had said they would follow her wherever she went. When she saw that in their eyes, she walked toward the forest, and they followed her at a little distance. The oarsmen watched them and then rowed off toward town: they were curious about what was going on back there, and they were also longing for the good, strong beer.

The three of them walked nearly all day. Sometimes they would stop, and Tora looked wonderingly at her mother. Her face seemed normal; she was just more beautiful and somehow distant from them. She seemed to be listening for something and had no peace.

Svein took Tora's hand as often as he dared, and she let him hold it. A couple of times he also got a friendly, searching look and a smile. His heart was full of that singular happiness, and he didn't think at all about Holme.

In the sunset, they saw the ridge were the cave was. Svein didn't know about the cave, and he looked in surprise at the dark opening. Outside lay several things, thrown from the cave—a sledgehammer, an ax, a hammer, tongs, drill bits, a saw, and a scythe.

Ausi signalled for the young people to stop, then got down on her knees and crawled into the cave. They heard her talking and whispering tenderly inside, so they sat down on the mossy boulder outside and waited hand in hand.

When she came out she said quietly that Holme was in there, and that no one would ever see him outside the cave again. She would stay with him. She was his wife and had a right to do that.

Tora and Svein looked at her in silence. They could hear and see that talking would do no good. Ausi's face was radiant and clear, but she looked at them as if from a great distance. She said, too, that Holme had thrown the tools out so they could be of use to someone else. That's how he'd always been.

They should go on now and not worry about her. If they wanted to close up the cave with stones afterwards, that would be good. Otherwise, wild animals would find their way in.

And the young people soon walked on. Tora didn't cry, but she kept turning around. Her mother, stately and beautiful, stood on the ridge watching them.

Tora knew that she would never see either of her parents again, but she walked calmly away. Svein's hand was numbed by her hard grip, and her tears fell quietly in the moss. He was thinking she was Holme's daughter, and he smiled proudly. For generations people would talk about Holme, his wife Ausi, and their daughter, who was Svein's woman.

When Ausi couldn't see them any more, she went back to the cave. She moved calmly and with dignity as she broke off branches to cover the opening a little until it could be shut up with stones again. She talked out loud into the cave as she did so.

When she was through, she looked around. She thought about the morning when Holme came running and dragged her with him to the cave after saving Tora from a wild animal's jaws. The memory of how much she had feared him made her smile. She hadn't known then that the silent and feared thrall was the finest man alive.

Thoughts swarmed inside her, but she couldn't let them out yet. She didn't want to make Holme wait too long. She dragged the branches within reach, looked around again, and crawled inside. The massive figure lay quiet and still inside, his face peaceful in the darkness. She lay down beside him, tenderly lifting his heavy, still head, and putting her supple arm under his neck. She ran her other hand over his body and soon found what she was looking for. The knife blade shone dully in the sparse light coming in through the cave opening. She didn't have to check to see if the knife was sharp. Holme never carried a tool or weapon that wasn't sharp and strong.

But she still had one more thing to do, the most important thing of all. She had to talk with Christ so that He would be prepared when she and Holme came to Him. She was certain that He would understand and receive them well. He could also see them here in the cave—something a wooden god surely never could have done. Holme hadn't had water poured on his head, and the priests said that without that a person couldn't reach Christ and have things good . . .

A thought made her carefully withdraw her arm and crawl out of the cave. She hurried along the slope to the spring, and a squirrel chattered angrily at her from the top of a spruce tree. She filled her hands with the cold spring water and returned to the cave. She crawled in carefully, raised her cupped hands over Holme's head, thought for a moment, and then said out loud, "Oh, Christ, now I baptize my husband in Your name so that he can follow along with me to You. He is much better than anyone else, more like You than Your priests are. We'll be coming soon." She thought a little more and added, "Better, except for the one You sent here first."

Satisfied and happy, she resumed her position, feeling the water on Holme's head moistening her arm. Everything was ready. There was plenty of time to talk with Christ about Tora once they got to Him. She was in good hands until then.

She had laid the knife on Holme's chest and now groped for it again. She wondered where Holme's fatal wound was—she'd like to stab herself in the same place. But she didn't want to change positions again, so instead moved only her upper body so she could get her arm and hand away from Holme's head. She aimed the knife and drove it in. The warmth gushed over her hand, and she smiled contentedly as she lay back down.

She realized that she had forgotten to pull the branches in front of the opening. Well, that did no harm; the young people would come back soon.

It got darker and darker in the cave, and soon she no longer had any feeling in her body. A pleasant fatigue engulfed her, and she wanted to fall asleep. But it soon passed, and the cave got lighter. The light intensified quickly, and she could see through the cave wall. Could it be Christ on His way to them?

It was early morning now, exactly like the first time. The stones on the slope bore light yellow stripes that faded away in the light around them. Butterflies fluttered about, and the water from the spring glistened brightly. There was still something alien about the scene, however, and she was a little frightened. She was still so alone.

At that instant, she saw Holme standing outside the cave. His face was peaceful, full of love, and younger than when he had fought in town. He looked warmly and tenderly at her, and she flew jubilantly into his arms. She felt herself enclosed by them, and then he carried her away over grass, flowers, and butterflies. She heard him say something about her needing to rest first. Then she would learn something very important and very pleasant.

After a couple of days had passed without Holme returning, the chieftain and priests began to hope that he had been fatally wounded. They also saw many signs of uneasiness among the heathens. They walked out often, looking across the water toward the king's farmstead and the mainland forest, and finally they sent messages to many places. The Christians saw the messengers return without success.

Svein's mother rejoiced with them, although she noticed uneasily that her son could no longer be seen at the heathen temple. She must be certain about his fate. And so she decided to go to the relatives' farmstead to look for him. The chieftain reluctantly gave her a couple of older men for help and protection on the journey.

She noticed from a distance that there were people at the farmstead. She was happy again, thinking that now she would return to town just once more, and then only to find out about Holme's wife and daughter. They were her thralls, and she would make sure they knew it.

The thought got her worked up, and she walked toward the new building without paying any attention to the men who were finishing up the work there. She didn't ask about her son but walked straight in through the door. From the hearth, she was met by a pair of surprised black eyes and she herself stopped in amazement when she realized it was the thrall's daughter. Svein's mother let loose an angry, triumphant hissing sound and rushed forward. Before Tora had time to react, she felt the older woman's hand in her hair.

But not for long. Svein's mother saw the dark eyes flash and felt a strong hand grab her wrist. When she felt the grip she remembered whose daughter it was in the midst of her rage. Her arm was twisted now so that her fingers lost their hold, and a sudden jerk cast her to the floor.

The men outside heard the racket but didn't have time to look in before the older woman came bounding out. Holme's daughter was chasing her, dancing a bundle of birch twigs off her back and head. They ran down the slope, the men laughing loudly and raucously as they went.

Tora returned soon, and the men praised her and talked about whose daughter she was. She was still furious, but that soon passed, and she smiled at the men, her white teeth glistening as she walked back into the house.

Just then, Svein came down out of the woods, and he saw a bowed figure on his father's burial mound. He stopped in surprise, but the men waved to him and laughingly told him what had just happened. They praised Holme's daughter and warned him kiddingly about provoking her.

He walked proudly and happily into the house but met a gaze that made him stop for a moment. The look asked angrily and proudly on whose side he was in this fight between the women. This was soon made clear to Holme's daughter. Svein stroked her hair with love, pride, and respect. For the first time she put her arms around him, and he lost his breath for a moment. She pressed against him, and he thought happily about a moment that would soon have to come. He also sensed that the look and those arms were like Holme's. Svein had to be either with her or against her. Although she was a woman, it could still be dangerous to be against her. The bowed figure on his father's burial mound witnessed to that. He knew that his mother's role had been played out, and he was glad.

A late summer cloud passed over the town on the island; the warring parties dispersed again without resolving the conflict, and the grinning wooden gods looked across at the Christian church. The Christian priests would flee this rugged land yet again, and what they called the heathen darkness would hover over it for a hundred years more.[12]

---

[12] The mission efforts of Ansgar and his successors are considered a mere episode, having little impact on Swedish history. Archbishop Unni of Hamburg renewed the mission in about 936 but likewise met with brief and questionable success. Unni died in Birka, perhaps by stoning, on September 17, 936, "the first precise date we know for domestic Swedish history" (Franklin D. Scott, *Sweden: The Nation's History* [Minneapolis: Univ. of Minnesota Press, 1977], p. 35). See also Ingvar Andersson, *A History of Sweden*, trans. Carolyn Hannay (New York: Praeger, 1956), p. 26.

Like two trails of blood, Christendom and the fight for freedom would proceed through the centuries side by side. The town would be destroyed, and for centuries, no one would know where it had been.[13] But the two trails that originated there have still not, a thousand years later, reached their destination.

---

[13] Birka essentially vanished at the end of the tenth century and was not rediscovered until the end of the seventeenth. See Björn Ambrosiani, *Birka on the Island of Björkö* (Stockholm: Central Board of National Antiquities, 1988).

AFTERWORD

They dominated most of the known world from the eighth to the eleventh centuries, earning themselves such descriptions as "wolves from the sea," devising such extraordinary barbarities as "the blood eagle," a particularly savage form of execution in which they cut the condemned man's ribs away from his spine and pulled his lungs out to form bloody wings on his back. Legend tells us that King Ella of Northumbria suffered this death at the hands of the Dane Ragnar Loðbrok in 867.[1] Other individuals, indeed whole cities, from Hamburg to Chartres to Dublin, likewise fell victim to the Viking raids. But while they had dire reputations as fierce pirates, the Vikings also created art and literature of rare force and beauty. They lost their piratical edge on the high seas with the advent of ships like the galley, hulk, and cog, which were much higher and less assailable in the water than the long ships, and for that and other reasons their way of life eventually died.[2] As they disappeared into history, however, the memory of their ferocity and the evidence of their literary and artistic skills retained their grip on the imagination of western Europe and America.

Their literature, austere, mysterious, "masculine" in the extreme, has been the main source of inspiration, particularly the Eddic and Scaldic poems, the Old Icelandic sagas, and Saxo Grammaticus's *Gesta Danorum*, together with the Old English poem *Beowulf*. In English and American literature we find Viking themes and stories manifesting themselves in, for example, the works of Thomas Gray (1716–71), Robert Southey (1774–1843), William Morris (1834–96), and J. R. R. Tolkien (1892–1973) on one side of the Atlantic, and in those of John Greenleaf Whittier (1807–92), Henry Wadsworth Longfellow (1807–82), Jack London (1876–1916), and Michael Crichton (1942–) on the other. In Scandinavian literature the Vikings understandably have a particularly strong foothold, their world appearing in a relatively unbroken line in works from such authors as Esaias Tegnér (1782–1846), Erik Gustaf Geijer (1783–1847), Adam

---

[1] Gwyn Jones, *A History of the Vikings*, revised ed. (Oxford: Oxford Univ. Press, 1984), p. 219.

[2] Magnus Magnusson, 'End of an Era,' *Scandinavian Review* 68, no. 3. (1980): 60. On the collapse of the Viking world, see Jones, *History of the Vikings*. Jones's is the standard history of the period.

Oehlenschläger (1779–1850), and Johan Ludwig Runeberg (1804–77) to Henrik
Ibsen (1828–1906), Frans G. Bengtsson (1894–1954), Vilhelm Moberg (1898–
1973), Halldór Laxness (1902–98), and Villy Sørensen (1929–2002).[3] The early
writers naturally engage in romanticizing and idealizing the Viking warrior,
turning him into a symbol of Scandinavian purity and strength, while later writers tend to take a much more sceptical, sometimes ironic, view. For Tegnér, the
Viking was a civilized, noble seafarer, but for Laxness, he was a grotesque parody
of a true hero.[4]

When Jan Fridegård (1897–1968), then, began writing about the Vikings,
he was working within an established tradition, even as he intended not to praise
the Vikings but to use them as a medium for social criticism.[5] His novel also fits
within a sub-group of that critical tradition, the group focused on Viking thralls.
Three Nobel Prize winners writing before Fridegård, for instance, the Dane Karl
Gjellerup (1857–1919), the Swede Selma Lagerlöf (1858–1940), and the Norwegian Sigrid Undset (1882–1949) treat thralls sympathetically; and strictly within
Swedish literature Fredrika Bremer (1801–65), Viktor Rydberg (1828–95),
Verner von Heidenstam (1859–1940), and Gustaf Fröding (1860–1911) all show
varying degrees of compassion for the Viking slave. Bremer does so in her play
about oppression and hatred, *The Slave Girl* (*Trälinnan*, 1840), Rydberg in his
attack on industrialism in his poem "The New Song of Grotti" ("Den nya Grot-
tesången," 1891), a reworking of the Old Norse *Grottasongr*, Heidenstam in his

---

[3] On the use of Viking motifs in European and North and South American literature, see Jöran Mjöberg, 'Romanticism and Revival' in David M. Wilson, ed. *The Northern World: The History and Heritage of Northern Europe AD 400–1100* (New York: Harry
N. Abrams, 1980), pp. 207–38. Mjöberg's *Drömmen om sagatiden*, 2 Vols. (Stockholm:
Natur och kultur, 1967–68) is the definitive work on the subject.

[4] See Tegnér's *Frithiof's Saga*, trans. Ida Mauch (New York: Exposition Press, 1960)
and Laxness's novel *The Happy Warriors* (*Gerpla*, 1952), trans. Katherine John (London:
Methuen, 1958). See also Runeberg's epic poem *King Fialar: A Poem in Five Songs* (*King
Fjalar*, 1844), trans. Eiríkr Magnússon (London: J. M. Dent & Sons, Ltd., 1912). And
for a classic Viking novel, see Bengtsson's justly famous *The Long Ships: A Saga of the
Viking Age* (*Röde Orm*, 1941, 1945), trans. Michael Meyer (1954; rpt. New York and London: Collins, 1986).

[5] Jan Fridegård (1897–1968) was born into a poor working-class family of seven
in Enköpings-Näs, an area in central Sweden just north of Lake Mälar. His father was
a *statare*, a farm laborer tied to a large estate and earning his wages partly in cash but
mostly in kind (stat). The brutal statare system, which arose in the eighteenth century to
support the aristocratic estates and survived until 1945, almost guaranteed illiteracy and
social immobility in its victims and has a pervasive role in Fridegård's work. Of his close
to thirty novels and his numerous short stories and essays, most are autobiographical,
depicting the lives of lower-class working people. See Robert E. Bjork, 'Jan Fridegård,'
Dictionary of Literary Biography 259 (2002): 60–68. The thralls in his viking trilogy seem
clearly to represent the oppressed statare.

mildly critical depiction of slavery in his novel about eleventh-century Sweden, *The Tree of the Folkungs* (*Folkungaträdet*, 1905, 1907), and Fröding in his radical reinterpretation of the Old Norse legend of Weyland in his poem "The Smith" ("Smeden," 1892), which I will discuss below. No one before Fridegård, however, concentrated so much interest on the Viking thralls and what he felt had to be their inevitable fight for freedom.[6]

Fridegård had little evidence for substantiating his portrayal of Viking slavery, just a brief study or two by some of his contemporaries, and so most of the story and much of the milieu in the Holme trilogy Fridegård created himself.[7] The backdrop for Fridegård's anti-ideal saga basically develops out of three different kinds of sources: archeological descriptions of the Viking period, such as a Norwegian museum catalogue and reports about excavation sites; cultural studies, such as a 1938 work on Nordic religion and Christianity; and a ninth-century saint's life chronicling the career of Ansgar, the archbishop of Hamburg who conducted the first recorded mission to Sweden in ca. A.D. 830[8] The first kind of source allows Fridegård to create a believable atmosphere for which he has often been praised.[9] From descriptions of buildings to those of agricultural techniques and burial practices, Fridegård has been fairly precise, making only occasional and understandable errors as when he refers to horned helmets, which Vikings never actually wore. To insure the right historical flavor, Fridegård even takes

---

[6] Nobel Prize winners: e.g., Gjellerup's plays, *Brynhild* (1884) and *Kong Hjarne Skald* (1893) and Lagerlöf's stories 'The Legend of Reor' ('Reors saga,' 1893) in *Invisible Links*, trans. Pauline Bancroft Flach (Garden City, N.Y.: Doubleday, Page, 1899) and 'Astrid' (1899) in *The Queens of Kungahälla and Other Sketches* (*Drottningar i Kungahälla*, 1899), trans. Claud Field (London: T. W. Laurie 1917). On these works and Undset, see Mjöberg, *Drömmen om sagatiden*, vol. 2, pp. 285–86, 452ff. Bremer: in *The H—Family: Trälinnan: Axel and Anna and Other Tales*, trans. Mary Howitt, 2 vols. (London: Longman, Brown, Green, and Långemans, 1844). Rydberg: see Wilson, *Northern World*, p. 234. Heidenstam: trans. A. G. Chater (New York: A. A. Knopf, 1925). On the Viking slave motif in Scandinavian literature, see Mjöberg, *Drömmen om sagatiden*, vol. 2, pp. 285–90.

[7] Ebbe Schön, *Jan Fridegård och forntiden. En studie i diktverk och källor* (Uppsala, Sweden: Almqvist & Wiksell, 1973), pp. 61ff., discusses some of the popular works on Viking slavery that Fridegård may have read. For discussions of thralls in the Viking period, see Peter G. Foote and David M. Wilson, *The Viking Achievement: A Survey of the Society and Culture of Early Medieval Scandinavia* (New York: Praeger, 1970), pp. 65–78 and Ruth Mazo Karras, *Slavery and Society in Medieval Scandinavia* (New Haven: Yale Univ. Press, 1988).

[8] Schön, *Fridegård och forntiden*, pp. 23–53, offers a thorough analysis of Fridegård's sources.

[9] See, for example, Erik Hjalmar Linder, *Fem decennier av nittonhundratalet*, 4th ed. [Vol. 2 of *Ny illustrerad svensk litteraturhistoria*] (Stockholm: Natur och kultur, 1966), pp. 589-90.

the names of his characters from rune stones in the Uppland area of Sweden and
limits both dialogue and the use of archaisms to a minimum, since either device
could easily make the novels sound false.[10] The second kind of source material, cultural studies, enables Fridegård to establish a primitivistic or naturalistic
atmosphere that he felt was so important for a period not, as yet, fully restricted
by the Christian antipathy to sexuality. For example, he draws heavily on Helge
Ljungberg's *Nordic Religion and Christianity: Studies in the Nordic Religious Shift
during the Viking Period*, which provides a thorough analysis of the pagan temple
at Uppsala and the nine-day festival of sacrifice that used to take place there.[11]
In creating a primitivistic atmosphere, Fridegård aligns himself with authors
such as Sherwood Anderson (1876–1941), whose *Dark Laughter* (1925) he greatly
admired, and D. H. Lawrence (1885–1930), whose *The Plumed Serpent* (1926)
may have influenced his erotic descriptions in *Land of Wooden Gods* and *Sacrificial Smoke*. Fridegård's "primitivism" in these novels further augments their sense
of historical accuracy and verisimilitude since the books describe a past era and
sensibility.

The third source that Fridegård used in writing his trilogy is Bishop Rimbert's *Vita Anskarii (The Life of Ansgar)*,[12] and this source, unlike the other two, he
modifies for his own purposes. While he frequently follows Rimbert quite closely,
he just as frequently deviates severely from the *vita*. Some of his inaccuracies may
be inadvertent, such as his anachronistic depiction of Christ as a frail, effeminate
godhead, an image that was the product of the late, not early, Middle Ages.[13] But
others clearly are not. Ansgar, for example, did not neglect the poor, as Fridegård
implies throughout *People of the Dawn* and *Sacrificial Smoke*, but instead founded
a hospital for them in Bremen and "gave away for the support of the poor a tenth
of the animals and of all his revenues and a tenth of the tithes which belonged to
him, and whatever money or property of any kind came to him, he gave a tenth for
the benefit of the poor." Neither would Ansgar have countenanced the kind of lust
for money that Fridegård's priests display, especially in *Sacrificial Smoke*. Rimbert
tells us that Ansgar gave strict orders to missionaries "that they should not desire

---

[10] Schön, *Fridegård och forntiden*, pp. 152–53; pp. 30, 52.

[11] Helge Ljungberg, *Den nordiska religionen och kristendomen. Studier över det nordiska religionsskiftet under vikingatiden* (Stockholm: Hugo Gebers förlag, 1938); Schön,
Fridegård och forntiden, pp. 95 and 113.

[12] For an English translation, see Charles H. Robinson, *Anskar: Apostle of the North*,
801–65 (London: Society for the Propagation of the Gospel in Foreign Parts, 1921).

[13] On Christ as Germanic hero, see Ljungberg, *Den nordiska religionen och kristendomen*, p. 95; Axel Olrik, *Viking Civilization* (1930; rpt. New York: Norton, 1971), pp.
141ff.; chapter 8 ('Christ as Poetic Hero') in Stanley B. Greenfield and Daniel G. Calder,
A New Critical History of Old English Literature (New York: New York Univ. Press, 1986);
and G. Ronald Murphy, *The Saxon Savior: The Germanic Transformation of the Gospel in
the Ninth-Century Heliand* (Oxford: Oxford Univ. Press, 1999).

nor seek to obtain the property of anyone" but rather "be content with food and raiment."[14] And finally, Fridegård's implication that Christianity exacerbated the problem of slavery instead of solving it does not bear scrutiny. Modern historians, in fact, tell us precisely the opposite.[15] Fridegård has obviously made deliberate changes in Rimbert's account of the period for a political agenda that is anarchist in origin and demands a rereading of history. Since little history actually exists for slaves, and none for the rebellions they raise in the trilogy, Fridegård creates a story fabricated in many particulars, but based on a socialist understanding of the processes of history and, from his point of view, therefore true in its essential outline: oppressed people necessarily rebel against their oppressors.[16] As an anti-ideal designed to undermine a political and literary image of Sweden's past, which venerates the Viking and ignores the thrall, the Holme trilogy remakes Nordic history to create a new ethos.[17] In Fridegård's new myth, Holme functions centrally as a representative of the rising proletariat in Sweden, and the interconnections Fridegård establishes among him and the other characters in the novels become of paramount importance.[18] They are the focus of Fridegård's higher purpose of reinterpreting history through anarchist ideology and are what make the trilogy a serious work of social and philosophical criticism.

To understand how Fridegård uses Holme to advance his cause, we must look closely at Gustaf Fröding's "The Smith," a poem that greatly impressed Fridegård.[19] In forty-eight lines, Fröding recreates the Old Norse legend of Weyland (Völundr), the king of the elves and a skillful smith, who, along with his prize sword, was captured by the Swedish king Nidud. Nidud, wanting to take advantage of Weyland's skills, had Weyland's hamstrings cut so he couldn't escape and then isolated him on an island where he had to make treasures for Nidud. When Nidud's two sons came to see Weyland work, he cut off their heads and made their skulls into silver vessels for Nidud, their eyes into jewels for Nidud's wife, and their teeth into a necklace for Nidud's daughter. Through artifice, a laughing Weyland then raised himself aloft and out of reach.[20]

---

[14] *Anskar*, chapter 35, p. 112; chapter 33, pp. 104–5.

[15] See, for example, Foote and Wilson, *Viking Achievement*, pp. 77ff.

[16] Schön, *Fridegård och forntiden*, pp. 61–79.

[17] Schön, *Fridegård och forntiden*, p. 51, says that Fridegård sometimes wrote in conscious opposition to Tegnér's *Frithiofs Saga*.

[18] Schön (*Fridegård och forntiden*, p. 28) observes that the story about Holme 'is to a certain extent to be regarded as a kind of social myth where Fridegård, with the help of his imagination, tries to explain the origin of the struggle of the proletariat' in Sweden.

[19] Schön, *Fridegård och forntiden*, p. 50. Mjöberg, *Drömmen om sagatiden*, 2, pp. 291–92, asserts, but does not really show, the importance of Fröding's poem to Fridegård's trilogy.

[20] For a translation of 'The Lay of Völundr' or 'Weyland,' see Carolyne Larrington, trans. *The Poetic Edda* (Oxford: Oxford University Press, 1996), pp. 102–8.

In his rendition, Fröding dispenses with the specifics of the Weyland story, focusing instead on the idea of the smith's rebellion against his oppressors. The poem opens with the poet dreaming he is walking through a coal-black forest with tree tops like iron and a wind that causes the surroundings to quake, not whisper. The path he walks on is strewn with soot, not covered with grass, and there he hears one noise that sounds like people tramping heavily and another that resembles the muffled sound of a sword clashing against a dagger. As he dreams, the poet discovers that he is near Weyland's valley and that the sound he hears carries the warning of impending storm "and the feud of the mighty powers" ("och de väldiga makternas fejd"). When he hears the clanging of a hammer and sees sparks rising, he moves forward to investigate, but all he finds is a scraggly, hunched over, dishevelled smith, with low forehead and crooked back, a mere thrall laborer, "one of the thralls who live in the cellars / beneath the overlord's tramping heals" ("en av trälarnes folk, som i källrar bo / under herrarnes trampande häl"). The poet thinks the man is a modern, harmless smith. But then the smith rises, becoming tall, noble, and straight. His mighty arm strikes with its tool at the smithy's iron roof, "and heavy as a mountain the hammer fell / and like thunder was the roar of the blow" ("och tungt som ett fjäll föll hammarens slag / och som åskan var slagets dån"). Weyland has been a thrall smith for a thousand years, says the poet, but now he fashions the sword of revenge that will destroy the dwelling of the gods. The dreamer then realizes that the forest is actually a modern factory that will one day feel the force of Weyland's revolt. It, like the forest, is filled with a noise like the clashing of sword against dagger, and soot covers its walls and roof as well.[21]

Fröding transforms the thrall smith in the course of the poem in three specific ways, all of which have importance for Fridegård's Holme trilogy: first he changes the bent and scraggly thrall smith into a massive, noble figure; second he turns the nameless, insignificant, unattractive slave into the legendary Weyland, who is capable of leading a revolution; and third, after changing the smith into Weyland, he also conflates Weyland with the Nordic god Thor, whose hammer makes thunder and protects gods and men from their enemies. Fridegård, I maintain, uses the same pattern of transformation in depicting Holme.

Holme's transformations into a noble figure and into a figure capable of leading a revolution are easy to apprehend. Although Holme is never bent and scraggly, he does crouch in *Land of Wooden Gods* as an animal would (pp. 5, 7, 9) and is even likened there to various animals (e.g., an owl, p. 6; a dog, p. 19; a wild animal, p. 93), as well as to a sub-human shadow (p. 6) and ghost (p. 8). He also has broad cheek-bones (p. 5), reminiscent of Fröding's smith's low forehead, and has a primitive, animal-like walk (p. 43). After he has established himself

    [21] G. Michanek, ed. *Gustaf Frödings Poesi* (Stockholm: Wahlström & Widstrand, 1993), pp. 421–22.

as a respected smith in Birka, however, such imagery rarely occurs. [22] A change in Holme's relationship to his antagonists coincides with the disappearance of animal imagery. His stature, strength, and capabilities become magnified as the trilogy progresses, and he, like Weyland, becomes larger than life.

The outcome of his first major, life-threatening confrontation in *Land of Wooden Gods* seems doubtful from the start. After taking refuge in the cave with Ausi and their baby, Holme is discovered by the most powerful and feared warrior from the settlement, Stenulf, who orders all of them to come back with him. Holme refuses, a fight ensues, and Ausi, expecting to see Holme fall at any moment, takes action.

> Ausi crept out and grabbed the spear leaning against the cave entrance. Holme had been moving in a half-circle, and Stenulf, following him, had his back to her. Ausi took the spear in both hands, rushed forward, and thrust it into Stenulf from behind.
>
> A severe jolt almost knocked her off her feet, and the spear shattered in two. Stenulf had swung violently behind his back with his sword, catching the spear in the middle. As he did so, he lost balance, reeled, and was unable to parry Holme's blow fully. The ax grazed his neck.
>
> Inexplicably, the fight stopped. Stenulf sheathed his sword and, with a look of arrogance at the thralls, walked up the ridge toward the settlement. Blood pulsed from his neck . . . . (25–26)

Stenulf bleeds to death, clearly not the result of Holme's superior might. Holme never will know if he could have defeated Stenulf and will never feel proud of his dubious victory.

In the rest of the trilogy, however, neither Holme nor we have any doubts about his abilities and superiority to all his foes. His strength is manifest and feared throughout, and Geire's demise in *People of the Dawn* is swift because of it. Unable to draw his sword to fend off Holme's attack, he feels himself in Holme's grip and "could feel death in [its] incredible power. He felt himself rise into the air, saw the sky and the stone walls flash before his eyes, and then everything was dark and quiet" (232). And in *Sacrificial Smoke*, a band of invading Vikings scatters before Holme's charge: "The invaders began leaping out of the way of this raging giant . . . His reach exceeded theirs, and the power in his blows made their weapons fly from their hands" (344).

A change in Holme's relationship to other human beings also takes place as the trilogy progresses; Holme moves from committing selfish, brutal acts, to being moved by mercy and understanding. In *Land of Wooden Gods* we are

---

[22] Animal imagery recurs when Holme is back at the settlement or fleeing from his persecutors in *Sacrificial Smoke* (i.e, 'pig,' 'night animal,' 'wolf' and 'fox'). He is also compared to a troll on one occasion.

told that Holme, like Stenulf before him and Geire after him, had raped Ausi. During Holme's fight with Stenulf, Ausi remembers the incident. "She hadn't been able to do anything to defend herself. She thought [Stenulf] was going to do it again once, but it turned out to be Holme instead. Though she feared and hated Holme, she had been glad it was him instead of Stenulf" (25). Holme also commits three other acts of brutality in the first volume that shock the reader and that Holme will come to regret later in the trilogy. On one occasion, in ret-ribution for the chieftain's trying to kill Holme's baby, Holme hurls a rock at the chieftain's own child, hitting him at the base of the neck and permanently maiming him (20). On another, wanting a house that once was his, Holme con-fronts the current and rightful inhabitant, ordering him out, then killing him when the man objects. "There was no sound except the ax blow and the soft thud when the man hit the floor. Immediately Holme grabbed him and dragged him out into the woods" (116). And, most disturbingly, on the third occasion Holme puts Ausi's child by another man out in the forest to die. The child is the result of the orgies in honor of Freyr in Uppsala, and Holme wants no part of it. "But deep in the woods a tiny blue face shone rigidly and questioningly back at the moon, which sank gradually among the dense branches of the spruce trees. The baby's new mother — cold — had not taken long to lull it to sleep" (113).

In *People of the Dawn*, however, Holme would commit no such act. He has the chance, for example, to kill the two men responsible for carrying his baby into the woods to meet certain death, but he foregoes it because "they were alone and old now and had a right to stay and fend for themselves" (159). In the same novel, he leads starving thralls to the Christian storehouses and doles all the grain out to them, totally neglecting himself (153). This selflessness and concern for others develops into a full-fledged vision of freedom, without violence, for all humankind in *Sacrificial Smoke*. The transformation that begins within Holme eventually has ramifications for all around him as he becomes a revolutionary leader.

The third transformation of Holme, into a kind of Thor figure, is by far the most complex. It develops simultaneously with the other two, beginning, curi-ously enough, with the Stranger in *Land of Wooden Gods*, and ending with the conflation of Holme, the Stranger, Christ, and Thor by the end of the trilogy. The Stranger, first of all, represents a primitive, "socialist" kind of Christianity that is egalitarian, non-materialistic, and dedicated to converting society from the bottom up.[23] In the Stranger's case, he begins with the thralls, going "down among the workers and the overburdened" as Christ once did (46). This socialist ideal has an obvious affinity with what Holme later develops in the trilogy, for he too works for an egalitarian society beginning with the thralls. Never forgetting

---

[23] See Ljungberg, *Den nordiska religionen och kristendomen*, pp. 77ff., and Schön, *Fridegård och forntiden*, pp. 124–25.

the time he spent in servitude, he divides the smithy's earnings equally among all who work there (134), "associated with [thralls] as equals" even though he was free (141), and makes sure in handling out grain during the famine that every one, baptized or not, gets an equal share of food (153).

Other aspects of the Stranger's character and description, however, tie him still more closely to Holme. Both he and Holme, for example, come from distant lands, which makes them somewhat mysterious (13, 37); both seem to some to be sorcerers (13, 37, 41); both have striking eyes (e.g., 42, 45; 7, 15, 19); and both have a powerful effect on Ausi, who perceives another similarity. The Stranger "must have been closer to Christ than those who came after him" and Holme, too, "was a lot like Christ" (210) in helping the poor (223) and defending the weak (269). Holme probably would not have appreciated the comparison, but she makes it nonetheless and solidifies Holme's identification with Christ and the Stranger as the trilogy develops. The Stranger, for instance, actually becomes Christ. As Ausi walks through the market town in *People of the Dawn*, she has a revelation:

> Suddenly she stopped. Something was lighting up and expanding inside her, and she was breathing heavily. She saw everything now. The stranger had been Christ Himself, come to earth once more. He was a gentle and good as the sun; he tolerated everything without complaint; and He wanted nothing for himself. He endured death without fear. He was Christ, and he had come back for her sake. (165)

Ausi also feels that Christ and Holme live inside her ("With Christ and Holme living peacefully together within her, who could do her harm?" [169]), and she knows too that "for a long time she had belonged only to Holme and Christ" (178). In addition, Ausi observes, all three men are tormented and eventually die for their revolutionary faiths. The Stranger and Christ had both been tortured to death (165), and both Holme and Christ "had been beaten and persecuted; that was why He was on the side of Holme and the thralls" (238). Holme, more like Christ than his priests, was willing to offer his own life "if it meant saving his thrall companions" (333).

Holme's faith and substance partake of more than the primitive Christianity represented by the Stranger. They partake, as well, of the Nordic religion as represented by Thor. Here again, I believe, Fridegård takes liberties with his sources in order to advance his view of history as he transposes his paradigm for Christianity's development—from egalitarian to elitist—onto Nordic paganism. We have no evidence, after all, that the Norse gods were undemocratic in bestowing their favors on their subjects, as Fridegård says they were. Instead we have considerable proof that Thor was the god of common men and peasants, perhaps even thralls.[24] He was, in fact, more like the Weyland/Thor figure in Fröding's poem than the battle god in the trilogy, and Fridegård fashions Holme in the Fröding mold in distinct, though subtle ways.

Fridegård first creates a broad and loose association between the god and Holme by making the latter a smith as well as a thrall. Holme is not just any smith, but one who, like Weyland, "could do anything with his hands, coming as he probably did from across the sea where people had magic powers" (12). In addition, Thor was the patron of smiths, a fact that may account for the otherwise curious transformation that Weyland undergoes in Fröding's poem, and the thralls' weapon and tool, the ax, was considered "a bolt from the thunder god" (255) and was almost as strongly associated with Thor as his hammer was. That Holme actually uses both the hammer and ax in battle brings an even closer association between him and Thor. The silver amulets representing Thor's hammer may have been made in conscious opposition to symbols of the Cross, and Holme uses his hammer at least twice against Christian symbols.

In *People of the Dawn* "Holme ran without a sound toward the Christians; before anyone knew what had happened, he had smashed the baptismal font to bits with his sledgehammer" (152). He later topples the bell tower, caves in the church door, and finally demolishes the Christian altar with it: "the holy relics bounced high into the air and landed in the hands of thralls" (181). Holme's hammer, it seems, becomes Thor's, and his acts also reflect those of the god, to whom men turned for protection from Christ. Furthermore, consciously or not, Fridegård draws the parallel between Holme and Thor still tighter by alluding to Holme's intimidating power. In legend, Thor challenges Christ to battle, but Christ backs down before Thor's superior might.[25] In *People of the Dawn* Ausi knows that "Christ was powerful, but who could stand up against Holme?" (133). Holme renders all gods, "both the old ones and the new one," powerless (139). Finally, Fridegård likens Holme to a wooden god twice (104, 200), portrays him as the leader for "everyone who still believed in the ancient wooden gods" (323), and later places him in Thor's traditional spot in the middle of the heathen temple during the final confrontation with the Christians (331).

Holme, of course, never fully becomes Thor, just as he never fully becomes Christ. His life is far too rooted in a socio-economic, rather than a religious or spiritual, reality for him to be either. Instead, he rises up a noble, straight-backed, and clear-sighted man, with his thoughts fixed on the welfare of his fellows. His ultimate vision, then, fleetingly realized through Ausi's eyes in her dying moments, is not that of the destruction coming with a Ragnarök or Armageddon but of the creation of a just and different world. That vision gives him his

---

[24] See E. O. G. Turville-Petre's chapter on Thor in *Myth and Religion of the North* (New York: Holt, Rinehart, and Winston, 1964), pp. 75–105.

[25] Turville-Petre, *Myth and Religion*, p. 84; p. 90.

strength and stature, and the new myth that Fridegård creates through Holme thus proceeds not from a godhead, Christian or pagan, but from an idea—that to all mankind belong freedom and equality. Fridegård has rewritten myth in his Holme trilogy to give the proletariat a history and a hope. In the distant past, in the beginnings of Scandinavian society, lie the beginnings of a better future.

—

A slightly expanded version of this essay was published as "Medievalism in the Service of the Swedish Proletariat: Jan Fridegård's Viking Trilogy." *Studies in Medievalism* 8 (1996): 86–99.